THE CRITICS RAVE

"Sensational Shirl Henke . . . American romance."

—Romantic Times

"A true shining star of the genre."

—RT Book Reviews

"Shirl Henke mesmerizes readers with the most powerful, sensual and memorable historical romances yet!"

—RT Book Reviews

"Shirl Henke is one of the brightest stars in romance. . . . Her engaging characters and talent for storytelling will grip readers from the first page to the last."

—Katherine Sutcliffe

"The lively dialogue, biting repartee and sizzling sensuality crackle through the pages of this delicious and fast-paced read. Henke captures you from page one . . . A quick charmer of a read!"

—RT Book Reviews on Yankee Earl

"Readers will need oxygen to keep up . . . Shirl Henke knows how to spin a heated tale that never slows until the final safe kiss."

—Midwest Book Review on Wanton Angel

"Another sensual treat for readers who like their romances liberally laced with both danger and desire."

—Booklist on Rebel Baron

"Wicked Angel is a clever blending of humor, romance, and history into a powerful Regency tale . . . another powerfully entertaining Shirl Henke novel to savor."

—Amazon.com

A NIGHT OF PLEASURE

Amber followed a circuitous route to the opposite side of the house, then dismissed the maid with a smile of thanks. She stood inside a small retiring room before the assignation chamber's hidden door. The light beneath it went dark. She heard the rustle of covers and thought of Robert St. John, lying naked on the large bed. The image would not quite come into focus, but her mind held a shadowy vision of that long, lean body stretched across the mattress.

It will be dark. He cannot see your face.
He is here only to please you.

Other *Leisure* books by Shirl Henke:

WHITE APACHE'S WOMAN
BROKEN VOWS
McCRORY'S LADY
A FIRE IN THE BLOOD
NIGHT WIND'S WOMAN

Wild West Trilogy:
THE RIVER NYMPH
PALE MOON STALKER
CHOSEN WOMAN

American Lords Trilogy:
YANKEE EARL
REBEL BARON
TEXAS VISCOUNT

Blackthorne Family Trilogy:
LOVE A REBEL . . . LOVE A ROGUE
WICKED ANGEL
WANTON ANGEL

Colorado Couplet:
TERMS OF LOVE
TERMS OF SURRENDER

Discovery Duet:
PARADISE & MORE
RETURN TO PARADISE

Shirl Henke

Love Lessons at Midnight

LEISURE BOOKS NEW YORK CITY

For
the Rochats,
Thank you for letting us be a part of the family.

A LEISURE BOOK®

July 2010

Published by

Dorchester Publishing Co., Inc.
200 Madison Avenue
New York, NY 10016

ISBN 10: 0-8439-6363-8
ISBN 13: 978-0-8439-6363-2
E-ISBN: 978-1-4285-0892-7

The name "Leisure Books" and the stylized "L" with design are
trademarks of Dorchester Publishing Co., Inc.

Printed in the United States of America.

10 9 8 7 6 5 4 3 2 1

Visit us online at www.dorchesterpub.com.

Love Lessons

at Midnight

Chapter One

"After spending the past two years trying to drive me out of business, you now wish to hire me?" Amber Leighigh Wolverton studied the man standing in her private quarters through narrowed eyes. When his face flushed red as a spring tulip, she felt a keen tickle of satisfaction.

"Not you personally!" Robert Emery Crispin St. John, sixth Earl of Barrington, quickly replied in a strangled voice. Clearing his throat, Rob imagined what he was certain must be the madam's cat-in-cream expression, even though he could not see her face. He felt tongue-tied as a schoolboy, hardly the fiery orator who held members of the House of Lords spellbound. Reaching inside his waistcoat, he took out his purse.

"Pray, put your money away. I do not accept payment before I have a clear understanding of what a gentleman wants. Not all fantasies are . . . ah, acceptable here. If what you propose is suitable, there will be time enough to discuss cost."

"I believe you will find my fantasy to be rather mundane," he said with a trace of irony.

She stared at him, again noting his nervousness. "Allow me to be the judge of that."

All he could see of her face was the glow from her eyes. The only light in the large, opulent room was provided by a small branch of candles positioned directly behind her. A part of him wished he could see her more clearly, but perhaps it was better that he did not, lest he lose his nerve and give over this gin-witted scheme. However, he could discern the outline of her body and it was splendid.

She wore a gown of some dark shade. Blue? The soft fabric

clung to her pale shoulders. A matching sapphire necklace glinted at her slender throat. Although he took no interest in women's fallalls, he recognized the quality and elegance of the gown and its wearer. Swallowing for courage, he answered her question. "I want instruction from the most skillful female in your employ."

"The women in my employ await instruction by the gentlemen, not the other way around," Amber replied dryly, her curiosity more piqued than ever.

The earl paced across the thick emerald carpet of the opulently appointed office. "If I merely wished a compliant woman, I could damn well afford a mistress," he burst out in frustration, feeling his face flame anew.

"Ah, but if you kept a mistress, how could you rail in the House of Lords against immorality?" Amber watched the tic in his jaw as he clenched his teeth. Was he implying what she thought he was?

"I do not rail against immorality. I speak out against criminality," he replied stiffly.

"But you believe my establishment to be criminal?"

"Most bordellos are criminal, even exclusive ones. But the scandal sheets would have it that your, er, establishment is unique. Every rake in the ton comes here to live his own peculiar fantasy."

Amber quickly interjected, "Not all the rakes in the ton are accepted here, m'lord. I have refused some *most* peculiar fantasies because I do not permit violence, involve children, bestiality, opium eating, drunken bacchanals, or any other odious things that you and your friends in Parliament might imagine."

Rob watched her slender body stiffen ever so slightly. Lady Fantasia's demeanor indicated that she was displeased. Well, he was not exactly all cock-a-whoop himself! "I intend no offense. If I believed you allowed abusive behavior, I would not have come to you with my . . . request."

"I am immensely relieved by your good opinion."

Ignoring her sarcasm, he swallowed and plowed doggedly ahead. "I have investigated your establishment. According to all reports, your courtesans are educated, of sound health, and well trained in the pleasure arts."

Amber raised her chin as proudly as the wife of a marquess, which she was. "They possess all those qualities and beauty, besides." She waited for his next move like a chess player, which she also was. *This is humiliating the stiff-rumped devil.* She felt another tickle of satisfaction.

"I am considering marriage within the year." His face flushed with heat. Damn, why did his swarthy complexion betray him as if he were a bran-faced boy? "I wish to please my wife . . . as much as befits a gentleman to impose himself upon a lady."

She could sense his intense discomfort growing apace. "And you believe a courtesan would prove the best instructor."

"Only if she were completely honest with me as the . . . instructions progressed."

"Ah, then you expect not only skill but honesty. The latter is not a trait members of your reformist cadre usually assign to those in my profession."

"I am willing to pay for honesty. That should suffice." The moment he snapped out the words, he regretted them. "I did not intend an insult," he said.

She rolled the crystal tumbler filled with excellent French brandy between her palms. He had declined to imbibe with her. A moralizing prig . . . or a man desperate to keep a clear head? She wondered. Taking a sip, she said, "Give me leave to doubt what you intended, but"—she waved her hand dismissively—"it signifies nothing. You will pay handsomely for this . . . honesty."

"I have been given to understand that you are a woman of your word," he said, trying not to sound grudging.

"A compliment? I shall return it, m'lord. You are to be commended for your intentions. Most men do not give a fig for their wives' satisfaction in the marital bed."

"I am not most men." He bit off each word.

Amber studied his face in the dim light. "No, you most certainly are not," she agreed. The earl was the most impossibly handsome man she had ever seen. The broadsheet sketches had not begun to do his physical beauty justice. Worn longer than current fashion, his thick black hair framed his face in unruly waves. Piercing green eyes bored into her while the heavy dark eyebrows above creased in a frown. His nose was long, elegant, and straight, his jaw bold and masculine, but his mouth, ah, that mouth could be wickedly sensual . . . if he ever smiled. Did he? She wondered.

His eyes glowed with fiery intensity. Even tense and angry, he was arresting. He should have had women falling at his feet in a swoon. What would make such a man believe he required sexual tutelage? Somehow she knew it would be unwise to ask. "Very well. What you propose is acceptable."

"There is one thing more . . ." His voice faded.

"And that would be?" Amber found herself hoping that he was not going to spoil everything with a less than wholesome addendum.

He paced across the room, raking one hand through his already tousled hair. With his back to her he replied, "The bedchamber must be darkened."

"If you have indeed investigated my establishment, you know no woman in my employ would ever stoop to blackmail," she said sharply. "Not even of so tempting a target as a confidant of Mr. Wilberforce and his 'Saints.'"

"I realize some of my associates in Parliament would be shocked to learn I am here, even more dismayed by what I have proposed. But I did not intend to accuse you of blackmail."

"What then?" Amber knew she was toying with him but for some reason could not resist. He appeared to steel his nerve to face her, grasping the back of a Chippendale chair in a whitened grip. His long, strong fingers were lightly dusted with black hair. Suddenly she felt guilty . . . and something else. She dismissed the disturbing train of thought when he spoke.

"I would be more comfortable in the dark—and I am certain my future lady will prefer to maintain her modesty."

Amber noted the way he had quickly added that last thought. She nodded gravely, wondering if he had some concealed disfigurement, a scar perhaps? *No, he is as green and uncertain as he appears.* Although she did not know the reason why this should be so, she determined that she would find out. But she had tormented the man quite enough. "You are a most . . . considerate man, m'lord."

"When do we begin?" he asked, eager to be quit of what was becoming an increasingly uncomfortable conversation.

She leaned back in the Robert Adams chair and tapped her chin thoughtfully. "I shall require a bit of time to select the woman best suited for your needs. Say, three days. Will that fit your schedule?"

He fought down a sudden urge to bolt for the door, devil take his cork-brained idea. *You've come this far. Only hold fast for another moment.* "Quite," he replied with a stiff nod.

"Now you may take out your purse, m'lord." Lady Fantasia allowed herself a bemused smile. "For the initial payment . . ."

Rob slipped from the back entrance of the House of Dreams wearing his great coat with the collar turned up, not only against the night wind, but also to conceal his identity. If his presence here ever became known, he would be quite properly dished up. Not only would he lose the good opinion of the reformers whose help he needed in Parliament, but he would lose the widow he intended to court.

What would she think if she knew I was going to receive love lessons from a Cyprian? Somehow he doubted that she would consider his motive before turning away in disgust. The interview had not gone smoothly, but then he had not expected that it would be anything but devilish awkward. Yet, the place and Lady Fantasia were not what he had expected.

The location on Alpha Road was a newer but exclusive residential neighborhood that afforded privacy, as did the triple lot with its high stone walls and elaborate gardens. The area was called St. John's Wood, an irony that did not escape him. As he made his way around the twisting walk, Rob could not begin to imagine what went on in the topiary maze during warm weather. Best not to dwell on satyrs chasing naked females through the shrubbery!

The house was built in the neoclassical style, an elegant three-story edifice of simple white brick. Inside, the décor was understated yet opulent, nothing such as the lurid visions of crimson-flocked wall coverings and animal-skin rugs he had imagined. Rather, the clean lines of Robert Adams furniture and muted colors of oriental carpets gave the place a feeling of uncluttered welcome and excellent taste. How strange a contrast in a house where men acted out sexual fantasies.

Indeed, the place was more subdued and tasteful than many of the mansions in Mayfair with their clashing mélanges of Egyptian, Turkish, and Chinese furnishings. Just thinking of the Prince Regent's monstrosity at Brighton made him wince. Excess had become the byword of the era.

The "lady" herself, mysterious, aloof, sharp witted, was unexpectedly elegant, not at all the garish bawd he had imagined. Considering her speech and manners, she was well educated. He had heard the speculation regarding her identity. She went to considerable lengths to conceal it in the dimly lit chamber. Recalling how her slender body filled out that dark gown so gloriously, he knew she would be the center of male attention at any fashionable gathering.

What had made a beautiful woman from good family turn to such a sordid business? Freedom from wifely duties? The thrill of flaunting decency? Perhaps her family had fallen in dun territory and she needed the money. She was a mercenary female, no doubt of it. He had paid an exorbitant sum and would owe more when the tutelage was complete.

He would have preferred never again to face the woman to whom he had confessed such an intimate . . . inadequacy. But he knew he would have to do so if he intended to go through with his plan. Whom would she select for his lessons? What did it matter? He had stipulated that they be in darkness, intuiting that a lady such as Verity would prefer it that way. Certainly Credelia had insisted on it . . . for all the good that did. He suppressed the painful memory, but then images of Spanish women in flickering firelight took its place. Those encounters had been rare and utterly unsatisfying, too.

Yet here I am once more, paying a woman to lie with me.

He pushed the thought aside. His long-held monkish existence would come to an end within the week. For good or ill, he had committed to go through with his plan. He reached the gate, and the keeper opened it for him, showing no interest in studying the guest's face. The well-oiled hinges swung without a sound.

Rob was grateful for the thick fog smothering the city. It obscured the narrow tree-lined lane at the rear of the expansive grounds where an unmarked black coach waited for him. Frog, his footman, jumped agilely from the box and opened the door for him the moment he materialized from the mists. The lane led to Alpha Road, which was deserted on the inclement night. In moments, the clattering of hooves sounded on the cobbles, leaving the sixth Earl of

Barrington alone inside the carriage with only bitter memories for company.

•

"You would not have believed it, Grace," Amber said as she crossed the oriental carpet in Grace Winston's private quarters and approached the liquor cabinet. She quickly poured her friend and mentor a glass of her favorite port. Unlike Amber's simple neoclassical taste, Grace preferred ornate French court furnishings in gold, white and pale blue.

"Pray, do tell me something I would not believe," Grace said with a dry chuckle, accepting the proffered port. She settled back in her Louis XV brocade chair and waited until Amber took a seat in the matching piece across from her. The founder of their establishment was a handsome woman in spite of the years that had turned her once chestnut hair silver-gray. A slight plumpness held facial wrinkles at bay and a skillful touch with paints allowed her to look a well-preserved forty-five when in fact she was already far past the distressing age of fifty. "What does the earl want?"

"Robert St. John requires instruction in how to please a woman in bed. Can you credit that?"

Grace's round blue eyes widened. "Never say it! That troublesome young devil is handsome as Lucifer. I've always wondered why there were no rumors about women in his life. Of course, being associated with those Clapham zealots and Mr. Wilberforce . . . Lord save us from religious reformers! Ah, such a waste," she murmured, shaking her head.

"Well, he now wishes to worship at a different shrine," Amber said.

•

"I vow if I were young enough, I would be happy to be his priestess." Grace gave a rich chuckle. "Why ever has he waited this long? He must be at least five and twenty."

"He is duty-bound to marry and produce an heir."

"That scarcely requires lessons," Grace said with a snort.

"It has been my experience that lack of skill has never had a deleterious effect on randy young men."

"He is concerned that he satisfy his wife . . . in the dark, so as not to upset her delicate sensibilities, although I suspect 'tis his own that are really at issue."

Grace studied the young woman who had taken the place of the daughter she'd lost in her youth. Amber was lovely as a spring rose with dark cherry-red hair and golden eyes to match her name, but those eyes were all too often haunted by her past. A thought flitted across the old madam's mind. Leaning forward, she asked, "You truly believe St. John is afraid of bed sport?" *As are you.*

"Why else would an avid reformer associated with rigid moralists chance coming here, even under cover of darkness?" Amber asked rhetorically.

Inclining her head, Grace agreed. "Indeed. If word of such ever reached those 'Saints,' the uproar would make Prime Minister Percival's assassination seem a flea bite. It would appear Barrington is a most considerate man, to risk all for love. In the dark, hmmm . . ." She tapped her chin with her index finger and stared at her young protégé.

"You look to be evaluating me as if I were a side of mutton and you a butcher," Amber said suspiciously.

Grace tossed down the remainder of her port and chuckled. "A lamb to the slaughter? No, not at all the thing."

"What, then?" Amber asked.

Grace leaned forward in her chair, her playful expression turning suddenly earnest. "Only think, if you are correct and he is so green and so considerate of a lady's sensibilities . . . might he not be the perfect one for *you* to instruct?"

Amber reacted as if Grace had slapped her. "I have never taken a man to my bed since I fled the marquess! You have never asked such a thing since you rescued me."

"Tut, I would never have you do anything against your

will," Grace said reassuringly. "But who was it returned from her education on the Continent with the idea of making an ordinary bordello into the House of Dreams? A place where gentlemen could fulfill their secret fantasies . . . Lady Fantasia?"

"My idea was born of studying classical literature. It has proven wildly successful." To her own ears, Amber sounded as if she were defending her honor—as if a woman who worked with courtesans had any to defend. Best to shift the conversation. "You know I had to assume a false identity here in London to prevent my husband from finding me." She shuddered as the vile marquess's face swam before her eyes.

"Yes, an ugly rotter, Eastham is, inside as well as out," Grace agreed, then added smoothly, "But the earl is devilish handsome, young, and in need of a skilled teacher."

"Considering my limited experience, I am scarce qualified."

"Your qualifications are sterling."

Amber raised her hands in frustration. "An addlepated boy and a brutal man twice my age. There's sterling experience if ever I've heard it."

"Pish, I explained the finer points of our art to you so that you could assume control of the business. You, in turn, have instructed the most exclusive courtesans in London."

"I've instructed them in history, literature, and deportment, given them a small bit of the education you afforded me. I hardly possess anything like actual experience with a patron."

"My point exactly." Grace leaned forward, practically rubbing her hands in excitement. "Do you not see it? We have trained women to give men pleasure. This is a man who wishes to give a woman pleasure. A rare opportunity for any of our sex and a golden one for you, child. A handsome, earnest young lord, yours to command. You could ask anything of him and he would comply. 'Tis every woman's fantasy."

"I am in the business of providing fantasies, not living them," Amber said defensively.

"We, all of us, require a fantasy or two to survive," the older woman replied in a gentle voice. "You might think of it as a fantasy come true for the both of you. He will do only what you ask, everything you ask . . . if you dare."

Her sly smile was not lost on Amber. "I neither want nor need a lover," she protested, starting to pace just as St. John had done. The moment she realized what she was doing, she sank onto the chair once more.

Grace waited patiently. "The man is principled, sexually innocent, young, and handsome. You may never again have this chance, Amber. You have dealt with a stupid boy and a vicious older man. There is much you have yet to experience."

"Burleigh has quite turned your head, dear Grace, but I do not expect to find such a paragon." Grace's lover, a baronet, was a widower who spent many nights sharing her bed. She often visited his isolated country estate.

"You will never find such a paragon lest you have the courage to seize what is offered when 'tis offered. Pray, to whom were you going to assign this 'odious' task?" Grace asked.

"I told Barrington that I would need three days to select the woman who best suited his requirements."

"See that you do, hmmm?"

Amber made no reply, but left Grace's quarters deeply disturbed. She did not see the wistfully sad smile on the older woman's face.

Amber tossed and turned in her lonely bed, unable to chase Grace's idea away. By the following morning, she was honest enough to admit to herself that the thought of becoming the handsome earl's teacher had lurked deep in the back of her own mind before her mentor suggested it. In spite of his stiff-necked pride and self-righteousness, he had come to her at great personal risk, asking simply to learn how to be a good husband. His embarrassment was keen. Few men would humble themselves that way.

Before she made any rash decision, Amber wanted his past looked into very thoroughly. Every potential patron of the House of Dreams was investigated by a Bow Street Runner in her employ. At present, she knew very little about Sinjin, as men with the St. John surname were often called. There was the gossip bandied about the ton. He had fallen heir to Barrington through a series of untimely deaths, and allied himself with reformers in Parliament. His personal life was above reproach.

Until last night.

Amber carefully composed a letter, then rang for Clifton, her footman, to deliver it to his cousin Clyde at Bow Street. Having dispatched that task, she opened the *Morning Chronicle* to learn what was going on about the ton. On the second page, Barrington's name caught her eye. He was scheduled to give a speech on child labor the day after next. The journalist, Mr. William Hazlitt, anticipated an invigorating presentation by one of the brightest lights ever to grace either chamber of Parliament since the demise of Charles James Fox.

Amber put down the paper and considered. One of the cook's helpers had lost her voice while working as a small girl in a match factory. The toxic fumes from chemicals had eaten the lining of her throat. After rescuing the child from such a horrid environment, Amber was curious to hear how the earl's speech would be received in the House of Lords.

Admit it, you want to see him in the hard light of day to better take his measure. Amber put aside the disturbing thought along with the newspaper and rang for a light repast to break her fast.

Securing a seat in the gallery of the House of Lords was not an easy task for a woman, but as Lady Fantasia, Amber knew many highly influential men in the government, although they knew nothing of her true identity. By late afternoon, she had a voucher from Lord Twilling that would grant her admission.

Perhaps by then she would learn more about the earl from her Bow Street Runner. She had but three days to make the most important decision of her life since accepting Grace's offer of shelter as a frightened seventeen-year-old runaway wife.

Chapter Two

Clyde Dyer had been a Bow Street Runner for two decades and worked for Grace Winston ever since his cousin Clifton had found employment at her fine establishment. Like his cousin, Clyde was completely discreet. It was no mean thing to delve into the affairs of the Quality, searching for any secret vices that would bar them admission to the new madam's fantasy world. If one whisper concerning their application to the House of Dreams were to become public knowledge, it would do irreparable harm to the establishment. Although many prominent gentlemen gave not a fig that their carousing was known, others jealously guarded their privacy.

Clyde wished to keep his position. Lady Fantasia paid very generously.

He scratched his shiny bald pate and settled into the wooden chair that protested against his rotund body's weight. The walls of the crowded room were filled with drawings of assorted villains for whom rewards were offered. He cleared a space on one of the cluttered desks and read the letter, being careful not to allow anyone nearby to get even a glance at its contents.

The Earl of Barrington had applied to Lady Fantasia's! *What a breeze that would raise if the scandal sheets found out.* He chuckled to himself, wondering what the reformer's fantasy might be. No, it was not his place to dwell on that. He set to work in his usual methodical way.

* * *

Wolf's Gate, Northumberland

Lytton Wolverton, seventh Marquess of Eastham, stared out at the bleak day. An icy wind blew down from the hills, making a mockery of spring in the barren north lands of his ancestral home. He preferred the isolation. Everyone who worked on the large estate, even those in the small village nearby, owed their lives and livelihood to the marquess. His authority had never been questioned.

Except by one chit of a girl. His first wife.

Amber was most certainly dead. But what if she were not? The thought had given him no peace in the ten years since she had run off with nearly a hundred pounds pilfered from Mrs. Greevy's household expense money. Neither his housekeeper nor he would ever forgive such perfidy.

Beyond that, if Amber had somehow managed to survive, his second marriage would be bigamous and his heir illegitimate. Unthinkable. Emma had died birthing a lusty, strong son who would one day be the eighth marquess. He cared nothing for his second marchioness's death. Indeed, he had no interest in the sniveling babe, given into the care of his younger brother and sister-in-law. He would reclaim the boy when he was old enough for instruction.

Wolverton looked down at the crumpled paper in his fist, uncurling his blunt fingers from the soft velum. Damn, could Hull be right? He found it impossible to imagine a cold, haughty miss like Amber surviving in such a harsh life. She who had not possessed the wit to appreciate being a marchioness! He cursed and threw the balled-up missive at the fireplace, but it bounced off the andiron without igniting and rolled across the stone hearth as if mocking him.

"Is aught amiss, m'lord?" Mrs. Greevy asked. "I saw the post rider."

The marquess turned toward the door. His housekeeper

was a reedy, thin woman with a hatchet face. She wore her iron gray hair pulled into a mercilessly tight bun. Her stringy limbs were deceptively strong and the cold light in her narrow eyes made them glow with malevolence.

"He brought disturbing news from London, Elvira."

Mrs. Greevy studied the man to whom she had given her youth and life's devotion. The marquess wore his straight, salt-and-pepper hair clubbed back in a queue. He was a tall, heavy-boned, broad-shouldered man at the brink of midlife. His face looked to have been chiseled from granite. The Roman nose and high forehead bore the Wolverton stamp, as did his mouth. It was wide with thin lips that turned downward, closed tightly over large straight teeth. His gray eyes, framed by heavy black eyebrows, swept from her to the spot where the letter lay.

"Pray, what did the message say?" she wheedled, drawing as close as she dared. When she had first come into service at Wolf's Gate, he had taken her to his bed, but quickly tired of the plain, skinny serving wench. Elvira had married the chief butler and risen to become the marquess's housekeeper and a confidante of sorts. A taciturn man who preferred solitary drinking, Eastham had no close friends and only his younger brother, whom he detested.

He stared out the mullioned window, as if weighing whether or not to reply. At length, he said, "Hull thinks he may have found her."

She gave a sharp intake of breath before she was able to control her emotions. *No, it cannot be. Not after all these years.* "In London? How ever could she manage?"

Eastham gave a snort of disgust. "If his report is to be believed, she is a courtesan."

"It would explain much." Her tone was snide.

"You can credit it, then?" he asked. "She detested marital duties. Defiant, unnatural chit. No, it simply isn't possible."

"A flighty gel like that one, a thief, who knows what she might do?" Elvira said, carefully.

Eastham spat a series of guttural oaths and slammed his fist down on the oak windowsill. The panes made a brittle protest. "Demme, after all these years! I dare not chance her being alive, no matter how unlikely the possibility."

"If she is, Hull can kill her," Elvira replied with a feral light of hope in her eyes.

The marquess shook his head vigorously. "No! I shall have that pleasure."

She could read his expression and knew that he was visualizing the torturous games he could enjoy before he killed Amber. Elvira hid her hands in her apron so he could not see her clenched fists, not that he would pay any attention to her now that thoughts of that cherry-haired bitch crowded his mind.

"Summon the rider and have him wait outside the study door," he instructed her with a dismissive wave, turning his back on her.

As she walked stiffly from the room, he sat down at the large oak table against the wall and reached for a pen and paper. Perhaps this was good fortune. At last he would know that she was well and truly dead, just as everyone in Northumberland already believed. For this time when she returned to Wolf's Gate, she would never leave . . .

St. John's Wood

Amber sat by the bay window facing the small arbor that shielded her quarters from the outside. She could enjoy the lovely spring morning with no prying eyes to see her face in daylight. Hiding her identity had become second nature over the years. As far as anyone knew, Amber Leighigh Wolverton, Marchioness of Eastham, was dead. She took a sip of her morning coffee, strong and black just as she liked it, and broke the seal on Clyde Dyer's missive.

"It would appear that Barrington is everything he purports to be," she murmured to herself as she quickly read the Bow Street Runner's report. There was a brief mention of his spending some time in seminary before he bought a commission as a captain and went to war. She smiled. The seminary would go a ways toward explaining why so sinfully handsome a man had led such a monastic life. Also why, perhaps, he allied himself with unpopular reformist causes.

Tonight he would arrive at midnight for his first "lesson." Amber had considered all the courtesans at the House of Dreams, finding one reason or another to reject each. Hannah was too bawdy, Cicely too old, Lilly had a teasing manner he might not react well to, Claudia was too haughty . . . yet each of them was skilled and capable of doing what he requested. So were the others.

Amber had spent the last three days fretting about whether she dare do as Grace suggested, but was no closer to an answer. She glanced over at the document that would grant her admission to the Gallery of Lords. It lay propped against a sterling candelabra on the pier table across the room. The looping flourishes of penmanship on the velum seemed to taunt her.

"'Tis past time to make a decision. No further dithering as if I were some lack-wit," she murmured, arising. She reached for the bellpull. When her maid arrived, Amber said, "Bonnie, lay out my clothing. I will be going abroad this morning."

The maid bobbed a curtsy. "Which mourning gown do you wish?" she asked.

"The lighter bombazine. The day promises to be warm," Amber replied. "Please have Mr. Boxer bring the carriage around at half past the hour and inform Jenette."

Bonnie nodded and scurried away. She was a tiny thing with carrot-red hair and dense freckles, quick to learn and eager to please. She had been barely eleven years of age when Amber rescued her from the streets. Trained as a lady's dresser and now seventeen, she possessed the skills to work for the nobility or a wealthy Cit. Amber had offered to find her a good position, as she had for many other of the children she had saved, but Bonnie had chosen to remain with her benefactress.

Whenever Amber went outside her safe haven, she dressed in full mourning clothes, black from head to toe with a heavy veil on her bonnet, shielding her face from the public. Not only was it a precautionary disguise, but it also afforded her deferential treatment with few questions asked, even by the most addlepated people. She had just finished tying her bonnet and stepped back from the Girandole mirror to inspect her appearance when Jenette tapped on the chamber door.

"I see you are properly attired for the House of Lords," the Frenchwoman said with a jaunty tilt of her head. Her voice was low, musically accented. Jenette Claudine Beaurivage, daughter of Baron Rochemonde, had survived a date with Madame Guillotine by guile and good fortune. The rest of her family had not been so blessed. "Will you never tire of black?"

Sighing, Amber replied, "I detest it, but—"

"It serves you well, I know, *ma coeur*," Jenette said with a fond smile. "Are you armed?" The tall, slender blonde had been a spy against Napoleon before her flight, as adept at assassination as she was at seduction. She had become Amber's personal bodyguard, able to enter places with her friend that the retired soldiers in Lady Fantasia's employ could not.

Amber raised her reticule. "I would not dare leave it behind lest you scold."

"And you continue your practice shooting and reloading?"

"Not for the past few days," Amber replied distractedly.

Sensing her companion's mood, Jenette asked, "Has your unease anything to do with this zealot we are going to hear this morning?"

"I am interested in what the Earl of Barrington has to say

about child labor. As to whether he is a zealot . . . I shall reserve judgment."

Jenette frowned. "You had best beware of that one. He condemns places such as this and would see us closed down if it were within his power."

Amber laughed at Jenette's unintended irony. She had told no one save Grace about Barrington's midnight visit. "There is no other place 'such as this' in the Great Wen. Still, let us be grateful that neither Parliament nor Prinny possesses such power."

"True, but that has not stopped this earl and Madame More and Monsieur Wilberforce from attacking you as if you were a common bawd!"

"Don't work yourself into a pet, Jeni. I only wish to hear his legendary oratory and judge his sincerity for myself."

"Why do you concern yourself with such a man?" the Frenchwoman asked suspiciously. "I have heard that he is very handsome," she added, giving Amber a speculative look.

Amber appreciated the protection of her heavy veil, which hid the sudden flush blooming on her cheeks. "Perhaps we will better be able to judge if his character is equal to his physical appearance after he speaks." She tried for a careless Gallic shrug. "Perhaps not. But Parliament should act to prevent the exploitation of children."

"Pfft," Jenette said with a true Gallic shrug. "They only consider Mr. Peel's proposal to form a commission for the study of child labor. In spite of your earl's vaunted oratory, it will come to nothing. You are not the only one who reads the *Morning Chronicle*."

"I bow to your cynicism, my dear," Amber said curtly.

"Yet you will go?"

"Yet I will," was the determined reply. "Mr. Boxer and his arsenal await below." She practically stomped down the stairs. *This is insane. I should not do this.* The warning voice echoed inside her mind.

"Whatever would we do without our formidable sergeant major?" Jenette said gaily, ignoring the high dudgeon her questioning had induced.

Waldo Boxer, formerly with the Coldstream Guards, waited patiently at the door. The squat, sturdy man with the ruddy complexion and unfashionable chin whiskers smiled at the women with a twinkle in his pale blue eyes. "Good morning, m'ladies," he said as he opened the carriage door and assisted them inside before taking his place next to the driver. Like Jenette, he performed double service as servant and bodyguard.

The House of Lords met in the former Court of Requests, one of many chambers clustered about Westminster Hall. Boxer took a seat in the anteroom. Both he and Jenette observed those in line as they presented their vouchers for entry to the proceedings. Amber was well concealed by her veil. No one appeared to give the widow particular notice, but a few admiring glances were cast her companion's way. The beautiful Frenchwoman ignored them.

Amber and Jenette climbed the marble stairs to one of two balconies at opposite sides of the long, rectangular room, which had been refurbished for the peers. Painted a deep red, the chamber was supposed to exude gravitas. In fact, the intense color only made the space seem smaller. The press of people on the upper level contrasted with scant attendance on the floor.

"It would seem that the peerage has far less interest in the exploitation of children than do the citizens whom they supposedly serve," she murmured disdainfully to Jenette.

"I wager the Cits are more concerned with protecting their cheap labor supply than in seeing that Parliament cuts it off." Jenette's whisper was filled with the world-weary tolerance of one born of the Ancient Regime.

"A new day is dawning in England," Amber replied. "And I wager we shall see the reformers triumph."

Brass chandeliers dripped hot wax, adding more heat in the unventilated room. As she took a seat on a wooden bench in the second row, Amber resisted the urge to employ her fan. No, she dared not do anything to call attention to herself. *He will not recognize you, you paper skull!* She scanned the floor, looking for Barrington.

Jenette's jaundiced eye swept across the assembly casually, but she was, as always, on guard for any threat to her friend. "*Mai oui*, that must be your earl," she whispered to Amber. "There could be no other with the beauty of an archangel."

Amber followed Jenette's eyes to Robert St. John as he strode down the aisle. He looked even more handsome in harsh daylight than he had the night they met. Her breath caught, hitched faintly, and she tightened her grip on the fan at her wrist.

"You have perhaps met this one before?" Jenette's tone was dulcet.

Amber was saved from framing a reply when the opening of the debate began with a loud and bombastic speech from a Tory peer who heaped vitriol upon the Honorable Mr. Peel of Commons for the audacity of proposing the Parliament interfere in matters of labor, industry, and the natural order of Society.

"Fustian, I believe is what you English call it," Jenette whispered behind her fan.

As Amber nodded, there was a slight commotion at the gallery entrance. A lady, perhaps in her late twenties, took a seat in the front row directly below them. She was accompanied by an elderly gentleman. The silver blonde wore a half-mourning gown of lavender silk that complemented her delicate complexion. A widow and her father, Amber guessed, turning her attention back to the floor. The speaker had completed his remarks and took his seat.

"The House recognizes the Right Honorable Earl of Barrington," the leader said as Rob rose and walked to the center of the floor. Amber followed every step he took, straining to hear when he began to speak in a low voice.

"My lords, you have just heard an attack, not merely on a man, but on an idea—the idea that protecting English children from vicious enslavement is absurd and unnatural. Please allow me to describe what is truly unnatural, indeed unholy and utterly evil." As he spoke, his voice gradually rose in power and intensity. "Little boys as young as five years of age are sent down into the black bowels of the earth to mine coal. They swing heavy picks and other implements that ill fit the hand of a child. They toil before sunrise. They toil until the sun, at least, receives its well-deserved rest in the heavens. But these boys never see the sun, nor do they share its rest.

"Little girls as well as boys of the same tender age live out their brief lives in huge, filthy mill houses tending dangerous machinery, often sixteen hours a day until they faint with exhaustion and hunger. I have seen on the streets of London the results of this vicious practice—five-year-old beggar children missing hands, arms, feet, legs—appendages that were ripped from their tender bodies by mechanical looms. Those even less fortunate, although that may be a point of debate, die when sheer fatigue causes them to fall into the machinery, where they are ground alive. Ground like sausage!

"Who among you has not employed a sweepster to bring his climbing boys to clean out the many chimneys in your homes? Do you know that these small children are sold by their starving parents? As surely as Africans are slaves in America, these children are slaves right here in England! Their English owners prod them into the soot-stained confines of chimneys, employing lighted torches to the soles of small, bare feet."

By this time, there were visible shudders of revulsion, grimaces of disgust, and, pointedly, sniffs of disdain from various of the listeners. Amber leaned forward, enthralled by the passion of his message and the power of his voice. Its richness melodically filled the chamber, mesmerizing even those who were angered that he would describe such cruelties so vividly.

Jenette noticed the beauteous widow seated in front of them. Although it was against the rules, she appeared to be making notes on a small tablet she had taken from her reticule. "An admirer such as yourself?" she whispered to Amber.

Amber blinked and forced herself to look down at the woman who was closer to her than to Jenette. When she read the contents on the page, her lips curled with contempt. "I think not," she hissed through gritted teeth, returning her attention to the floor where the earl was closing his remarks. As soon as he had finished, the blonde woman and her companion rose and made their way from the gallery.

"You are angry—oh, I do not mean only with the horrid evils your earl so stirringly decried—but with the woman. Why?" Jenette asked

Amber's eyes remained fixed on Robert St. John when she replied, "The vacuous creature was composing menus. And please reframe from calling him *my* earl."

Jenette studied her for a moment, then said, "I wonder, eh?"

Amber's head snapped around. "I believe it is time to depart. All we will hear in rebuttal is indeed fustian."

They followed the old man and younger woman down the stairs. As they waited their turn while a line of carriages pulled up, Amber and Jenette discussed the earl's speech. "Well, he spoke with force and clarity," Amber said.

"*Oui, certainement*, I could not agree more. The man is *magnifique!*"

Overhearing Jenette's remarks, the blonde's escort murmured loud enough for them to hear, "Demned Frenchies everywhere. We delivered them from the tyrant. Why do they not go home?"

The blonde made a shushing sound. "Father, please," she

said, pulling him toward a carriage whose footman was opening the door.

"How insufferably rude," Amber said, loud enough for the old curmudgeon to hear.

Jenette only laughed, patting Amber's arm. "*Alors,* if only I had a home to which I might return, perhaps I would oblige the English gentleman."

Amber could see the wistful sadness in her friend's eyes that gave the lie to the fanciful rejoinder. "What would I do if you left me, Jeni?"

"You could return to France with me, *ma coeur.* Your French is every bit as excellent as your English." Just then their carriage arrived. As Boxer assisted them inside, Jenette said, "I would be spared such fools as that Englishman if only I could erase my wretched accent."

"Never say it," Amber remonstrated. "Men find your voice lilting, enchanting."

"Ah, yes, the perfect lover of every English gentleman's imagination, a French aristo," Jenette replied dryly.

Amber felt a tremor sweep over her. Could it work? Dare she try? When they reached their residence, Amber escaped Jenette's shrewd gaze and locked herself in her chambers. She paced for several hours, hearing his voice, seeing the brutal images his words evoked, the righteous anger he truly felt. He was as beautiful and as wrathful as an archangel. And noble to the core of his heart.

She sucked in a breath. Could a French noblewoman be his fantasy lover?

Chapter Three

*O*n the stroke of midnight, Rob entered the House of Dreams by the rear door for the second time. As arranged, he walked down the deserted hallway to Lady Fantasia's quarters. The door was ajar. He tapped discreetly and she answered. "Please come in and have a seat."

As at their first meeting, she sat in shadows. He fought the urge to walk over to her and take a good look at her face. Did it match her clipped, cultured voice? Some instinct honed on the battlefield made him resist. This was no woman to anger.

Amber could sense the tension in his body. He was wound as tightly as a spring on a timepiece. So was she, but she had spent many trying years learning to conceal it. *I am in control here. This is a secure place where I belong.* But once she was in bed with him . . . She pushed the frightening thought aside and took a calming breath, knowing her lines as well as the best-trained actor at Drury Lane.

"After some consideration, I have selected a young woman who will suit your needs perfectly," she began.

Rob felt his fingers tighten around the wooden chair arm. "Then tell me where I am to meet her and—"

"Do not rush your fences, m'lord. 'Tis the downfall of most men." She could see his face flush as he forced himself to settle back in the chair. "You must know a few things about Gabrielle. She is a French émigrée, forced from her home by the tyrant. All of her family are dead, her birthright gone. She was . . . ill treated before her escape and has little reason to trust men. She is not a courtesan. I have explained your requirements and Gaby is agreeable. She will be as grateful for the darkness as will you."

Rob muttered an oath of outrage. "A woman who was abused—and you want me to . . . to . . ." He stammered to a halt.

"Precisely. She has known cruelty, but you will show her kindness. Every woman knows what pleases her . . . if only a man is willing to go slowly and take instruction regarding what she wants. You are blessed with one who is willing to tell you what she wants."

He turned the idea over in his mind. Perhaps this was a stroke of genius. His throat constricted as he asked, "This would be her fantasy, then?"

Amber nodded, not trusting her own voice for a moment. What he said was far too close to the truth for comfort. Gathering her thoughts, she continued. "You may rest assured that a young woman such as Gabrielle will not feign pleasure. She would not have any idea how to do so . . . but culmination may take . . . several visits. Do you agree to these conditions?"

It was Rob's turn to nod, speechless.

"Gabrielle may be nervous. Stroke her, kiss her, above all, ask her what does and does not please her as you proceed."

Swallowing for courage, Rob answered, "Yes, yes, I can do that." *I will do that.* "Perhaps it is not so very different from getting a skittish mount to trust one."

Amber felt an unexpected tinge of humor and released a husky chuckle. "Were you perchance in the cavalry, m'lord?" she asked, already knowing the answer from her Bow Street Runner's report.

"Two years on the Peninsula," he replied. "I have been told I have a way with animals. If only it could be transferred to women!" he blurted out, then felt his face flame and cursed silently.

"Perhaps women and mares do have a bit in common, but do not be disappointed if Gabrielle fails to whinny for you."

Under other circumstances, Rob would have appreciated her glib retort. But the situation was far too painful. "If she tells me what to do, I will do it," he gritted out.

"I apologize, m'lord. It was wicked of me to tease. Now then, I have told Gabrielle only that you are one of France's liberators, a major in the British army. That fact alone has given her the highest regard for you."

He had, in fact, been a captain, but it did not signify. All he wished to do now was begin this insane venture. Perhaps it would work . . . perhaps it would fail. He had to take the risk. His whole future hung in the balance.

Sensing his unease, Amber made a dismissing gesture with her hand as she said, "Gabrielle will come to you within the hour by a private entrance. This will allow you to gather your thoughts as you disrobe," she added quickly lest he protest the delay. She required time to bathe with a fresh lilac scent so that he could never recognize her by the attar of roses that she normally wore. "Go to the last door on the right at the end of the hall. It has but one candle that you are to douse after you remove your clothing. I trust you do not require the services of a batman to do so?"

Rob almost overturned the chair in his haste to rise. "I am quite capable of disrobing." She made no mention of a nightshirt. He was too embarrassed to inquire. If a robe was there, he would don it. If not . . . He sighed and turned to meet his fate.

As soon as he was gone, Amber stood. Her legs were so weak they almost gave way. She gripped the pier table behind her for support and took a deep breath, then walked unsteadily to her changing room. Bonnie quickly removed her gown and undergarments, then stood by as her mistress sank into the scented bathwater. She had worn no perfume that day, so her hair did not require washing. That might have raised some awkward questions.

When she stepped from the bath, Bonnie floated a sheer

silk night rail over her head. The few pins holding her heavy mass of hair slipped out easily. Amber shook it free, feeling the weight tickle her back before Bonnie held up a robe. As she slipped it on, she thought of her parting remark to the earl. The irony of having a dresser while he had none was rich, but she found no humor in it.

With Bonnie leading the way to make certain the hallways were clear, Amber followed a circuitous route to the opposite side of the house, then dismissed the maid with a smile of thanks. She stood inside a small retiring room before the assignation chamber's hidden door. The light beneath it went dark. She heard the rustle of covers and thought of Robert St. John, lying naked on the large bed. The image would not quite come into focus, but her mind held a shadowy vision of that long, lean body stretched across the mattress.

It will be dark. He cannot see. He is here only to please you.

No amount of rationalizing was going to make this any easier. Amber reached for the knob, turning it to meet her fate.

Rob heard the door and tensed as it opened. He caught the faintest outline of a slender feminine shape in the very dim light behind her. Then utter blackness once more enveloped the room. He cleared his throat and whispered, "Gabrielle?"

"*Oui, mon commandant,*" she replied in soft, melodic French, judging by the sound of his voice that he sat on the left side of the bed. Feeling her way, she drew nearer. He was so close she could feel his body heat, hear the sound of his breathing. She slowly stretched out her hand. It touched the hard muscles of his shoulder. "I will sit on the bed with you, please?" she asked.

Her voice was soft, thickly accented yet delicate. Somehow it put him slightly at ease. "Yes, of course," he replied, feeling the mattress shift ever so slightly as she sat beside him. After waiting for what seemed a long, awkward moment, he asked, "What do you want me to do?"

"I . . . I am not certain. First, perhaps we talk a little, *oui?*"

The faint essence of lilacs teased his nostrils. "What do you wish to talk about?" he asked in a strangled voice.

"I thank you for allowing the darkness. You do not mind?" she asked.

"Not at all. In fact . . . I—I requested it," he admitted.

"Then you understand a lady's . . ." She appeared to grope for the right word, then said, "How a lady would feel."

The awkwardness grew. "I will try my best to understand."

"Then . . . then we begin. May I touch your face—to read it like the Braille writing?"

"You can read Braille?" he asked.

"Not truly . . . but I can imagine how it might be."

"You must have sensitive fingertips," he said with a smile, feeling the awkwardness fading. "Yes, please, touch my face."

Following the sound of his voice, she placed her fingertips on his cheek, caressing it until she heard his breath catch. She moved up to those wickedly arched eyebrows, then to his eyelids, following the narrow blade of his patrician nose. Using both hands, she dug her fingers into the thick curly hair of his head. When she traced the bold line of his jaw and touched his mouth, she felt a smile curve his lips.

"What do you read?" The question seemed to ask itself.

"You are very handsome, *mon commandant*, and good of spirit." Her voice sounded as breathless as his.

"You have lovely soft hands. May I touch your face now?"

"*Oui.* I would like that, I think."

His hand was large and warm, the fingers careful as they glided across the satin of her skin. Her nose was slim and delicate, her eyes thickly lashed, her chin pointed a bit. He tried to imagine what she must look like. A beauty, certainly. Then he felt a tiny ridge across her left cheekbone, about a half inch long, so small he almost missed it. A scar?

The thought of someone harming this lovely creature infuriated him.

The instant he touched the scar, she felt him pause, then tense. "Does my imperfection displease you?" she asked hesitantly.

His fingertip caressed it delicately. "No, but the one who did this, I would like to kill." When she stiffened, he quickly said, "I apologize. I did not intend to bring back painful memories. Will you forgive me, Gabrielle?"

She took a deep breath and pushed back the ugliness. *It is past. Over. This is now*, she reminded herself. "There is nothing to forgive. Only let us forget all else for this night. It belongs only to us, *oui*?"

"To us. No one else," he echoed, waiting. He could feel his erection, so quickly growing rock hard, something that had not happened since . . . No, he pushed back his own painful memories. *"Gabrielle will not feign pleasure. But culmination may take several visits."* He wondered if he could endure several moments, much less visits. Yes, he could. He would. He must. Then her soft voice broke into his jumbled thoughts.

"Perhaps you could kiss my hand?" she asked, cupping his jaw until he took the hand and pressed its back to his lips. *"Non,"* she whispered, turning it so his mouth touched her palm. When he kissed it, heat coursed up her arm. She had been told a woman's palms and wrists were sensitive, but she had never imagined how much so! Eager for more, she moved her hand across his lips until his mouth touched the pulse at the base of her inner wrist. "There, oh!"

He could feel her pulse race when he plied his lips against it. Her tiny gasp of excitement elicited an unexpected surge of satisfaction. Taking the initiative, he raised her hand gently and let his mouth travel up the inside of her arm. When her free hand cupped his shoulder, he felt her nails dig into the muscles. *Like a kitten kneading in pleasure!* The experience was utterly new, heady, wonderful.

"Does this please you?" he asked, certain that it did.

"*Oui.* Perhaps . . ."

"Yes," he drawled, falling under the spell of her soft French accent, eager for further instruction.

"Perhaps you would try kissing my neck and throat . . . *s'il vous plaît?*"

The pulse points. Of course! What felt good on her wrist and arm would also feel good there. He moved his mouth to the curve where her shoulder joined her neck and kissed her silky skin until he found the tiny hollow at the center of her throat. "Do you like that?" he asked, his heart hammering in his chest.

"I think it would be better if you made the kissing softer, like the wings of a butterfly," she murmured near his ear.

Pausing to control his excitement, he repeated the caresses slowly, letting his lips dance across her throat. She threw back her head, allowing him greater access, now holding on to him with both hands gripping his shoulders. Rob felt the tips of her breasts brush against his bare chest. This brought the fire he had tamped down raging to sudden life. He fought the irresistible urge to pull her into his arms and roll onto the bed.

She knew they were poised at the brink of an abyss. The tips of her breasts tingled from the feel of his chest muscles. It would be so easy to give in. His whole body had grown tense with lust. But the faint male musk of his arousal reminded her that doing the deed so quickly would help neither of them. Her lazy, delicious haze of pleasure dissipated.

"Lie back, *mon commandant,*" she commanded cajolingly. "We must go slowly . . . lightly . . . softly. Here, I can feel your heart pounding," she whispered, pressing her palm against the springy hair on his chest, pushing him onto the mattress.

He complied, lying on his back in the center of the bed. She sat beside him, gently holding him down, feeling the thrum of his racing heartbeat. "Now . . ." She waited, hoping he would continue to defer to her wishes, giving him time to do so.

"Now?" he finally echoed hoarsely.

"Now I will read more of your body. I need to become accustomed to how it feels . . . to how you are made."

If she touched his fully aroused sex, it could frighten her and it most certainly would undo his struggle for self-restraint. But before he could say anything, she knelt on the bed and ran her hand over his chest. "I think my heart may burst free and explode," he said raggedly.

"I would not wish you harm, *mon ami*. Does this not please you?"

"Ah, Gabrielle, it pleases me all too well."

"Then I will continue, for it pleases me, too." She felt the cunning pattern of hair and the hard muscles. He was young, powerful, all male, and, she hoped, completely hers to command. She glided her hand up to his collarbone, tracing along it, then around one broad shoulder, feeling the biceps bulge as he clenched his hand into a fist. She could sense that he was fighting for control. "You are a strong man, *mon commandant* . . . and very beautifully made, I think."

Rob had never been vain of his looks. In fact, the subtle and more often not-so-subtle invitations in women's eyes had always made him uncomfortable. Yet her simple declaration pleased him greatly. "I am glad you think so, Gabrielle," was all he could reply. The barest essence of her perfume again teased his nostrils. It was torture. It was paradise, all at the same time. He waited for her to say something. When she did not, he asked, "What do you wish me to do now that you have . . . read my face and body?"

"W-would you kiss my lips?" she asked hesitantly, scooting closer but keeping one leg over the edge of the mattress. She wanted to trust, but it was nearly impossible. Her right hand remained resting lightly on his chest.

He sat up and took her hand in his, once again pressing

his lips to her palm, then kissing his way softly up her arm. Like butterfly wings. The thought hammered in his brain. Soft. Slow. She made a low hum of pleasure as he reached her throat, brushing it once more with his mouth. He framed her face with his hands and tilted his head to place a chaste kiss on her lips, being careful not to press too hard. Then he withdrew, still holding her face, feeling the heavy silk of her hair spilling over his fingers.

"Did you like that?" he asked.

"*Oui* . . . but . . ."

"I was too rough." His heart constricted. When she gave a tiny, mischievous chuckle, he was so startled that he dropped his hands from her head, tangling them in her hair. "What amuses you?" he asked, trying not to sound as frustrated as he felt.

"Oh, please forgive me, *mon ami*. I did not mean to anger you, but it is only that you were not . . . rough at all. I mean . . . well, I have been told that a man's lips should move over a woman's, brushing, teasing. Please . . . I do not mean to be bold, but . . ."

"Very well," Rob replied, taking her face in his hands once again. He could feel the blush heating her cheeks. This time he did as she instructed, turning his head back and forth to caress her mouth . . . brushing, teasing, still careful. He was rewarded when her hands stole up his arms and held his shoulders. *Remember the butterfly wings.* After a moment, he raised his head and asked, "Am I doing this correctly?"

"It is most excellent. Now you could kiss me again, please, but open your mouth . . . perhaps just a little bit, so you can touch my lips with your tongue. I have heard that such a thing feels very . . . agreeable." The courtesans called it French-kissing, when two tongues dueled, openmouthed. Grace had explained that it was far more than "agreeable." Somehow she had never thought it sounded appealing . . . until now.

"Let us find out if such kissing is indeed agreeable," he whispered raggedly. He sought her mouth and brushed against it, opening his enough to let his tongue rim her lips. She moaned quite distinctly this time, clutching his shoulders until her nails dug into the muscles as she leaned into his kiss.

Oh, good heavens above, Grace had been right! The tingle that began on her lips spread all over her body. She pressed her mouth to his, harder, then opened her lips. Would he understand what she wanted?

What could he do but enter the sweet chamber into which he had been invited? He let the tip of his tongue dart tentatively inside. Her teeth were smooth and even, the taste of her as pure as spring water. When she did not pull away but opened wider, he dared to touch his tongue to the tip of hers before withdrawing, breathless. "Is this agreeable?"

"*Oui!* But I think we need a better word than 'agreeable.' Your tongue . . . when it touched mine . . ."

"You mean like this?" He knelt on the mattress and lowered his head over hers, taking care to keep enough distance between their bodies so as not to alarm her with his erection. He kissed her again, slanting his mouth, opening it for another foray between the barely parted seam of her lips. He teased at them and she parted them quickly, making him bolder this time when he slipped inside. *Butterfly wings! Butterfly wings!* He let his tongue dart and dance against hers until she returned the caress in his hungry mouth.

They kissed for a breathless moment, then two. Both were eager, experimenting with tastes and textures never experienced. She felt as if lightning had struck her, setting her on fire. Oh, such a sweet burning! Such a dangerous addiction! His staff, rock hard and desperate, brushed her thigh at the height of their kissing frenzy. He had her hair tangled in his hands, holding fistfuls of it as he bracketed her head, kissing her as she had never been kissed before.

This is going too fast, too far! If she did not stop him soon, everything would be ruined. She was suddenly afraid. He was starting to lose control. She knew what she must do. Steeling her willpower, she pulled away, testing to see if she could break through the haze of his passion. For one panicked moment, she feared it would not work.

Rob felt Gabrielle's hands pressing against his chest, her head turning away from his impassioned kisses. He released her, panting and breathless, trembling. "I . . . I am sorry. Please forgive—"

"*Non!* Do not be sorry. There is nothing to forgive," she whispered fiercely, feeling an ache of emptiness that unbalanced her. "But if I am to teach you how to control your pleasure so that you may bring equal pleasure to a woman, then we must stop . . . for tonight."

Rob sighed and sat back on his heels in the middle of the big bed. "You . . . you are not frightened by me? I did not repulse you?" He felt his ardor wilting as quickly as his erection.

What would ever make him think he could repulse a woman! She vowed to find out. "*Oui*, I am a bit frightened by my own feelings, but you could never repulse me, *mon commandant*. In fact, you are a pupil most . . . *exceptionnel*. You have quite mastered kissing, I think."

He digested that, for this once wishing they did not have to be cloaked in darkness. He wanted to read her expression. Her voice sounded earnest, almost girlish at the last. "You enjoyed my kisses—truly?"

"*Vrainment. Oui*, truly, I did. Only consider this until you return to me tomorrow night. We do not want our passion— I mean, your passion—to carry us too far, too quickly. We must go slowly, softly at first—like—"

Rob sighed. "Like butterfly wings, I know."

After slipping through the hidden door into the retiring closet, Amber leaned against the wall, composing herself.

The mirror in the corner showed a bright flush on her cheeks, tangled hair, and huge, wild eyes. She took a deep breath, trying not to listen to the sounds of the earl dressing beyond the door.

I must get away from here . . . from him! When she heard the door to his room open and close, Amber reached for the bellpull. Almost instantly Bonnie stepped inside, curtsying nervously, her eyes downcast as she waited for instructions.

"You may tell Sergeant-Major Boxer to put away his brace of Manton pistols and retire for the night. I will not require his services."

When Bonnie left, Amber collapsed against the wall. She had thought she might need protection from the earl. Her laugh was soft and bitter. She never imagined that she would need protection from "Gabrielle."

Chapter Four

In the jumble of policing jurisdictions in London, Bow Street was the busiest. On any given day, dozens, even hundreds of people passed through its chambers, some willingly, many under physical restraint. Sullen young pickpockets, crafty old bawds, and drunken toffs, offenders of low and high degree, awaited deliverance to the courts. Mingling with them were an equally diverse group of law-abiding citizens seeking redress. Staid bankers and plump boarding-house matrons eyed non-propertied slum dwellers with disdain, often shoving ahead of them in the ill-formed lines that crowded the railing. The runners were adept at listening to one supplicant while tuning out the babble of sound surrounding them.

That morning, a slattern from the Billingsgate fish market reeking of "blue ruin" gin related how she had been robbed by the emaciated boy she held in one red, meaty fist. She twisted his shirt collar so tightly he made strangling noises. Close by a man in a clean but cheaply cut wool jacket wrung his hands, trying to avoid contact with her while waiting his turn. A drunken Corinthian whose doe-skin inexpressibles were stained with claret brayed in a nasal voice, demanding he be placed at the head of the shortest line.

Alan Cresswel had been a runner for over two decades, a long time in a hard and dangerous job. Tall and rangy, he had once possessed considerable speed, an asset while learning his trade. Now his wind was all but gone. However, over the years the clever fellow with the pockmarked face had made a reputation for himself around Westminster. He honed survival instincts and learned how to turn a tidy profit, often with clients who were not law abiding. As long as they could pay, Cressy was happy to work for them.

"Come along, what is it now?" he asked over the din, inspecting his next petitioner's appearance as he waited impatiently for a reply. The younger man shoved a shock of greasy straight tan hair from his high forehead. His clothing, while that of a gentleman, was certainly not made by a London tailor. He was of medium height, thin with a slight thickening around his waist that hinted at dissipation. His sallow complexion and the puffiness beneath his close-set eyes proclaimed it. A large nose with broken red veins moving across it like poorly spun spiderwebs was set in a long, angular face.

Out at heels chawbacons. Cresswel sighed. "Well, out with it," he said, irritated by the smirk on the young fellow's face.

"If you are the chap known as Cressy, you can attend me in a quiet alehouse. What I have to say is not for common ears." He glanced disdainfully around the room.

Cresswel shifted slightly, looking up at the man. "Why should I desert me post for you?" he asked. When the complainant pulled a fat purse from his waistcoat and hefted it in his hand, the runner nodded. "Maybe I do 'ave a bit o' thirst," he said.

They made their way through the crowd and left the offices. As they walked, the stranger said, "I am Mr. Hull, late of Northumberland."

Cresswel had already deduced that from the accent. Among his repertoire of skills, he possessed an ear for patterns of speech. "What's this business 'not for common ears'?"

"I need some help with a runaway gel. Might be a deal of the ready in it for you."

"She be gentry?"

Hull snorted, peeling back his lips to reveal crooked teeth going to rot. "She's the wife of a bloody marquess, but she ain't a lady now. His Lordship sent me to fetch her."

Now Cresswel became truly interested. A bloody marquess. Yes, lots of the ready, he would wager on it. "The Hare and Hound's just round the corner. We can talk real private."

The interior of the public house was dark and smelled of spilled ale and rotting wood, but it was quiet. The owner knew Cresswel and quickly ushered them into a small room. After serving them pints of foamy liquid, the barkeep closed the door and departed. Hull pulled the pouch from his waistcoat and tossed it on the table. The runner picked it up, nodding. "Now, where's this here woman live?"

"A fortnight past, I chanced to be at White's on St. James Street," Hull said, self-importantly.

"I know where all the gents' clubs is located, 'less they put wheels on 'em this mornin'," Cresswel interjected impatiently. "But I'd give odds she ain't in any of 'em."

The smirk on Hull's face vanished at the cheeky reply. "I learned where she resides when a member described her," he snapped. "He was foxed, talking loudly to his companion. The chit's in some crib called the House of Dreams."

Cresswel's jaw dropped. "Crib, my arse! It's all the crack! Most expensive bordello in London, it is. Every lord and cit with enough blunt be pantin' to get inside. And lots of 'em don't make it. That's where your run-off marchioness is?"

Hull nodded. "This baron saw her in the hallway of a private area where he was not supposed to be. He had just relieved himself in a pot of greenery. Chit didn't see him, but he saw her. Then the madam's guards caught up with him and tossed his arse out the front door. He kept remarking to his friend on the odd color of her hair. Dark cherry red. Said she was a real beauty. Not too many like that, I'd warrant. He even mentioned a scar the marquess gave her—a little nick on her left cheekbone. Obviously I shall require help to get her out of the place."

Cresswel digested the information. "That ain't going to be a brace of snaps. The gels what work for Lady Fantasia is guarded closer than Prinny."

"Lady Fantasia?" Hull echoed, scratching his head. "I recall that baron saying something about her—no one ever sees her face, some such rot."

"No rot." Cresswel scratched his chin thoughtfully. "I don't know about stealin' a whore from that woman. 'Er guards is all veterans. Fought ole Boney. A mean lot, they are."

Hull's eyes narrowed and he hunched forward over the table. "You ain't met the marquess. Nobody is meaner than that one."

George Berry's grocery emporium boasted the finest teas and coffees from the far reaches of the British Empire, not to mention the very best spirits to be had in the city. The wealthy, Quality and Cits alike, traveled to St. James Street to make their selections. Rich, strong coffee was one of Amber's indulgences ever since she had been introduced to the beverage while traveling in Tuscany. Feeling a need to get away from the House of Dreams, she decided to spend the morning amid the fragrances that reminded her of her first taste of freedom.

While Boxer waited patiently outside, she and Jenette walked up and down the aisles, examining the merchandise. When Amber took a deep breath, her friend said with a chuckle, "I do believe you would apply coffee beans in place of fine French perfume if given the choice."

Opening a tin of beans from Java, Amber sniffed. "What a novel idea. Yes, perhaps I should start a new fashion that will become all the kick, as the toffs say."

As they ambled along with a clerk following obsequiously

behind them to carry the "widow's" purchases, Amber suddenly froze. Jenette stared at her. "What is amiss, *cherie?*" she asked, reaching into her reticule for the Forsyth percussion-lock pocket pistol she carried.

Amber held up her hand to silence her friend, then whispered, "Nothing." From the far end of the aisle she could hear Robert St. John's voice, cordially greeting a lady. Their voices drew nearer. *I'm well disguised. He has never seen my face.* Yet her heart hammered almost as hard as it had the night past when Gabrielle instructed him, naked in her bed. In an attempt to blot out that unsettling image, Amber seized a box of tea and perused its wooden stamp as if examining a Faberge egg.

Jenette kept her hand on her pistol inside the reticule, listening to the man's voice. Where had she heard it before? But of course, the handsome earl whose impassioned speech had so moved Amber! As he turned the corner of the aisle with the lady, Jenette read the tension in her friend's body. Not wanting to appear as if she were gaping, the French-woman also picked up a tin and examined it, but could not resist saying, "He does cut a dashing figure in those tightly fitted breeches and the kerseymere tailcoat. I wonder how well he rides."

Her suggestive tone was not lost on Amber. "I am quite certain I would not know," she said, unable to take her eyes off the way his broad shoulders and long legs flattered the tailor's art. He moved down the aisle with pantherish grace, attending the slender blonde who was speaking.

"Mr. Berry blends my teas to precise instruction," his companion said in a soft, whispery voice. "Oh, Elgin, do be careful!" A little boy no more than two years of age leaned away from the nursemaid carrying him. One chubby fist swiped at a stack of small tins, knocking them to the floor. "Phoebe, you were to watch that he did not touch anything!" she scolded the servant. "Now look what has happened. I feel a complete cake," she said, looking at the earl as several clerks came scurrying.

"'Tis natural for a child to possess curiosity, Lady Oberly, and you are not a cake," he replied, grinning at the child whose face clouded when he was restrained by the young nursemaid struggling to hold him.

"I try not to indulge him too much," she said over Elgin's wail. "But we do love outings such as this . . . until some, er, difficulty occurs. I suppose you will tell me 'tis natural for disasters to follow all little boys." The lady gave the earl a mischievous smile.

Watching the exchange set Amber's teeth on edge. They were flirting! This was the woman he intended to court when her mourning period was finished. Paying no notice to the two women at the opposite end of the aisle, the earl raised his hands, palms up, and replied, "I grew up with two older cousins. We created disasters that would put this small, er, difficulty in the shade."

When Elgin continued to cry, his mother instructed the maid to take him to their carriage. The clerks made swift work of restacking the merchandise as Jenette whispered to Amber, "That is the one who writes menus while the earl speaks."

"Now we know for whom she composes them," Amber replied more tartly than she intended.

"Perhaps we should leave," Jenette suggested, but Amber shook her head. Some perverse instinct held her rooted to the floor, eavesdropping as the handsome couple continued chatting.

"It was so fortunate that I chanced to meet you here, Lord Barrington. I would have your opinion on a new blend of tea that I shall introduce at my dinner party on Friday next."

"You are out of mourning now?" he inquired as they strolled past Amber and Jenette.

"Yes. I do miss the baron, but he has been gone for a year.

'Tis time that I rejoin society. Please say you will favor me by attending," she cajoled.

"I should be delighted. Now, where is this marvelous new tea blend?"

As they disappeared around the next aisle, Jenette asked dryly, "Why do I disbelieve she chanced to meet him here? She has set out to have him. *Quel dommage!* She might succeed." The Frenchwoman observed Amber's reaction.

"She is of his class, beautiful, and has proven herself capable of bearing the earl an heir," Amber replied, trying to keep her tone neutral.

"There is nothing such as a babe in arms to win a man's heart—providing, of course, that the arms belong to a servant," Jenette said scornfully.

"'Tis the English custom to use nursemaids. At least she brought the child with her."

"The better to appeal to your earl."

"He is not *my* earl. I wish you would leave off saying that," Amber snapped, still clutching the tea in her hand.

"Take care you do not get the splinter through your gloves," Jenette said with a knowing smirk. "You have, perhaps, a small *tendresse* for this earl, *oui?*" Her shrewd gaze bored in on her friend's averted eyes.

"Do not be ridiculous. I merely applaud his concern for children." Although she had never before kept a secret from Jenette, Amber had not told her he was a patron. It was too painfully . . . personal. If not for Grace, Amber never would have gathered the courage to become involved.

Ignoring Jenette's gibe, she placed the small wooden box on the shelf and stalked ahead. So, that vacuous blonde was the woman he intended to court . . . the woman he wanted to please in bed once he had made her his countess.

"I do not like her," Jenette said, as if reading Amber's mind.

"I do not like her, either," Amber admitted, vowing to have Lady Oberly investigated.

The young clerk gave them her name—Verity Chivins, Baroness Oberly. Before the earl visited Gabrielle that night, Amber wanted to speak with him, perhaps learn what he knew—or thought he knew—about his baroness. "You will be late for your appointment with Madame Velange if we do not hurry," she said to Jenette.

"There is ample time," the Frenchwoman replied, sauntering down the aisle, selecting special treats and tossing them into the basket the clerk held.

Amber gritted her teeth. The earl had been dressed for riding and it had just begun to rain when they approached the grocery. She had an idea, but it would only work if she could leave Jenette at the modiste for her fitting and then have her driver head toward Portman Square. "If we do not hurry we shall be soaked before we reach the carriage. 'Tis starting to rain much harder," she said, looking out the bow window at the front of the building.

With a careless shrug, Jenette capitulated. "As you wish, *ma coeur.*"

When Amber paid for her purchases, she was delighted to see the baroness still had Barrington dancing attendance on her at the tea blending table. He paid no heed to her or Jenette. It was not unusual for men to ignore a woman veiled and dressed in black, but Jenette's beauty usually turned heads. The earl appeared well smitten with Baroness Oberly.

Once Jenette had been handed down and entered the French modiste's shop, Amber instructed Boxer to return to St. James Street instead of heading directly home. Knowing the direction of Barrington's city house, she intended to find him as "accidentally" as had the baroness. What could be more natural than to offer a ride in a closed carriage when it was raining?

If he accepts, then what shall you do? She knew she was playing with fire. This was unwise, but something compelled her to speak with him away from the place where he would meet

Gabrielle tonight. Perhaps she would not run across him on London's busy streets. What if he had not gone directly home but to his men's club, or tailor, or . . . wherever? Just when she was about to tap on the roof and instruct the driver to return home, she saw him mounted on a splendid black stallion.

The earl stood out in the crowd, guiding his horse through the throng sloshing along Oxford. While others hunched down in the rain, scurrying hither and yon to escape, he rode as if the skies were not pouring cold spring showers. She leaned out the carriage window just enough to call out to him.

Rob recognized the crisp, cultured voice calling his name over the seething babble of street vendors and cursing draymen. Lady Fantasia? Then he saw the veiled woman in the expensive, unmarked black coach. Of course, if she hid her identity on her own property, she would do so in public. He cut across the press of soaked pedestrians, rigs, and riders.

"Might I offer you a ride in this beastly weather, m'lord?" she inquired.

Had he seen her somewhere today? The severe bonnet with its heavy veil looked vaguely familiar. As if she had cued it, the rain turned into a downpour. "That would be most kind, if you are certain it is no inconvenience."

"I would not have stopped if it were, m'lord. Please tie your reins to my carriage and come in out of this deluge," she instructed.

Looking about the busy street, Rob did as he was bid and climbed in the open door. The coach's interior was commodious, upholstered in deep black velvet. In the dim light, the black-clad woman seemed to blend into the squabs. "Still careful to conceal your identity, I see," he said as he took a seat across from her. "Might I ask why?"

"You may ask, but I will not answer," she replied.

"Was there perchance a Lord Fantasia whom you mourn?" he asked.

"I do not mourn," she replied sharply, then settled back and tried to focus. Sitting so close to him in confined quarters during daylight was insanely dangerous. She took a steadying breath.

"The first time we met, 'twas I who was nervous. Now it would appear our roles have reversed." He smiled ruefully, recalling his awkward interview with the mysterious madam four days past. Had one night with Gabrielle given him this new confidence . . . or was it Lady Fantasia's shift in demeanor? *She is vulnerable.* The thought surprised him.

She watched as he brushed glistening droplets of water from his dark hair and jacket. His presence seemed to fill the space. The aroma of damp wool blended subtly with a faint hint of horse and the male essence of him. She rearranged her skirt, tucking her slippers beneath the hem to avoid touching his Hessians. His long legs stretched across the space between them.

When he felt the carriage start moving into the traffic, he said, "You may tell your driver—"

"He knows your direction." At his raised eyebrow, she replied, "Recall your first visit when I told you all patrons are discreetly investigated."

"So you know my city house is not overly far from your establishment. What else might you know?" He peered at her veiled face, wondering again if it matched her splendid figure. The urge to reach across the coach and lift the veil on her bonnet was almost irresistible. The older man sitting next to her driver would probably shoot him. Both fellows had a military bearing about them.

"Would it surprise you to learn that upon occasion I attend parliamentary speeches?"

"I suspect there are many things about you that would surprise me," he replied honestly. "Did you hear me speak?"

"I was in the gallery when you described the abominable

exploitation of children this past week. You were most impressive."

"I thank you for your kind words, but my oratorical abilities, such as they are, have had little effect." He had been correct. She had surprised him once more. This topic was the last one he could have imagined.

"Do not look so amazed. Even a 'frail flower' requires diversion, and since there were no cock fights or bear baitings scheduled for that day, I decided a session of Lords would serve almost as well. I've often found it difficult to discern much difference between political debate among the Peers of the Realm and the crowing and roaring of bestial combat."

Rob blinked, then threw back his head and laughed. "I detect a cat-in-cream tone in your voice. You tease my earnest efforts."

"Hardly. I quite agree with Mr. Hazlett regarding your skill. However, the majority of your colleagues must have taken Mr. Swift's satiric reference to infant cannibalism in his *Modest Proposal* quite literally. Abusing children is not the natural order of things, nor should it ever be."

"Have a care now. You sound like a bluestocking holding forth in her salon," he replied, amusement in his voice.

"As an adherent of Mrs. More and Mr. Wilberforce, you would have no use for intellectual salons, would you? Too much sinful vanity in such places."

"I support Mr. Wilberforce on abolition. But he is blind to barbarity here at home and I have often taken him to task over the issue."

"And Mrs. More?" she asked.

He pulled a face. "She believes the poor should be rewarded in the next world, not this one. I am not persuaded that starvation is a prerequisite for heaven."

"Then you attend other than reform gatherings?"

He shrugged. "Where ideas are freely exchanged . . . and

political alliances are forged, I have been known to lurk, yes. Even to lift a toast or two when the occasion warrants."

His smile lit up the dim interior of the coach. How charming he was now. She compared him to the nervous, angry man who had come to her four nights ago. "Might I offer you some cognac, then?" she asked, opening a hidden compartment beneath the armrest to reveal a small crystal decanter filled with amber liquid and a set of glasses. "After being soaked in the rain, you might catch a chill. It would be an unconscionable waste to lose a reasonably enlightened man. The nation has too few of them."

Rob laughed. "You are a most gracious hostess, Lady Fantasia. Since I, too, would dislike thinning the ranks of 'reasonable enlightened men,' I'll be delighted to share a cognac with you."

She poured a small amount in a glass, amazed that her hands remained steady, but when she reached out to give it to him, her gloved fingers touched his warm flesh and she nearly dropped the drink. He had removed his wet gloves and she could see those marvelous hands, remember how they . . . No! She quashed the erotic image. Those feelings belonged to Gabrielle, not Lady Fantasia.

As she poured herself a glass, he said, "I would not have imagined your interest in politics."

"I, too, have been known to lurk," she replied dryly, feeling the burn of fine liquor steady her nerves. "Indeed, even to skulk."

He raised his glass at her bon mot and took a sip with a chuckle.

"Are you a Whig or a Tory, m'lord?" she asked.

"Agreeing with neither on the whole, I hold no party affiliation," he replied.

"Then you belong to both Whites and Brooks?"

Rob smiled. "Also Boodles."

"Because the food is far superior?"

He nodded. "I did possess vices before I arrived at your door," he said. It was suddenly easy to admit such a thing to her. "I am obviously no saint, plaster or otherwise, Lady Fantasia. What of you, hmm?" he could not resist asking. Would she answer?

The turnaround question took her off guard for a moment. "Mrs. More would not approve, but my mentor and I have rescued a few women from the same abuses you so stirringly describe in Lords. None who have chosen to remain under my roof have been forced to do anything against their will. My guards and footmen are, almost to a man, former soldiers, turned out by our Regent's government when the war was won."

"You've done well to offer them work. Neither Prinny nor our great hero Wellington have even offered them gratitude."

"One cannot eat gratitude," she replied tartly. "Have you ever given shelter or employment to anyone in need?"

"From time to time. I find it difficult to turn away from a crippled child begging on a street corner. My cousin runs a school for them at my seat in Kent."

Amber blinked. "My, you are filled with surprises, m'lord. Noblesse oblige?"

He gave a bitter scoff. "Haven't you heard? Noblesse oblige has been guillotined."

"Regrettably, the revolution in France has had a dampening effect on our country . . . but I believe there is always hope. You must, too, else you would not labor as you do in Parliament."

"Are you, like Gabrielle, of the nobility?" The question popped out before he could reconsider asking.

"If ever I was, 'tis long past." She made a dismissive gesture with her hand. He was too perceptive for comfort. She must tread very carefully.

"Were you 'rescued' by that mentor you mentioned earlier?"

"Suffice it to say, Grace Winston is the mother I never had in childhood." It was madness to bandy words with such a clever man. She was relieved when the carriage pulled up in front of his city house, an elegant redbrick structure. "We are here, m'lord. I bid you good afternoon. Gabrielle will await you at midnight."

Rob was about to thank her for the gracious rescue when her words jarred him. How could he have forgotten Gabrielle? Memories of her passionate kisses and soft little moans of pleasure flooded his mind and body. He had been wild with frustration when she had halted their passion last night. How extraordinary that a mere conversation with the English madam had so distracted him!

"I greatly appreciate the ride and the cognac. You are most kind," he said as he stepped down and untied the reins of his horse from the rear of the carriage. Sketching a bow to the lady in shadows, he bid her good afternoon.

As the carriage pulled away, he thought of the lady in shadows and the lady in darkness . . . to whom he would go tonight.

But neither of them was any longer a lady, he thought sadly. Somehow he knew that they were blameless in the loss of their virtue. Sighing, he climbed the steps and entered the foyer of his lonely house.

Ever efficient, Clyde Dyer reported back to Amber early that evening. The earl's baroness was indeed a widow. Her husband, Charles, had died the past year of a lung inflammation, leaving her alone with a baby and a family whose fortunes were in decided decline. Was she a fortune hunter who would break the earl's heart?

"That is no concern of mine," she muttered savagely as she crumpled the report and threw it onto her escritoire. But she was concerned. Very much. Dare she caution him about the baroness? No, she dismissed that insane idea the instant it popped into her mind. A bordello madam presuming to warn a peer about avaricious women! He would stalk out of the place and never return.

Amber felt as tense as a drawn bowstring. What could she do? Looking at the ormolu clock on the mantel, she saw that it would soon be midnight.

And she would become another woman.

He entered the chamber with more assurance than he had felt the night before. Undressing eagerly, he doused the light and stretched out on the large bed. As he lay alone in the dark, all thoughts of the English madam vanished like the wisps of smoke from the candle.

Gabrielle's soft fragrance would soon tease his nostrils, her silky touch inflame him. Butterfly wings! Butterfly wings! He gathered all the self-control he could muster for the night ahead.

By the time he heard the soft swish of the opening door across the room, he was rock hard. His breath came in barely stifled gasps. Then a small, cool hand touched his face, caressing his brow, brushing the hair back.

"*Mon commandant* is happy that I have returned, *oui*?"

"Do we resume where we left off last night?" he asked hoarsely.

"Hmmm . . ." She appeared to consider as she placed one knee on the mattress. "A woman is not a . . . how would you compare it . . . a coffee grinder? Left sitting half filled with beans, one can simply begin to turn the handle again and, voila, it starts just where it stopped before."

"Then tell me, how does a woman work?" he asked.

"We begin with kissing my wrists . . . then my arms . . ."

"Then your throat . . ." His voice was muffled as he took

her hand in his, turning it palm up to start the butterfly wings beating once again.

He only prayed that he had learned his lessons well enough to progress beyond kisses this night.

Chapter Five

Moving slowly, he continued kissing her palm and fingertips while he sat up on the bed facing her. Then he proceeded up her arm until his mouth finally reached her throat. He felt the madly beating pulse in the tiny hollow at its base. She was as excited as he! A surge of pure joy jolted him. She trembled and moaned softly when he buried his hands in her hair. "'Tis like silk," he whispered, gently tugging her head back. "I would love to know its color."

Neither wanting to lie nor daring to tell the truth, Gabrielle arched her neck to distract him with an invitation. When he nibbled his way over her chin to her lips, she eagerly waited for the next kiss. But he stopped. "What is wrong, *mon cheri?*"

Rob remembered the libation he had shared with Lady Fantasia only a few hours ago. "I taste of cognac. Will that disturb you?" he asked.

Gabrielle felt a deep warm glow at his consideration. She bracketed his face with her hands. "All that disturbs me, *mon commandant,* is that you have stopped. I would taste this cognac . . . to see if it comes from a fine chateau," she whispered. "We French are experts."

He rimmed her lips with the tip of his tongue; then when she opened to him, he made a delicate invasion. Their tongues danced, tentatively at first, then with increasing ardor. He could feel her hands buried in his hair, tugging at his scalp. She gave herself so eagerly, returning his kisses with fire. When he felt the lush softness of her breasts brush his chest, his arms naturally pulled her closer.

Gabrielle almost panicked. He was big, powerful, male. She could feel that power in his embrace. *But he is also kind and gentle.* Pulling her mouth free, she murmured against his throat, "Let us try something new . . . *s'il vous plait?*" She placed her hands against his chest and separated them. As before, he released her immediately, although she could tell by his breathing that he did not want to do so.

Rasping, he asked, "What is this new thing . . . please?" His fingertips lightly traced circles on her upper arms, as much to distract himself as to please her. He felt ready to spill his seed without so much as a touch on the rock hardness of his erection.

"Kneel facing me," she commanded softly.

He complied. When she took his hands in hers and placed them around her breasts, he gasped. "They are not large . . ." she said hesitantly.

"They're perfect," he murmured, feeling her nipples through the sheer silk of the tempting concoction she wore. He squeezed gently, or what he thought was gently.

Gabrielle wrapped her small hands around his wrists, making a shushing sound, restraining him. "You must begin slowly, softly."

"Yes, butterfly wings," he whispered ruefully, letting his fingers glide around the upthrust mounds until he could feel the nipples tighten and hear her breathing catch. She arched forward, encouraging him.

"You must learn to feel a woman's reactions. Does she offer herself or draw back . . . how does her body move? How does she . . . breathe?" she said, trying to be pedantic, but he was teasing her nipples so they burned and tingled, growing ever more sensitive. She guided his hands so that he cupped a breast in each palm as if weighing them.

It seemed natural to let his thumbs press on the tips and make circling motions. "Do you like this?" he asked raggedly, feeling certain she did. He felt an irresistible urge to use his mouth on them, but before he could ask, she spoke.

"It is time to remove this barrier between us," she said breathlessly, reaching down to lift up her gown.

Rob could feel the whispery fabric brush against his erection and groaned, but fought the urge to push her backward onto the mattress and proceed. If the room had not already been ink black, he would have felt blinded by his need. No—butterfly wings, he reminded himself . . . butterfly wings! She placed the silk in his hands and guided him to raise it slowly over her head, lifting her arms to assist him. Then he sent the soft bit of fluff sailing away in the darkness. She was as naked as he!

"What now?" he asked, unable to stop his hands from returning to her breasts.

"Let us explore . . . I will go first, *oui*? Then you follow."

"Oh, *oui, mai oui*," he replied as her nails raked lightly over his chest. He never imagined that flat male nipples could feel such sharp pleasure.

She felt his heartbeat pound as she pressed her palms against his hard pectorals, delighting in the crisp hair sprinkled across them. "You speak French, *mon commandant?*" she asked, certain he did because all educated Englishmen learned, with varying degrees of skill.

"Well enough, I suppose," he replied raggedly in that tongue.

His accent was very good. "Then let us continue making love . . . in the language of love," she said in flawless Parisian French. She moved her hands up to his shoulders and glided over the flexing steel of his biceps, holding on to him, dizzy with breathless excitement. "Now it is your turn," she whispered.

Following her lead, he glided his palms over her bare breasts, down her rib cage, to the narrowness of her waist.

" 'Tis so tiny I can span it with my hands," he said in wonder, drawing her closer as she held on to his shoulders.

Gabrielle loved hearing him speak French in deep, breathless whispers. Arching her back, she raised her breasts like an offering, using one hand against the back of his neck to draw his head downward.

He groaned when his mouth found a hardened nipple and suckled on it. She gasped, seizing his head with both hands. When she grabbed fistfuls of his hair and drew him closer, she writhed with the scalding pleasure. "The other one . . . do not neglect the other one," she whispered.

Rob moved from one breast to the other, using his tongue as he had done during the kissing instruction. Her sharp little cries of pleasure lured him on to bolder action. He nuzzled the vale between her breasts and brushed her nipples with his lips, tugging gently on them with his teeth, then drew a pear-shaped globe into his mouth until she moaned.

After several moments of the exquisite ecstasy, Gabrielle knew she was slipping over the edge. He murmured soft love words to her in French as he lavished her breasts with caresses that stole her reason. She must not let her own body's hunger, her desire for this man, blind her. He had come to learn what was required to bring a lady to culmination. A *lady* . . . She felt a sad, sudden twist deep inside her and knew it was her heart's pain.

She also knew she must do what was right for him. There would be reward enough for her before their assignations ended. Ever so slowly, now feeling assured that he would follow her lead, she pulled away with a breathless murmur. "Lie back and I will lie beside you."

Breathing hard, he lay down but kept his arm around her waist, pulling her to his side. He was careful not to let her near the painfully sensitive hardness of his sex, which was straining for—and so dangerously close to—release. He wanted to ask her if she felt as he did . . . but was damned if he knew how, or even *if*, a woman achieved the same kind of release as a man.

In his limited experience, he had never known one who genuinely did, although the Spanish camp followers had feigned pleasure. But then they had gotten up and walked away as soon as they were paid. This felt a world apart from those brief and tawdry encounters. He reached over and stroked her breasts, letting his hand trail down her belly, so soft and flat, toward the apex of her thighs. When he drew near the mound, he hesitated.

Gabrielle knew this was the moment. She would find out if he could bring her what she had only been told existed . . . what he wanted to give the woman he intended to marry. *Please, let it be possible!* Taking a shuddering breath, she said, "Do not be afraid, my love." She moved his hand over her mound, into the soft curls. He sucked in his breath.

He heard her breathing grow ragged when he touched the heated center of her body and felt her petals. "You're wet," he said in English before he could think better of it.

"Pleasure . . . excitement causes a woman to . . . to release moisture," she reassured him.

He rubbed his fingers delicately against her satiny heat until she cried out when he separated her petals.

"Ahh!"

He stopped. "Did I hurt you?"

"No, no! Please, continue . . . only go softly, slowly. . . ." She guided his hand until his fingers, those long beautiful fingers, found the rhythm she craved. He patiently stroked her, his senses newly attuned to the subtle nuances of her body. She arched her hips against his caresses, urging him on without needing to say a word, although her small moans and gasps of excitement spoke volumes.

Suddenly she tensed and then shuddered, almost coming up off the mattress with a keening cry. Her hands clawed at the sheets as she felt—really, truly felt for the first time in her life—that culmination she had only heard other women describe. Words could never do justice. . . . Her world spun out of control for what seemed like an eternity.

Rob knew the rhythmic pulsing he felt at her core must mean she had achieved release. Surely a woman could never feign such a thing. In spite of the intense ache of his own unfulfilled needs, he felt jubilant. He had given a woman pleasure—real pleasure, not the cold, lifeless acceptance of a wife's duty or the counterfeit fervor purchased with silver.

"Did I please you?" he asked, praying he was right.

In answer, Gabrielle rolled across his chest and began raining kisses over his face and neck, crying joyously, "Yes, oh, yes, a thousand times yes! It was . . ." Words deserted her, so she used her mouth another way, kissing him deeply, with such fire that he groaned and wrapped his arms around her.

"Now," she murmured against his throat, "it is time for you."

Rob started to roll her onto her back, but then stopped as a sudden thought struck him like a lightning bolt. Why had he never thought to consider it before this! "Gaby . . ." How in bloody hell did one ask about preventing conception? Courtesans knew, but Gaby had not been with a man since being raped. "Have you . . . ? What I mean is . . . could my seed take root inside you?" he blurted out, then cursed silently for his awkwardness.

"Lady Fantasia has shown me what to do. Never fear, my major, I am protected—but you are kind to ask," she murmured, caressing his cheek and drawing him closer once more.

Rob required no further encouragement. He parted her legs, prepared to enter her, but she pressed her palms against his chest. Stifling another groan, he stopped . . . barely. "Please, have mercy, Gaby," he whispered fiercely.

"Oh, I intend to be very . . . merciful," she whispered in

return. "Now lie back." He complied. "Remember what I said about exploring bodies . . . hmm?"

A smile touched his mouth in spite of his extremity. He was learning far more than he ever could have imagined. What a remarkable creature his lady in darkness was!

She sat up and let her hands glide down his chest, following the narrowing arrow of body hair over the hard muscles of his abdomen. . . . "You are very strong," she cooed breathlessly, pausing only long enough to feel his body tense in anticipation. "And very much a man." Her hand closed around his staff, grasping it, feeling its heat. "It is so smooth . . . and long."

"Does that please you?" He could barely get the words out.

"All of your body pleases me. Women enjoy the freedom to touch, to become familiar with a man's body . . . to admire its power . . . provided . . ."

"Provided . . . ?" He spoke through gritted teeth now.

"Provided the man has a body as splendid as yours."

He had never imagined touching his naked body could bring a woman pleasure. Oh, women admired his face and form in public, but that was entirely different. She leaned over him and kissed him, her breasts pressing against his chest, her hair spilling around his shoulders like satin.

"Now," she murmured against his mouth, wrapping her arms around his shoulders. He rolled on top of her without breaking the kiss, his hands caressing the curve of her spine, the flair of her hips. He worshipped her body as she had his. How could any woman resist parting her thighs, inviting him? "Please, come inside me . . . but . . . do not end this swiftly as nature urges you to do."

He paused at the entrance to paradise, aching yet amazed. "You can . . . you can do it again—this way?" he blurted out.

"Not this time, I think . . . but your pleasure will be greater if you prolong the culmination . . . and I have not been taken by a man in so long that . . . you might hurt me if you rush."

He felt a wave of tenderness mixed with the breathless excitement that inflamed him. "I would never hurt you, Gaby," he whispered.

Ah, yes, you will . . . but not in the manner you imagine. "I trust you, my love," she murmured.

Tamping down the fire raging through his blood, he brushed the head of his staff against the creamy moisture of her petals. They felt swollen. She made a slight sound—discomfort or excitement? He was not certain. Setting his jaw, he held still for a moment, waiting for her signal. "Are you all right?"

The concern in his voice made her heart ache for his sweet intensity. "Please, this feels wonderful," she whispered, burying her mouth against his shoulder.

When she arched and clamped her thighs around his hips, he pressed down, easing an inch into her. Then he forced himself to stop. She was incredibly tight, every bit as much as—no! He would not think of Credelia now, lest his manhood desert him. "My little one," he murmured in French as he kissed her temple, her nose, then her mouth, urging her to return the fevered caresses.

His mouth was magic, but his staff was stretching her, bringing back the old terror . . . yet she realized that this time there was no pain. She was not exactly certain what it did feel like, other than fullness, the merging of his body with hers. *Concentrate on the kisses!* She felt him ease a tiny bit deeper, shaking with the strain of holding back when she knew he wanted to blindly plunge.

But he will not do that. He will not cause you pain. She arched her back, allowing him to move deeper, accommodating slowly to his size and hardness.

Rob felt her tightness enveloping him. Losing control

would be all too simple. But he would never forgive himself
if he hurt this sad, loving woman. Gaby had suffered so
much already. Holding on to that thought, he eased in a
tiny bit at a time, waiting for her body's signals that she
wanted him to proceed. The creamy moisture still slicked
his path. That was a good sign . . . was it not? He kissed her
deeply and sank farther into the drowning well of bliss.

When her nails dug into his shoulders, he stopped. "Am I
going too fast?"

Gabrielle shook her head, murmuring, "No, no . . . I feel
like Cook's Christmas goose being stuffed. He has a very large
hand, our cook. And you have a very large . . ." A small
breathy laugh surprised her. She had not intended to say that!

"Flattery, Gaby?" he managed to ask. Rather than un-
manning him, her disingenuous humor only increased his
ardor. "Perhaps it is not that I am so large as that you are so
small," he said hoarsely.

Without speaking she had to use her body to communi-
cate so that he would understand what his bride wanted,
even if the lady was too shy or inhibited to speak. One gentle undulation of her hips seemed so natural that she felt
certain any woman at this point would react the same way.
It produced the desired result.

Rob buried himself completely in her, then held still, letting the blissful feeling wash over him, struggling to control
his passion. *Your pleasure will be greater if you prolong the
culmination.* She was indeed the perfect teacher for him.
After a moment, she gave another gentle lift of her hips. He
raised himself and stroked very slowly downward. His reward was a soft sigh.

That was encouragement enough for him to begin slowly
thrusting, feeling her reactions, alert for any indication that
he was causing her discomfort. Quite the opposite, she
clamped her thighs tightly around his hips and kissed him
hungrily, urging him on with breathless little moans. Her

hands splayed across his back, her fingers kneading his flexing muscles.

Deep inside her, Gabrielle felt that delicious scalding urge start to build again. But she knew she could not ask him to wait for her. Sweat slicked his powerful body, yet he moved slowly, carefully, savoring the pleasure he was giving as well as receiving. For now, the fulfillment of their joining would be enough for her. After all his patience and the gift he had already given her, she must reciprocate.

There would be time enough for them to climb the heights together another night. She arched, digging her nails into his back as she returned his kisses fiercely. He thrust faster, harder, almost bringing her along with him, when she felt him shudder and his staff swell deeply inside her, then pulse its life into her body.

Rob had never before experienced such ecstasy. All past encounters paled to insignificance, utterly forgotten as the intense release washed over him like a great tidal wave. One slim woman possessed the power to bring him to such heights. As his heartbeat thundered, he collapsed, rolling to his side so as not to allow his weight to crush Gaby. When she continued to cling to him, it felt natural to hold her in his arms, stroking her hair, raining soft kisses across her face.

"I was too rough . . . at the last . . ."

"No, darling major, you were not too rough," she said softly, placing her palm against his chest, feeling a small thrill as his heart hammered beneath the hard wall of muscle.

She no longer felt afraid of performing this act with him. That gave her a sense of tender power. But thanks to Grace's instruction, it would give her nothing else. In time would she come to regret taking measures to prevent conception? *Do not think of that. Think only of the time you have with him now.* . . . His soft murmur carried her away from the bittersweet melancholy.

"You were right . . . about going slowly. But I could not bring you with me this way, and I want to do that . . . if I can."

Gabrielle smiled in the dark. If only he knew how close he had come. "I am quite positive that you will. That is why we have many more lessons, yes?"

"Oh, certainly yes," he murmured fervently, nuzzling his face in her perfumed hair. "Can you . . . that is, would you stay with me for a while, Gaby?"

Dare she? He felt replete and wanted to hold her. She wanted to hold him. *But he is not yours.* He would one day belong to his baroness, and Gabrielle knew he would be a faithful husband. After a brief time she would never see him again. Another pang squeezed her heart. Why not seize whatever she could during these midnight trysts? "Yes, I will stay for a while, my major."

They lay on the big bed in the darkness. Neither spoke for several moments, although thoughts whirled through both their minds.

"It must have been quite difficult, coming to a new country," he said. "You are very brave, Gaby."

"Not so brave. I have been frightened much of my life," she responded before she realized how much she was revealing.

He stroked her hair. "Yet you are here . . . with me. And I do not frighten you."

"You were an English soldier, not a French soldier," she replied, skirting the truth that lay beneath her disguise.

"Not all French soldiers are evil men. Not all English are good," he said darkly.

She sensed the undercurrent in his voice. What had his experience in Spain done to him? "But you are a good man. . . . Others, they were not?" she prompted.

He tensed, weighing his reply. Something about lying in the darkness with this remarkable woman made him want to answer. "No, there were others who were brutes. . . . I caught a junior officer, a lieutenant . . . in a despicable act."

"He forced a woman?" she asked, feeling his horror, remembering her own.

"She was little more than a child."

So had she been. "That is truly horrible. What did you do?" She could not stop herself from asking. He needed to tell her—tell someone, for she doubted he ever had spoken of this before.

"I arrested him. Our colonel convened a court martial. He was found guilty. I was placed in charge of the execution."

His narrative came out in a burst of short, pain-filled sentences. "You knew this lieutenant well?"

"No, he had only recently arrived. But I took the coward's way out and wrote to his father, telling him that his son had died a hero's death."

"That was a kindness. The lie should not trouble you." She caressed his chest, feeling the steady strum of his heartbeat.

"I said I did not know the lieutenant, but I do know his sire, a colleague in Lords. A good, decent man. Our paths cross from time to time, and when they do, this sad, proud father insists that we drink to his gallant son. I drink. Later when I'm alone, I get sick."

"You punish yourself for an imagined sin. You are too good for this world, I think. Let God sort out good from evil. That is His task. Not even a member of the great English House of Lords dares usurp it."

He was startled by the purging chuckle that rose from deep in his chest. "Has anyone told you, my little one, that you are a very wise woman?" He gathered her in his arms and placed a soft kiss on the tip of her nose. "I feel as if I could tell you anything."

The warmth of his voice made her wince. He would trust

Gabrielle with his darkest secrets . . . but she was a complete fraud who could never tell him hers. "I will never betray a confidence, my major," she murmured sadly.

"My name is Rob, Gaby . . . and perhaps . . . one day I will tell you why I came to this place, where I was so blessed to meet you. Will you call me Rob?"

The words were like a dagger to her heart. As she started to slip from the bed, she paused to kiss his lips softly, then said, "Yes, Rob. I will wait for you tomorrow night."

And she fled silently through the darkness.

Chapter Six

The fog blanketed London like a foul tattered cloak worn by an old man who never bathed. Alan Cresswel sat in the back of the Hare and Hound, his big hands surrounding a mug of foamy brown ale, something to warm his innards against the spring chill. If Hull did not show himself by the time he had drained the tankard, he would brave the vile weather and return to his lodgings. "An' I'll keep what he's paid me, devil take the promise o' more," he muttered.

In truth, in spite of the lure of money, he did not like the risks involved in kidnapping a woman from the House of Dreams. Just as he started to slide from the splintery bench, he spotted Hull peering through the smoke-filled room. He waved the Johnny Raw over to him. The out-at-the-elbows bumpkin irritated him, smirking and putting on airs, all self-important because he had gotten some crazy old marquess from Northumberland to send him on this fool's errand.

"Give me a pint of your best," Hull said to a serving wench, pinching her arse until she squealed and gave him a hard look. He slid behind the table and squinted at the runner. "What have you learned about this House of Dreams, Cressy old fellow?"

Cresswel could tell Hull had already drunk more than one pint. "I learned to keep me voice down in public places," the runner replied as Essie set a pint on the scarred table with an angry thunk. She looked from Hull to him, expecting that he would pay. "Give the gel 'er due, Mr. Hull," he said firmly.

His face flushing, Hull tossed a coin on the table that

barely covered the price of the ale. "No sport around this place," he groused, quaffing the ale, then pulling a face.

Before the chawbacon complained about the ale, Cresswel said, "Whoever yer cherry-haired chit with the scar be, she must ne'er leave the 'ouse. Pity that drunken baron didn't giv 'er name."

"Considering the circumstances when he saw her, I doubt he heard it," Hull said with a sneer. "If we can just get inside—"

Cresswel leaned across the table. "You got apartments to let?" he asked, tapping his temple with a finger. "Ain't no way we gets inside the 'ouse o' Dreams without endin' up dead. The gel 'as to go outside. I had the place watched. Lots o' women come and go. None lookin' like 'er."

Hull uttered a particularly foul oath and slumped against the hard plank wall behind him. "She has to come out sooner or later. You just want more money, don't you?" he asked.

Cresswel stifled the urge to reach across the table and grab the young fool by his throat. "Oh, yer marquess, 'e'll be payin' me plenty o' blunt when all's said and done. There is another way o' it." At that, Hull perked up. "One woman comes out real regular, always veiled, dressed in black. . . ."

Hull's eyes narrowed and a crafty smile smeared across his face. "You mean that Lady Fantasia?" He cackled drunkenly.

"Keep yer voice down," Cresswel admonished for the second time, furtively glancing around to make certain no one was paying attention. If word got back to the House of Dreams . . . he did not want to think about the consequences. Satisfied that no one appeared interested, he continued. "Why else would the madam never allow nobody to see 'er face—not even 'er high-water customers . . . less she's ugly as a Billingsgate hag . . . ?" He paused craftily. "Er she hidin' from 'er husband?"

"It makes sense. How do we kidnap her, if not from the house?" Hull asked.

"Good weather, she rides, out past St. John's Wood. Another woman, a Frenchie, always with 'er. And a bodyguard. A Coldstream veteran, tough old bugger, but we can deal with 'em," Cresswel said.

"Yes, we can," Hull replied, rubbing his hands together.

The runner could see he relished the prospect. For the money? Or was there something more between him and the marchioness? "This gel, she know you, Mr. Hull?"

Hull's face, already red, darkened even more. " 'Twas so long ago, she will not recognize me."

Considering how dissipated the younger man looked, that was probable. "Just watch you stay back when we snatch 'er. If she gives a yell, you might could end up real dead."

Hull's laugh was nasty. "I intend to stay alive to deliver the bitch into that old man's hands."

Cresswel suspected what Hull wanted to do on the long journey to Northumberland . . . if he dared to risk angering the deadly marquess. But that was none of his concern as long as he was paid for capturing the marchioness.

After a restless night, Amber took her morning coffee, trying to soothe her guilty conscience. If "Rob" ever found out that Gabrielle was Lady Fantasia, he would never forgive her. She stared out the window at the spring rain, dreary and chill. It perfectly suited her mood. Such rain brought lovely verdancy but at a cost, just like her duplicitous game with the earl.

She set her cup in its saucer and massaged her aching scalp. What to do? Should she tell Grace? She knew her mentor was eager to hear how the "lessons" were progressing. Jenette sensed her attraction to the earl. Either or both women would be happy to lend a sympathetic ear. But she was not ready, or indeed able, to talk about her dilemma.

"One thing is certain. I cannot have him come for his Gaby tonight." Her conscience was simply too raw. She sat down at her escritoire and composed a terse note, then rang for Bonnie.

Within the hour a messenger delivered an unmarked sealed missive to the earl's city house. Puzzled, he opened it and read the brief lines, dropping it numbly when he had finished. It was from Lady F, indicating that Gabrielle was ill and could not meet him for several days. Without taking time to consider the consequences, he yelled for Frog to fetch his stallion.

He was soaked to the skin when he reined in at the front gate of the House of Dreams. The street was deserted, but Rob did not care if all of the Diamond Squad were witnesses. A guard whose posture and demeanor indicated military experience stood in front of the closed heavy iron bars.

"Let me pass, man," Rob demanded.

"I am very sorry, sir. No gentlemen permitted during daylight hours. House rules," the guard replied.

"Do you think I am here for a dalliance?" Rob asked. "I must see the Lady Fantasia. She sent me a message regarding an important matter."

The guard shook his head. His greatcoat was soaked, but he sheltered an intimidating blunderbuss beneath it protectively, keeping the powder dry. "No gentlemen admitted without instruction from the lady."

Rob narrowed his eyes, then snapped in his most imperious officer's voice, "Soldier, you will go at once to inform your lady that the major is at her gate. She will grant permission to admit me."

"B-but, Major, sir, my post . . . I cannot—"

"I will stand your post. Now go! I am not used to repeating an order, soldier." He could sense the young man was on the verge of saluting. Instead, the young guard turned and slipped through the gate, trotting rapidly toward the house. Rob waited until he was at the front door, then grabbed the bars of the gate and shoved it open.

He thundered up to the front steps and leaped from his mount. Barging through the door, he pushed the startled guard aside, blunderbuss be damned. At the same moment an older man of solid build with gray hair and the set jaw of a seasoned campaigner appeared to block his path. The man who had ridden guard on her carriage in the rain? Rob was in no mood to care.

"Now, m'lord, you know this is not permitted," he said patiently, yet with steely determination.

"I don't give a damn what is permitted. I will see Lady Fantasia at once."

From the top of the stairs, Amber looked down in horrified amazement. The earl was dressed in soaking wet buckskins that molded to his broad shoulders and long legs, his hair a wild tangle beneath a slouch hat with rainwater dripping off the brim. The expression on his face was anguished and angry at the same time.

She had seized a bonnet and veil when she heard Boxer responding to the guard's excited cry. Quickly covering her head, she called out, "The Lady Fantasia is at your service, m'lord. Sergeant Major, please allow him to pass." With a swish, she turned and headed for her study. She could hear his swift footfalls on the steps below her.

As soon as they reached the room where they had first met, Amber whirled around and slammed the door behind him furiously. "You bird-witted, beetle-headed clodpole! Have you lost your mind? After all we have done to protect your identity, you ride up to the front gates, raising such a breeze that everyone in London will know you are a patron by nightfall! What were you thinking?"

"I was thinking about this," he said, pulling her note from inside his buckskin jacket. He threw the damp missive on her desk. "You said Gabrielle is ill. Has she a fever? Is your leech attending her? I will place her under the care of my personal physician."

"You are the one who should be under care—of the State Secretary of Lunatics and Idiots! You have risked your whole career, your future, everything."

Rob removed his hat and realized that he was soaking the fine woolen rug. But he did not give a fig. He combed his fingers through his hair to remove it from his face. "No one will recognize me in country clothing. Besides, on such an evil day, the street is deserted. Now will you please let me see Gaby?"

Gaby! Amber grew even more furious. The stubborn fool cared enough for his counterfeit Frenchwoman to risk everything for her. What would he do if he ever found out she did not even exist? She turned and walked over to the window, composing herself. "You would humiliate and embarrass her, forcing your way into her quarters in daylight. She is no practiced courtesan."

"Demme, madam, I know she is not a courtesan," he raged. "But I must know that she . . ."

Her shoulders slumped. What could she do? Then inspiration struck. "Perhaps my note was too . . . terse, not sufficiently informative. Gabrielle is experiencing . . . to put it baldly, m'lord, 'tis her time of the month. You do understand what that means?"

Rob felt his face heat beneath the icy-cold rainwater dripping from it. "Oh, my sweet Lord! A thousand pardons, Lady Fantasia."

Amber felt a small bit of vindictive satisfaction upon sensing his acute embarrassment. It served the rotter right! "I see you do comprehend," she said dryly. He sketched a hurried bow and spun on his heel to quit the room, but then paused with his back still to Amber.

"Lady Fantasia, I would that Gabrielle not learn I have made an ass of myself."

Amber did not feel charitable as she snapped, "The girl is

inexperienced. If you do not bray much, she will not discover your secret. Now go!"

Late that afternoon, two magnificent bouquets of hothouse roses arrived from the finest florist in London. The one addressed to Gabrielle was deep crimson. The one for Lady Fantasia was yellow.

Grace sipped her tea and studied Amber through lowered lashes. This had been their morning ritual ever since her young charge returned from the Continent. They normally discussed the preceding night's events, planned for what was to happen that evening, and in general gossiped as if they were a dearly close mother and daughter. But Amber had avoided coming to her apartments ever since her first night with the earl.

When Barrington had forced his way inside and created such a breeze, she had expected Amber to come and explain. Nothing of the sort had happened. After waiting patiently for another week, she decided it was well past time to find out was happening between them.

Something was certainly amiss. Grace spoke with Jenette and others close to Amber, gathering what information she could. According to Jenette, Amber had been behaving in a most peculiar fashion for the past fortnight, but Amber had told her nothing about her relationship with Barrington. Perhaps the canny Frenchwoman sensed it. She confided to Grace that there was a glow about Amber, like that of a woman newly awakened sexually, satiated, yes . . . but there was also a tension in her body and a sadness in her eyes. It worried Grace even more, for she had been the one who suggested that Amber become Barrington's tutor.

Determined to get to the bottom of the mystery, she had knocked on the door to Amber's quarters early that morning. Dressed in a deep blue brocade robe, the sleepy-eyed younger woman had called for her to enter, expecting Bonnie. Although Amber had looked somewhat dismayed, she had admitted Grace, who carried the tray with tea for herself, coffee for Amber, and scones for both of them.

While breaking their fast, they made desultory small talk about business for a few moments while Amber drank her coffee and tore off tiny bits of the crusty scone, eating almost none of it. At length, Grace asked bluntly, "Has he not pleased you in bed?"

Amber almost choked on a swallow of hot coffee. She had known that she must eventually explain everything to Grace . . . if only she had an idea of how to do so when she did not understand the bizarre dilemma herself. She coughed, gathering her thoughts, then replied, "He is quite the apt pupil, perfect for Gab—for my purposes." As she caught herself, Amber felt the flush stealing over her cheeks. She cursed, knowing Grace had caught her slip.

"I take it your pose as the French émigré has convinced more than Barrington," she said dryly.

"I'm deceiving him, Grace. He believes I've survived rape, war—"

"You *have* survived rape and a war every bit as terrible as the one in Europe."

"I am a runaway wife, no matter the justification. He trusts Gabrielle so much he has told her—me—to call him Rob." She leaned back stiffly. "Me he calls Lady Fantasia." She spat out the words, recalling his wild ride to Gaby's sickbed.

"So the Lady Fantasia is jealous of his French lover," Grace said, turning the conundrum over in her mind.

"No!" Amber exclaimed, but the older woman made a dismissive gesture.

"He has pleased you all too well, and now your heart is involved. That was always a risk, dear child, but I had hoped . . . Who knows?" She paused. "Barrington might not give you up when he weds."

Amber shook her head. "Even if he were not too honorable to keep a mistress, I am not Gaby. She is not me!"

"Therein lies the problem, and the solution since you are both women. Barrington must see you in the bright light of day. He must become as attracted to Lady Fantasia as he is to his Frenchwoman."

"Gaby has a distinct advantage over Fantasia," she replied. "She is his lover. I cannot compete."

"According to the *Chronicle*, he is highly intelligent and interested in social reform. You have much in common. Engage his mind. If the earl is half as noble as you credit, he will appreciate discourse as much as . . . intercourse." She smiled at her bawdy bon mot, then compounded it, suggesting, "Invite him to ride with you. 'Tis a lovely day for an outing and you have not ridden this week past . . . at least not on horseback," she added with a chuckle.

Amber threw down her napkin and stood up, pacing to the bow window and looking out at the woods surrounding their property. "That is an addlepated notion. How could it possibly help to socialize with him? If he learns how I have played him . . ."

Grace followed, placing her arm around Amber. "In time, he must learn—and he *will* understand. If he is half the man you believe, how could he not? Come, now, you have fallen into such a brown study. Everyone remarks on it. If ever you are going to sort out your feelings about Barrington, you'll not do it by avoiding him."

"Since I have bedded with him, I am scarce avoiding him."

"Ah, but that is when he meets Gabrielle in darkness. That does not signify for the purpose at hand. He will enjoy sparring with you."

Amber remembered their encounter in her coach. He did enjoy their verbal fencing. "It would be presumptuous to invite him to be seen in public with a widow. Whatever pretext could I use?"

"According to what Jenette told me, you might employ his baroness's trick."

Amber threw up her hands. "I have already done so after I saw him at Mr. Berry's grocery. He would never believe another chance encounter such as that."

Grace considered for a moment. "Then send a message and tell him you wish to speak with him about some political matter. Suggest a ride this afternoon, if his schedule permits."

Amber paced, thinking. The courtesans at the House of Dreams were well educated and often discussed politics with their patrons, many of whom sat in Parliament. "Only yesterday Claudia did pass along a rumor regarding Mr. Cobbett, which might interest the earl."

Grace patted her arm in a motherly fashion. "Most clever. Get Barrington in Fantasia's debt. You must spend time with him before your French rival sees him again." *And Gaby will most certainly hunger do so very soon, ere I miss my guess.*

Rob recognized Lady Fantasia's flourished handwriting on the note. Thanking his footman, he closed the door to his library and broke the seal, considering his humiliation after the last time he read a message from her. "What now?" he muttered.

> *My Dear Lord B,*
> *At the risk of alarming you with another terse note, I invite you to join me for a ride this afternoon. The area north of St. John's Wood is open country with no city traffic. I shall be passing Hempstead at one. Be at ease. The matter is political, not social.*
> *Lady F*

He stared at the missive, uncertain whether to be angered at her presumption or pleased by her wit. Glancing at his desk, where he had been laboring over a speech he was to present the first of the week, he considered the bright spring sunshine splashing over the papers. Perhaps a ride would be just the thing to clear his head. The tall case clock in the foyer struck eleven. He would have just enough time to change and ride to Hempstead by the appointed hour.

A political matter. He considered what it might be. With a woman as well educated as the madam, the possibilities were infinite. *Admit it, you enjoy her company and wonder why such a bright, clever woman must hide her face.* He also enjoyed the beauty of her slender body. His conscience twinged. He was being disloyal to Gaby.

No, by damn, he owed loyalty to neither woman. The House of Dreams and its inhabitants were only a means to an end. He should be thinking of Lady Oberly's dinner the day after tomorrow, not riding . . . of either sort!

Yet as he guided his big black down Alpha Road, he could not conjure the image of the baroness's pale blonde beauty no matter how hard he tried. He had met her scores of times, yet two women whose faces he had never beheld filled his mind to her exclusion. What was wrong with him? He reminded himself that Lady Oberly was lovely and kind. *But has she ever engaged you in a discussion of consequence the whole time you have known her?*

His troubling thoughts ended when he passed through the tiny hamlet of Hampstead and saw the madam mounted on a splendid blaze-faced bay. Lady Fantasia waited beneath the shade of a large oak. She wore a severely tailored black riding habit that showed off her slender curves to excellent advantage. A jaunty small hat accented with a single peacock feather perched on her head. He could not discern the color of her hair because of the heavy veil drooping to her shoulders.

"Ever the lady of mystery, Fantasia," he said as he reined in beside her. "The veil quite spoils that fashionable bonnet."

"I see you have elected to leave your fashionable bonnet behind," she could not resist teasing. "I do hope it was not ruined in the rain." He was bareheaded, his hair clubbed back with a few loose waves caressing his brow. "Your buckskins have obviously survived quite serviceably." The "country clothes" were not as revealing as they had been soaking wet, but she appreciated how they fit his lean body all the same.

"Most uncharitable of you to mention my ill-considered ride. As to the hat, it has survived, thanks to my valet. He was almost as cross with me as were you for drenching my wardrobe." In spite of his embarrassment over the incident, he found himself chuckling with her.

As they turned their horses and cantered down the lane, Rob noticed a rider emerge from behind a clump of alder bushes a discreet distance away. He recognized the gray-haired man who had blocked his way to the stairs with such serious determination that morning. "Your groom has a military bearing," he said.

"Sergeant Major Boxer spent twenty-one years in the Coldstream Guards before he came to work for me."

"He looks to be a man not to cross."

"I assure you he is that and more," she replied as Boxer trailed them. She tilted her head up and let the warm sun seep through her veil.

She sat the sidesaddle with expert ease, as if born to ride fine horseflesh, reinforcing his certainty that she had come from a good family if not a titled one. He wanted to ask but decided that she would not answer and it might spoil what could be a most pleasant outing. She broke into his thoughts with a question.

"Do you, perchance, read Mr. Cobbett's *Political Register*?"

"Only at night after drawing the drapes within the privacy of my study, yes," he replied dryly.

Amber watched his face from behind the safety of her veil. His smile was so seductive it was akin to being seditious. "He can be a bit inflammatory," she said lightly.

"A deal more than just inflammatory, but we agree on many issues such as the treatment of veterans and the plight of the poor—most especially their being used as a politically destabilizing force."

"Some in Lord Liverpool's government would say the speech you gave in Lords on child labor was a deal more than just inflammatory," she replied. " 'Tis a good thing you are a peer, else you might have ended up in Newgate with him a few years back."

Rob nodded. "I mislike the way Liverpool and his home secretary have subverted the rights of our citizens. Cobbett said nothing to merit spending two years in prison—without benefit of so much as a mockery of a trial."

"Then perhaps you should warn him that Sidmouth has a list with his name on it . . . again."

He turned his head and stared at her. "This is the political matter you wanted to discuss?" When she nodded, he asked, "How the devil do you know the home secretary is plotting to imprison Cobbett again?"

"Although I will never divulge their names, a few very influential members of Parliament are patrons of the House of Dreams. Upon occasion they discuss things outside the fantasy world."

That made sense to him. Then a disturbing thought occurred. Would Gaby share his confessions with Lady Fantasia or any of the other women? No, he felt quite positive she would never betray him. "Cobbett has always spoken of traveling to America," he mused aloud. "Perhaps I shall suggest now would be an opportune time to make such a journey."

"You are acquainted, then?"

"I do lurk in places where interesting ideas are discussed,

remember?" he said, smiling at her. Although he could not see her face, he felt the warmth of her return smile through the veil.

Neither of them noticed when Boxer's mount came up lame. The sergeant reined in and dismounted to examine the horse's hoof, then took out a knife to dislodge a sharp pebble from it. As he worked on the animal, his mistress and her companion disappeared around a curve in the lane. It was a tranquil, safe area, so he was not disturbed . . .

Until he heard loud yells and pounding hoofbeats over the chirping of birds.

Chapter Seven

From the concealment of a thicket of untrimmed box-woods, Cresswel and his confederate watched the trio ride down the deserted country lane. They had followed the veiled woman and her guard since she left her bordello, waiting for the best opportunity to kill him and abduct her. When she met a gentleman, the runner was infuriated with his bad luck. Not expecting to have to deal with a second man, he had brought only one cutthroat from Whitechapel. Hull waited back a quarter mile away with the final payment in exchange for the woman.

The moment Cresswel saw the guard fall behind, he whispered to Jem, "This be our chance. You know wot to say. I'll take out the gent, then watch for 'er guard 'n shoot 'em when he comes round. You grab the chit." At Jem's nod, they kicked their horses into a gallop and swooped from the brush up to the road.

Rob heard the thunder of hoofbeats as two riders with pistols drawn broke from cover. One yelled, "Pull up 'n give us yer purses." It seemed like a robbery, which would be rare enough in this area, but he did not like the fact that they wore no masks, nor the way the second man slowed down. The big, rangy fellow was preparing to shoot him while the one who had spoken neared Fantasia. He cursed himself for going unarmed.

There was no help for it. He nudged his stallion into a full gallop and stretched his body low on the black's neck, charging directly into the man who was trying to seize her reins. A shot whistled over his shoulder just as he crashed his big mount broadside into the thief's scrawny nag, sending horse and rider tumbling to the ground. The man's gun went flying into the brush. Fantasia backed her horse expertly out of the way as the downed horse scrambled to its feet and raced off in terror.

Rob expected Boxer to handle the man whose weapon had been discharged. He dived from his mount and tackled the thief on the ground before he could retrieve the unfired pistol. The fellow drew a knife from his sash and made a clumsy slice at Rob, who jumped agilely to one side, then kicked the weapon from the squat, burly man's fist. His opponent scrambled to his feet. Rob seized him by his filthy jacket with one hand and landed a hard punch in his thick gut with the other. Beneath the fat was substantial muscle. He grunted but did not go down.

Rob punched, ducked, and punched again, landing lightning-swift blows to his thick foe. Just as the barrel-like man tried to take another swing, the earl ducked beneath it and sent his fist upward, slamming it into his opponent's throat. As the burly man crumpled to the ground, another shot rang out. Busy fighting, Barrington had not seen the fellow on horseback pull another pistol from his sash and take aim at his back.

Rob whirled around in a crouch, expecting that Boxer had dispatched the second man, who indeed dropped his pistol and slumped in his saddle. But then he saw Boxer urging his mount around the curve in the road, too far distant to have fired. He turned to Fantasia, who calmly held the reins of her sidestepping mount in one gloved hand while the other held a French LePage percussion-lock pistol, still smoking. She had pulled away her veil, revealing her face!

"Jem, here!" the man she had shot yelled out, but when the short man clambered to his feet, his companion calmly shot him, then kicked his nag into a gallop and vanished into the bushes.

"That one was going to kill you," she said, sliding the pistol into a hidden pocket at the side of her riding habit.

"I thank you that he did not succeed," Rob replied.

"Boxer, see if you can catch him!" she yelled at the sergeant major, who galloped into the brush in pursuit, his Manton pistol out and ready to fire.

Both Rob and Fantasia heard the fellow on the ground groan. A red stain widened across his chest, and blood bubbled at his lips. Rob knelt beside him. "Who is the man who shot you?" he asked. The thief's hand gripped the earl's arm for a moment, as if he wanted to speak. Then his hold loosened. His head lolled to one side. "I wish we could have learned who the other man was. He killed this one to prevent him from talking."

"Damnation," Fantasia said. "I would not have misjudged my shot if this skittish beast had behaved. We would at the least have had two bodies for my runner to identify." Tightening her hold on the reins until the bay calmed, she dismounted. She knelt beside the earl and looked at the dead man's face.

"Have you ever seen him before?" he asked.

"Never. I could not forget anyone that ugly." She turned and looked up at him. "Do you have enemies from your army days? Or perchance because of your unpopular opinions in Parliament?"

Rob shook his head, trying not to stare at her face. "Wilberforce has made many more enemies than I. He has considerably more influence in Parliament. Yet no one has attempted to kill him. It would make no sense that any political foes would want to see me dead, either. I trust you believe me when I say there are no compromised women or cuckolded husbands lurking in my past?" he asked dryly.

She smiled at him. "No, I do not think that is likely."

The mysterious Lady Fantasia was incredibly lovely, more so than he could ever have imagined. Her wide golden eyes, slender nose, and ripe full lips were framed by red hair the color of dark sweet cherries. He had longed to see this face ever since their first meeting. That desire had only grown as he had come to appreciate her wit and intellect. Now he was shocked by a sudden carnal urge. How appalling. How would his sweet, sensual Gaby feel if she knew he lusted after her benefactress?

What would Lady Oberly think!

"Your reputation among the saints remains intact," Amber replied nervously, realizing that she had made a serious mistake. The earl was studying her face. Could he see Gaby in her? She was grateful that Grace had taught her to apply paints to conceal her scar. He had become a very perceptive lover and knew every inch of her body, including the mark on her cheek. Gabrielle had taught him too much about women for him to be easily fooled. Swallowing hard, she steadied her hands, then replaced the veil, trying to gather her scattered thoughts.

"I did not expect you to be so young and beautiful," he said, then could have bitten his tongue. "That is, a woman of your intellect, your wit, and . . . er . . . organizational skills . . ." he blurted out, realizing he was making a horrid bumble bath of it.

"How old did you imagine one must be to operate an establishment such as mine? Must I need resemble Medusa and shuffle along on a cane? How old are you, m'lord—no more than three decades, I would wager."

The tart inquiry brought a heated flush to his face. "I am eight and twenty," he replied stiffly.

"Yet you have had a successful military career and are poised to become a significant voice in Lords."

"A man's lot is different," he replied stubbornly now.

"I took you for other than a clunch-headed male. What a most contradictory man you are, m'lord. Bravely charging an armed thief and bringing him down with your bare hands, then back to braying again."

"I think these ruffians were after you," he stated, ignoring her pointed barb. "I was merely in their way."

She smiled grimly. "You have honed your verbal skills well in Parliament, to shift my attention away from your, er, ill-considered comments."

"Why would you need to conceal your identity if you are not hiding from someone?" he persisted.

His intent gaze and nearness disturbed her almost as much as the idea he forced her to consider. "My reasons for concealing my face are my own," she snapped. Amber stood, praying her legs would not give way before she could reach the bay. *It cannot be! Not after all these years . . . surely . . .* She would have to speak with Grace. And Jenette. They had warned her never to assume she was safe until the marquess was dead. At six and forty, the vicious beast could live for decades yet.

Rob watched her step away from him and give her still-skittering mount's reins a firm tug. Immediately, he followed, chastened that he had upset her. "I have ill repaid you for saving my life. Please forgive my prying. Are you certain you feel able to ride?"

"I have Star under control now. It would be best for both of us to get away from the smell of blood."

"You have never killed anyone, have you?" he asked gently.

"No, but not for want of trying," she replied. "I assume you have . . . considering that you were in the war."

He was not the only one who excelled at debate. "Yes, but 'tis not something I would care to do again. I hope you are never forced to take a life."

There was one life she would sell her soul to take, but she would never reveal that to Barrington . . . nor had she done so to anyone else save the two women and the sergeant major, who understood her reasons. "Perhaps Boxer will catch his quarry and we will solve this mystery," she said with a calmness she did not feel.

"Unfortunately, I doubt that's likely. His horse appeared to be favoring his right front hoof as he gave chase."

When Rob cupped his hands for her booted foot, she quickly swung up into her sidesaddle, eager to leave the place. "Boxer would never have fallen behind unless the animal was injured," she said with a frustrated sigh. "I did not notice he was missing until we were set upon."

The earl mounted his big black, saying, "Nor did I. We were quite engrossed in conversation. It is not only I who owe you my life, but perhaps Mr. Cobbett will owe you his as well."

"Please do see that he heeds the warning. Now I would like to return to Hampstead and wait for the sergeant there. The day has lost its luster for me. Would you be willing to alert the authorities about the dead man without involving me? They will not question the word of an earl."

"Certainly. Out for a ride, I chanced upon a dying ruffian whom I had never seen before. Which, narrowly interpreted, is the truth."

"I certainly would not wish to place the burden of lying upon your conscience, m'lord," she said, a bit of her former jauntiness returning.

He looked over at her profile, that strikingly beautiful face once again hidden behind the veil. Who had terrorized her so badly as to drive her into a life of hiding? Her words about killing troubled him. *"Not for want of trying . . ."*

On his way to Lady Oberly's dinner that evening, Rob mulled over Fantasia's disturbing words and the consideration that someone wished to kidnap or kill her. Who? She was hiding some dark secret buried in her past and refused to speak about it. As his carriage pulled up in front of the baroness's city house in Mayfair, he forced himself to focus on the enjoyable evening ahead.

This was to be his new life, if Verity Chivins became his countess. He had received every indication that she returned his interest since he had been introduced to her several months ago after worship at St. Paul's. Still in half mourning for her husband, the widow had been comely and gracious. Her warm smile had attracted him immediately, as had the rambunctious little boy peeping from behind her skirts beneath a nursemaid's watchful eye.

He had put off marriage for too long. He was the last of the St. John line and must have an heir for Barrington. Meeting the lovely widow seemed providential. Fixing that thought firmly in mind, he entered the foyer of the old city house for the first time. An ancient butler took his hat and ushered him into a small sitting room, explaining that he was the first to arrive. Lady Oberly would be down shortly.

The years had worn the luster off the marble floors, and the wallpaper hinted at a bit of mildew in the east corner, but the room was cheerfully decorated in pink and white with several large sprays of spring flowers adding a welcoming fragrance. The ornate furniture was piled with tasseled cushions, and the walls were covered with miniatures of Oberly ancestors. A bit cluttered, perhaps, but charming in its way.

"Do you approve, m'lord?" his hostess asked, gesturing at the walls with one gloved hand.

"'Tis a delightful house. I detect your touch everywhere," he said, taking her proffered hand in his for a chaste salute. She was dressed in pink, the delicate color both vivid yet soft enough to flatter her pale silver-blonde hair and porcelain complexion. The gown dipped low at the neckline, revealing the bounty held beneath by a high-waisted sash of deeper pink. White lace dripped from the shoulders and adorned the hem in a double row.

"I am so happy that you were able to find time in your busy schedule to attend my first entertainment since my period of mourning has ended," she said.

"If I had not found the time, m'lady, I would have made it," Rob replied.

"Barrington, still busy tilting at windmills?" a brash voice boomed from the door. "I hear you have raised quite a breeze in Lords," her father said as he approached. A tall man with thinning gray hair, a hooked nose, and narrow dark eyes, Viscount Middleton had an unctuous smile.

"Now, Papa, you promised me, no talk of politics until the ladies have retired from the dining table," Lady Verity said as the two men shook hands.

"I would be pleased to debate any issue on which we disagree, but only on the floor of Lords, sir," Rob offered with a smile. He found the baroness's elderly father to be crusty but tolerable.

Middleton made a dismissive gesture. "I have better things to occupy my time than being cooped up in Westminster's crowded chambers. Do you ride to hounds when you are in residence at your country estate?"

"Fox hunting has never been my sport, but I do enjoy fine horseflesh."

The conversation turned to a new foal out of Rob's prize-winning mare, a far safer subject than politics. In moments the other guests began arriving, Lord and Lady Chaldyce, who were cousins from the Middleton clan, Lady Babbington, an elderly countess who immediately attached herself to the baroness's widowed father, and a young baronet and his bride, from the Oberly side of the family.

They all spoke of the weather—too rainy—and agreed that the season would nevertheless be quite splendid. But the major topic of conversation as they were seated at the dinner table was the impending divorce scandal between Lord Byron and his wife of scarcely more than a year.

"Poor dear Annabella, I do not know whatever possessed her to marry such a rackety fellow," Lady Babbington said with a sniff of disdain.

"Well, he's gone off to the Continent now and I say good riddance. Wild-eyed revolutionary. France deserves the likes of that one," Middleton pronounced.

"He's deep in dun territory, I know that to be true," Penelope Chaldyce whispered as she sipped a tiny bit of the beef consume.

"Probably drank up all his earnings from the scribbling he does," her husband added snidely.

"Oh, dear, I confess that I do enjoy some of Lord Byron's verse," Verity said. "It is really quite romantic."

Before Rob could inquire what poem had caught her fancy, the young baronet said, "Byron has more probably given his money to dangerous men such as that Wilberforce chap."

"I do not see how Mr. Wilberforce's battle to abolish slavery can be construed as dangerous," Rob said as the soup course was removed and fillets of trout were served.

The baronet leaned forward, waving his fork. "Do you realize that the whole economy of our Caribbean colonies is based on it? And the raw materials from America for our mills—who would pick that cotton, eh? Abolition would destroy our national wealth, Lord Barrington. How can you not see it?"

"Well, I certainly cannot see why those poor white wretches lying idle in our crime-ridden tenements should not pick the cotton. We could send them to our colonies— and to America," Lady Chaldyce said brightly, smiling at her own cleverness.

"We have no way to force free men to labor in sugarcane or cotton fields, my lady, or, if innocent of a crime, to deport them to another country," Rob explained gently, as several of the other gentlemen chuckled condescendingly.

"A pity the earl is correct," Middleton said. "Wish Wellington had thought to ship those Froggies to the sugar plantations after Waterloo, eh, what?"

"A splendid idea," Chaldyce said.

Verity clapped her hands. "Now, gentleman, please, let us forgo further political discourse. It quite disturbs the digestion, and I have labored long over the menu for this dinner. We are having a splendid rack of spring lamb and a trifle with fresh fruit before the savory completes the meal."

"You are very wise, m'lady. Politics can indeed give one indigestion. I know from experience," Rob replied, raising his glass in a toast. "To our charming hostess, and her return to society."

"Hear, hear," echoed around the table as he exchanged smiles with the baroness.

Rob could see that Chaldyce and the baronet remained spoiling for further verbal jousting. He would be happy to oblige when the ladies retired, leaving the gentlemen alone with their port. Lady Chaldyce was an addlepate. Rob hoped that Lady Oberly did not share her uninformed opinions. Of course, he had no idea precisely what the baroness's opinions were. She appeared, like many women of his class, to have no interest in political matters, only hearth and home. The meal had been superb, her household ran smoothly, and she was a good mother.

What else did he require in a wife? Thoughts of Fantasia's razor wit and keen interest in Parliament vied with Gaby's sweet passion and acceptance of his sordid past. He shook himself mentally for thinking of them. They were who they were, and as such, could never share any part of his future. He must focus on the woman he hoped to make his countess.

Just before the ladies excused themselves from the table, a servant approached the hostess with a whispered message. She smiled brightly and said, "Please have Phoebe bring him at once." Turning to her guests, she said, "I would like to bid my son good night here at table so that you may meet him—if that is acceptable to everyone?" Her eyes met Rob's, looking for approval.

"That would be delightful," he replied. The others chorused agreement with varying degrees of enthusiasm.

In a moment the sleepy boy was brought into the dining room, his heavy-lidded eyes blinking beneath the bright glow from the chandelier. "Here's Mommy's good boy." She planted a kiss on his curly head, then said, "This is my son, Elgin."

"I doubt you remember me but we met amidst a great crash of tea tins," Rob said to the toddler, who should have been asleep hours ago instead of dressed in a satin suit, all turned out for inspection. But Lady Verity was a proud mother, he assured himself.

"Elgin, do you remember the Earl of Barrington?" Lady Verity asked as the maid rocked the boy, who shyly hid his face.

"A bit of foolishness, this. Send the child off to bed, Verity," his grandfather said gruffly.

"As you wish, Papa," she replied, reaching up to pat her son's head.

Finally awakened by the sound of the old man's voice, Elgin twisted in Phoebe's arms and launched himself at his mother. Verity tried to avoid the chubby little hands, but he seized hold of a white lace ruffle on her gown with a squeal of delight. A bit of drool escaped his mouth, dripping onto her lush bosom as she pried his hand free.

"Phoebe, I've told you repeatedly to hold him securely so this could not happen. Now see what you have done," Verity scolded, looking at the damp spot and crumpled bit of lace. She dabbed at the spot with a napkin and smoothed the sleeve, dismissing the red-faced nurse. "Please put Elgin to bed immediately."

When Phoebe turned to go, the little boy, already tired and out of sorts, saw the pink and white confection disappearing from his reach. Frustrated, he emitted a muted cry. As the nurse left the room, she crooned to him and his distress quickly abated.

His mother's cheeks matched her gown as she straightened and attempted to smile bravely. "I do apologize for that debacle," she said, looking over at Rob. "It would appear every time you see my son, he is in the suds. I hope you understand," she added hesitantly.

"What child would not reach out for his mother, especially one as loving as you, m'lady?" Rob asked. "It is late and the lad is tired. There's no harm," he assured her.

Around the table everyone chorused agreement, although Middleton muttered darkly about mollycoddling the next Baron Oberly. Rob noticed Lady Oberly's hand still nervously smoothing her gown as the conversation resumed.

Amber sat at the bow window in her private quarters reading the *Morning Chronicle* while she sipped hot black coffee. She noted a brief piece buried at the bottom of the second page. A thief from Whitechapel named Jemmy Starling had been found shot through the chest outside Hampstead. The report speculated about why a flash house denizen would venture into the countryside but drew no conclusions. She placed the paper on her lap and stared at the shrubbery outside being drenched in a heavy spring rain. The weather suited her mood.

Just as Barrington had surmised, Boxer had been unable to catch up with the man she had wounded. Her bodyguard was profusely apologetic and dispirited for what he perceived as a grave failure to protect her, no matter that she had assured him he was not at fault. When they arrived home, she had gone to Grace and told her about the attack. The older woman had immediately summoned Clyde Dyer, asking him to look into the incident. The runner quickly learned the thief's identity. Now he was searching for Starling's companions. Perhaps one of them might, for some coins, give over the name of Jem's murderer.

A light tap sounded on her door, but before she could inquire who it was or bid them enter, the door swung open and Jenette burst into the room. Her lovely face was flushed with anger. "You almost die—or worse—and you do not send for Jenette!" she accused, glaring down at Amber. "Grace, she tells me two men attacked you."

"You had gone to the opera with Lorna and her patron and did not return until quite late. Was I to spoil your sleep with my news? 'Tis all right, Jeni. The earl knocked one fellow from his horse and I shot the second ruffian. You would have been proud of me, my friend."

Jenette made a dismissive sound. "I merely instructed you how to fire at a target. Shooting at a man who shoots in return, that is brave and takes great courage, *ma coeur*. And your earl, he is brave as well as beautiful, that one. He speaks for the poor with great eloquence. Bold yet kind, which makes him twice the danger to your heart."

Amber's eyes flashed. She had not told Jenette about her masquerade as Gabrielle. "How did you know that I was . . ." She could not ask the question.

"That you have taken him to your bed?" The Frenchwoman finished her trailing question.

"Grace!" Amber accused.

"*Non*, she did not whisper a word. The years I spent spying against the Corsican taught me how to use my eyes . . . and ears. I am *sans honte*, without shame, when I must protect those I love." She shrugged unrepentantly. "You did not think to fool me . . . not after we went to hear your earl give his fiery speech, eh? I saw how you watched him."

"I wish you would cease calling Barrington *my* earl. Just because I have taken him as a patron does not mean—"

"Oh, after avoiding men all these years, now on the sudden, you choose this one to make love with and he is only a patron. *Non.* You listen to his speeches, give him carriage rides, and go on country outings with him. You—"

Now it was Amber's turn to interrupt. "How did you know that I gave him a ride in the rain? Boxer would never have said anything."

Jenette smirked. "Why should he not? I only ask him if you returned home without incident after leaving me at the modiste. He volunteers the rest."

"I should know I can keep nothing from you, my friend."

"Do not be angry with the sergeant major. Already he blames himself for yesterday, but we all knew one day the beast, he would find you."

"You speak just as Grace did. They could have been robbers."

"Robbers! And what would men from Whitechapel do on a lonely country road? Rob the sheep?"

"Perhaps they were sent to silence Barrington. Eastham may not be involved." She knew her voice lacked conviction.

"Grace says that Monsieur Dyer investigates. He will follow the stench of Eastham, not of sheep, mark me."

Chapter Eight

*T*hroughout the day, Amber fretted about the earl, who was scheduled to arrive for his next "lesson" that night. How could she pretend to be Gabrielle after the harrowing events of yesterday? Revealing her face to him had been an incredibly foolish blunder. He had not realized the truth, but if she continued spending time with him as Fantasia, it would be only a matter of time until he did.

"I have no excuse that I dare use to put him off. He would only come storming in again, demanding to see Gabrielle," she murmured to herself. She was confused because there was a part of her that was eager, nay, hungry, to spend another night lost in passion. Was she becoming as hopelessly addicted to his body—and indeed to his mind—as an opium eater to the drug? All too soon, their liaison would end. He would court his vapid baroness after returning to the world to which he was born . . .

The world to which you were born, too. That reminded her of the marquess. She swallowed bile. No, that evil brute had no place here. She would seize all the joy she could with Robert Emery Crispin St. John, Earl of Barrington . . . Rob.

Her earl . . . if only for a brief interlude.

Rob paced like a caged tiger across his study, watching the rain drench peonies and sweet woodruff. His gardener would be displeased by the broken branches and debris flung from the trees that marred the perfection of his handiwork. The earl had always enjoyed a good, cleansing storm, upon occasion even venturing out to ride during a downpour. He smiled ironically, recalling how he had eagerly accepted Fantasia's offer of shelter in her coach, when he certainly did not require it.

But he had wanted to talk with her. The woman had been a fascinating enigma from their first awkward interview. If Gaby was sweetness and fire during their "lessons," then Fantasia was arrogance and ice during their "debates." But as he began to spend time with her, he sensed a wary vulnerability beneath the clever wit and erudition. She was one of those "unnatural political females" men such as Byron detested. There had certainly been a time before he became engaged in the reform movement when he would have agreed.

Certainly Lady Oberly would not approve of "political females." But she was the perfect woman for a man in his position, he reminded himself. Did it matter if bills pending in Parliament held no interest for her? Her first commitment was to home and family. She would be a fine wife and mother, just as his own mother had been. Then the scene with young Elgin last evening intruded. The baroness had tried to conceal her distress when her only child did what he and his sisters had always done—reach out for their mother, who always picked them up. Abigail St. John did not care if they damaged her dress. Of course, his mother never had the money to afford nursemaids, being the wife of a priest in a modest country parish. But then, she did not have many dresses, either.

The invidious comparison bothered him. Should he court Lady Oberly? He wanted a loving wife and mother for his children, but he also wanted a companion who shared his interest in bettering the world. Fantasia was not only witty but well read, as radical a reformer as he had ever thought to be. *You could marry her no sooner than you could wed Gaby, fool!* As if either one would consider such a misalliance.

He stared through the rain-spattered window glass just as the sun broke through the clouds, unable to forget Fantasia's face, with its wide golden eyes and delicately arched eyebrows, high cheekbones, and lush mouth. "Damnation, admit it, you want to taste that mouth, not hear it speak," he muttered to himself. Saying the words aloud made him feel even more disloyal to Gabrielle than he already felt.

Fantasia was an infamous courtesan cloaked in mystery. At first he had convinced himself that he simply enjoyed verbal sparring with her, nothing more. After they survived death together, she had revealed her incredibly lovely face. At that moment he knew he had been deceiving himself. He desired her. When he made the decision to have a courtesan teach him how to become a good lover, he had never imagined that he would fall under the spell of not only his teacher, but her mentor!

The tall case clock struck the hour. The sun was sinking through the branches of the oaks outside. He had an appointment with Gabrielle at midnight. Did he wish to make love to her . . . or to Fantasia? Would the madam want him in her bed? Although he possessed great self-confidence in the political arena, Rob was not a vain man. She enjoyed conversing with him and had gone out of her way to find occasions for them to meet. They had much in common, unlikely as that would have seemed to him before he became acquainted with her. But that did not mean she returned his ardor.

To find out, he must pay her an early visit before he met Gaby in the darkness again . . . if he met her. She had already taught him more than enough to satisfy a lady. Yet the thought of saying good-bye to Gaby pained his heart. Was he going mad? He was torn between two women of the demimonde and disillusioned with the very lady for whom he had sought their help in the first place!

By the time Rob reached the House of Dreams, dusk was gently blanketing Alpha Road in a cool, spring haze. After

Frog drove around to the rear entrance, the earl climbed down from the carriage and started walking toward the door. Some activity was going on in the surrounding woods. He could see the flicker of torchlights and hear voices, even the clang of swords, for heaven's sake. Some rich man playing out his fantasy?

A scant few weeks ago he would have condemned such activity as immoral, or at least, foolish. Now he simply shrugged. Gaby's relaxed French attitude had mellowed him. *Forget Gaby. What are you going to say to Fantasia?*

When he was admitted, the footman nodded discreetly at his request to speak with her. Shortly a carrot-topped serving girl led him upstairs into the sitting room. "The mistress will be along shortly, sir," she said, bobbing a shy curtsy and scurrying away before he could thank her.

Rob looked around at the pale cream walls and rich green carpet, touched the smooth simplicity of the walnut furniture. No drawing room in London was more elegant or tasteful. Like the lady herself. He compared this room to the pink clutter of Verity's home, then dismissed the thought as inappropriate.

Think about what you will say to explain your untimely arrival. Vexed because nothing came to mind, he suddenly seized upon his early morning conversation with Cobbett. At least that would provide an opening. Then what?

Bonnie knew that her mistress had never before taken a patron to her bed. She approached Lady Fantasia in the library, not certain that she had done the proper thing by admitting him to her private quarters. But she dared not turn him away. "That fine-lookin' gentleman's here, askin' to see you, m'lady." Her face flamed as red as her hair. "I put him in yer sittin' room," she said. "Is—is that all right?"

Amber almost overturned the inkwell, which would have spilled all over her bookkeeping ledger. Carefully righting the inkwell, she laid aside her pen after dropping a blob of ink over the neat columns of figures. "Oh, of course, Bonnie. Did he say why he's here?"

When Bonnie shook her head, Amber dismissed the maid, instructing her, "Please see if Jenette requires any help."

She toyed with the idea of concealing her face from him, but dismissed it. He would surmise that she was afraid of him and she could not allow him that advantage. Besides, he had seen her face in bright daylight and given no hint that he knew she was Gabrielle. She smoothed her gown, then walked down the hallway. As she reached the door to her sitting room, she paused with her hand on the cool brass knob.

Turn it, you lackwit! With as regal an air as she could muster, she plastered a smile on her face and opened the door silently. She had caught him unaware, studying the Turner landscape on the far wall. He was so splendidly handsome her heart stuttered in her breast. His black kerseymere breeches and cutaway jacket were expertly tailored to fit his tall, lean frame. The snowy cravat at his throat contrasted with his swarthy complexion. Night-dark hair waved around his face, in disarray, as if he had been combing his fingers through it.

When she glided into the room, he turned and fixed her with those dark green eyes. Sparks seemed to shoot between them as she met his gaze. With a hitch in her breathing, she said, "Good evening, m'lord."

Rob had been startled by her cultivated, musical voice interrupting his reverie. Staring at her body swathed in sheer gold silk proved his undoing. The fabric clung to her hips and molded around her breasts. Its low neckline revealed wickedly soft cleavage where a lone topaz pendant nestled. "I see you have forsaken hiding your face from me," he commented boldly as he advanced a step toward her.

Amber stood rooted to the floor, her gold eyes answering the heat in his green ones. What would she do if he kissed her? He would know. *I must break this spell!* She decided upon a direct attack, asking, "Why are you here so long before your lesson with Gaby?" He stopped, his complexion darkening just as it had done at his first halting attempt to explain why he had come to the House of Dreams.

Rob cursed silently. What had he almost done! "I, er, I wanted to inform you that Mr. Cobbett has taken your warning to heart. He and his eldest son sail with tomorrow's tide," he blurted out.

She tilted her head. "Excellent. Sidmouth will not—"

Before she could complete the sentence, Bonnie burst through the partially closed door, wringing her hands, a look of wild alarm on her freckled face. "M'lady, come quick! Robin Hood has sliced open the Sheriff of Nottingham's bum! There be blood everywhere!"

What else could go awry this night? No, she dared not tempt the Fates by asking that. "Tell Jenette that I will be there immediately," she instructed the maid, who ran from the room, so upset by the sight of blood that she forgot to curtsy. From the corner of her eye, Amber saw Rob take a step toward the door. "Please remain here, m'lord. Have a glass of brandy—or an entire bottle for all I care—but do not leave this room."

Before he could respond, she seized a shawl hanging on a wall peg and rushed out the door. Rob decided he was not thirsty . . . but he was curious. Something must have gone dangerously wrong at the revels in the backyard. "Robin has cut up the Sheriff of Nottingham, eh?" he murmured to himself with a chuckle. His amusement was cut short when she ducked her head through the partially closed door. She had draped the wrap over her hair and face for concealment.

She quickly commanded, "What I said was not a suggestion, but an order, sir."

Rob stepped closer to the door. "But I have battlefield experience. I may—"

"Sit!" With that she vanished down the hall.

"I am not a dog," he muttered, slipping out the door. Even in the army, he'd never been good at following orders. He was careful to stay well behind her lest she catch him being insubordinate. The wooded area behind the house was lit by a series of torches, positioned among the budding oaks and hawthorns. Rob made his way down the twisting path in the gathering twilight. As he neared the scene, he ducked behind a large yew hedge to watch. The "players" were all dressed in medieval costumes, some as lords and ladies, most in forest green.

A man writhed on the ground, groaning and crying out, "'E's sliced off 'alf me arse! I be bleedin' to death!" A short, plump man in green tights that ill flattered his spindly legs brandished a sword over his prostrate victim. "You degraded poltroon, most fortunate are you that I administer so light a chastisement to one who dared lay hands on the fairest blossom of Sherwood Forest," he declaimed grandly, as he gathered a stunned young woman to his side with his free arm. Pointing the blade at the downed sheriff, he asked her, "Art thou unharmed, dearest Maid Marian?"

Rob stifled a guffaw. Although he did not recognize the Sheriff of Nottingham or Maid Marian, he knew the would-be Robin Hood, a wealthy merchant who held a seat in Commons. It would be best if the merchant never learned he had a fellow member of Parliament witness his fantasy.

Apparently Fantasia felt the same, for she and Bonnie knelt quietly at the side of the injured sheriff, attempting to ascertain the damage without interrupting the action.

As a distraction, a tall slender figure wearing a scarlet jerkin and tights cried out in a throaty French accent, "My lord Robin of the Hood, we must depart hence before the sheriff's villains descend upon us." Startled by the intrusion, Lord Robin whirled around, sword raised, while he still clutched the woman at his opposite side, he accidentally sheared off the top of a ridiculous feather on his compatriot's cap. Had not "Will Scarlett" ducked quickly, he would have been beheaded by Robin's clumsy victory flourish.

The red-clad figure danced back as Maid Marian seized her hero's arm, directing his weapon downward. "Oh, my darling Robin, you have saved me from a dreadful fate and suffered many a bruise to do so. Come with me and I will kiss each of those precious aches away."

The adoring female caught Robin's attention immediately. Will Scarlett nodded encouragement to her as she kept one eye on Robin's sword, the other on Fantasia and Bonnie as they attempted to deal with the thrashing victim.

"Yea, away we go!" the peerless leader said, now ignoring his adversary on the ground as he was herded farther into the trees by Marian. Rob could hear her cooing, "Yes, my love, I will worship every bruise you have received on my behalf. . . . I will kiss them ever so slooowly." She drew out the last word in a breathless whisper that carried on the night air.

"Ooh, please kiss my bruises—every one—ever so slooowly. Oh, my, that would be the cow's thumb!" Robin replied excitedly. Will Scarlett followed them into the darkness after relieving Robin of the wayward blade. The legendary hero handed it over without protest, too absorbed in having his bruises thus tended.

Rob doubled up trying to stifle his laughter. *This is more entertaining than an evening at Covent Garden!*

"Ralph, do lie still so we may see how badly you're hurt," Fantasia said to the fallen sheriff, who continued to thrash.

"Do like m'lady says, Ralphie. I seen me brothers' bums aplenty. Yers is no different," Bonnie scolded, trying to pry his hand away from his injury.

Will Scarlett returned to the scene, sword in hand. He gave the moaning man a swift kick in his good buttock with the toe of his boot, saying, "Lady Fantasia, this blubbering dolt has only been nicked." Bending over, Will slapped the sheriff's hand away so Bonnie and her mistress could see the wound. "Such a huge *bebe*," he scoffed.

Upon closer inspection, Rob could see that the legs in those tights were most certainly feminine. The voice, although a low timbre, belonged to a woman as well, obviously a French woman, but not his Gaby. *Gabrielle . . . what am I going to do tonight?* Momentarily distracted, he barely listened when the red-clad female called out, "Corporal, where are you?"

Rob blinked as a brawny youth stepped from behind a tree. It was the guard from the front gate whom he had ordered to summon Fantasia the day he thought Gaby was ill. Like the others, he, too, was dressed in medieval costume. He said, "I were afraid to stop the play, Lady Jenette. The patron—he was enjoyin' it so much."

"You did well, Corporal," Fantasia said, rising and dusting off her silk skirt, now satisfied that the wound was minor in spite of the blood. "Please assist Ralph indoors and take him to the housekeeper. She will stitch him up."

Ralph started to protest, "No, no woman ain't . . ." Fantasia's quelling glare silenced him. The corporal helped him stand and walk while he clutched his rump once more. All the other characters in the farce melted away in various directions.

Fantasia turned to the woman Rob had heard her call Jenette. "I am so relieved that you are not harmed, Jeni. How on earth did our patron get an edged weapon? The ones we rent from Drury Lane are dulled with guards on the tips."

The Frenchwoman pulled the cap from her head, spilling dark blonde hair about her shoulders. She inspected the remaining half of the feather. "This was no actor's property, but Boxer would not allow a mere female to be in charge of weapons," she huffed, then added, "I did not cheat Madame

Guillotine in France to be beheaded in England. Blame your human mastiff."

"This would appear to be an unfortunate week for him," Fantasia said with a sigh. She turned to a worried Bonnie and said, "Please find Mr. Boxer and ask him to come to my office immediately."

As the maid bobbed a curtsy and left, Fantasia said to the Frenchwoman, "Jeni, would you see that our patron is . . . ah, being well soothed?"

The blonde threw back her head and gave a deep laugh. "*Cherie*, would you have me observe his bruises being kissed ever so slooowly? No, *ma coeur*, that is certainly *not* my fantasy!"

Rob stepped from behind the hedge and leaned against an elm trunk, unable to stifle his laughter at Jeni's bon mot. "Nor would it be mine," he said to Fantasia.

Amber saw Rob and froze. "I told you to remain in my office."

"Ah, I see you will not be left alone, so I take my leave," Jenette said with a mock bow, skipping quickly away.

"Jeni, come back here at once," Amber cried.

"Only remember, *cherie*, 'ever so slooowly.' Au revoir." Her laughter faded rapidly.

Amber turned her fierce glare from her retreating friend to the earl, who approached, still laughing at the mad scenario he had just witnessed. "I imagine the poor Mr. Boxer's rump will be as well chewed as my own," he said.

Amber was furious. He had disobeyed her order and seen one of the fantasies turn into a humiliating disaster. More distressingly, his tall body looming over her in the torchlight did strange things to her heart. Backing up a step, she asked sweetly, "Did our near tragedy here provide sufficient amusement? We must be more entertaining than a carriage wreck, m'lord."

Remembering the cleanly sliced feather on the nimble

Frenchwoman's hat, Rob quickly realized that this could have indeed turned into a tragedy. "I intended no insult. Please, do not be angry. I'm truly sorry, but the scene was just so . . . well . . . unexpected. Robin of the Hood was certainly caught up being Maid Marian's hero."

Amber's anger died as she considered how the fat little merchant had looked in bright green hose and jerkin. Her lips twitched. "I suppose it was a bit amusing."

"Yes, but Lord Robin would be better suited for the role of Friar Tuck."

Amber chuckled and shook her head. "Our patrons usually wish to win the fair maiden, so being a monk would not serve."

"I can understand why being Robin would be preferable." He stepped closer to her. "After all, Mr. McGilvey's bruises are now being 'ever so slooowly' kissed away by the beauteous Maid Marian."

She was acutely aware of his nearness. The tension between them was palpable on the heavy night air. Sounds of soft laughter echoed in the distant woods, adding to the sensual allure. His eyes met hers and he held her gaze, mesmerizing her, rooting her to the ground. They were completely alone . . . and he knew the patron! The thought quickly jarred her out of the trance.

"Upon your honor as a gentleman, m'lord, please promise that you will never reveal his presence here or breathe a word about what occurred tonight." She was quite certain he would never do such a thing, but exacting the pledge allowed her time to collect her scattered wits.

Rob realized that she had deliberately broken the spell cast between them. He was Gabrielle's patron. She was the Lady Fantasia, mysterious and untouchable. "Of course you have my word," he replied stiffly, offering her his arm. "After all, who am I to intrude into another's dream?"

She rested her fingertips lightly on his arm and they

walked. But with her other hand she once more held the wrap across her face. Now she required a diversion. "This is, indeed, the House of Dreams, m'lord. But not all of the dreams are amatory. A few seek to heal the wounds inflicted by reality."

Rob's flash of anger was replaced by curiosity. "Without jeopardizing the identity of a patron, could you explain that?"

She lowered the shawl and gave him a genuine smile. "Yes, I believe I can do so. There is a young woman in residence here whose indifferent father died, leaving her to the mercy of a greedy cousin who possesses none. As luck would have it, I was approached by a wealthy man of middle years, a widower still grieving for his long-dead daughter, a girl who would be about Lorna's age. I am fulfilling a dream for both of them."

"You are certain this grieving father has no ulterior designs on the young woman?" he asked, his tone dubious.

"M'lord, cynicism ill becomes you. Of course I had him thoroughly investigated before allowing him to meet Lorna. She is a virgin and will remain so until her new father proudly bestows her on a worthy suitor. Strange, perhaps, but true."

"M'lady, I am beginning to believe that strange is your milieu."

Amber laughed. "Come now. I have a staff meeting to conduct."

Chapter Nine

*A*mber dealt with the near disaster quickly, learning that a new guard had seen they were one sword short and took it upon himself to substitute his own for the "play." After dismissing everyone else, she gave him a good tongue-lashing and exacted a promise never to tamper with Boxer's equipment again. She was certain the sergeant major would administer an even more vigorous verbal flogging and watch the youth closely in the future.

Alone at last, she paced in her bedroom. Should she ring for Bonnie and prepare for midnight? She knew it was folly for Gabrielle to go to him after what had transpired in the woods. But she could think of no excuse that would not make him suspicious. The nervy ache in her heart unsettled her even more than the base physical craving to feel his hands on her body once again. No, she reminded herself, not *her* body. Gabrielle's body.

The two must forever be separated if she was to retain her soul and her sanity. Gabrielle had so little time before her Rob left. Somehow that was even more difficult to bear.

As Rob lay alone in the darkness awaiting Gaby, thoughts about the farce played out earlier in the evening spun in his mind. If he had never come to this place of fantasies, he would not be faced with the dilemma confronting him. He desired two women he could never have, yet seemed destined to marry a woman who no longer held the slightest appeal.

The hidden door opened softly and his troubling reverie

faded when he smelled the soft scent of Gaby, his lady of darkness. He felt her slip into the bed with him and stretch silently alongside him. He caressed her flat belly, slowly moving up to her breasts while he nibbled soft kisses over her shoulder to her throat. "I feel your pulse racing, Gaby," he murmured.

"I . . . I have missed you, my heart," she said in French, turning into his embrace like the petals of a flower opening to the sun. If only they could be together in the light! But that would never be. "Please love me, Rob, love me."

Was there a desperate plea in her voice? He could not be certain, but his confidence had grown greatly during the past weeks of instruction. He raised himself over her and placed his weight on his elbows as he lowered his mouth to hers, feeling her legs open as his knee pressed against the insides of her silky thighs. This was so beautiful, so natural . . . so glorious. How could he ever feel this way with another woman?

But you must. He firmly reminded himself of that fact, then pushed the sad thought to the back of his mind while he rained swift, light kisses over Gaby's delicate face. Butterfly wings! He no longer had to remind himself to go slowly, to restrain his passion and wait for her body to send its sweet signals to his. She did not take long.

She kissed him back with searing intensity, opening her mouth, letting her tongue duel with his. Her hips arched in invitation. Suddenly he wanted to prolong the moment, to lose himself in Gaby's yielding body until his confusion over Fantasia, his future marriage, all else was forgotten. After teasing her ear with his tongue and nipping the lobe with his teeth, he murmured, "We have all night. Let us take our time. . . ."

He feasted upon her smooth firm flesh, moving his mouth down to her breasts, taking one nubby tip between his lips and suckling, then moving to the other. He loved hearing her little moans, feeling her nails digging into his back. She allowed him free access to her naked flesh. A wildly erotic idea formed in his mind, something he would never dare do with a wife . . . but with his passionate Gaby . . .

Somehow he knew that she would accept it. She would accept anything he did. Her passion was real, not feigned. It had nothing to do with her position in the House of Dreams, any more than it did with the money he paid for his "lessons." This was honest pleasure mutually shared. Why not explore it to the fullest?

This is your only opportunity!

He trailed soft, wet kisses down her belly, pausing to tease her navel with the tip of his tongue. Then he slid down on the big bed, cradling her hips with his hands. The kisses moved lower yet until he was nuzzling her mound and kissing the sensitive skin on the insides of her thighs. Ever so slowly he centered his quest, searching for that vital place where a woman's magic was seated. His hand had found it. Now his tongue did the same, ever so delicately.

Gabrielle had heard the courtesans speak of this, but she never imagined her Rob would dare to experiment this way. She should stop him—this was nothing he would ever do with his baroness! She felt duty-bound to stop him. . . . *But I am not Verity Chivins!* Still, she shoved him away, whispering raggedly, "No, you must not—this is very wicked . . . ah . . . ooh!" Gabrielle knew the battle of conscience was lost . . . she was lost, drowning in a sea of unimagined bliss.

Rob felt her hands push him away at first, then quickly stop. He paused only an instant as her halfhearted refusal turned to whimpering pleasure. Then she dug her fingers into his hair and pulled him closer, urging him to continue. He found the pulsing little bud and laved it as she arched and moaned with exquisite excitement.

Her hands tugged almost painfully at his scalp, but he was unaware of it, completely caught up in the wonder of making love so unselfishly. He felt an overwhelming combination of joy and power . . . power in giving freely and in knowing that his gift would not be refused but accepted with equal fervor.

Gabrielle lost all sense of time and place, aware only of Rob and the ecstasy he gave her. All too soon the now familiar contractions began and she sobbed, desperate for the culmination, yet at the same time wanting this bliss never to end. When it finally crested, she cried out his name and clamped her thighs against his head.

After her body collapsed back on the bed, replete, Rob planted a light kiss on the soft curls of her mound, then slid up to lie beside her. "Sometimes wickedness can be very good, do you not agree, my sweet Gaby?"

"I have never . . ."

"Neither have I," he murmured. "But it seemed like a good idea when I thought of it."

"You know it was . . . how much I enjoyed it . . . but my Rob, I have left you unsatisfied. I will—"

"No, you will lie back," he ordered when she reached for his pulsing staff that pressed against her hip.

When he removed her hand and rolled on top of her, she said, "You have become quite the bossy one, eh? Now that the naughty student teaches his teacher, he gets—how do you English say it—too big for his breeches."

Rob could not contain his laughter. "Gaby, when I am with you I am always too big for my breeches." She pounded on his back with her fists, sputtering in indignation until he said, "Now, dear heart, unclench those little weapons. After all, my naughtiness is all your fault. You have given me the gift of confidence."

"Perhaps, but God or Satan has given you the gift of arrogance, my wicked angel," she retorted.

Rob heard the hint of laughter in her voice as he began kissing her. She responded, opening her thighs to him. It felt so right to laugh and talk amid caresses, but soon their passions flared beyond words. At her urging, he slid into the wet heat of her body and slowly stroked until she again writhed and arched, saying, "Now, my heart, my Rob, come away with me now!"

He let go, plunging deeply, harder and faster as her sheath contracted around him. The sun, the moon, and all the planets collided in one blinding explosion of pure light. The entire universe shattered. He rolled onto his back, holding her so that she lay on top of him while they fought to regain their breath.

Gabrielle pressed her face against his throat, half afraid that he would feel the wetness of her tears. She could never make him stay, but how could she bear to let him go? Pushing the bittersweet pain away, she pressed soft kisses on his neck and combed her fingers through the crisp hair on his chest. Swallowing for courage, she said, "You have become the very best of lovers and now you reverse our roles. You teach me . . . although it began the other way."

"What I did, making love to you that way . . . I was not certain at first . . ."

She kissed the corner of his mouth and whispered, "Why did you do something that you cannot do with . . . a wife? Was it because of who I am, where we are?"

"No, you are my sweet and innocent Gaby. Life has not been kind to you, and the fault is not your own. Never think of where we are when we make love, or feel any guilt because you are not 'a wife.'"

The way he said the word *wife* so disdainfully filled her with curiosity. Not for the first time, she wondered why he had come to the House of Dreams to be instructed in making love. He was beautiful of face and body, also of soul. His instincts were to be gentle, to please a woman, not simply to satisfy his own desires. He was a rarity among men—that much she had learned from Grace and many of the women in this place.

Swallowing for the courage, she asked, "Why did you feel you could not please a wife?" Rob remained silent. "Oh, I have no right to ask such a thing! Please say that you will forgive me, my heart."

He stroked her hair as he replied to the question. "Because I did not please my wife."

"You have been married, then?" She was taken aback. How had Dyer missed this vital fact! "Oh, if you do not wish to speak of it, I will understand."

"Perhaps it's best if I do," he replied thoughtfully, still stroking her hair. "You see, I was the son of a second son. My father's elder brother held the title and had two heirs. My father was a priest. I grew up expecting to follow in his footsteps. During my first year in seminary, my family was approached by hers to arrange our marriage. She was the daughter of a baronet. I was but eighteen and as virginal as Credelia, who was a year my junior.

"Still, the marriage should have worked. My parents had a similar arrangement made for them and they were devoted to each other. I have three sisters, married and quite content. I expected to assume my father's position in our parish upon ordination, and to raise a family of my own. . . ."

This explained much about his life that she had not known. "What happened with this Credelia?" The question seemed to ask itself. Gabrielle knew the fault could not have been his and she was angry.

"She could not abide my touch," he replied bitterly.

"How could such a thing be? Did she love another?"

"No. We courted briefly. She seemed very much in agreement with the match, a pleasant and pretty girl. There was no other man. What I learned in the months following our marriage was that she enjoyed attention, but holding hands and receiving bouquets of spring flowers were the extent of it."

"Girlish things," Gabrielle said softly.

"She was seventeen."

"Many girls are wed younger than that," she said, repressing a shudder of remembrance.

"The fault may have been mine. No, not 'may have.' It was my fault! I—I was nervous on our wedding night. Clumsy. When kisses and cajoling failed, I tried to remove the barriers of night garments, starting with my own. She became hysterical. She pulled her night rail tightly around her body like a shield and rolled away, huddled in a ball of misery in the darkness. I put my nightshirt back on and tried to fall asleep while she sobbed on the opposite side of the bed.

"In the morning she asked that we no longer sleep together. I thought that if I gave her time to grow used to living under the same roof with me . . ." He sighed. "After several weeks, I explained that her duty as a wife was to allow me to be a husband. I returned to her bed."

"So she did her duty," Gabrielle said, feeling unutterably sad for Rob.

"She lay stiffly beneath me. I . . . I could feel her revulsion every time I touched her. After a few months, she locked her bedroom door and told me she would kill herself if I ever . . ." His voice faded away.

Somehow she felt certain the spoiled child he had married had not killed herself. Gabrielle caressed his cheek. "Did you divorce her then?" she asked softly.

"No, that would have broken my parents' hearts and created a scandal. Since I felt increasingly ill suited for a life in the church, I bought a commission and went to the Peninsula, which you already know."

"Your wife, what became of her?" she asked guardedly.

"Two months after I left she died falling down a flight of stairs. The accident was caused by an overdose of laudanum. Apparently, she was reeling drunk on the vile stuff. I did not learn until I returned that she was with child."

His flat tone of voice masked what she knew must be unbearable anguish. No wonder he felt inadequate as a lover. A boy raised in a religious household wed to a girl who detested his touch and sought refuge in drugs. "Credelia was too selfish to intentionally kill herself."

"Perhaps if I had not run away to war. If I had stayed and tried—"

"No!" she interrupted angrily. "You are not to blame. She killed your child. You are the one who was wronged, my heart," she said, holding him, offering the comfort of a loving embrace. "I have heard of women such as this... unnatural ones who shrink from any man. Sometimes it is because they have been treated cruelly as children."

"No, Credelia was beloved by her parents. Her father was a wealthy landowner who lavished everything on his wife and children. She was given whatever she wanted." He gave a mirthless laugh. "My father was taken aback when hers approached him. Why would the daughter of a baronet wish to marry the son of a poor priest?"

Gabrielle thought she knew the answer. "Because she had seen you and thought you were splendid to look upon. She asked her father for you just as she would ask for a new dress or a fancy carriage." His hum of agreement told her that she had guessed correctly. "She wanted a handsome husband, but she did not want to be a wife."

"That was long ago, best forgotten. I have never dared to tell anyone what I have shared with you. I am sorry for unburdening myself this way."

"You have not placed a burden on me. I am humbled by your trust and will never betray it."

He kissed her brow, then her cheeks and the tip of her nose. "I know that, Gaby."

His soft words cut like a knife. Gaby. She had betrayed him already with her deception. *Who am I? Gaby . . . or Fantasia? Or Amber, whose husband is very much alive?*

When his kisses grew more heated again, she pushed the confusing thoughts to the back of her mind and returned his passion with a hungry despair. Soon he would be gone forever, but tonight . . . tonight belonged to them.

Northumberland, Wolf's Gate Castle

Eastham cursed and smashed his hand on the table as Edgar Hull stood rigidly in front of him. "You are an incompetent imbecile!" he railed. "You have hired a kidnapper who could do the job no better than your own pitiful attempt a decade ago."

"The fellow's a Bow Street Runner."

"Who, you now say, requires more money. Do you believe I can shake it off trees for you to live the high life in London?"

"It's not for me. I have to pay for information." The main point of enduring the ugly confrontation was to extract more of the ready from the clutch-fisted marquess. He did enjoy the vices of the Great Wen and was, by damn, owed a little pleasure in exchange for the abuse Eastham heaped upon him, not to mention the long ride back to this wretchedly bleak place.

"If you have paid this runner so well, why has he failed so abysmally?"

"How was he to know that the harlot was armed and could shoot? Or that she would have a rendezvous with one of her patrons? Fancy-looking toff, he was. Bold as brass, too."

The marquess turned his back on Hull, stroking his chin as he considered what to do next. Shooting a runner while on horseback sounded quite like that damnable hussy he had married. She had always been far too coming for a proper female. Then another thought occurred to him. "We may be able to use this 'fancy-looking toff' to bait a trap for her if she spends time with him outside her filthy bordello. Have you any idea who he is?"

"I didn't recognize him," Hull lied. He had not even seen the man, only heard Cresswel describe the incident while his wound was being dressed. At the thunderous look on the marquess's face, he quickly added, "But I will find out his identity. Cressy owes me a favor. Him being a runner and all, he'll be able to do it."

"See that he does, posthaste!"

Hull only prayed that Alan Cresswel survived the ugly gash the bullet had torn across his side so that he could collect his favor.

Amber had never seen Grace behaving so nervously. She had been working on account ledgers that morning, trying not to think of Rob, when her mentor knocked and said she had brought coffee and freshly baked crumpets with Cook's strawberry jam. While she closed her book and removed the inkwell, Amber watched Grace fuss, setting the tray on the small table by the window. She poured two cups of a rich black brew and handed one to Amber.

Knowing that Grace far preferred tea, Amber considered remarking on it, then decided it might be wiser to simply wait and see what her old friend wanted. She accepted the cup and took a sip. "Heavenly. Thank you."

Grace took a sip and swallowed manfully, then tried not to grimace. Lud, how she detested coffee! But she knew if she waited for Cook to steep tea, she would lose her courage. "Now," she began, "er, do have some jam on that crumpet before it gets cold."

Amber sighed. "Grace, dear friend, why is it that I think you have a concern that is far more important than a cooling crumpet?" *Please do not let her ask me anything about Rob!*

"I fear I do," Grace confessed, setting aside her coffee cup. "You must not feel obligated . . . but you know what a detestation my dear Burleigh has always had for the diamond squad."

Amber smiled. "He has, upon one occasion or another,

remarked on it, yes." The crusty baronet much preferred living on his rambling country estate. He was well and truly a farmer and horse breeder. Being all the crack in a starched cravat and skintight breeches was the worst fate he could imagine. Burleigh Chipperfield was never happier than when he wore muddy boots and a belcher around his neck to wipe the sweat from his face as he walked his fields.

"Every man has his fantasy," Grace blurted out, startling Amber.

Thoughtfully, Amber replied, "I suppose that is true. Does his have aught to do with the upper ten thousand?"

Grace nodded. "Yes. Oh, my, after confessing it to me, he made me swear that I would never tell you . . . but it would be so much fun for him . . ."

"And it involves me." The response was not a question. Amber waited.

"You are the only one he would not feel uncomfortable with . . . er . . . fulfilling his fantasy." She leaned forward, a gleam starting to twinkle in her eyes as she warmed to the explanation now that she was nerved to reveal it. "Burleigh was quite surprised to receive an invitation to the Chitchesters' masquerade ball to open the season."

"That would be a singular honor. Invitations are quite coveted in the ton." Left unsaid was how a mere country baronet, albeit a man of substantial property, had come to be on the guest list when he had no interest in the ton.

"I know, why should he have been so favored? Well, Burleigh has a cousin who is quite the mushroom. He is heir to a sizable estate and will be the next Viscount Caruthers. But that is no matter," she said dismissively. "The invitation came because he is willing to marry the Chitchesters' eldest granddaughter."

"The one they call Medusa?" Amber asked. "He is a mushroom, indeed. She is not only on the shelf, but pushed to the rear of the cupboard. Yet, if she found a husband . . ."

"Just so. He secured the invitation for Burleigh, simply to irritate him, knowing how the dear fellow detests any rarified social occasion, least of all a masquerade. It was to impress, without the slightest expectation that Burleigh would actually attend."

"Where does Burleigh's fantasy enter into this Banbury tale?"

Grace shifted in her chair a bit uneasily again. "In a moment of wry good humor, he told me that it would be a lark to attend—with you on his arm. His cousin would be flummoxed to see him with a lovely young woman—of course," she hastily added, "only Burleigh would know his lady was from the House of Dreams. He never imagined that I would dare to ask you to do this. In fact, he will be quite put out that I have done so . . . but only consider, all the while the two of you dance, gossip will swirl about you. No one would ever imagine who his mysterious young lady is."

"And both of us could laugh at the ton's pretensions, a country baronet and a courtesan at a duke's ball."

Seeing that Amber was warming to the idea, Grace said, "You are the only one who could do this. Even if I were young enough, I could not serve. Far too many in the Chitchesters' circle would recognize me, even masked, since I was quite the infamous madam in my younger years. But wearing a mask and a wig to cover that remarkable hair . . ." She paused a hopeful beat. "Do you not see the humorous possibilities?"

Chapter Ten

*A*mber did see the wicked humor in snubbing her nose at the proprieties of the ton, the diamond squad who had banished her to cruel exile because of their horrendously hypocritical rules. Before she could reply, Grace continued her explanation.

"Of course, we would send along a host of our most trusted guards for your safety, but at such a public place I believe you would be in no danger or I would never ask, even for Burleigh. In fact, once he learns that I have shared his jesting wish with you, he will probably fall into an apoplexy."

Amber grinned. "But if I were to refuse, you would never tell the dear man, would you, you dry boots?"

Grace actually blushed beneath her paints. "No, I would not. You do see why no one else but you could do this, not even Jenette?"

"No, Burleigh would not be comfortable with anyone but me." Amber considered. "This will be great fun."

Grace became thoughtful. "Now that I have asked you, I am reconsidering the matter. It is too dangerous. If by any chance some distant member of your family were in London for the season and recognized—"

"You said yourself, how could anyone? I shall have on a mask and will conceal my scar with paints as always. Remember, I never had a season. No one in London has the slightest idea who I am. Grace, Burleigh is not the only one who would enjoy a bit of revenge on the ton."

Knowing the circumstances of Amber's marriage, Grace nodded reluctantly.

"Do not be in such a brown study. I shall wear a wig to conceal my hair—and powder it beneath just to be certain no odd red strands peek out. Pale blonde, a silvery tan, hmm, what do you think?"

"Well, we have two weeks to decide," Grace replied, pleased in spite of her misgivings. How Burleigh would relish this!

For her part, Amber welcomed the adventure. It would take her mind away from Rob. She expected any day that he would send a note, or appear in person to pay what he owed and terminate their business. What would she do then? Uncertain, she decided to use her voucher for the Gallery of Lords one more time. It thrilled her to watch him speak. To see him move in daylight, after he shared the darkness with Gaby.

Amber was not the only one preoccupied with their dilemma. Rob held thoughts of Gaby and Fantasia at bay during the days by burying himself in work, writing speeches, conferring with various members of Lords and Commons, and attending political rallies. On several occasions when delivering a speech on the floor of Lords, he caught himself glancing up at the galleries to see if a lady dressed in black was present.

His sleep and his concentration had suffered in recent weeks. Friends and political associates commented on his apparent distraction and asked what was wrong. There was no answer he could give. Nor could he explain his distraction to Lady Oberly when they met with increasing frequency at social gatherings.

He had no further reason to see Gaby. The kind of love they made now was far more passionate and bold than would be at all seemly in the marriage bed. She had taught him everything he needed to know and much more. He should thank her and tell her good-bye. Perhaps tonight?

Rob instantly dismissed the idea and returned to work on a speech for today's session in Lords. He would attempt to expose the corruption of Newgate prison guards and the deplorable conditions that many of the incarcerated endured. His hard-won resolve to focus on work was interrupted a quarter hour later by a messenger with a note from Verity Chivins.

Once her bright cheery invitation to ride on Rotten Row would have delighted him. But her talk of fashions, what went on at Almack's, or the latest gossip about Lord Alvanley's gambling debts and Brummel's exile were becoming increasingly taxing. He dashed off a reply, explaining that he would be on the floor of Lords today. She had attended several of his earlier speeches. He invited her to do so again, but in his heart, he honestly hoped she would decline.

After arriving at Westminster, Rob reviewed his notes and waited his turn to take the floor. Just as he was recognized to speak on that warm afternoon, he saw the baroness and her insufferable father seated in the first row of the gallery. A widow dressed in black and wearing a heavy veil sat directly behind them. Fantasia and Verity were both watching him, sitting scant feet apart!

All thought suddenly fled as the horrifying possibilities flashed through his mind. What if some devilish urge led Fantasia to speak to the only other woman in the gallery? When he blinked and looked down at the notes in his hand as if he had never seen them before, Lord Realton cleared his throat and said, "We await your pleasure, m'lord. You do have some wisdom to impart to your peers, do you not?"

Rob shoved his notes into his pocket and forced himself to focus on the matter at hand. "Most certainly. Please forgive me, m'lord." He bowed stiffly to his political foe whose bacon-faced countenance smirked openly. "My lords, I am here to discuss a grave miscarriage of justice. Two worlds exist side by side inside the cold, gray walls of Newgate. . . . ."

Somehow he completed the speech and responded ably during a heated debate on the prison reforms introduced in Commons. By the time the session drew to a close, he was relieved to see the baroness and her father had departed. He knew the issue, and any others discussed, held no interest for Lady Oberly. She had come only to please him. The baroness was encouraging his suit . . . if he ever began it. Now he had grave doubts that he should.

Perhaps I could ask Gaby's advice tonight.

No! He had to wean himself from depending on her sympathetic ear. Better the tart, acerbic wit of Fantasia. She was nothing if not blunt and practical, a woman who had seen a good deal of life. Dare he confide to her his change of heart regarding his chosen bride? He stuffed his notes into a leather satchel and quickly made his way through the noisy throng of peers, receiving congratulations from a few and caustic comments from many.

When Frog pulled his carriage up to the door in the Old Palace Yard, he retrieved a pistol from inside the coach, sliding it into the waistband under his coat. Then he instructed the driver to return home without him. He quickly found Fantasia awaiting her chaise and cut across the crowded melee of carriages and pedestrians. Without giving a fig for the potential danger, he approached the "widow." "Good afternoon, m'lady," he said softly.

Fantasia spun around abruptly and whispered, "Are you mad? What will the gossipmongers make of this?"

"No one knows your identity." *Including me.* "I should simply tell anyone who inquires that you are a distant cousin from Kent, recently widowed."

She could not resist smiling when a thought suddenly occurred to her. It was a good thing that he could not see her expression through the heavy veil. "Are you concerned that I might have spoken to your baroness?"

He frowned. "How did you recognize the woman I intended to court? I never gave her name."

Amber noted the choice of words. The woman I *intended* to court. Had he changed his mind about the vacuous little fortune hunter? She hoped so as she replied, "When I had you investigated as a potential patron, she was, er, noted in the report. It is quite apparent that she has set her cap for you." She made a dismissive gesture. "But you evade *my* question and I asked first."

She was teasing him. His frown softened into a smile. "After due consideration, I decided to trust your discretion. You would never betray a confidence."

"Ah, but at first the thought did distress you, did it not? Else why did your legendary eloquence desert you when given the floor by that pompous ass Realton?"

"I have been a bit distracted here of late," he confessed. "Would you be so kind as to give me a ride home once more?"

"You are taking a grave risk, Barrington," she said softly, her heart racing.

"You are my third cousin Angela Whitfield from Kent. What could be improper in my accepting a ride in an open carriage with a widow?" he asked with sternly proper bow. Only the dancing green light in his eyes gave the lie to the stiff words. "No one need know that I was rather ungraciously forced to beg for the honor."

"Well, today wishes do indeed become horses and beggars will ride." She gave his direction to her driver, then turned to the earl. "Please assist me up." The moment his hand touched her arm, Amber felt as if lightning had struck. She quickly averted her gaze and forced herself to remain calm while climbing into the carriage. Because the day was so lovely, she had taken the open carriage, which meant he had to sit beside her. The smaller vehicle had only one seat. When he climbed up, the crisp, masculine scent of starch and shaving soap teased her nostrils.

She did not dare to look at him as the carriage pulled out into St. Margaret Street. The busy afternoon traffic impeded their progress as her driver was forced to rein the horses every few yards. Rob was very careful not to allow his body to touch hers. The confined space on the small seat made it difficult. He had to straighten his long legs and brace his feet against the footboard to keep from brushing against her. What cork-brained impulse had made him ask for this ride? Her rose perfume had an instantly arousing affect on him. What should he say? What *could* he say?

"Perhaps this was not a wise idea after all, Fantasia," he finally managed.

She turned from staring at the motley press of humanity and faced him. "Do you intend to court the baroness or not?" There. It was out in the open. Did she sound jealous? What did it matter? He had begun this gambit.

His chuckle was rusty. "You are awake upon every suit, to take notice of my slip. You are also honest." He paused, gathering his scattered thoughts. At length he replied, "I'm no longer certain about Baroness Oberly's . . . suitability. Her appeal from a distance was far greater than it is now that she is out of mourning and we have spent several social occasions together."

"She is vacuous and her father is a mean-spirited ogre who was insufferably rude to my friend Jenette when last we were here."

"You do not sugar the medicine," he said with a sigh. Feeling it would be unchivalrous to reply to her accurate assessment of the baroness, he said, "The viscount detests everything French, making no distinction between Bonapartists and Royalists. We do not get on all that well, although he tries to temper his dislike of my politics for his daughter's sake. Was your friend Jenette the charming Frenchwoman who played Will Scarlett?"

Amber could not believe she had dared to ask him about the baroness—and that he had replied without growing angry at her presumption. What did that mean? Rather than ponder such a disturbing question, she replied, "Yes, that was Jeni. She is a remarkable woman."

"Was she the one who taught you to shoot?"

Amber nodded, once more aware of how he filled the carriage with his presence. To shift her dangerous train of thought, she turned and looked back. "Boxer was behind us, but in this traffic I cannot see him."

Rob, too, turned back and spotted the sergeant major some distance behind them. "He's making his way closer as rapidly as possible. I wondered at his absence when we left the building. Do you never travel without him to guard you?" What enemy could she have made who could be this dangerous?

"Sometimes others such as Jeni accompany me, but there is always someone," she replied, hoping he would not press her further.

Her driver was suddenly forced to turn the light carriage sharply in order to avoid the cart of a street vendor. Amber tumbled against the earl's chest. Instantly his arms reached out to steady her. He did not immediately release her, but stared at her face as if he could see through the veil.

"I detest the need for your disguise," he said in a husky voice.

"Not nearly so much as I."

"You are a strikingly beautiful woman. Why—"

She placed one gloved hand over his lips and felt her fingertips burn through the soft fabric. "Do not ask what I cannot answer. Tell me instead about your misgivings regarding the baroness."

Rob fought the desire to remove the bonnet and kiss her.

This was insane. The woman he desired in that way was Gaby. He shook his head to clear it, then leaned back against the seat and said, "I find her conversation lacking . . . wit . . . but that is the least of it." He outlined the events at Lady Oberly's dinner party. "It is as if she brings the child out to show that she is capable of producing an heir. That sounds insufferably vain of me."

"Not vain, true. Jeni said the same thing when we chanced upon the three of you at Berry's grocery. A nurse-maid will raise that boy and any other children she may have."

"You were there when poor little Elgin pulled down those tins? I did not see you."

"No one takes note of a widow veiled in black."

"You must be very weary of hiding. Can you not confide in me? You can trust my discretion. I have trusted yours."

For one insane instant she almost unburdened herself. What a relief to tell him all of the dark, ugly secrets that haunted her nightmares, but she quelled the impulse. "'Tis not a lack of trust, m'lord. It is—"

She was interrupted when a band of ruffians suddenly surrounded the carriage. Amber could hear Boxer's shouted warning from a distance, but it was too late. One vile-looking fellow with shoulder-length strings of greasy hair and hands the size of bear paws seized the horse's harness while his scrawny companion pulled her driver from his perch. Two more piled onto the open carriage from Rob's side while a horseman reined in beside Amber.

Amber dug into her reticule as she screamed to draw attention, but in the noisy press of people at the busy King Street intersection, the gawkers who paid any mind did nothing to aid them. Rob raised his foot and kicked one of the invaders squarely in the chest, sending him flying backward to the pavement. From the corner of his eye he caught the gleam of a blade and ducked an instant before his second attacker sliced open his throat. He used his arm to shove the knife away, then punched the man's face.

As they struggled, the horseman leaned down and tried to scoop Amber from the carriage. She twisted away as her right hand found her pistol. Without removing it from the reticule she aimed and fired, but in the struggle the bullet missed its mark, leaving only a charred rip beneath her attacker's arm. With a snarled oath he reached out once more, knowing she could not have a second weapon in such a small bag. Hearing the shot, the crowd panicked. Pedestrians, street vendors, and carriages scattered pell-mell in all directions.

Ever since the attempted kidnapping, Rob had begun to carry his Egg pocket pistol everywhere but on the floor of Parliament. He yanked it from his waistband and used the blunt barrel to smash his attacker in the temple. With a yelp the man fell from the carriage. Rob turned at the sound of the shot and saw Fantasia holding on to the seat with one hand while she writhed and kicked to keep from being thrown across her kidnapper's saddle. The man who had disposed of their driver now climbed over the bench with the whip in his hand.

Rob grabbed the end of the braided leather and gave a hard tug, overbalancing the ruffian, who tumbled headlong into the carriage. Placing his knee on the sprawled attacker's back, he aimed at the horseman, but Amber was between him and his target. He reached over and pulled her out of the brute's grasp, then fired his pistol. Her attacker fell from the horse as it reared up, whinnying in terror.

The big fellow holding the carriage horse saw that things were not going as planned. He released his grip and fled into the crowd, as did his companions whom Rob had repelled. The last one still thrashing on the floor of the carriage was their prisoner now. Rob used his spent pistol to club him insensate, then leaped from the vehicle to where the man he had shot lay. By this time the crowd had thinned sufficiently for Boxer to reach them. He quickly seized the harness of their carriage horse and calmed the frightened animal while the kidnapper's mount ran down King Street.

"Is the blighter dead?" he asked Rob. A large red stain had quickly soaked through the man's filthy ragged shirtfront.

"Unfortunately, he is, but the one inside should survive." Rob looked up at Fantasia, who was standing over the unconscious fellow, calmly reloading her pistol. "Are you unharmed?"

"I am in far better condition than that one," she said, looking at the dead man sprawled on the cobblestones. "Sergeant Major, we'll require Mr. Dyer's services as soon as you see to poor Alfie. Is he badly injured?" she asked, biting her lip. The boy was one of a group of climbing boys Grace had rescued many years ago, a favorite who had been thrilled when he learned to handle horses and became one of their drivers.

Alfie had struck his head when tossed from the driver's seat. He was on all fours, trying to stand. Boxer quickly assisted him, dusting off the younger man's jacket. "There you go, lad." Turning to Fantasia, the sergeant major said, "He has a bit of a bump. Had worse, ain't you, Alf?" The boy smiled gamely and nodded as he rubbed the swelling on his forehead. "Are you able to drive, boy?" Boxer asked.

"Yes, sir, Sergeant Major Boxer."

Rob stood up and handed Alfie the whip he'd taken from the unconscious man in the carriage. "Keep the horse calm while I secure this miscreant," he said, rolling the unconscious man on the floor.

By this time a crowd was beginning to gather, curious about the mayhem now that the violence was apparently over. Keeping a wary eye on them, Rob pulled a well-worn leather belt from around the kidnapper's waist while Fantasia climbed down so that he had room to work. The earl bound the kidnapper's wrists and ankles together behind his back, then shoved him flat on his stomach. Alfie returned to the driver's seat and took the reins from the sergeant.

"What do you want us to do with 'em, Lady Fantasia?" Boxer asked.

Rob interjected, "Perhaps it would be wise to have the sergeant major see you home while I borrow his mount to take the dead man to Bow Street. I shall explain that I was set upon by thieves and defended myself."

"Then we can question our prisoner here in private," Boxer added with a wicked smile, obviously relishing the idea.

She considered, then nodded. "Very well. But once you are cleared of any blame for killing that ruffian, have Clyde Dyer come to my home. He may know the identity of the prisoner as well as the dead man. I shall want him to investigate."

Rob looked at her. She appeared a bit disheveled but over all amazingly calm after such a harrowing ordeal. "I should think you would. This is the second attempt to kidnap you within the month." Left unsaid was who had hired this scum to do her harm. He was determined to find out if the Bow Street runners could not.

As the earl and the sergeant major loaded the dead body over Boxer's horse, they did not see the tall figure slouched at the back of the crowd, watching the scene. Hull cursed in silent rage. While Cressy was laid up with a bullet from that damnable bitch, here that toff appeared again to ruin a second attempt!

Hull had ventured into Seven Dials where he found a gang of thieves whose leader bragged that he would kill any guards the woman had and make off with her. "I've seen how well that went," he muttered savagely beneath his breath.

He watched impotently as the elusive marchioness once more slipped from his grasp. The toff rode up toward Bow

Street with the dead gang leader while the older servant climbed into the chaise with her to guard their prisoner. They headed out of the city toward St. John's Wood and the House of Dreams.

It was most fortunate that only the dead man had seen Hull. If he had lived, he could have described the man who paid him.

Lady Eastham would have known immediately who he was.

Chapter Eleven

Disheveled and trembling, Amber climbed the stairs to her private quarters, praying that she would not encounter Grace or Jenette. She had to bathe and steel herself before she began questioning the man Boxer now held in the mews at the back of the property. Grace would be frantic when she heard about another attempt to kidnap her, in broad daylight, virtually within sight of Westminster! Both women were quite certain Eastham was behind the first attempt. At that time, she had tried to convince herself that it was impossible. How could he have learned that she was here? She had been so careful. But a second attempt . . .

Eastham has found me.

She looked down at her torn black day dress and could not wait to rip it from her body, along with the hated bonnet and veil. Lord above, how she loathed black! She had almost made it to the sanctuary of her door when Jenette saw her from down the hall.

"*Ma coeur*, what has happened? You look like the house cat who has fought with a badger!" She quickly closed the distance between them and held Amber at arm's length, inspecting her tatty appearance.

Sighing in resignation, Amber replied, "Come inside. I will explain while Bonnie draws a bath." She quickly outlined what had happened and explained that Clyde Dyer was coming to assist in questioning their prisoner while the maid filled a tub with warm water. Bonnie's freckles appeared dark and large against the chalky pallor of her face as Amber talked. Jenette's eyes narrowed, but she remained calm.

"Let us see what this, this *batard*, this animal will say to us, *oui*?"

Amber sighed. "I suspect Eastham is behind it, but I doubt the fellow we have will know anything other than that some intermediary paid them a pittance to kidnap me."

"It is, I suppose, a place to begin, this intermediary. But it would be far wiser to go directly to the source. Northumberland," Jenette replied as Amber sank into the tub.

Splashing water, Amber sat up and stared at her friend. "No! Grace tried that several times after she first took me in. You know how it turned out. One man was killed, and two others narrowly escaped with their lives. The marquess rules that area with a steel fist. No one will say a word to an outsider and Wolf's Gate is impregnable."

Jenette made a snorting sound of disgust. "A dozen men are not equal to one woman . . . provided the woman is *moi*." When Amber started to protest, her friend shushed her and continued. "You know that I became the spy after my family was destroyed by the Tyrant. I survived many years working for your government. I am good at this, *oui*?"

"You saved my life and helped me escape Napoleon's web, but that was in France—"

"And I shall yet be French . . . in Northumberland. I shall, how do you say it?—cut a dash in the wild north as la Comtesse de St. Emilion, an émigré who has escaped France with great riches and wishes only to live the quiet life now. . . ."

Amber could see Jeni's eyes gleam with a hard, calculating light. She had lost everything during Napoleon's dictatorship, but she had survived by her wits. Knowing it would do no good, Amber nevertheless protested. "It is too dangerous, Jeni."

Her friend gave a Gallic shrug of dismissal. "So is crossing Piccadilly at four in the afternoon. Within the fortnight I will know how we deal with *le diable* . . . for once and all." She grinned at Amber. "Grace will be happy to give me the 'riches' for my charade, *oui*?"

With that, she turned and left Amber sitting in the cooling bathwater.

That evening the "comtesse" set out in an elegant coach bound for Northumberland on an expedition of reconnaissance. She had been outfitted with a splendid wardrobe by her courtesan friends, carried a goodly portion of Grace's jewels, and was attended by four trusted servants, two veterans, and two émigrés she had brought to work at the House of Dreams.

As midnight drew near, Rob sat in his study, fortifying himself with a glass of cognac. What a wretched day this had turned out to be. He had spent an hour at Bow Street explaining away the body of the man he had shot. Once Clyde Dyer arrived, he was respectful of the Barrington title and possessed enough common sense to release him after having him sign some papers for the magistrate. The runner identified the dead man as a notorious criminal from Seven Dials who led a gang of the lowest sort of thieves and killers.

After the earl explained privately about the Lady Fantasia's involvement, the runner accompanied Rob to St. John's Wood. They spent several hours questioning the cutthroat, but it was obvious that he had never seen the man who had hired his dead leader.

Dyer took the kidnapper into custody. Then the earl returned to his city house to bathe and prepare for his meeting with Gaby at midnight. Once Fantasia was certain their prisoner could yield no information, she had excused herself before Rob could question her about this second incident. He was certain she knew who was behind both attempted kidnappings. That was why she hid her face in public and never ventured from her home without armed guards, even going so far as to carry a pistol in her reticule.

He finished the cognac, vowing that he would find out who her enemy was and deal with the villain. Perhaps Gaby might know something useful. "Best to tread lightly there," he muttered to himself. Questioning Gaby about the woman who had saved her from destitution might be awkward at the least.

Considering awkward matters, how was he going to figure out what he felt for Gaby and Fantasia . . . and Lady Oberly, who had unwittingly precipitated the whole dilemma? He was starting to think he and the baroness did not suit. She had sent by a note while he was at the Bow Street station, saying how much she had enjoyed his speech, although she could not quite understand why he was concerned with "the criminal element" as she put it. She and her father had left before he finished speaking.

"What will we discuss if I court her, once the topic of Elgin is exhausted?" he asked the empty room rhetorically, staring disconsolately at the crumpled missive lying on his library desk.

As his carriage headed away from the city, he decided he would ask Gaby. Perhaps it was the darkness . . . or the satiation after making love, but whatever the reason, he always found it natural to reveal his inmost thoughts without embarrassment. No one, not even his beloved mother and sisters, knew about the debacle of his first marriage. Deeply religious and steeped in country virtues, they would be horrified if they ever learned how he had been spending his nights the past weeks.

"They'd wear out their knees praying for me," he murmured wryly. Odd, but the guilt that had plagued him when he first went to the House of Dreams had become a thing of the past. Something else to ask Gaby about?

While the earl was looking for advice, Amber was looking for respite. She desperately needed the all-consuming distraction of a night's passion as Gabrielle. After hanging over her head like the sword of Damocles, her past had at last come crashing down upon her. And now her closest friend was risking her life by walking into the wolf's den. She shuddered just thinking of Eastham's gray ugly castle and the marquess himself, brutal, ruthless, and evil beyond imagining. Amber tried to assure herself, even as Grace had earlier assured her, that no one was better suited to taking care of herself than Jenette Claudine Beaurivage, the only surviving daughter of Baron Rochemonde.

Rather than fret heedlessly, she needed this night of mindless pleasure in her lover's arms. But what of the bitter price when he was gone? Dismissing that thought, she slipped off her robe and tossed it on the chair in the small dressing room. She could tell the candle in their chamber had been doused. Silently opening the door, she stepped inside and made her way to the bed. "Rob?" she said softly.

"Here, Gaby." He sat up on the edge of the bed, eagerly reaching for her. "Your skin is like silk," he breathed, brushing light kisses across her belly as he cupped her derriere with his hands, gently kneading the firm little globes.

When the tip of his tongue swirled around her navel, she purred with pleasure, leaning back and gripping his head with her hands, burying her fingers in the thick inky waves of his hair. Even in the darkness, she carried the image of his face and body etched indelibly in her mind. She would remember it always.

"Gaby, Gaby," he murmured her name as he pulled her down onto the big, soft bed with him so that she lay on top of his body, her face nestled beneath his jaw. She kissed his throat as he ran his hands down the delicate curve of her spine, tracing each vertebrae with deft fingers.

"You have mastered butterfly wings so very well, my major," she murmured.

"I have had a very fine instructor," he replied, rolling them onto their sides facing each other.

When he cupped her breast and thumbed the nipple, she gasped, knowing where his hands moved, his mouth was certain to follow. It did—one breast, then the other, tugging, swirling, suckling as she arched and writhed, trapping his hardened staff between her thighs. She could feel her own wetness and wanted him to come inside her, to bring on oblivion, but Rob had other ideas.

He rolled over her, braced himself on his elbows, and framed her face with his hands. Then he rubbed his nose against hers, adjusting in the darkness until he found her fluttering eyelids. He pressed his lips against one, then the other, murmuring, "Your lashes are thick and long." He kissed her forehead. "Your brow high and noble." When his mouth brushed against her temples, he whispered, "I feel your blood pounding." His lips danced across her cheekbones. "Mmm, high, elegant cheekbones. You are a beauty, little Gaby. How I long to see you in daylight." The moment he said the words, he could feel her body stiffen.

"No!" The instant she spoke, Gabrielle knew that she must explain in a way he would understand and accept. "I mean . . . I cannot bear for you to look at me and I at you . . . and then have to part, as one day soon, we must. Let the beauty of these nights be my secret treasure to keep, yes?"

Rob stroked her cheek, thinking about that inevitable parting, something he had been pushing to the back of his mind for weeks now. It was well past time already for him to say good-bye. But he knew he could not bring himself to do it. "I do not want to think about parting, Gaby, although someday we must. These nights will be my treasure, too."

He brushed soft kisses all over her face and ran his fingers through her long, silky hair, trying to memorize the feel of her. Then his lips reached her mouth and he took possession of it.

Gaby opened for the hot, sweet invasion, twining her tongue with his until they were both breathless and hungry. She cupped her hands around his shoulders, arching her head back as his kisses moved to her throat and down to her breasts once more.

"I could feast on you forever," he said raggedly.

Gaby pulled one of his hands away, guiding it down lower to the hot aching core of her body. "Feel where I hunger for you the most," she whispered.

He touched her petals and creamy wetness proclaimed her readiness for his invasion. Ever so slowly he used his fingers to tease and stroke, leaving her panting. Then he carefully inserted one finger inside her tightness, tantalizing her as she bucked beneath him. Just as quickly, he withdrew and ran his wet hand over the curve of her hip, down one leg.

Sitting back on his heels, he held her slender ankle in his hand, raising her leg. "I wonder, how would it feel if . . ." His words trailed away as he teased the sensitive arch of her foot with his tongue, then sucked on her toes, one at a time.

"You are most . . . inventive," she whispered hoarsely while he kissed his way up her leg and then released it, repeating the exercise with the other one.

"Such perfect legs. If the insides of your arms are sensitive . . . turn on your stomach," he commanded gently as a new idea blossomed in his mind. She complied.

When his mouth touched the back of one knee, she moaned. Satisfied, he moved to the other, then nibbled his way up to her buttocks with tiny licks and bites. This was more erotic that he could ever have imagined. He drew out the pleasure, slowing her frantic race to finish, much as she had admonished him to do when first they began "the lessons."

Without thinking, with an instinct as old as time, she raised herself onto her hands and knees, presenting her backside to him as she whispered, "Come into me!"

He responded the same way, realizing that this was probably the most primal way a man took a woman. Would it please her? The moment he guided his staff to her creamy welcome, he knew it would please him . . . greatly. Slowly he penetrated her from behind, waiting to see if she could accommodate him in this new position. She wriggled her bottom, emitting small moans and gasps that he knew meant she wanted him to continue.

When he finally seated himself fully inside her sheath, she let out a small "aaah" and braced herself, pushing against him. That was all the encouragement he required to withdraw and stroke inward, repeating the glorious motion in a slow, steady rhythm. He kneaded her buttocks as he moved, then let his hands glide around her waist and upward to cup her breasts, feeling the hardened tips of her nipples pebble in his palms.

Bringing her such pleasure increased his own twentyfold.

She arched her spine and moved backward and forward with each thrust. Never before had he been able to bury himself so deeply inside her. The heat and pleasure grew, but without contact to the bud that triggered her release, she could not join him. With wisdom as old as Eve, she reached for his right hand and guided it over her belly to the place she wanted him to touch.

At once, he understood. His fingers found her and grazed the wet satiny flesh until she stiffened and cried out his name. He could feel her sheath contracting around him and knew it was time to follow her to bliss. With another stroke he arrived.

They collapsed on the bed, panting and satiated, lying on their sides, still joined like two spoons in a drawer. He held one hand possessively over her hip and kissed her neck, murmuring, "Gaby, Gaby . . . you inspire me . . . I never imagined . . ."

"I . . . I did not know anything such as that was possible . . . I think we have imagined ourselves . . . together. You understand, yes?"

"Yes," he whispered in French, feeling completely at peace.

Finally he stirred, rolling onto his back and pulling her to his side, where she nestled contentedly. He played with a lock of her hair, then said, "It seems so natural to speak of what we do . . . to talk afterward, without feeling embarrassed or awkward."

She felt the same . . . as Gabrielle. But what of Fantasia? And what of Amber, whom he would never know at all? "For as long as you are with me, I am happy when we make love and when we talk," she finally managed, leaving unspoken their parting. Enough had already been said on that subject.

Rob did not want to dwell on the disturbing thought, either, or on why never coming to the House of Dreams again made him feel desolate. He must focus on the future, on his duty to the Barrington title. "I require some advice, Gaby," he began hesitantly.

She could hear the uncertainty in his voice. "If I can help, my heart, only ask."

"A woman of your class, would it matter that . . . that you were raised in France—instead of England, I mean? No, that isn't what I mean . . . ah, bloody he—" He stopped himself, then apologized for his atrocious language. "I'm making a muddle of this," he added, frustrated. "Do you think an English lady of rank would be able to talk in bed the way we do?"

Gabrielle swallowed her tears. "You mean the lady you will one day marry, the one for whom you came to this place?" She was proud of the steadiness of her voice.

"I suppose so," he said with a sigh, tracing small circles on her shoulder, absently. "But the problem is, I can't imagine what I shall say to her . . ."

"You mean in the dark, after you make love?" she prompted when his voice faded away.

"I cannot imagine this naturalness, her willing ear, exchanging confidences. Would any lady want this, Gaby? Am I asking too much?"

She tried for one of Jeni's shrugs, knew she failed miserably. "I think some ladies would grow accustomed in marriage to talking after making love . . . with a lover such as you for a husband. Think of all the wonderful things you have to tell her—your work in Parliament to help poor children, to reform the prisons, to—"

"She has no interest in politics or reform," he said flatly. "We discuss the weather, tea blending, the newest fashions. She tells me the latest gossip about Prinny and Alvanley. Once those topics have been exhausted, we seem to have little to say to each other."

"She has no interest in your work, then?"

"None that I have discerned, which is probably for the best since her father is a rabid Tory who detests any whiff of change. She does have a little boy from her first marriage."

"She is a good mother, yes?"

"In a titled English mother's sort of way, I suppose she is. The boy's nursemaid spends more time with him than his mother does."

"You were not raised in this manner?" she asked.

"No. My father was a second son, a priest in a country parish. The Barrington title and all its social obligations fell to his elder brother and his sons. They grew up with nursemaids and tutors. My sisters and I were in our mother's charge. We ate our meals with our parents and took our lessons in Papa's study. It was a simple life of religious devotion and family pleasure. What of your childhood, Gaby—before Napoleon, I mean? I'm sorry if I brought back sad memories. You do not have to answer," he quickly added.

"No, it is all right." Having no happy moments from her own childhood, she borrowed from Jenette, who often spoke of growing up in the French countryside. "My parents sound much like yours, although my father did inherit the family title. Oh, to be sure, we were not religious, but we were loving and happy, my brothers and my sister and I. They are all gone now. . . ."

He rubbed her arm and pressed a kiss on her temple. "Gaby, I am so sorry if I have made you sad."

"No, you have not made me sad. There are many good things locked in my heart that I shall treasure forever."

He smiled in the dark. "Those were my mother's words after my father died of a fever. Then we lost his brother and my cousins to cholera three years ago. . . . Edward and Kenneth spent summers with us when we were boys. . . ."

"You, too, have lost much, Rob. Your mother, does she still live?"

"Yes, with my eldest sister and her family. I will visit them as soon as Parliament is out of session."

"Would your mother approve of this lady you will marry?" The moment she asked, she wished to take back the most inappropriate question.

Rob considered his reply. "I honestly do not know. She understands that inheriting the title has changed my life, and not all for the better," he added darkly.

"I had no right to ask such a thing. Please forgive me."

He chuckled softly. "Ah, Gaby, there is nothing to forgive. My lot in life is scarce a burden. When I think of my cousins dying so young . . . and the starving children on the streets of London . . ." He sighed.

"You try to make it better for them, do you not? I have heard Lady Fantasia say that you rescue children and take them to your country estate."

"Your mentor has rescued more than her share of people in need, men, women, and children. I am grateful that she found you, my little Gaby."

"Mrs. Winston taught Lady Fantasia to help others, and I was saved."

"Lady Fantasia is a most remarkable woman."

"Why do you say that, my heart?" What would he say about her? No, he did not know *her*. He only knew about a mysterious woman who operated a house of fantasy. Not Amber. Never Amber.

"The Lady Fantasia is brilliantly educated, possesses a

razor-keen wit, and . . ." He started to say she was beautiful, not the wisest thing when lying in bed with a woman to whom he had just made love.

"And?" she prompted, unable to resist.

"She is kind." An inadequate reply, but the only one he could think to use.

Kind! Such a bland word. What did it mean? He probably had as little idea as did she. Gabrielle would never know what he truly felt for her. If he was unwilling to speak of his feelings for Fantasia, what could he say about his "tutor"? He could not stay with either of them, even if he had wished it, for they did not really exist . . . and he was duty-bound to wed a proper lady.

She felt the tears thicken her throat and forced them back. Rolling up, she pressed her palms against his chest and began kissing him. "We have done enough talking with words. Now it is time for our bodies to speak once more."

Alan Cresswel slumped in the corner of the Hare and Hound waiting for Hull. It had been two weeks since the fool had initiated the disaster at King Street. Two of the ruffians who escaped after their leader was killed had beaten Hull and, if not for the timely intervention of a charley, would have killed him. Cresswel felt it served the chawbacon right. Only someone with apartments to let would have hired a pack of petty thieves from Seven Dials to kidnap a well-guarded woman.

He peered through the smoky gloom toward the front door, cursing beneath his breath when a sharp pain in his side reminded him of the long ugly gash from the bitch's pistol. Now he had an account to settle with her himself. Where the hell was that clodpole?

At length, Hull sauntered into the pub, leering at the barmaids, who all gave him a wide berth. He spied Cresswel and headed in his direction, barking out an order for a pint of ale as he approached.

"Ye're late, gov'. I got me better things to do 'n wait on ya," the runner said, still rubbing his aching side. "Now, where's the blunt? Spend it all in Seven Dials?"

Hull could see the smirk through the haze. He straightened up and pounded the table just as the barmaid set his pint down. "I waited for you while you lay abed with a bullet in your side. Shot by a woman," he added spitefully.

"Shut yer trap!" Cresswel snarled. "You got that purse 'er not?"

Hull tossed a small pouch across the table. "Because you botched the job, I was forced to hire others."

Counting the coins, Cresswel looked up and flashed a nasty grin. "They didn' do so good, did they, now? Heard you was rescued by a charley from Harbie 'n Fish. Mean enough boys, just not smart." He leaned over the table. "Now, 'ere's wot I got planned . . . soon's me side 'eals up. . . ."

Hull chuckled malevolently. "You want to run the bitch to ground because she shot you. Once you do it, just don't get any ideas about damaging the merchandise. Leave that for the marquess."

Chapter Twelve

*A*re you certain you do not wish to turn back? We do not have to go through with this," Sir Burleigh said to Amber as they stood in the doorway to the Chitchesters' ballroom, waiting to be announced. He glanced back to the cochere where three guards in her employ watched warily as their carriage started to pull away. The former soldiers would wait just outside in the unlikely event of trouble. "I cannot believe I allowed Gracie to convince me to follow through with my foolish whim. 'Tis too dangerous."

Amber smiled at the kindly older man. A bit above middle height, the baronet was as strong as an oak. He had a sun-darkened face marked by time and the elements, but nothing could dim the brightness of his keen blue eyes, framed by bushy white eyebrows. His thatch of unruly white hair was unfashionably long, clubbed back in a queue. Seeing the worried frown creasing his brow above his mask, she patted his arm in reassurance. "'Tis not a foolish whim, but a marvelous idea. We are well protected. I shall enjoy a taste of the season I never had and we both will laugh behind their backs," she whispered.

An impressive-looking footman pounded his staff on the polished marble floor and intoned, "Sir Burleigh Chipperfield of Hertfordshire and the Honorable Miss Livingston."

"Miss Livingston of nowhere," Amber whispered as they climbed the stairs into the glittering press of people to take their place in the duke and duchess's receiving line. She had made up the name based on her detestable childhood nurse-maid, Henrietta Livingston, long gone to what Amber hoped was a suitable reward in the next life. Peering through her feathered and jeweled mask, she could see the puzzled looks on the revelers' faces. A buzz of whispers filled the air. What was that odd country baronet doing at such a prestigious ball—squiring a mysterious woman young enough to be his daughter?

"The chap in the silver satin whose face is turning from red to puce is my cousin Elberd, soon to join the Chitchester clan," Burleigh said to her.

"Only if no one learns of our little joke at their expense. Not even to find a husband for that harridan granddaughter would the duke and duchess endure such an affront," she murmured with a chuckle.

"Do look at the woman. Medusa, indeed," he murmured, nodding a greeting at his angry cousin.

"I understand she has a disposition to match her looks," Amber said.

Burleigh could see the surprise and chagrin on Elberd's face. Arrogant fool never believed his cousin would have the gall to accept the invitation, mixing with the diamond squad. Barely able to make himself heard over the music and babble of voices surrounding them, he muttered in her ear, "Heavens have mercy, staring overlong at that woman might just turn a man to stone."

The Chitchesters' eldest granddaughter wore her kinky tan hair twisted into long locks. "When she frowns and turns to scold your poor cousin, her hair swings about her shoulders as if it were indeed live snakes," Amber said.

Chitchester shuddered when "Medusa" stamped her foot in pique, causing his cousin to jump backward. "He is a prig and a mushroom, but still I pity the man," he said as they moved forward in the line.

Eventually they were presented to their host and hostess, who had so many guests that they merely nodded perfunctorily while Burleigh and his lady made their bow and curtsy, then moved on as the next in a seemingly endless line stepped forward. Once away from their hosts, Amber looked around the room, which was quite impressive. A dozen huge chandeliers dripping with crystal glowed brilliantly with the light cast by hundreds of candles.

At the far end of the vast space, two dozen musicians plied their art on a white satin dais decorated with pink bows. All around the pink marble floor, six-foot-high urns overflowed with flowers in a profusion of colors. Servants carrying heavy trays laden with delicacies, wines, and stronger spirits wended their way through the press of chattering guests.

"I vow I have not seen so much satin and jewelry since Prinny wed Caroline of Brunswick," Burleigh said. "The glitter fair blinds me."

"You attended the royal wedding?" Amber asked.

The old man grimaced. "Much against my will. My mother was still alive then and forced me to escort her to London for it. How she obtained the invitation, I have no idea."

Amber laughed, imagining how he must have detested the ordeal. "Everyone is grandly tricked out," she said as a lady wearing more plumage than a tropical parrot trailed past them.

"Bedizened, I believe is the word Gracie would use."

She agreed that most of the guests were dressed in frightfully bad taste. Men with embroidered satin waistcoats stretching painfully over their large paunches bowed to women whose turbaned heads would have put an Ottoman pasha to the blush. Ruffles, bows, pleats, and plumage accented by endless yards of lace had replaced the simple, elegance of ladies gowns from the preceding decade. Fashionable or not, Amber detested the latest fashion. Smoothing her gloved hand over her unadorned skirt, she inventoried the guests sporting jewels of every hue—dazzling blood rubies, ocean-blue sapphires, forest-green emeralds—and all around the room, the white brilliance of diamonds. Even the masks were encrusted with precious stones.

Amber's gaze swept across the sea of humanity to the area reserved for young ladies in the marriage mart. With wide eyes and sparkling cheeks, the girls were soaking up their first season under the watchful eyes of predatory mamas. She had been cheated of that opportunity. Would she have been so excited? Was she ever so naive?

Best not to dwell upon the past. As they made their way to the area where many couples were waltzing, she asked Burleigh, "Are you prepared to put Grace's lessons to the test?"

I fear I shall tromp your feet," he said dubiously now that the moment was at hand.

"I shall risk it. Will you favor me with this dance, sir?" Amber asked gaily.

"If I can draw breath enough to keep from choking. Lud, I've mucked out many a stable that smelled better than this," he muttered.

The warm evening and tight press of the crowd created a suffocating combination of perfumes, hair oils, and snuff, blended with the distinct odor of unwashed, perspiring flesh. "Not every gentleman has adopted Brummel's enthusiasm for daily bathing—or his fashion sense," she replied, wrinkling her nose and laughing. This was an adventure that allowed her to escape thinking about Rob, or Eastham. She was not certain which of them caused her the most distress, one who would leave her, one who had found her.

Burleigh took her very carefully in his arms when they reached the dancing area and they whirled around to the lilt of the music. If she had been one of those young women having their first season, would someone as handsome as Rob have asked her to dance? No, there was no man as handsome as the earl, and when she was seventeen he was a poor seminarian, already wed to a spoiled girl. She shook off the sad thought and gave herself over to enjoying the music.

"Grace would make a splendid caper merchant," she said to Burleigh. "She has taught you well."

"She was more exacting than a drill instructor in the army. I'm accounted to have fair skill at country dance, but this waltzing is quite another matter," he averred, counting his steps carefully in time with the music.

As his confidence grew, they laughed and enjoyed the waltz, unaware of the couple discussing them from across the room. "Everyone is wondering who she can be," Lady Oberly whispered to Rob from behind her fan. Then, glancing at her father to be certain he could not overhear, she added, "Lady Richardson said she might be a Cyprian! Can you credit that?"

Rob watched the old man and the striking young woman. She was small and slender, her heavy butter-yellow hair pinned up in a simple pile of curls that trailed over one shoulder. Unlike most of the ladies' busy attire, her gown was severely cut without any trim or ruffles. The soft spring-green silk fell from a high waistline to the floor. Her only adornments were the emeralds, a teardrop necklace, and earrings.

"She scarce looks like a Cyprian," he whispered back.

"And how would you know about such females?" she asked a bit waspishly, tapping his arm with her fan.

Rob smiled wryly, aware of the unintended irony. "I merely meant the way I would imagine such a creature might look," he assured her. In fact, there was something vaguely familiar about the way the woman moved so gracefully around the floor. Her partner was stiff and overly careful of his steps, but it was obvious that the lady had been born to dance. "Perhaps I shall ask her to favor me with a waltz and find out if the rumor is true," he said with a grin.

The baroness's breath caught. "Oh, you would not dare!" Her expression had turned from the gleam of gossip to genuine distress now.

"No, I was but making a jest. Please forgive me for oversetting you." He was finding that Verity Chivins possessed less sense of humor than a turnip.

After a few more desultory exchanges about the ladies' gowns, the heat, and speculation about whether Prinny would favor the Chitchesters with his presence, several of her father's Tory friends joined them. The baroness excused herself for a trip to the ladies' retiring room, obviously as bored with her father and his cronies as was Rob.

The usual arguments about taking harsher measures against the Luddites and keeping the lower classes in their place droned on. Rob made no comment, but instead found his attention drawn to the glow of pale green silk. The blonde stood across the floor, surrounded by several young gentlemen vying for a dance while her escort beamed approval. She accepted an invitation from one thin toff in a yellow satin jacket that clashed distressingly with his sallow complexion.

As they whirled around the floor, Rob again felt that frisson of recognition. Then he realized that she looked and dressed much the same as Fantasia. The hair was wrong, but . . . No, surely he was mistaken. Then she changed partners, laughing and bantering with her admirers. After observing her exchange bon mots with several more toffs, he knew he was not mistaken. The delicious joke almost made him laugh aloud. If only the proper ladies gossiping around the room knew how truly they had struck the mark!

His amused reverie was broken when the baroness returned. She took hold of his arm, smiling guilelessly up at him. If she was distressed to catch him watching the "Cyprian," she hid it well. "I fear Papa feels quite overcome by the heat. We must leave, Lord Barrington. It has been quite delightful dancing with you," she added demurely.

As was proper, he had escorted her out for one dance, not daring a second, which would have given notice that he was courting her. Two months ago he would have done it. Now he held back. "The pleasure was all mine, Lady Oberly," he said, giving her gloved hand a chaste salute. "I am sorry your father is not feeling quite the thing. A pity you must depart so early."

In fact, the earl was relieved. When she and her father were announced, he realized that he was obligated to socialize with them. His only reason for attending the ball had been to discuss a key political matter with several members of Lords. He never intended to stay after he spoke with them.

The baroness sighed. "I do so miss dancing . . ." she hinted broadly. When he merely smiled and made no comment, she nodded graciously, saying, "Perhaps another time?"

"I shall look forward to it," he replied evasively.

As Amber waltzed with Sir Toby, she caught sight of the earl kissing a lady's hand. Although her back was turned, Amber was certain the voluptuous little blonde in the turban was his baroness. Rob's simple black mask could not conceal his identity, not with that slightly overlong dark hair waving around his hawkishly handsome face. In his plain black jacket and breeches, he looked like a sleek panther set loose in a roomful of peacocks. The white cravat at his neck emphasized his swarthy complexion, and the very severity of his wardrobe showed his tall, slim body to excellent advantage. Even his waistcoat of dark green brocade was an understatement amid the multicolored florals and purple and puce satins favored by most of the ton's "tulips."

What was he doing at a frivolous event such as this? When she agreed to Grace's plan, it never occurred to her that Barrington might be here, or that his baroness would be stalking him. So much for an evening to take her mind away from him! Surely he would not recognize her. No, she quickly dismissed that possibility. Masked and wearing a wig, not even her own mother would have known her. She focused on what her dance partner was saying, trying not to look at Rob again.

Across the room, the baroness's father harrumphed loudly and said, "I feel light-headed, m'dear. We must be off. Barrington." The old viscount bowed bruskly in farewell to Rob, then turned away. His daughter was swept along as he stalked toward the entry.

Rob forced himself not to look toward the dancers, but instead watched Verity Chivins. Her gown of pale rose was the latest fashion, with ruffles at the hem and around the neckline. She wore a turban with several matching rose feathers on it. Her taste was perfectly suitable for the occasion, but he had noted that since her coming out of mourning, her wardrobe was fussier and less appealing.

Why am I now so critical of a woman I had every intention of marrying? He knew the answer.

As soon as she and her father were gone, he felt the pull of Fantasia and turned to the ballroom floor once more. She danced a far more sedate quadrille with yet another "pink" while her escort looked on. Was he a patron of her establishment? A relative, perhaps her father? No, Rob dismissed that idea. What male relation ranking high enough to receive an invitation to this event would countenance a daughter in her profession?

Whatever was going on, he felt irresistibly pulled to find out, even though he knew there would be consequences when the gossip reached the baroness. His step never faltered. Was he mad? When the music ended and she made her curtsy to her partner, Rob reached her side. Her back was to him, but she must have sensed his presence.

Amber turned abruptly and looked into green eyes that glowed merrily from behind his mask. How could he possibly have recognized her? Then another even more distressing question flashed into her mind—had he recognized Gaby?

With a calm she was far from feeling, she asked, "Have we met, sir?"

Rob bowed politely and placed her arm over his, leading her out as the music resumed, relieved that her escort made no objection. "The wig fooled me for a bit, but now that I've scented your rose fragrance, I know we have met, m'lady," he said as he took her in his arms and they began to waltz.

She glanced about the room. "Where is your baroness?"

He chuckled. "So you do admit we have met. As to that lady, she has gone home with her ailing father."

"You must know the gossip will reach her."

He shrugged. "Perhaps. I could always say I recognized my distant cousin from Kent. It would be rude not to ask you to dance, after you have just come out of mourning."

"But only one dance. We would not wish to give the appearance of impropriety, after all," she replied, charmed by his teasing.

"Do you think the duchess would force us to wed if we danced a second time?"

"No, she would simply have me tossed out, once she learned my identity."

"If Her Grace learned your identity, she would know more than I do."

Ignoring his barb, she said, "Your friends in Parliament will be scandalized."

"Those who attend soirees such as this are not counted among the Saints."

"My, you have fallen from grace, then, to no longer consider yourself one of them. Should I feel guilty?"

"Not at all. I never counted myself among them, but came here to discuss Mr. Peel's police proposals with Lord Treving and Sir Philip Ridgeway. That done, how could I resist the opportunity to learn more about you?"

"You know where we met, m'lord. That is sufficient," she replied. To deflect his probing questions about her past, she asked, "How did such a serious reformer learn to dance?" She sensed the stiffening of his body before he replied.

"It was to please my first wife, who is now deceased." His voice was flat.

Only Gaby knew of Credelia. Amber said, "I am sorry, m'lord. Please accept my apology for bringing up such a sad matter."

"It was a long time ago," he replied thoughtfully, realizing that memories of his dead wife no longer had the power to wound him. Was it because he had cleansed his soul with Gaby? He held Fantasia in his arms, not Gaby, he reminded himself. But some connection between them niggled at the back of his mind. He tried to focus on the way she moved with him through the waltz, wishing he could close his eyes and savor the feeling of holding her. But that was something he could not do on the crowded floor.

I dare not stay in his arms a moment longer. Amber could sense that he was comparing her to Gabrielle. He had never held Fantasia this way. Her relief was palpable when the dance ended. "Let us speak of happy things such as what a splendid group of musicians the duchess has employed," she said as he escorted her to back to her elderly companion.

Ignoring her gambit, he asked, "Happier things such as why you are here, surrounded by drooling young pups?"

"As long as the drooling young pups can dance without giving me fleas, they are tolerable enough," she replied.

"You counter every move without giving away anything. I should think you would be a formidable chess player, m'lady."

"I am. Would you like a match, Barrington?" some insane urge made her ask.

"Yes, I would enjoy that a great deal."

"Shall we say tomorrow . . . at one?"

He had a political meeting in the morning, but it would end by midday. "I will see you at one, then."

She attempted to take her leave, but he insisted on

returning her to Burleigh. There was no help for it. She would have to introduce them and hope for the best. The baronet bowed politely to the earl after being presented, one white eyebrow raised subtly.

Knowing from Grace exactly who Barrington was and how Amber came to meet him, Chipperfield remarked, "You have previously met . . ." He leaned forward and added in a very low voice, "At the House of Dreams." His eyes twinkled.

Rob did not know whether to be appalled or to laugh out loud. He chose the latter. "Are you a patron living out a fantasy here, perchance?" he countered.

"What better one could there be for a crusty old fellow like me? I am the envy of every man in the house. I have brought the most beautiful lady in London to the ball."

"Spanish coin, Burleigh," Amber protested. "Consider all the young ladies in the bloom of their first season."

"He does not give you false flattery. None compare to you," Rob said. "You are the most beautiful lady in London—in spite of a wig concealing your magnificent hair." The moment the words escaped his mouth, Rob knew he had revealed too much . . . and betrayed Gaby, whose face he would never see.

As Lady Fantasia, Amber had schooled herself never to blush, but she could not control the heat tingling on her face. "Now we move from Spanish coin to court holy water," she said with a low chuckle. But her gaze locked with his and she saw the blaze of desire in his eyes. They played with fire . . . and both of them would be burned before this was finished.

Burleigh watched their exchange with a troubled expression. He would have to discuss this with Grace. Unless his eyes were deceiving him, the two young people were falling in love. And neither was free to love the other.

Rob finally broke away from her and turned to the older man. "A pleasure to meet you, sir. Enjoy the evening and your fantasy. You could not have chosen a more worthy lady to share it." To Fantasia, he said, "Until tomorrow at one?"

When she nodded silently, he kissed her hand and walked away.

Burleigh watched her stare after the earl. *Perhaps my little joke on the ton has proven more costly than either of us imagined, child.*

Chapter Thirteen

Rob spent a restless night filled with strange dreams that awakened him repeatedly. At one moment he would feel Fantasia in his arms as they glided in a waltz, the lights blazing all around them. Next, he would be loving Gaby in the darkness. Next he would light a candle and find Fantasia's cherry-red hair spread across the pillows . . . as if they were the same woman. The images twisted and merged over and over until he finally tossed aside the covers and got out of bed. He paced across his large bedroom, naked in the moonlight that poured through the open draperies.

He had never slept without a nightshirt in his life until he made love to Gaby. Now he could not sleep with one. He pulled on a light robe and stood staring out at the small courtyard fountain in the rear of his city house. Combing his fingers through his hair, he cursed, trying to sort out the dreams. What the hell did they mean—if anything?

His French lover was nothing like the cool, calculating madam. Whatever her mysterious past, Fantasia was English to her fingertips, keen witted, practical, even lethal when the need arose. If she knew a word of French, she had most probably picked it up from that French courtesan he had encountered in "Sherwood Forest."

Gaby's French was far too natural for even the most exclusively educated English finishing school miss to emulate. Her gentle spirit had been grievously wounded, yet her inherent sweetness and honesty shone through. That could be no act. Fantasia parried every question he asked with another of her own. She traded barbs with him rather than exchanging confidences. On the other hand, Gaby invited open conversation, speaking of her tragic past and drawing out his own unhappy experiences. She healed. Fantasia, he was certain, could wound. She would fight like a wild creature and give no quarter if cornered.

Then why did he suddenly feel as if they were the same woman? How absurd to flatter himself by thinking a woman who had built such a lucrative business would choose to bed him when she had dozens of employees to perform the task. No, Fantasia had selected Gabrielle because he and the émigré had both been scarred by their first sexual experiences. He, not Fantasia, had proposed that the lessons be in darkness. She had only agreed that Gabrielle would probably be more comfortable that way, too.

He knew the scent of each woman intimately, Gaby's soft lilac, Fantasia's much bolder attar of rose. Even more primal, he knew the female essence that defined each, something intangible but most certainly distinct. It made no sense for Fantasia to perform such an elaborate charade. What possible motive could she have?

"None," he muttered. "'Twas nothing more than the nightmare, making you muzzy-headed."

Below the open window, the fountain tinkled musically, as if laughing at him.

Amber knocked on Grace's door discreetly, knowing that Burleigh had spent the night. But he never dallied once the sun rose. Grace had requested that she come here at ten. Her mentor called out for her to enter. After her night with Burleigh, Grace had a satiated glow about her, but Amber could see that she felt troubled in spite of it.

"Please have a seat. I had Bonnie send up a tray for us," Grace said, gesturing to the comfortable rose damask chair across from hers. Between them on the low table sat two pots, one of tea, one of coffee, and a basket filled with the cook's delectable croissants.

"Have you summoned me to account for how I cavorted with Burleigh last night?" she asked, smiling as she sat down and poured herself a cup of steaming coffee.

"The dear man told me everything," Grace said, her expression devoid of all humor as she sipped her tea. "You waltzed with Barrington."

"The earl recognized me and whisked me onto the floor before I could protest. There was no harm in it," she replied.

"You know otherwise. I can see it in your eyes. Burleigh, bless him, is a very shrewd judge of people, one reason he has sat on the assizes for so many years. He is certain that you and the earl are in love."

Amber almost dropped the cup. Instead, she set it in its saucer with an unseemly clatter. "That is absurd. If he's in love with anyone, it's Gaby, not I."

"The earl could tell from across the crowded ballroom that you were the woman he knows as Fantasia. He came directly, as you put it, to whisk you onto the floor because he could see through your very good disguise. Burleigh observed the way the two of you laughed and talked and danced . . . how you exchanged glances when you parted. You are in love with him. He with you."

"We already discussed this when you convinced me to invite him riding. I admit that I am guilty about deceiving him as Gabrielle . . . and, yes, I have come to greatly enjoy *making* love with him. But I have no illusions about a permanent relationship. Nor does he, either with Gabrielle or Fantasia."

"But you are in love with him." It was not a question.

Amber sighed. "Yes, I suppose I am," she finally admitted aloud. "There is nothing to be done about it. You of all people understand that."

"Will he marry his baroness?" Burleigh had also observed a bit of interplay between Barrington and a woman wearing "a turban larger than herself," as he described the widow.

"I am no longer certain. Ironic that he should have come to Gabrielle to learn how to please the woman he intended to court. Now it seems he finds her less than a paragon. But that does not mean he is in love with Gaby."

"He has confessed this dislike to 'Gaby,' has he not?"

"He merely told her—me—that they have little to discuss besides fashions and ton gossip. She has no interest in his work."

Grace brightened. "Yet he delights in verbal fencing with you, and you're certainly in agreement about political reforms."

"With the exception of bordello closures," Amber replied wryly, rubbing her temples as a headache came on.

"Can you not see it? His Gaby is the perfect lover and confidante in bed. You are the perfect politician's wife, an informed, witty English noblewoman. Such a combination is every intelligent man's dream."

"Are you not leaving out one or two small problems—such as the fact that I am already married and the proprietor of a notorious house of courtesans? Not to mention that if he ever learns how I have deceived him, his male vanity will make him hate me." *No, not his vanity, but the violation of his very soul!*

Grace leaned back in her chair. "I doubt he could ever hate you once he understands the reasons you became Fantasia and Gaby."

"But I am Amber Leighigh Wolverton. Not Fantasia! Not Gaby!" The headache throbbed wickedly now, in full bloom. "We can never marry."

"Not as long as Eastham is alive. . . ."

Amber's head jerked up. "What are you suggesting—that we murder him to free me?"

"He has attempted to kill you twice in the past fortnight. Now that his spies have found you here in London—"

"We do not believe there is any choice," Jenette said as she stepped into the room silently and closed the door. She was still dressed in dusty travel clothing and appeared to have been in her coach through the night. "As soon as I returned, I spoke with Grace. We have decided what should be the plan." She walked over to the table and took a croissant, biting into it with gusto.

"I suppose I was not to be consulted about this 'plan'?" Amber asked.

"Do not be the foolish one, *ma coeur*. Of course, that is why you are here, *oui*?" She daintily wiped a crumb from the corner of her mouth with a napkin, then pulled up a small Louis XV chair and sat down.

Grace rang for her maid, requesting a fresh pot of coffee and a third cup as Jenette, like Amber, favored the vile stuff. They were likely to be locked in debate for some time. Burleigh had been wise to take his leave. Of course, he did not know about Jenette's plans, nor did Grace intend to tell him. He would only insist on being part of it, and that would never do.

The three women sat facing one another. "As the eldest, I imagine it is my place to moderate this discussion. First, Jenette, please tell Amber what you have learned in Northumberland."

"Eastham has had you declared dead. There is a body beneath a headstone with your name on it in the family cemetery." Jenette could see a shiver run down Amber's back as the implication sank in.

"Some poor girl from the countryside was killed because she bore a passing resemblance to me," Amber said, clutching her cup so tightly she almost snapped the delicate handle. "I see Mrs. Greevy's hand in that. She is as evil as the vile beast she adores and she has charge of all the household help. She probably selected the victim herself."

"Most likely. No one would speak of it, but all in the village fear her. With you dead, the *batard* no longer had to explain your absence. If anyone suspects you ran away, no one speaks a word. I and my servants made friends with the villagers. From them we learned much in the past weeks. Your grieving widower, *le cochon*, wed another young girl the year after you 'died.' She, too, died when his heir was born."

Amber shuddered, remembering how Eastham had tried to get an heir on her. "I am so grateful that I was not that poor girl, may God forgive me."

"Only thank *le bon Dieu* you were not she. There are the rumors as well that she did not die in childbirth."

"Why would Eastham kill her? He should have wanted a spare to his heir, would he not?" Grace asked.

"He would not bother if she did nothing to anger him," Amber replied. "But Mrs. Greevy . . ." She looked over to Jenette.

"*Oui*. Such is the gossip. The housekeeper buys poisons from the village apothecary . . . for rats, she tells him. He does not believe her."

"She was once Eastham's lover, long ago. I believe she would kill any woman who stood between her and the marquess."

"So," Jenette said, wiping her hands on a napkin and crossing her arms over her chest. "We have two vipers to . . . how do you say, *exterminer*—exterminate." She sounded out the verb carefully.

"Ten years ago Grace sent good men just to investigate. Some died," Amber said to Jenette.

"But they were mere men. And now Eastham has an heir—a son who would be declared a *batard*."

"If word got out that you were still alive, the unfortunate

child would be illegitimate and unable to inherit the title," Grace said to Amber. "That is why, now that he has found you, he will not rest until one of you is dead. I would prefer that it be him."

"*Oui*, he will stop at nothing to protect the boy's legitimacy. We must strike first."

"What do you propose, to raise an army?" Amber asked. "There is no way into Wolf's Gate."

Jenette smiled but her eyes were cold. "I have myself been inside, and needed no army. Eastham wishes a second son . . . now that he meets me. I will find the best time . . . to deal with him."

Amber jumped from her chair. "No! It is far too dangerous! Mrs. Greevy must already be mixing her poisons. If Eastham does not kill you, she will."

Jenette shrugged. "I am careful to eat only what she serves her lord. Now I make him wait while his greed and desire grow. I am all alone in this world, with much wealth and a fine title. Even I tell him I have a son who is with tutors. When I return, he eats, how do you say it? Out of my hand?"

"Jeni, no! I will not permit it. You cannot just—just murder him," Amber said, appalled and frightened for her audacious friend.

A shadow fell over Jenette's face. "*Ma amie, alors*, I have killed many times before."

"In self-defense or to save a life, not this way," Amber protested, grasping Jenette's hand.

"This *is* to save a life—yours," Grace said.

"But he has a child now." The moment she mouthed the words, she realized that they rang false.

Jenette gave voice to Amber's thoughts. "He would make the poor *enfant* into a monster like himself."

"Eastham's young brother and his wife have been given charge of the boy until he is out of leading strings," Grace interjected.

"Lord Oswald attended our marriage. He and his wife were kind to me," Amber admitted.

"He would become the child's guardian. And be a much better father, *oui?*" Jenette asked rhetorically.

"The matter is settled, then," Grace said. "Jenette will take Villiars and as many other of our servants with military background as she requires. They will pose as her retinue. Once she takes up residence at a small country estate that I am negotiating to rent, Eastham will leave that hellish fortress of his and pay her court. Then"—Grace gave a shrug that was almost as fatalistically Gallic as Jenette's best—"we shall let matters take their natural course."

"I cannot permit it. 'Tis like walking into the jaws of hell itself! I of all people should know." She shivered, biting her lip until it bled. "No, you *will* not do this."

"Ah, *cherie*, how are you to stop us? Warn Eastham? *Non*, I think you will remain here in London and, as Grace has said, let matters take their natural course. . . ."

She and Grace exchanged a quick glance. Anticipating Amber's reaction, they had already arranged with Clyde Dyer and Boxer to watch so that Amber could not foil their plans.

Rob had just returned from a gathering at Brooks with several members of Commons to discuss legislation that would create a citywide police force. When his footman answered a knock at the front door, the earl immediately recognized his mother's voice as she greeted his elderly butler, Settles. "What the devil is she doing here?" he murmured aloud.

Abigail St. John was the dearest, most gregarious, and quite alarmingly keen-witted woman he had ever met. If she knew nothing about the House of Dreams yet, he would have to tread most carefully to keep her from finding out. He shuddered at the prospect, then quickly jotted a note to Fantasia, offering his apology for having to postpone their afternoon chess match. As he rang for his valet to send it out, he realized that he should also cancel his assignation with Gaby tonight. No, perhaps he could make it after his mother retired. She always kept country hours. If he stayed out after his political meeting this evening, she would be none the wiser. Donning his jacket, he headed downstairs to meet her.

He observed her from the landing, trying to detect her mood. She certainly sounded cheerful. He sagged in relief. She did not know. "Mother, what a delightful surprise! Why did you not tell me that you were paying a visit? I would have sent one of my carriages. Is everyone well at home?" he asked.

Abigail turned as Rob walked across the foyer with open arms. She met him halfway, stretching on tiptoes to hug her tall son. "Your sisters and their families are all well," she said, patting his arm affectionately.

"How did you travel?" he inquired, already suspecting the answer.

"Why, by public coach, what else?" she replied. "Just because you have become the earl does not mean that the rest of us will change our ways. We're simple country folk, Robert. Public conveyance is quite satisfactory. I met the sweetest young couple, recently married. They were traveling to London for him to assume a position as a clerk."

Slight of stature with simple tastes and plain features, she nonetheless attracted people like bees to a honey tree. Her warm blue eyes and broad, ready smile had always cheered the dourest of her husband's parishioners and offered comfort to any in affliction. She wore her gray hair in a simple coronet of braids and favored practical dark colors that did not show soil when she cooked or worked in her garden. Her only adornments were the small gold cross on a thin chain about her neck and her narrow wedding band. There was a shrewdness in her eyes that belied her merry nature. She possessed the ability to see through deceit and to detect goodness. Many people made the mistake of thinking her flighty because of her talkative nature and propensity for striking up conversations with strangers of all stations.

"I hope I am not imposing, Robert, but I read in the *Chronicle* that this session of Parliament will end shortly and I wanted to spend a bit of time observing the season before you returned to Kent."

Rob blinked. "You are most welcome here anytime, Mother, but why on earth would you care about the season?" he asked as a footman took her one modest trunk to the guest room at the head of the stairs.

She clucked patiently. "For my granddaughter—your niece Esther—who will turn seventeen this winter."

"Bernice's eldest? She was but a child last I looked," he said, shaking his head. "I suppose I should have looked more frequently—or posted a sentry. If she is of an age, of course, I shall sponsor her come-out."

"Now that you are an earl, I imagine you have many duties . . . and also, I fear, many nieces."

"Six, last I counted," he said glumly as they walked into a small receiving room with comfortable furniture. He knew little about such social events and had never set foot in Almacks, although once he became Barrington, he had received a voucher. Would his lack of interest be held against Esther?

Abigail's laughter rang down the hallway. "At least you have the number of your nieces correct, even if you cannot remember their ages. Girls do grow up, Robert."

Rob rang for his butler and ordered a noon meal for them, then asked, "Would you like to rest a bit or freshen up before we eat?"

"I may be a grandmother, but I remain strong as a plow horse. We have much to discuss."

"I shall have to find out what is involved in introducing a

young lady to society," he said distractedly. He had no idea about where to begin.

"I am not certain 'tis wise for Esther to do this, Robert. That is why I have come a year early. If your poor uncle Reginald and his sons had not passed so tragically, the gel would never have had the thought in her mind. She would have married among the gentry in Kent just as her mother and aunts did. We are country people. I do not want her hurt, Robert."

"So you decided to see if the ton is as wicked and snobbish as everyone at home believes it to be."

She nodded. "Would it be too great an imposition for you to introduce me to some of the ladies of your acquaintance? Perhaps that Baroness Oberly you mentioned in a recent letter?"

Ah, so now we get to the heart of the matter. "Why do I believe that you are more concerned with my marrying than you are with Esther's having a season?" he asked wryly.

Abigail sighed. "I never could dissemble with you, could I, Robert? I confess that I want not only to protect Esther, but to protect you as well—whether you believe you require it or not," she added before he could protest.

Rob raised his hands in resignation. "I suppose your arrival may be more timely than you thought. I would value your opinion of the baroness."

"Second thoughts, Robert?" she asked shrewdly.

"When first we met, she appeared quite the perfect woman to become my countess, a sweet, charming young widow with an infant son. . . ."

"What has happened to change your opinion?"

Gaby? . . . Fantasia? . . . Lord help him if he mentioned them! But how could he explain anything when he was so confused? He paced across the oriental rug and stared out the bow window at the busy street outside. Gathering his thoughts, he replied, "I have found that she has little interest in my work—or any of the reforms to which I am committed. Oh, she and her father attend my speeches in Lords now and then, but he is quite the Tory and sees any attempt to better the lot of the poor as radical and destructive of the social order."

"I take it she has not expressed such harsh sentiments, else you would never have considered her," she said.

"No, she has expressed no sentiments whatever regarding politics. She has a very limited understanding of the desperate conditions under which so many of our people live, even though she does have a kind manner with those in her employ."

"She only attends the debates in Lords to gain your favor. Hmm," Abigail said, stroking her pointed little chin.

"Perhaps I flatter myself overmuch to think that. I do not know."

Abigail shook her head in frustration. "Robert, Robert, you have never had any idea of your worth—and I do not just mean your title, a burden only recently come to rest on your shoulders. You are good, kind, noble of spirit . . . and unconscionably handsome!" she added with a smirk.

Rob was shocked and it registered on his face. "Mother! If I acted upon such an inflated sense of worth, I would be vain as those toffs who spend half the day on their toilets before venturing out to promenade. Recall how Father cautioned about vanity?"

"I have little fear you will ever succumb to vanity," she said dryly. "But you have turned women's heads since you were a lad. Why do you think poor Credelia begged her father to allow her to marry below her station?"

Rob winced. No one in the family had the least idea how disastrous their marriage had been. As far as his mother knew, Credelia had died in a tragic accident that robbed him not only of his wife but his child as well.

"Oh, dear heavens, please forgive my bringing up such

painful memories, Robert. I realize that your unhappiness with her kept you from considering a second marriage until inheriting the title forced you to do so." She placed her hand on his arm gently, noting his expression of surprise, then apprehension.

"Did you think me incapable of linking your spoiled young wife's behavior and your going off to war? You had no money to purchase a commission. I did not have to ask your uncle to know he had given it to you. And I am certain only the most extreme circumstances compelled you to do so."

"I had hoped to spare you," he said simply.

She hugged her son, then looked up into his troubled eyes. "Robert, you are too noble for your own good. So much has happened . . . since Credelia died. I wanted you to come to me and talk about your losses, but you were off in Spain, then preoccupied by your duties as Barrington. There never was time. Now we shall make some. First, you must arrange for me to meet this baroness and take her measure."

Rob chuckled ruefully. "If you had had charge of Wellington's armies, the war would have been won in half the time."

Chapter Fourteen

$\mathcal{A}$s Abigail and Rob shared an early dinner, he described the gentlemen in Parliament he worked with—and those who worked against their causes. She was excited when he told her he would participate in a debate the following afternoon.

When she asked if she might attend, he replied, "These things can become, er, acrimonious. I do not think—"

"Balderdash, Robert. My ears shall not fall from my head if I hear a harsh word or two. I vow I've heard far worse from my second son-in-law when his new gelding dumped him on the ground Friday last. I am greatly interested in what members of Parliament think about the terrible unrest in the countryside."

"You mean the Luddites who go about smashing machinery? Many rail against them but few understand or care why the poor benighted devils do as they do."

Abigail's brow furrowed and her eyes flashed. "Then they are either blind or foolish or incredibly hard-hearted!"

"I shall allow you to observe the debate only if you promise not to pray aloud from the gallery for thunderbolts to strike down my opponents," he said with a smile, adding, "However, silent prayer would be welcome."

"I will do no such thing, aloud or under my breath," she replied primly, pleased that she would get to see her once shy son actually speak before the peers of the realm.

Although she would never admit it, his mother was exhausted by her long and arduous coach trip. After a few delicate yawns, she made her excuses and retired for the night, eager for tomorrow.

Rob had explained that he was going out for a political gathering at one of his clubs that evening, which was true. What he neglected to tell her was that after the brief meeting, he would go to the House of Dreams . . . and Gaby. With so much emotion roiling in his soul, he wanted only the blind solace of the flesh. He knew that was selfish of him, but he also knew that she enjoyed their nights together as much as he.

After leaving Brooks he ruminated in his coach as the driver headed for St. John's Wood. What would his mother think if she had any idea about his moral shortcomings? He should feel horribly guilty . . . but he did not. Gaby and Fantasia were good women. What he shared with each of them felt somehow . . . right. If that damned him as a lost soul, he was powerless to change his fate.

After he undressed in the assignation chamber to wait for Gaby, he doused the candle, plunging the room in darkness. "How can I bear to leave her . . . and never again to spar with Fantasia?" he murmured softly to himself.

What he truly wanted was a woman with Gaby's innocent sensuality and Fantasia's keen intellect, a woman who could share every facet of his life. Increasingly, he was certain that woman was not Baroness Oberly. How the devil was he going to have his mother meet her without giving the impression that this was a prelude to courtship?

The disturbing consideration was interrupted when a dim flash of light signaled Gaby's arrival. She quickly closed the door before he could catch a glimpse of her. He strode toward her in the darkness. Having memorized the furniture placement in the room, he knew it better than his own sleeping quarters in the city house. With a breathless greeting, he embraced her and felt the warm reassurance of her arms around her neck. Her head tipped back and her lips parted eagerly when he lowered his mouth to hers.

They kissed hungrily as his hands splayed over the delicate curve of her back, caressing every tiny bone. Her nails dug into his shoulders as their hips met in an undulation as old as time. Wordlessly, he scooped her up and stepped over to the bed. When he bent over to lay her across it, she pulled him down with her, whispering, "Please, come inside me, my Rob. I need you. Now!"

He was not alone in his need for the solace of blind passion. She had spent the day worrying about Jenette and Eastham—and how to stop her friend from undertaking such a deadly subterfuge. Hoping for a distraction, she had looked forward to the chess match that afternoon. Then when he sent his regrets, she worried that he might end both of his liaisons at the House of Dreams.

Now he was here, his naked flesh pressed to hers.

What more was there to ask for than this moment? Gabrielle gloried in it, guiding his hard staff into the wet heat of her body. She arched and gasped as he filled her, stretching her flesh, gliding in glorious friction. "Yes, Rob, yes," she whispered hoarsely, locking her legs around his hips.

They moved in a frenzy, the desperation each felt resounding in the other. He rolled onto his back and raised her upper body so that she could ride him the way they had accidentally discovered some time ago. His hands cupped her breasts, then glided down the curve of her tiny waist to cup her buttocks as they rose and fell while he thrust upward in counterpoint.

Her fingernails clawed at the hardness of his chest, then raked through the springy hair covering flexing muscles. She tossed her head back, arching against the impossible pleasure of each stroke. "Slower, please . . . I do not wish to end this . . ."

"Let me suckle you," he whispered, holding her hips immobile, then resuming a much slower pace.

She braced an arm on each side of his head and lowered

her upper body so her breasts hung over his face, suspended like fruits ripe for plucking. His mouth was hot and sweet as he took one nipple, then the other, feasting on the hard points until she whimpered in pleasure.

The sounds she made, tiny, indistinct mewls, sent the blood singing through his veins. He seized a fistful of her hair and guided her mouth to his for another soul-robbing kiss. Her tongue darted inside, bold and saucy for an instant, then coy and inviting as it retreated. He followed inside her mouth, twining his tongue with hers. Free of the restraint of his hands on her derriere, Gabrielle once again increased the pace, raising and lowering her hips, twisting and rolling as she felt the great onrush of culmination begin.

"Come with me, my love," she whispered raggedly into his mouth.

"How could I not?" Rob rolled them over and plunged deeply, feeling the contractions of her velvety sheath drawing him to spill his seed. He let go of all the control he had schooled himself to learn over the past weeks. Assured that she would be with him in surfeit, he felt free to surge to the stars. He kissed her hard, pressing his body the full length of hers as the world exploded around them.

Neither cared.

He rolled over and brought her with him so she nestled across his chest. They lay, limp and panting. A light sheen of perspiration slicked their skin in the cool night air. Gabrielle glided her hand over the muscles of his shoulder, loving the hard, smoothness of his body. He was a horseman who spent hours outdoors. He had spoken about riding across fertile fields and working with breeding stock on his estate. Would he return to it and his family when the session of Parliament ended? Would the baroness pursue him?

Those are not questions I have the right to ask.

If he wished to speak more about his conflicting emotions regarding Lady Oberly, he would bring the matter up. If he did not . . . To keep herself from such troubling thoughts, she began nibbling kisses in the crisp hair on his chest while she caressed his face with her hand. When her lips grazed a hard male nipple and she tugged at it with her teeth, he let out a soft growl of pleasure.

"You are an insatiable little minx, are you not, Gaby?" he asked in a husky voice.

"Does this please you?" She could tell that her ardor pleased him mightily by the hardening of his staff as it pressed against her thigh.

"I am here to please you, remember?"

"Well . . . it would please me if we could begin all over again . . . only this time slowly, softly, like—"

"Butterfly wings," he whispered with a chuckle, brushing a soft kiss against her ear. Then he used the tip of his tongue to trace the outline of the small shell, sending shivers down her spine. "Yes, we can do this for as long as you wish, my darling Gaby."

"You know all . . . there is to know . . . all any woman . . . could ever want . . . ever imagine," she gasped out between small hitches in her breathing as he laved her throat with his tongue and massaged her scalp with his fingertips. Then his hands roamed across her back, gently lifting the mass of her tangled hair away so that he could caress her dewy skin. He rolled them onto their sides and raised himself up over her to press kisses from her throat to her breasts, then down lower until he reached her navel. He devoted exquisite attention to it, making her writhe and arch.

"I must taste like the salt block in Cook's kitchen," she murmured.

"Did I ever tell you how much I enjoy salty delicacies?"

He continued soft caresses, using his hands and his mouth, moving over every inch of her body, leaving her a quivering mass of pure bliss. While her body basked, her mind whirled. If only this could go on forever. If only they could close out the whole world and just be . . . suspended in time and space. But no, they had tonight.

"Tonight, we have tonight. No one can take this from us," he murmured.

She had no idea that his thoughts so closely mirrored her own until he spoke. "Yes, tonight must be enough . . ." she whispered back, letting body overtake mind as she returned his kisses and caresses, marveling anew at the contrast between her soft body and his hard one, her smoothness and the abrasion of his body hair. Yet for all his strength, he cherished her body, fierce with passion, gentle with . . .

Love?

No, never love! He had said that they had tonight. Implicit in that was an eventual farewell. His duty was to leave. But not tonight. She wrapped her arms around him and held him fast, kissing him deeply. After a long while, they became one and rode again to the pinnacle together. Neither thought about the price of tomorrow.

Rob left his mother beaming as one of the attendants assisted her up to the gallery in the House of Lords. Then he spent several minutes glancing over his notes before slipping them into his jacket. Several of his foes took their seats across from his, glowering at him and muttering none too softly about "lovers of rabble" and "disruption of the social order ordained by the Almighty." He glanced nervously up to see if his mother had overheard them take the Lord's name in vain, and was grateful that she had not.

If only Lord Teesdale and his cronies minded their manners during the debate! If only sheep were not stupid! Engrossed in the opening arguments, he did not see a second lady come late and take the only remaining seat in the gallery, which happened to be next to Abigail. The second female was a widow, austerely garbed in black from head to toe, heavily veiled.

Amber had read about the proposals put forth by Mr. Peel to reform the policing system—or lack thereof—in London. The mishmash of competing jurisdictions and bribery led to a thriving industry of thievery. The "flash houses," as they were called, were not only refuges for cutthroats and street whores, but served as recruiting centers for children who learned to swill·gin, pick pockets, and sell their bodies just to keep from starving. She wanted to listen to Rob's proposals for stopping the abuse. But even more, she longed to see him move and hear his voice in the bright light of day.

When Rob was recognized, he rose and began to speak. "We need a unified force immune from bribery, overseen by the governing authorities. Trained professional men must close down the flash houses. They are schools, not where the young learn to read and write, but where boys learn to steal and girls to sell themselves. How long must this continue before we act?"

As he elaborated the abuses and remedies with exacting and dramatic detail, Abigail leaned over and whispered in the widow's ear, "I see you are as taken with the Earl of Barrington's presentation as am I."

Amber looked at the elderly woman in the gray gown. Although of good quality, the day dress was utterly unadorned save for a small gold cross that hung suspended on a fragile chain. Her bonnet also was without feathers or any of the fallals so in fashion now. But her face was lively and kind. *Grace, if she had been given the chance to be a country lady.* Smiling at the whimsical thought, she replied, "He is quite a marvelous speaker, awake on every suit. That vile Lord Teesdale has yet to tangle the earl with words, and not for want of trying."

"Do you follow the debates often?" Abigail asked, warming to the young widow, who appeared quite well informed regarding political matters.

"I subscribe to the *Chronicle* and the *Times*. Whenever I

read that the Earl of Barrington will speak, I try to attend. We share a concern for aiding the poor, especially children. I greatly admire his keen intellect and strong moral compass."

"Have you ever met him, seeing that you have so much in common?" Abigail inquired.

"No," Amber replied, almost too quickly. *We have far more in common than ever you could imagine.* Even in disguise, she would never link herself to him in this place. "That is, although I would be honored, he is an earl and I but a poor widow."

Abigail patted her hand sweetly as Rob once more began to speak, rebutting yet another Tory lord's diatribe about "the rabble."

As the afternoon wore on and the arguments on the floor became more heated, Abigail and Amber traded whispered commentaries on the fallacies of Tory social policy and the earl's piercing wit in tearing them apart. When the session finally concluded, the two women rose and started to make their way from the gallery. Amber was prepared to thank the lady for her lively discourse, but her companion spoke first.

"I have a confession I feel I must make, my dear." When Amber cocked her head, Abigail whispered, "That handsome young rascal with the razor wit is my son."

Amber almost tumbled over the gallery railing to the floor below. "You are his m-mother?" she asked.

Abigail smiled. "That is the usual way it works, I believe. And now," she said, taking the widow's arm, "I am going to introduce you."

Without appearing horribly rude and yanking her arm away, Amber could do nothing but allow the older woman to guide her downstairs. The Widow St. John was deceptively strong for such a birdlike little thing. "I really must go. Your son is surrounded by his political friends and I—"

"Nonsense. He will be delighted to meet you. I am certain

of it." With that Abigail began wending her way through the press of much taller gentlemen, holding the delightful young widow's arm firmly. If the baroness was as unsuitable as she suspected, this lady might be the perfect anecdote! How fortunate they had met.

Rob saw his mother's slight form appear. Members of Lords stepped aside, as if she were Moses parting the Red Sea. He smiled and walked over to greet her. That was when he saw the woman behind her. His mother had Fantasia's arm in the kind of grip she had often employed to subdue unruly schoolchildren—even boys a head taller than she. He stopped dead in his tracks, his mind completely numb.

A beaming Abigail St. John said, "You were brilliant, Robert!"

He nodded woodenly, replying, "I hope I acquitted myself well, Mother." Then he turned to Fantasia, who remained a prisoner of Abigail's grip. "M'lady," he said, bowing politely.

"Oh, my, have you already met?" his mother asked with a puzzled frown.

"Yes," Rob replied

"No," Amber said at the same time.

Now Abigail's frown evaporated as she swiveled her glance from the flush stealing up her son's face to the star-tled posture of the young lady. Whatever was afoot, it was obvious that the two were attracted to each other. Smiling once more, she said, "I was so eager to introduce the two of you that I neglected to learn your friend's name. Robert, please introduce us."

Rob swallowed, trying to dislodge the knot forming at the back of his throat. "Lady Smithton," he said.

At that precise instant Amber blurted out, "Amber Leighigh." Immediately horrified consternation struck her. What on earth had possessed her to give her maiden name? She had not uttered it in over a decade. Amber Leighigh Wolverton was dead and buried in Northumberland—and

needed to stay that way! Recovering her wits, she said, "I
had forgotten that we both attended one of the more fre-
quented political salons."

Rob nodded. "Ah . . . yes, Lady Aberley's."

At his hesitation, Amber again spoke too quickly, saying,
"The Berry sisters."

Then in unison they said, "Both!"

Now Abigail chuckled. "Well, there appears to be a bit of
confusion here," she said, arching one silvery eyebrow as she
studied the darkening red beneath her son's sun-darkened
face. She was positive that if she could have seen the widow's complexion, it would be flushed as well. An intriguing
mystery . . . one that she intended to solve. "It does not matter where you have met, but I would prefer to know your
name, my dear," she said kindly to the agitated young widow.

"I have used an assumed name at salons because I am
newly widowed—it would not be proper for me to meet gentlemen outside of my immediate family . . ." Amber's voice
trailed away in abject embarrassment, which she hoped would
satisfy the earl's shrewd mother.

"Smithton is a common name," Rob chimed in awkwardly.

Without giving either of them the chance for further pre-
varication, Abigail whispered to her son, "That dreadful
Lord Teesdale is bearing down on you. You shall have to
deal with him." She patted his arm. "I know how crowded
your schedule must be as the session draws to a close. Do
attend your duties, only refrain from breaking Teesdale's
nose as you did the Harper boy when you were a lad."

Rob stood rooted to the floor as the Tory headed directly
toward him with a sullen expression on his face. At the moment, the earl would have been relieved if Prime Minister
Liverpool and Home Secretary Sidmouth had him carted
off to Newgate—or better yet, he would be delighted to
break Teesdale's nose!

Without paying her son the slightest mind, Abigail turned

to the widow. "This is a beastly hot day. I have heard that a place called Gunter's in Berkeley Square sells the most delicious ices in all of London. My dear, would it be too great an imposition to ask you to accompany me there?"

Amber looked pleadingly to Rob, but Teesdale intruded, rudely ignoring her and Rob's mother, demanding a meeting with members of Commons to discuss compromise legislation. "I should be delighted," Amber managed to reply. "My carriage driver will be waiting in the courtyard."

"Splendid," Abigail replied, nodding farewell to her son. She could see that he was distressed but she quickly hurried her young companion off before he could break free of Teesdale. She was relieved when he let them go without further protest.

Once they were settled in the luxurious interior of the "poor widow's" carriage, Abigail turned to her and said, "In spite of being perceived as a country bumpkin, I am a fair judge of character, my dear . . . Amber, is it?"

Amber recognized the shrewd light in those blue eyes. *Little escapes this woman's attention.* "Yes," she said with a sigh. Perhaps a bit of the truth could be fashioned into a believable tale. "I have not used my true name for many years. My husband was brutal and I hold no fondness for his memory, nor would any of his family welcome me."

"Do you have children?" Abigail asked, concerned with the obvious pain in Amber's voice.

"No."

The terse reply spoke volumes. "No family of your own, either?"

At this, Amber smiled inwardly and her voice softened. "No, although I have an abundance of friends who have become more dear to me than my own blood."

Abigail knew there was far more to Amber's sad history but did not press. "It is a great blessing to have friends. I would like very much to be one."

"I would be honored, Mrs. St. John."

"Please, call me Abigail. I have spent my life in the country as a clergyman's wife. I never imagined becoming the mother of an earl, until my brother-in-law and his two sons passed away."

Although Amber knew how keenly Rob felt the losses in his family, she could not reveal any knowledge of the tragedies. "It must have been very difficult for you and the earl."

"I am a woman of faith, child. One day we shall all be reunited. For now, I look forward to seeing my son settled in life. He is a good man, struggling with a fate he never expected to have thrust upon him."

"He has done extraordinarily well in Parliament," Amber replied cautiously. Was Abigail matchmaking? What a tangle that would create—a parson's widow confronting the proprietor of the ton's most infamous house of courtesans! She had to divert the conversation in another direction, but before she could say anything more, her coach stopped under an oak tree across from Gunter's shop.

Boxer swung down from his seat next to the driver. He examined the busy street, paying particular attention to the carriages and closed coaches of other customers. In a moment an attentive waiter approached the coach.

"Would you and Peter enjoy an ice, Sergeant Major?" Amber asked.

"That would be most kind, m'lady," the crusty older man replied while his eyes continued to scan the busy street.

"Strawberry, correct?" she asked, knowing his preference.

"Very good, m'lady."

Abigail had been observing the older military man carefully. Most interesting. When Amber asked what flavor of ice she preferred, Abigail replied, "Whatever selection you deem suitable will be lovely." When the ices were brought to their coach, the women settled back to enjoy the treat. Abigail watched Amber raise the veil on her bonnet just enough to allow her to eat the confection. *She is afraid of something . . . or someone.* In time, she would gain Amber's confidence and learn what it was. "You are a very beautiful young woman, my dear."

"You are most kind," Amber replied, directing her attention to the ice. The faster she ate, the sooner she could hide her face. It was folly to raise the veil, even if her hair remained concealed.

"I could not help but notice that you addressed your footman as 'Sergeant Major.' He has a military air about him." Gentle prodding often worked.

"Mr. Boxer was a sergeant major during the war. I employ a number of veterans in my home. They have served their country nobly and been ill repaid by His Majesty's government."

The "poor widow" could afford to hire numerous servants and owned a handsome carriage. She was obviously a lady of substance. "Robert agrees with you. He, too, has many former soldiers in his employ." She paused to dab daintily at her mouth. "I did notice that Mr. Boxer appears more bodyguard than footman, or am I mistaken?" she asked innocently.

This woman was entirely too keen of wit . . . just like her son. Amber smiled. "I fear you are mistaken. Mr. Boxer is simply protective of me because I have shown him kindness, nothing more," she said firmly.

Realizing her question had made Amber uncomfortable, Abigail said, "Robert has introduced a bill to award pensions to our brave soldiers. Are you familiar with it?"

"Yes, although I fear Lord Liverpool's government has no intention of allowing the royal treasury to waste money on common soldiers. The earl's proposals have fallen on mostly deaf ears, no matter how eloquently he speaks, but that will not deter him."

"Indeed, Robert has obviously overcome the shyness that plagued him as a boy," Abigail replied.

"I find it difficult to imagine the earl in any way retiring." Amber remembered his acute discomfiture during their first meeting when she was Fantasia . . . and when she was Gabrielle. Distracted by those memories, she did not hear Abigail's reply. "Oh, I apologize, Abigail. I must have been woolgathering."

Abigail laughed merrily. "I said, Robert has grown quite bold and assertive. He carries the title well, and for that, I am grateful."

"Yes, he certainly does." Amber wondered if his nights with Gaby had anything to do with his increased self-confidence, but doubted it. After all, becoming a skilled lover had nothing to do with being a skilled debater in Lords. He had already become famous as a champion of the poor when they met . . . and a moral crusader intent on closing bordellos!

Abigail leaned forward a bit. "Have you by any chance met Baroness Oberly? I would value your opinion of her."

Chapter Fifteen

*A*mber almost choked on the last swallow of her ice. "I have seen the lady," she replied, "but I have never been introduced to her. Are you acquainted?" *Do you know Rob intends to court her?* She found herself hoping that Abigail had found fault with the baroness. Rob should not marry the vacuous and possibly avaricious female, but it was certainly not her place to say that.

"I have not met the lady, either, but . . . oh, dear, this is going to sound indelicate." Abigail scooped up the last bit of her ice and swallowed it, seeing that she had drawn Amber's interest. "Robert has considered—mind, only considered—paying the widow court. I fear that they do not suit. I was hoping that you knew a bit about her."

"I do know that her father stands against everything in which the earl believes. But I do not think she has any convictions regarding political matters." Amber felt it necessary to clarify that fact. When Abigail sighed in satisfaction, Amber wondered whether it was about the ice or her opinion.

"That is what he indicated to me, although he still wants me to meet her. And I must confess that I do require a lady to sponsor my granddaughter for next year's season. . . ."

Amber had a disturbing intuition that Rob's mother wanted *her* to volunteer for the assignment next year when her "mourning period" would be over. What could she say? She decided to deflect the conversation back to the baroness. "Are you concerned that it would appear the earl intended to go forward with his suit if you approached her?"

"Just so."

"I am certain the earl can find another lady—perhaps an older one," she hurriedly added. "There must be many who would be delighted to sponsor his niece. He is quite popular in the political salons. Perhaps Lady Aberley? Then you would not require any assistance from the baroness."

"Perhaps. I shall discuss it with Robert." Abigail knew when to press and when to defer. Although every instinct told her there was more to her son's relationship with the widow than either of them would admit, she would have to glean more information before she dared to meddle. She felt strongly that Amber was everything Robert required in a wife—intelligent, good-hearted, beautiful, and possessed of excellent breeding. Amber Leighigh was from the Quality. But why on earth had they pretended not to know each other?

Over the years as a parson's wife, she had found the best way to induce a reluctant parishioner into confessing what troubled him was to ask a simple question. "I know this may be too coming of me since we have just met, but how long have you been in mourning, my dear?"

Amber's mind raced. What could she say—ten years? She felt Abigail's shrewd blue eyes fixed on her and knew she had to fabricate another half-truth that would end any match-making hopes Rob's mother might hold. "I told you my marriage was not a happy one. Because of that, I have determined never to wed again."

"Never is a long time, my dear," Abigail said with a wistful smile.

"How long has it been since the earl's father passed?" Amber asked gently, although she already knew the answer.

"Eight years, but we were blessed to be together for over thirty."

"You are a charming, warmhearted lady who could have remarried, if you chose to do so," Amber said.

"When my husband passed, I knew I would never marry

again. But I was an old woman and you are young with your whole life before you. My reasons for being content as a widow are quite the opposite from yours. Robert's father and I shared a most blessed union and four wonderful children. We hoped our son and his first wife would have the same kind of marriage, but alas, he, like you, was not so fortunate. She died in sad circumstances and I fear for her soul."

Amber blinked. She should have known a mother as wise as Abigail would recognize the discord between Rob and the spoiled Credelia. "But now he must wed again because he is the last Barrington, willy-nilly."

Abigail cocked her head and smiled at Amber. "Do not make it sound so onerous. I admit that I was at first concerned because his devotion to duty might lead him to a second ill-considered match. That is the real reason I came to London. I intend to take this baroness's measure."

Amber read the determined sparkle in Abigail's eyes. *Best beware, Lady Oberly.* She could not resist a sly smile from behind the veil she had once more lowered. "I have every confidence that you shall determine if she is worthy of your son."

"Robert already has doubts, so I believe it will prove a simple task," Abigail replied serenely.

Her "simple task" would be to show Rob just how *unworthy* Lady Oberly was. "I wish you Godspeed."

Abigail took Amber's hand and squeezed it fondly. "Dear me, I have been quite thoughtless, taking so much of your time. Please forgive an old lady. You have been most kind to indulge me."

"Nonsense. It has been a great pleasure!" The moment she spoke, Amber realized that it was true. If only her own mother had been half so kind . . . But that was in the past, best forgotten. "I was fascinated by your comments during the debate this afternoon. You are a keen political observer and a Christian lady who practices the tenets of her faith."

"As are you, child." Abigail nodded resolutely. "I trust in

the Lord and pray for Robert and his friends in Parliament. But that does not mean that I shall be content to sit back and do nothing to help him."

Amber felt Abigail's penetrating gaze on her and knew her words held a double meaning. She would not be deterred in her matchmaking.

Giving the impression that matters between them had been settled—for the present—Abigail announced briskly, "Now, I shall have a servant summon a hackney coach for me and leave you to go about your business."

"I shall see you home in my coach—I insist," Amber replied. Before Abigail could object, her young friend signaled Boxer, saying, "Please take Mrs. St. John to the earl's city house."

On the drive, the women discussed various measures in Parliament, the Luddite unrest in the countryside, and the current government's suspension of habeas corpus. Before they knew it, the coach had pulled up in front of the earl's home. "I have greatly enjoyed our visit, Abigail," Amber said warmly as the older woman allowed the sergeant to help her down.

Abigail leaned toward Boxer and whispered loud enough for Amber to hear, "Since you did not ask for my direction, I assume your mistress already knew where my son resides." Then she winked at Amber before turning to walk up the steps.

Northumberland

Elvira Greevy seized the cleaver from the girl assisting the marquess's cook. "No, you stupid chit! This is the way you cut up a stew hen." She raised the sharp implement and brought it down in a deadly arc. The blade sank into the milky white skin with a sharp hiss, cleaving a thigh cleanly away from the lower back. The cowering girl watched mutely as the housekeeper quickly chopped the bird into pieces and tossed them into a pot bubbling on the kitchen hearth.

Seeing the horrified expression on the child's face, Elvira smiled malevolently, shoving the cleaver back into the serving wench's thin hands. "Watch you do not drop it and cut off your foot," she said, whirling away in a flurry of gray muslin.

Plying the blade had been a good way of easing her frustration. But not nearly as satisfying as if she could use it on that French bitch! The marquess was upstairs gloating over a missive he had just received from the whore. The comtesse was returning in a fortnight. Elvira's fury knew no bounds. After all these years of devoting her life to him, serving him selflessly, this was to be her reward—to give over her chatelaine's keys to some Froggy piece of fluff!

If that vain, strutting young aristo became Wolverton's new marchioness, Elvira would no longer be in charge of Wolf's Gate. Her mouth was filled with the sour taste of bile just thinking of it. As she stormed through the servants' quarters, everyone scurried to get out of her way. *We will see how long you last, you haughty outsider!* The housekeeper slammed the door to her quarters and walked over to the desk in the far corner of the spartan room whose only other furnishings were a narrow bed and a washstand.

She took a seat on the stool in front of the desk and then selected a tiny key from the heavy brass ring hanging at her waist. Opening a small compartment, she extracted half a dozen small vials and lined them up on the desktop. "Which one will give you the most subtle—and painful—death?" she mused to herself.

Over the past decade, Mrs. Greevy had become the most skilled practitioner of poisoning since Lucretia Borgia.

Downstairs the marquess sat back in his leather chair and sipped a fine port. He felt like celebrating in spite of the latest wretched report from Hull. He had just received a second far more cheering message from the Comtesse de St. Emilion.

When he married her, all the jewels and gold she had smuggled from France would be his. To sweeten the bargain the delicious Frenchwoman hinted broadly that she would soon share his bed. He was certain she would prove a lusty wench, able to give him more sons.

Of course, there was the matter of his damnable first wife. Amber. At first he had regretted that she was barren, but after a few months of her willful defiance, he wanted no offspring from her womb. Unnatural female. He frowned, considering Hull's series of disastrous attempts to kidnap her. Now the dissolute young pup possessed the temerity to send a request for yet more money. He smiled bitterly. What could he do? Hull had learned the woman's new identity and where she resided. Sooner or later he would succeed. Carrying the crystal glass with him, he walked over to the library table and wrote out another bank draft for Hull's expenses.

"One day I shall have the pleasure of watching her die a most unnatural death. . . . And in the meanwhile, I shall bed a woman worthy of bearing my heirs." He upended the crystal and finished the port, then threw the glass against the brick hearth. As the shards glittered in the firelight, he fancied they looked like the diamonds the comtesse wore about her lovely throat.

At his mother's insistence, Rob had accepted an invitation from Lord and Lady Montgomery to attend a gala. It was the sort of vapid, boring affair that ordinarily would not have held any appeal, but Baroness Oberly would be there and Abigail intended to meet her. He knew once his mother set her mind to a matter, there was no deterring her.

He was surprised to see that she had brought a lovely blue gown, doubtless borrowed from his sister Catherine, who was of a size with their mother. Abigail would never have considered spending money on silk and ruffles, nor did she own the sapphire pendant that hung around her neck. He knew Catherine's husband, a wealthy squire, had given it to his wife last Christmas.

"You will be the belle of the ball," he said to her as they stood in the receiving line.

"Nonsense. I am far too old to be the belle of anything. I feel . . . what is it they say . . . bedizened?"

"If you mean overdressed, only look about the room. Your gown is the most tasteful of any," he whispered.

"Why did fashions start changing from the soft, simple cuts of the last decade?"

"Perhaps English dislike for the Empress Josephine?" he suggested dryly.

"Or that poor Austrian child Napoleon divorced her to marry," Abigail replied. "I never did understand why sensible English people have always felt compelled to follow French fashion dictates."

"It was the French who introduced those simple gowns to which you are bidding a bitter adieu," he reminded her with a smile.

"Your debate skills do not require sharpening at my expense, you young rascal," Abigail said, tapping his arm with her fan.

Carrying a fan was another affectation his mother would never have used at home. She must be determined to see that his nieces all had suitable come-outs. He would have to discuss this with his sisters, he thought dolefully.

As they advanced in the line, he considered Fantasia's taste in clothes. No slave to fashion, she still wore elegant clothes that flattered her slim, lovely figure, without the distraction of ruffles and flounces. What did Gabrielle wear during daylight hours? he wondered. He had sent a note to her yesterday, canceling their "lesson" tonight. She, like Fantasia, knew that his mother was in the city and accepted that their time together had to be curtailed until Abigail returned to Kent.

Then what? Would he resume making love with Gaby and holding those disturbingly charged discussions with Fantasia? He no longer had any valid excuse for spending time with either woman. He should be courting a lady he could make his countess. As if on cue, the baroness and her father were announced. He watched his mother turn to study the young widow.

"She is very lovely, isn't she?" Her tone held a worried note.

"Yes, a delicate English rose," he replied. Verity wore a pale pink gown adorned with tiered white lace. At her throat she had a deep pink velvet ribbon with a cameo on it, her only jewelry. As the current styles went, her ensemble was charming, if a bit on the girlish side. Since coming out of mourning, she certainly did favor pink, he noted, remembering the décor in her home.

Could he live in her peppermint candy world? The thought held no appeal, especially when compared to the cool elegance of the cream and green that Fantasia had chosen for her home. *Her home is a bordello!* The reminder did not make the contrast any more favorable to the baroness. His thoughts were interrupted when they reached their host and hostess. After presenting his mother, he escorted her toward the floor to watch the dancing.

"Since this is a waltz, I assume you would prefer to wait for a reel?" he asked.

"You have learned to waltz?" she asked, amazed. Although naturally graceful, Robert had always been painfully stiff and uncomfortable putting feet to music.

"Please, Mother, I have been forced into acquiring a few social graces. Shall I teach you?" he dared with a gleam in his eye.

"Perhaps it would be better if you asked Baroness Oberly to dance," she replied.

Verity, with her father in tow, bore down on them from across the room. "How the devil did they get through the receiving line so quickly?" he muttered beneath his breath. Aloud, he said, "If I dance with the lady, that will leave you in the less than charming company of her father."

"I do believe I can handle one ravening Tory," she teased back.

Rob made the introductions and asked the baroness to dance, leaving the viscount to his mother's tender mercies. Lord help the man if he began spouting his ideas about the divinely ordained social order in England! She would have the old curmudgeon reduced to red-faced stuttering within moments.

After exchanging polite small talk with Verity during the waltz, he was happy when the piece ended. As soon as they rejoined their parents, Abigail took the young blonde's arm and leaned close to her, saying fondly, "I would love to have a little coze with you, my dear—that is, if your father and my son do not mind my whisking you away for a short while?" She inclined her head inquiringly.

Both gentlemen demurred, the viscount heartily, Rob with unvoiced reservations. What was his clever mother going to do? He watched warily as the two diminutive figures retreated into a small sitting area down the hall from the ballroom.

Once they had taken seats on a small sofa behind several large urns filled with flowers, Abigail said in a warm conversational tone, "Now, child, you must tell me all about how you and my son became acquainted. He speaks ever so highly of you."

Verity clapped her hands together in obvious delight. "The earl is a most remarkable gentleman. We first met at a small gathering my aunt Hortense held last winter. The dear lady shares his concern for the abolition of slavery—oh, but mark me, she is no bluestocking. In fact, she is complete to a shade, an absolute fashion arbiter." She fingered the lace on her skirt. "Of course, I had only entered half mourning for my dear Charles at that time, so I was forced to wear a deep shade of purple," she explained with a slight curl of her lip. "But in spite of that, the earl did not seem to mind how wan it made me appear. He is such a kind gentleman."

"I understand you have a child," Abigail said, not wanting to hear more about "offensive" colors.

"Elgin is the light of my life. Such an adorable little one. He will be two in the autumn. His nursemaids all dote upon him, and your son has fallen prey to his winsome ways as well. . . ."

As Verity rhapsodized on about how brilliant her son was, according to reports from those left in charge of his upbringing, Abigail noted that almost every incident the baroness related was secondhand. How often did she actually hold Elgin? Had she ever changed his soiled linens or sung him to sleep herself? Abigail doubted it. She suspected that the younger woman had used the child to gain Robert's attention. After all, his countess would have to give him an heir.

Having exhausted her repertoire on Elgin, Verity complimented Abigail on her lovely gown and remarked about the sapphire pendant's beauty.

"I must confess that both the dress and the jewel belong to my youngest daughter. Life in the country does not require the widow of a parson to wear such finery. I borrowed Catherine's clothing and some jewelry for the trip to London," Abigail said.

"That is a pity—oh, I did not mean to imply that your borrowing your daughter's things is in any way improper, but that you should not be allowed to have beautiful gowns and jewels of your own," Verity said. "After all, you are now the mother of an earl."

"You have exquisite taste, my dear, but such things are for the young and I am far from that," Abigail replied.

"I could never imagine a time when I will not want to be

all the crack—oh, that is, dressed in the very latest fashion," she explained at the older lady's a puzzled look.

"Life in the country is . . . different. Even Catherine wears plain cotton day gowns more often than any finery," Abigail said. "Do you spend any time at your late husband's seat?"

"Oh, my, no. It is far to the west, a dreary place near the Cornish border. My father's estate is closer, but in need of—" She stopped short. "What I mean is that Father dislikes the country, so we stay at our city house." Realizing that confessing a desire to use the earl's money to redecorate the viscount's manor would be ill advised, Verity cast about for a change of subject. Just then a snatch of conversation from passersby provided her with a new topic.

"I say, old chap, the proposed legislation to abolish the exploitation of climbing boys is long overdue," one gentleman insisted.

His companion responded with heat, "Climbing boys have been on the streets of London for generations. Why forbid them now? 'Tis against the natural order of things."

As they argued, oblivious of the women behind the palms, Verity said, "I could not agree more with the gentleman wearing that clever gold waistcoat. The natural order of things is that boys be allowed, indeed encouraged, to climb. Why would someone wish to pass a law against climbing?"

Abigail blinked. "I do not believe they were alluding to boys climbing, but to climbing boys, my dear," she corrected gently. *She cannot be so dim! Then again . . .*

"That was precisely what I was addressing, Mrs. St. John," Verity responded, dispelling any hope of misunderstanding that Abigail had held. "At Middleton Hall when we were children, my brothers climbed everywhere, into trees, on top of the stable roof, into the haylofts. Oh, they were ever so adventuresome!"

Give me patience, Lord. Abigail could see the baroness's

beautiful face beaming at her supposed cleverness. "I believe you did not hear the arguments clearly over the music from the ballroom. Those gentlemen were discussing legislation pending in Parliament regarding the little boys who sweep chimneys."

Verity realized she had been too eager to discuss a matter in which she had no interest. What went on in Parliament was best left to gentlemen, but if her future mother-in-law wished to discuss it, she must do so. "Yes, of course, you are correct. I misheard, but nevertheless, why would any member of Parliament wish to forbid the little sweeps from exercising their natural inclinations? All boys, even the poor, wish to climb and there are so few trees in London. Where would they climb if not up chimneys?"

Finding oneself at the bottom of a well, the wisest course, child, is to cease digging. "My dear, the climbing boys are very young, tiny children who—"

"But that only proves that they are most suited to do what comes naturally to them while they are yet small enough to fit." Pleased with herself, Verity failed to read the consternation in Abigail's eyes. "I understand that they are from the lowliest classes, but this must be a means of earning money to aid their families—and they can do so while engaging in natural play!"

Marie Antoinette possessed more sense! Having lived nearly three-score years, Abigail St. John was not surprised by much. But that Robert would ever consider this poor creature a candidate to become Countess of Barrington stunned her. As she steered the conversation back to fashions, something she knew the baroness would be far better equipped to discuss, she felt a small measure of relief. Her son had expressed doubts about Lady Oberly's suitability . . . and Amber Leighigh had come into his life. Perhaps the one had something to do with the other, she thought, smiling inwardly.

* * *

Rob had found it apparent on their carriage ride home last night that the baroness had not passed Abigail's inspection. Although his mother only spoke ill of anyone under extreme circumstances, she expressed a repugnance for the old viscount. She was also concerned about whether Verity would make a good wife for a man consumed with his work in Parliament since the lady possessed no interest in political matters.

The next morning he found her seated at the small escritoire in his study, busily at work. "What are you writing, Mother?"

Abigail raised her head and gave him a winsome smile. "Why, I am writing a note to that charming young widow, Amber Leighigh, inviting her to tea."

Chapter Sixteen

$\mathcal{R}$ob froze midstride. His mind raced. What could he say? That it would be a bit awkward considering she was a member of the demimonde? Or, that she was not really a widow? That she only wore black and veiled her face because she was hiding from some enemy who had tried on numerous occasions to kidnap or kill her! *Think, blast it all, think!*

Ignoring his tongue-tied response, Abigail chattered on about how delightful and well-informed she had found Mrs. Leighigh to be. The more he considered the matter, the more he agreed. Fantasia, whatever her real name, possessed every qualification for being his countess—except for one glaringly obvious disqualification. Still, she had always been very discreet about her identity. Perhaps no one in London had ever seen Lady Fantasia's face or knew her identity, except for the small coterie of loyal servants surrounding her . . . guarding her.

No! Whatever was he thinking? She had been a prostitute, albeit one of the highest order. Many of her customers must, at one time or another, have seen her face before she became the mysterious Lady Fantasia. Perhaps it was one such man from whom she now hid, who wanted to keep her as his exclusive play toy. Still, that left him with no acceptable explanation to deter his mother from inviting "Mrs. Leighigh" to tea.

He reached out for the missive, saying, "I shall have Frog deliver it at once. Perhaps I can join you this afternoon."

Abigail shook her head. The expression on her face was one she normally reserved for Maggoty. The big sheepdog he had owned as a boy always managed to track mud across the hearth just after the floor had been scrubbed. "You have a meeting this afternoon with Mr. Wilberforce, do you not?"

"I shall make my excuses and reschedule."

"No, you will keep your appointment with that good gentleman. I shall entertain Amber myself." The steely gleam in those blue eyes was formidable enough to halt Napoleon's legions.

Amber, was it now? Fantasia had certainly ingratiated herself with his mother, and Abigail St. John was not an easy woman to deceive. "What if she refuses?" *Which she most certainly will do . . . won't she?* He prayed she would.

Abigail smiled serenely. "I believe the lady will accept."

When Amber received the note, she was stunned. Why on earth had the earl sent his mother's invitation? He should have made up some Banbury story to convince her to cease matchmaking. She pressed her fingertips to her temples and massaged the ache starting to build. *Surely he does not want me to agree to this madness . . . or does he?*

Well, if he allowed the invitation to be sent, then he could live with the consequences. Abigail's primary reason for coming to London had been to see if Baroness Oberly would make a suitable countess for the earl. Amber hoped his mother was too keen a judge of character to approve of the vacuous female. Besides, she temporized, she really enjoyed Abigail's company and the older woman would soon return to her family obligations at home.

She would tactfully explain the impossibility of a second marriage between Barrington and herself, and that done, would learn Abigail's opinion of the baroness.

As she penned a reply, she considered how his city house might be furnished. The décor would be bold and masculine, spartan to a fault, she was certain. A tiny smile curved her lips. Would he make some excuse to remain at home when she arrived? He knew he could count on her utter discretion, but still . . . Their relationship had taken quite a few unintentional turns since they first struck what was to be a short-term business arrangement.

"We shall see how you deal with this, m'lord," she murmured as she reached for the bellpull.

That afternoon she was admitted to the lovely brownstone house. All she had previously seen was the front. Stepping into the foyer, Amber glanced around and was pleased that her guess about décor had been quite on the mark. With the exception of two small landscapes, the pale blue walls were bare of adornment. Polished oak floors gleamed beneath her feet and an octagonal rug in dark blues and greens was centered in the foyer. An Adams pier table on the far wall next to the winding staircase was the only furniture besides a cane umbrella stand by the door.

"This way, m'lady," the butler said with the deference he might show to a royal duchess. "Mrs. St. John awaits you in her parlor. If you will follow me, please."

As she climbed the steep wooden stairs, Amber held on to the smooth curve of the oak railing, looking ahead to the long hallway at the top. She could see three doors set on each side. Which room was Rob's? Did he sleep in the nude here as he did with Gabrielle? If so, she would wager he had only recently stopped wearing nightshirts. A small ripple of wicked pleasure curled deep inside her belly as the thought flashed through her mind. Then the servant tapped softly on the first door.

When Abigail bid her enter, Amber saw the cozy sitting room was furnished in the English country style with sturdy rounded chairs and a straight-legged table set for a light repast. The linen cloth on it was edged with tatting, most probably done by Abigail herself. Beyond the sitting room, a door opened to a sleeping chamber with a four-poster bed plumped with several pillows. Like the upholstered furniture in the sitting room, the bedcover was a soft blue edged with tatting.

"Good afternoon, Amber. I am delighted that you were so gracious as to accept my invitation," Abigail said, approaching her and giving her a warm embrace as the butler discreetly closed the door behind him.

"It was very kind of you to extend it." She raised the veil on her bonnet as she glanced around, noting several portraits on the walls. One was of a striking man who bore an incredible likeness to the earl, with the exception of his clerical collar and plain black long coat. He had the same green eyes, she noted. But these were open and utterly warm, with no secret fears or haunted past in them.

"That is my husband, Lucas. Robert is his very image," Abigail said softly, her voice warm with memories.

"I can see the resemblance," Amber replied. " 'Tis quite remarkable."

Abigail chuckled. "What a handsome man such as Luke ever saw in me, I shall never know, but I will always be grateful. Even as a girl, I was plain as a hedgerow."

Amber turned to her friend. "You are no such thing. Why, you have the loveliest eyes I have ever seen," she protested.

"My best feature, little doubt, but the rest of my face is bony and quite unremarkable. I'm too short and too thin by half to suit the tastes of most men."

"Although I do not agree with your assessment of your appearance, I'm certain that your husband judged you by the beauty of your soul."

"He was an excellent judge of character, as am I. Alas, I fear Robert, although a keen judge of men, has not inherited our perspicacity when it comes to women." She walked over to the table and said, "Please do have a seat. The cushions are quite comfortable. I made them myself."

Amber took the chair indicated as Abigail sat down across from her. Ignoring the leading remark about Rob's judgment in regard to women, she said, "I never even learned to embroider, much less sew a seam."

"Ladies are taught embroidery. Country women such as I learn sewing. Although Lucas's father was an earl, mine was a parson. We lived a simple life, but were content with such. Will you pour, my dear? I fear my brother-in-law's heavy silver teapot quite intimidates me. I should hate to drop it and smash such delicate china. All of this came to Robert when he inherited the title."

"Along with a great many responsibilities. I am certain he takes them quite seriously." As Amber spoke, she poured the tea into two of the thin porcelain cups, offering one to Abigail.

Both women busied themselves with lemon slices and sugar from the small loaf sitting beside a basket of freshly baked scones. A moment passed before Abigail said, "Robert does indeed take his duty most seriously—too seriously at times, I fear."

"How so?" Amber asked, sipping the tea and remembering the baroness's fondness for her custom blend of the nasty stuff.

"His rush to search out a proper woman to be his countess. At least I have peace of mind knowing that it will not be that poor child, Verity Chivins."

Amber almost smiled before stopping herself. "You did not think the lady suitable?" She studied Abigail over the rim of her cup.

Rob's mother gave a surprisingly indelicate snort. "The Lord forgive me for saying this, but the baroness has less sense than my father's old mule. Clarabelle could not plow a straight line with *two* men leading her. Every furrow was as wavy as the Atlantic Ocean! Lady Oberly confuses climbing boys with boys who climb."

As she explained the previous night's misunderstanding, Amber felt the laughter bubbling up inside her. "There are so few trees in London?" she repeated, struggling not to choke on the bite of scone she had just swallowed.

"Indeed. Can you envision her entertaining his friends from Parliament with such astute observations? You, on the other hand, would engage their interest and further his causes quite handily."

Now Amber did choke, coughing until she had to upend her teacup, drinking with unladylike gulps to wash down the lodged piece of bread. Abigail quickly stood up and came around the small table, thumping her on her back. "There, there, my dear. I did not intend to startle you, but I am a forthright woman—and a determined one. You are the wife for my son."

Regaining her breath, Amber rasped out, "No! I would not suit, not at all. We come from different worlds."

"Perhaps. You were obviously raised as quality while Robert was the son of a country parson. If your fortunes have been reversed in recent years, it signifies nothing. You are educated and concerned with the same issues as Robert. You possess a keen mind and ready wit, not to mention being head-turningly beautiful. I suspect the latter would be accounted an asset in a wife by many members of Parliament."

"You do not understand. . . ."

"Pray, enlighten me, then," Abigail replied gently.

Rob stood frozen on the other side of the door, the knob in one hand, the other raised to knock. How fortunate that his meeting with William and several other MPs had ended earlier than expected. He had overheard his mother's startling pronouncement and knew that he dared not allow this dangerous conversation to go any further. Rapping sharply, he entered.

"Why, Robert, what are you doing home so early?" his mother asked accusingly.

Foiling your plans . . . I hope. Fantasia looked dazed. Abigail's words had obviously shocked her as much as him. "I did not realize that my political affairs need conform to your schedule, Mother," he said, trying for a light tone.

While regaining her composure, Amber watched the interplay between mother and son. This could develop into quite a contest of wills. It would be wise for her to retreat and let them sort the matter out, but before she could say anything, he turned to her.

Bowing, he said, "Good afternoon, Mrs. . . . Leighigh."

"M'lord," she replied coolly, noting his deliberate hesitation over her name. A name he believed to be false. How ironic that it was truly her own. "I think it would be wise if I took my leave—"

"Certainly not," Abigail said firmly. "You are my guest, my dear, and this young rascal shan't spoil our coze."

"Mother—"

"Robert." Her abrupt interruption was flat.

The glacial tone and flashing eyes were warning signs that Rob normally would never have ignored, but this was not a normal situation. "I could not help but overhear your last words to the widow as I approached the door."

"Eavesdropping." Abigail tsked, shaking her head, primed for battle.

"I do believe the door was a slight bit ajar," Amber interjected, waiting to see if he required her help. *Let the beautiful devil sweat a bit.*

"You have placed Mrs. Leighigh in a most untenable position, Mother. She is still in full mourning and our association has been quite brief, and of a political, not social nature. It is far too soon for a discussion of remarriage, as I am certain the lady will concur." He turned to Fantasia.

Amber inclined her head in agreement, but Abigail was not to be put off. "Did you not tell me that your first marriage had been so unhappy that you vowed never again to wed?" Without waiting for a reply, she continued. "I know you would not find my son to be such a brute, although he can at times be a bit dense." She smiled sweetly at him.

Rob noted the wry twist of Fantasia's lips. *She is enjoying this!* "I will be the first to admit that I am no paragon, but that does not mean I require you to select a woman and then coerce her into marrying me."

Amber placed her hand on Abigail's, saying, "I know that you had no such intention, Abigail, and I am most honored that you consider me worthy to be your daughter-in-law, but the earl is correct in saying that we have known each other only a short while. Now, I truly must go. Thank you so much for your gracious hospitality," she added as she squeezed the older woman's hand.

Abigail held it for a moment, saying, "We shall continue this conversation at a later time." Then she winked at Amber and released her hand.

Rob assisted Fantasia with her chair as she stood up. "If I may, Mrs. Leighigh, it would be my pleasure to escort you to your carriage."

Abigail watched Rob and Amber descend the stairs and walk out the door. Once they were outside, she noted the way their heads drew closer as they held a whispered conversation. "What I would give to hear that exchange!" she murmured.

"I fear your mother intends to pursue the crackbrained idea of our marriage," Amber said.

Rob chuckled grimly. "Once she makes her mind up, there is no deterring her." He paused, then surprised himself by asking, "Do you really think it's a crackbrained idea?"

"M'lord! Have you taken leave of your senses—a woman from the House of Dreams marrying a peer!" She stopped abruptly and looked up into those cool green eyes, trying to read what lay behind them.

"Has anyone seen your face or do they know your

identity—any of the current patrons or men you . . ." His voice trailed off as he tried to find a way to phrase what he wanted to ask.

Amber understood his meaning and it was like a slap to her face. "I have never *had* a patron," she said coldly, knowing that he would not believe her.

"Then how did you become Lady Fantasia?" He cocked his head and studied her stiff posture, wishing desperately to see behind the veil that she had replaced before leaving his mother's parlor.

"I will not dignify that question with an answer, one you would never believe in any case. Let us not waste any more of each other's time." When she started to walk away, he placed his hand on her arm to restrain her. She felt a frisson of heat travel up her spine. *Must his touch always leave me this way?*

"Fantasia, wait. I am making another muddle just as I did the first night we met. I did not intend to insult you . . . it's just that I have felt on a few recent occasions that there was some . . . spark between us," he said, knowing he was fumbling awkwardly.

Amber's throat thickened with unshed tears. *Oh, my love, if only you knew your spark is my flame!* She swallowed and did the only thing she could think to do—lash out. "What of the spark between you and Gabrielle? She is your lover, not I." *Liar.* Her words had the desired effect. He dropped his hand as if burned and bowed curtly.

Just then her carriage pulled up and Boxer jumped off the driver's seat. Without a backward glance, Amber climbed aboard and they drove away. Neither she nor Rob saw Abigail at the upstairs window, watching the scene unfold. She smiled quietly and let the curtain fall back in place, shaking her head. Young people could be so foolish. Sometimes they required help sorting out important matters.

* * *

The following morning a post arrived for Abigail from Kent, informing her that her middle daughter, Diana, whose baby was not expected for another fortnight, had just given birth. Both mother and the little boy were doing well. With such joyous news, Abigail knew she must leave immediately, in spite of the unfinished task of bringing Robert and Amber to their senses.

Rob arranged for his best sprung carriage and a driver to take his mother home. After promising that he would return to the country as soon as the current session of Parliament ended, he waved farewell to her with profound relief. That left him alone, rattling about in the big city house. Although he had much work to do before the end of the session, Rob found himself unable to concentrate.

All he could think of was his angry parting with Fantasia . . . and his guilt about Gaby. The madam had been right to reprimand him. He was still plagued by the same dilemma, brought into even sharper focus because of his mother's meddling. Fantasia would, on the surface of it, make the perfect countess, but the gentle Gaby was the keeper of his darkest secrets, his confidante, his teacher. He wanted to have both women and knew he could have neither.

So he did what he must. He sent a note to Gaby, telling her that his mother had returned home and he would like to see her that night. Would he tell her good-bye? Should he pay Fantasia what was owed and end their association? As his carriage lurched through the foggy night, Rob honestly had no idea what he would do.

When Amber received his note, she was shaken, uncertain if she could pretend to be Gabrielle any longer. Every time she came to him in darkness, it grew more difficult to deceive him. But the hunger he had awakened in her could not be denied. Like a sleepwalker, she went to the secluded chamber, wondering if this would be the final journey. "Far wiser to end it," she murmured to herself as she slipped out of her robe and opened the door.

If he would not do it, she would . . . after one last night in his embrace.

Rob heard her, smelled her soft lilac perfume, and felt an odd combination of lust and sadness assault his senses. "Gaby," he said hoarsely, reaching for her. At the same time she reached out to him and their bodies entwined in the dark. Their hands caressed while their mouths met hungrily.

Both of them sensed despair in their desire and grew even more voracious because of it. He reached down and cupped her derierre. With her arms clutching his broad shoulders, she instinctively raised her legs, wrapping them around his hips while he backed her against the door. She could feel his hard staff pressing against her mound. He could feel the wet heat of her, opening in invitation. She gave one wriggling twist of her hips to position him.

He thrust.

They gasped in unison, clutching each other tightly, riding hard and fast, kissing feverishly. Her hand raked through his hair, clenching a lock until it stung his scalp, but he felt no pain. He slammed into her as she arched to meet every plunge, her wet flesh clenching to hold him, loath to release him for yet another time. She felt his face buried against her neck where it met her shoulder, his teeth nipping at the tender flesh, but she felt no pain.

When she pressed her back against the door, his hardness started a sudden violent culmination rippling outward from deep within her. She cried out his name, shaking like a sapling in a summer storm. As his staff swelled even larger, stretching her, the spasms of blinding ecstasy swept over him. Within a moment, everything exploded . . . and he stood with her in his arms. They were both spent, panting, unable to speak.

Holding her, he walked to the bed with their bodies still

joined. Placing one knee on the mattress, he laid her down gently and followed, covering her. He raised his upper body, leaning on one elbow, then ran his other hand over her breasts and up to her face. Cupping her chin, he traced his fingertips over her lips, nose, cheeks, eyelids, and brows.

"You are so lovely, Gaby." His mouth followed his hand, kissing her softly.

She could hear the sadness in his voice and knew that this would be their last night. A pang stabbed at her heart and she fought the tears thickening her throat. *I intended to end it. Why am I crying?* Gabrielle drew his head down to hers and kissed him with a slower, softer passion, murmuring endearments as he responded in the same manner.

"You are saying good-bye, my brave major." When he started to protest, she pressed her hand to his lips. "It is all right. I understand. This is how the Fates intended it to be. I am grateful for the time we have had . . . far more than grateful, for you have taught me so much."

"You have been the teacher, Gaby," he said in a husky voice. "Not I."

"We taught each other, I think, neither of us knowing quite what to do . . . both wishing to please . . . and in so doing, being pleased." She gave a small, sad laugh.

"Oh, Gaby, I will not desert you to spend your life in this place—I—"

"No, no. You are not the kind of man who takes a wife and keeps a mistress. I know you too well. I would never ask it . . . or wish it. This matter has been explained to me. I understand."

"But you cannot remain here. I will not let you become a courtesan," he said firmly.

She could hear the anguish in his voice and knew she must find a way to let him extricate himself. "I will not remain here, my Rob, but return to France. Our king has restored our family's estates to my cousin Jean Claude, with whom I was raised. Lady Fantasia sent agents who found him. I will have my life returned to me . . . and you will begin a new one here in England."

He caressed her face, trying to gauge the truthfulness of her words. "You are certain . . . ?"

"Yes, I am certain. But before we go our separate ways, there is this. . . ."

His reply was muffled by her mouth. As he returned the caress, their kisses were no longer swift and desperate, but slow and gentle this time. He whispered her name like a prayer. How could he bear to see her go? The thought fled as her cunning tongue insinuated itself delicately into his mouth. His twined with it and the kiss went on, their lips moving over each other's faces, exploring every nuance. She pressed a puckered nip at the corner of his mouth, causing him to smile. He rimmed her lips with the tip of his tongue and felt her return the smile.

Her hands glided over his back, nails brushing powerful muscles. She could feel his erection hardening once more. Pressing her palms against his chest, she whispered, "This time we do not rush, yes?"

"There is all night. . . ." He felt her soft fingertips thread through the hair on his chest, her palm press against the steady thrum of his heartbeat. To whom did his heart belong? Her? Fantasia? Or, impossibly, both at once? He did not know, nor at this moment, would he think of that. He would think of nothing but pleasing his lovely lady of darkness whose face he would never see, pleasing her for one last time.

"Your hair is like silk . . . your skin like satin," he murmured as he ran his fingers through the fragrant tangles of her long tresses and glided his hand over the curve of her hip. He memorized every curve, touched the soft skin of her concave belly, and placed his little finger inside her navel until she gasped with delight. When he cupped a breast and circled his thumb around the nipple, she moaned softly.

They made unspoken vows with their hands, mouths. Their bodies remained intimately joined as they exchanged murmurs of delight and warmly flowing passion, rushing nothing, exploring everything, each sensation, each response etched in their souls, treasures . . . perhaps one day to be brought out in dreams to lighten dreary times ahead.

When they finally resumed intercourse, it was spontaneously mutual. Both moved slowly, prolonging the gliding, glistening pleasure that danced between them. They knew each other's responses so well that every nuance of breathing, touching, feeling communicated to each other what was desired. Go slower. Move faster. Then slower once more.

The climb was steep yet not arduous. With every stroke they rose toward the towering heights as one. When the final culmination blossomed, it was incredibly like the petals of a flower unfolding in spring sunlight. She felt her whole body quiver. He knew he trembled uncontrollably. They floated back to earth gradually, holding each other tightly, speechless, breathless.

Wordlessly, he drew her to his side and pulled the covers over them. They slept for several hours, then made love again. Although the heavy velvet draperies were drawn tightly closed, Amber awakened with the faintest hint of light. Soon it would be sufficient for him to recognize her. It was time to leave. . . .

"Good-bye, my Rob. I shall always love you," she mouthed, then slipped from the bed as he stirred, vanishing through the door before he came fully awake. Any words exchanged after this would be between the earl and Lady Fantasia. She went to prepare for the inevitable.

As the door closed, Rob sat up in bed, shaking his head. He felt drugged by their passion and its even more incredibly gentle aftermath. The bed was empty, but he could feel the warmth where her slim body had lain, feel its heat lingering against his skin. The scent of lilacs hung suspended in the air like a promise . . . but it was a farewell.

Had he only imagined the words of love? Or had she spoken directly to his heart before slipping away? The dawn gave him no answer.

Chapter Seventeen

Amber spent the following day in her quarters, refusing visitors, even Grace and Jenette. A note arrived that afternoon from the earl. He requested permission to meet with her and settle his financial obligations. Steeling herself, she wrote a terse reply, asking him to come the following morning. Saying good-bye once as Gabrielle had been incredibly painful. Being forced to do so twice was cruel beyond bearing. Yet it must be done. She had no choice.

"At least I shall have time enough to repair myself," she said, glancing at the oval mirror hanging on her bedroom wall. The face staring back at her was chalky pale. Her eyes were red-rimmed with dark smudges beneath them. Biting her lip, she vowed that he would not see her this way. Lady Fantasia must appear to possess a firm, serene confidence. There could be no hiding behind a veil or in shadows this time.

At last she rang for a bath and had a good long soak, applying cold compresses to her ravaged face as she laid her head back in the tub. Finally satisfied that she had done all possible to repair her body, she called Bonnie and requested a dinner tray. Facing Grace and Jeni over the dinner table would have to wait until Rob was well and truly gone. The roasted pork and spring vegetables tasted like ashes to her, but she forced down as much as she could.

Before retiring that night, she took a sleeping draught, something she discouraged any of the courtesans from doing, and never did herself. Tossing and turning fitfully would only leave her in an even more vulnerable state when Barrington arrived.

The day dawned bright and sunny as if mocking her black mood. She selected a dress of buttercup yellow, determined to put on a bright facade for the meeting. Bonnie brushed her hair until it glowed with a deep cherry luster, then arranged it in a smooth chignon at the crown of her head. She wore a simple gold chain around her throat and matching gold earrings.

"Ya look lovely, m'lady," the girl said when Amber stood before the floor-length glass by her dressing table, inspecting her appearance.

She did not feel lovely, but smiled at Bonnie. "Thank you. Please bring me a pot of coffee and give my regrets to Mrs. Winston and Mademoiselle Beaurivage. I have little appetite this morning but will join them for luncheon. The serving maid bobbed her head and left. Barrington was scheduled to arrive at nine. She prayed he would be punctual as was his normal habit.

At the precise hour, she heard his voice down the hallway. When he knocked on the door, she took a moment to compose herself. Shoving away the ledgers she had been attempting to work on, she said, "Please come in, m'lord."

Rob looked haggard but had dressed carefully in a black kerseymere jacket and white cravat. The severe clothing only served to make him more handsome than any toff in embroidered finery ever could hope to be. He cleared his throat and said, "Good morning, Lady Fantasia . . . or should I say, Mrs. Leighigh?"

"Never speak that name again," she snapped, then could have bitten her tongue. "Please forgive me. I did not intend to be rude, but . . . the name could pose a danger to me if bandied around."

Her words were stiff, almost terrified. More of the mystery of her past, the past she refused to speak of. Well enough. He had no right to ask. "You have my word, I will never use it again. Now . . ." He cleared his throat once more. "I appreciate your agreeing to see me today. I assume Gabrielle has told you . . ."

"Yes, she has explained that your lessons are complete. You are to be congratulated, m'lord. We agreed upon a sum that was . . . rather exorbitant. But you have proven such an apt pupil that Gabrielle has prevailed upon me not to hold you to it."

He watched in amazement as she tore up the contract he had signed the night she explained about Gaby. "No, that is, I—"

"We are quits, Barrington," she said with a tight smile. "All is well," she added more gently. "Please give your mother my regards and explain that I have retired to the country to live in seclusion. I regret any hurt I may have caused her."

Rob nodded woodenly, hoping that he could forestall his mother temporarily, still quite uncertain about what he himself wanted to do about Fantasia. "I shall convey your good wishes to her . . . but there is another matter. . . ." He began pacing as he reached into his pocket and extracted a bank draft, almost crumpling it in his haste. Then he spun around and extended it to her.

"I told you, you owe the House of Dreams nothing further," she said.

"This is not for you, er, for your business . . . 'Tis for Gaby. I . . ." A wry smile twisted his lips. "This reminds me of our first meeting, how deuced awkward I felt, tongue-tied as a boy in leading strings. I want to be certain she reaches France and her cousin safely. If he refuses to take proper care of her, this will help." He stepped around her desk and laid the note before her.

She read the amount with raised eyebrows. Money to assuage his guilt? No, she knew him better than that. Without reading the earnestness in his eyes she understood he genuinely cared for his Gaby and wanted her protected, even though he could never see her again. "This is enough for a woman to live comfortably for the rest of her life. I cannot—that is, I know Gabrielle will not accept it."

"I insist," he said stubbornly.

"No—"

Their argument was interrupted when the door to her office flew open and Grace rushed in, her face red with excitement and her eyes wide with fear. She was still wearing a brocade robe and her hair hung around her shoulders in wild disarray. "Please forgive my interruption but—my God, his granddaughter has been abducted! Right in front of her governess—" She broke into tears, something Grace Winston never did.

"Please, Grace, sit down and explain," Amber said, rounding her desk to reach her sobbing friend. Taking her arm, she helped Grace to the sofa near the door and sat beside her. "Now, whose granddaughter has been abducted?"

Rob walked over to the small pier table and poured a small portion of Amber's excellent brandy into a crystal glass. He offered it to Mrs. Winston, saying, "Take your time, dear lady."

Amber nodded to him gratefully and accepted the glass, handing it to the older woman. Grace took a deep, calming breath and raised the glass to her mouth, then swallowed a sip before saying, "Burleigh's granddaughter has been kidnapped. He is at his daughter's home on Old Marylebone Road now. His note simply says that Millicent's governess took the child for a walk in the Old Marylebone Cemetery—'tis been used as a park for several years, you know."

Rob and Amber nodded as Grace took another sip of brandy, then continued. "Two bully ruffians suddenly leaped from behind some trees and knocked the poor girl down!"

"They struck Millicent?" Amber asked, aghast.

"No, no," Grace said, shaking her head. "The governess. They then made off with Millicent in front of everyone. That park is filled with nurses and governesses with their young charges. How brazenly depraved must these savages be to do such a thing? Burleigh knows you have a reliable runner and begs your help," she said to Amber.

"He will most certainly have it!" She patted Grace's arm and rose, walking to the wall to ring the bellpull. Then she scribbled a note of explanation, adding the direction of Burleigh's daughter's home with instructions for him to proceed there at once. Her footman, Clifton, appeared within a moment. "Please give this to your cousin immediately. We are in desperate need of his services!"

Clifton nodded as he took the note, leaving in considerable haste without asking questions. If the Lady Fantasia said a matter was desperate, that was all that was required. Clyde would know what to do when he received the note.

"Mr. Dyer will be able to locate the child," she said reassuringly to Grace. *If anyone can!* "Now, you need to lie down and rest. You're quite overset."

"I could not rest while that poor little girl is in the hands of fiends who run virgin houses." Grace's eyes were cold as she shuddered in revulsion. "I know what sort of men kidnap beautiful young blonde girls—and why, Amber."

At the use of the name, Rob blinked. *So her name really is Amber Leighigh.* He filed that away for future consideration. "Your fears are well grounded, Mrs. Winston. We shall not attempt to deceive you, but Fantasia is right. You should permit us to handle the matter. I have some knowledge of where such ruffians take children."

"I am most grateful, Lord Barrington," Grace replied earnestly.

"What do you know about child abductions in London?" Amber asked him.

"In order to write bills dealing with child exploitation, I have had cause to investigate various of these virgin houses that specialize in auctioning children, boys as well as girls." He sketched a hasty bow to Grace, then turned to Amber and said, "I'm going to speak with several people who have given me information about the most infamous bawds dealing in this vile traffic. I shall send word of what I learn regarding the granddaughter of Burleigh—?"

"Chipperfield. He is a baronet from Hereford. You met him at the Chitchesters' masked ball," Amber replied.

Rob nodded. "I recall him," he said. "He and your runner and I would do well to compare information as soon as possible. Time is of the essence."

"If you become involved, Sir Burleigh will know you are . . . acquainted with me," Amber said awkwardly, not wishing to think about the baronet's shrewd observations regarding her feelings for the earl.

"I do not care. Move to the point, he already suspects," Rob added obliquely. He reached for the door, then paused. "You have a number of seasoned veterans in your employ. It might be wise to have them prepare for a fight. I shall send word to my staff to do likewise since the authorities will not enter a place of business, no matter the cause."

With that he was gone. Jenette, who had overheard the last of the conversation, walked through the open door and said to her friends, "He is correct, you know. We must prepare to rescue the child ourselves. What of her father— would he be of any use?"

Grace shook her head. "He is a diplomat, posted to Paris currently. Even if he knew how to fire a pistol, which I warrant he does not, he is unavailable. Poor Pamela, she is quite alone. I wish I could offer her comfort, but . . ." Her voice trailed away sadly. She was the infamous Mrs. Winston, owner of an exclusive bordello, hardly fit company for a lady.

"None of us may comfort the child's mother, but we can do more useful things," Jenette said to Amber. "With the help of your men, you have snatched children from the streets and saved them from horrid fates, *ma coeur*. Now you have not only me to aid you but your earl as well," she said, looking at

Amber as if daring her to protest once again that Barrington was not *her* earl. When she did not, Jenette nodded approval.

"I shall gather my men, Jeni. Why don't you see to Grace?" she suggested.

"Will the both of you please desist in speaking of me as if I were not present. I have gathered my wits sufficiently to function. Go about your preparations. I shall await Burleigh and explain about the earl. Now, off with you," she said, shooing the younger women out of her way as she set the half-full glass of brandy on the table with a sharp click. She rose and headed for her quarters.

Within a half hour, all of Amber's men from military backgrounds and those possessing other fighting experience had gathered in her office. Jenette stood near the rear of the crowded room. A handful of the men knew she had been a spy for the English during the late war. None appeared surprised to see her there. Amber outlined what had happened and what might be required to rescue the child—if and when they learned where she was being held.

After the men had dispersed to prepare, Jenette remained behind. "I have been thinking . . ." she said to Amber, but before she could frame her idea, Burleigh knocked on the open door.

When Amber ushered him inside, she could see the haggard bleakness in his usually merry, kind face. The baronet was badly frightened for his only granddaughter, a beautiful child that she and Grace knew he doted upon. "Burleigh, you poor man, we are waiting word from Mr. Dyer. Please, have a seat. I shall send for Grace."

Chipperfield shook his head. "I have just spoken to her. She is as distraught as my daughter and I. Pamela's sister is with her and I've sent a messenger to Paris to fetch Randolph home. While we wait for Mr. Dyer and the earl to report, there is little else I can do but offer my profoundest thanks for your assistance. Since Pamela is already so overset, I have asked both of them to return here once they learn anything. I do hope that is all right."

"Of course, my dear Burleigh," Amber said, pouring a brandy for him, which he accepted gratefully. "It is a wise idea for all of us to put our heads together once we know where Millicent is being held. We shall rescue her," she said firmly, trying to convince herself as much as him.

A far calmer Grace reappeared, dressed in a day gown of purple linen, her hair smoothed into a bun at the nape of her neck. She sat beside Burleigh, taking his hand in hers. Amber explained that her men were preparing for the rescue and that she had received a message from the earl's man Frog, indicating that he, too, had been instructed to marshal further reinforcements.

"All we require now is to learn where our battle will be fought and devise a plan," Jenette said. "I have snatched innocents from Madame Guillotine on more than one occasion." She noted Amber's nod. Her friend had been one such.

They discussed various possibilities for a while, and then everyone lapsed into brooding silence, tense as they waited for the sound of hoofbeats. Several nerve-racking hours passed. Then Amber, who stood peering out the window, saw Clyde Dyer jump nimbly from a hackney coach. As soon as Boxer ushered him into the room, Burleigh said, "What has taken you so long, sir?"

"Well, Your Honor, these things always takes a bit of time. A fellow has to muck about in a few sewers. The governess, she described a little one-armed weasel and a clumsy, carbuncle-faced noddy. Has a good eye for details, that gel. Anyways, I asked about down in the Dials, and found out it were a sorry excuse for humanity called Stump Jenkins and his half-wit chum, name of Corker. They's been known to snatch more'n one little one off the streets, accordin' to what I been told. Bein' as this child is from a good family and looks like a regular little angel, they'll sell 'er to a virgin house."

"Virgin house! Good God, I thought such places were a great hum—that they employed chitty-faced young trollops, not children," Burleigh exclaimed as Grace and Amber exchanged grim glances.

Clyde replied, "Most do, Your Honor, but a few others is the genuine article. Lots of folks hungry out on the streets. Some will sell . . . they sell, so to speak, 'first rights' of their own little ones for three or four pounds. Boys as well as girls. But when scum like Jenkins snatch a particular prime 'un like your granddaughter, they intend to sell her to a bawd who pays lots o' blunt."

"Do you know the bawd's name?" Amber asked in a strangled voice, her worst fears realized.

"Got two of me best men fetching Corker 'ere right now. Nabbed 'em slick as could be goin' into St. Giles rookery. Jenkins slipped away but Corker, he ain't so quick. 'e'll tell us 'fore an auction's held. They always holds 'em late at night."

"An auction?" Burleigh echoed in an even more strangled voice.

Rob reined in his big black stallion after it clattered over the cobblestones at the rear of the House of Dreams, accompanied by his former sergeant, Seth Coulter, and five other seasoned campaigners who had fought with him during his years in Spain. They passed by several of Amber's men, who greeted the earl in discreet recognition. Coulter told the rest of their group to wait, then climbed the stairs after the earl.

Hearing the commotion, Amber rushed to the head of the steps. Surely he would not have returned in such haste with another man who must be a soldier unless . . . She dared not finish the thought.

"Have you—"

"I have just learned that there is to be a special auction

tonight," he replied, making a swift introduction of the sergeant as they neared the office.

Amber thanked the hard-looking man with the unstylish, heavy mustache and level gray eyes, then asked Rob, "When will this auction take place? Where?"

As they entered her office he replied, "The stroke of midnight tonight. At a virgin house run by a bawd named Motley Molly Chub." He nodded to Dyer. "Have you heard of her?"

"Indeed I 'ave, m'lord. Old Molly ain't only a bawd, but a smuggler. Owns a warehouse on the docks and a dozen 'ouses and gin shops round town."

"But then where is Millicent?" Burleigh asked in frustration, rubbing his hands together frantically.

The baronet's eyes fixed on the runner, who replied, "Me best guess is one of 'er bordellos called the Goat."

Rob nodded. "That confirms what I was told. Lots of men with far more money than morals frequent it to purchase children at auction."

Jenette's mouth was a thin hard line. "Where is this ordure?"

"In the theater district, sort of," Dyer replied. "On South Street just round the corner from Cyder Cellars where that actor Kean swills himself every night."

"We'll require a map," Rob said, looking at Amber.

She nodded and walked to a wall cabinet behind her desk. In a moment, she was spreading a map of London across the desk, after clearing off all the books and papers.

Rob and the runner studied the location. Dyer traced a line with one blunt finger. "This is Maiden Lane. South Street comes in just 'ere, m'lord. 'Bout 'ere's the Goat." He stabbed the map to illustrate.

Rob turned to Coulter, who stood discreetly behind him awaiting orders. "Sergeant Coulter, your opinion?" As his companion studied the map, Rob motioned to Boxer, who stood near the door, taking everything in. "And yours, Sergeant Major?" he asked.

Amber's head of security stepped to the desk and looked at the map, as did Jenette, who had spent considerable time poring over maps of Paris for similar reasons. Amber watched the exchange, saying nothing.

"I'd say we cannot just ride up to the place and risk drawing attention," Boxer said.

Coulter nodded agreement. "Close in, that neighborhood."

"We don't wants to alert ole Molly's boys," Dyer agreed.

"How many men do you have?" Rob asked Boxer.

"I have four men ready to ride on Lady Fantasia's orders," the sergeant major replied.

"I have six men. All together we would look like a troop of cavalry riding down South Street," Rob said, rubbing his chin thoughtfully. "We must split our forces."

Jenette surprised the men by leaning forward and tracing her finger over a route on the map. "Charing Cross and High Holborn?" she suggested.

Coulter's startled expression was filled with more than a bit of male superiority as he looked at the Frenchwoman, but Rob knew something of her background and suspected more. Amber interjected, "Jenette spent years eluding Fouche's Secret Police in the sewers of Paris. Heed her. No one is better at helping people escape."

Rob gave Amber a curious glance but said nothing. Had Jenette rescued Amber from the person or persons from whom she now hid? Another matter to consider later. He returned his attention to the intersection on the map that she had indicated. At once he understood what she meant. "Sergeant Coulter, we'll go east along Holborn to Drury, then south. Here"—he pointed to a turn—"then cut past the south side of the market and we'll be at the head of South Street. Boxer, your men go east. Take Maiden Lane to the bottom of South Street. If we all arrive at dusk, we'll have the cover of shadows and time enough to get the child out long before the auction."

"A pincer movement, like being back on the Peninsula," Coulter said, eyeing the Frenchwoman, wondering if that was what she, too, had in mind. Boxer only nodded his approval of the plan.

"Then we crash into that damnable den of iniquity and whisk my granddaughter away," Burleigh said with rising enthusiasm.

"Won't be all so easy, Your Honors," Dyer interjected.

"Are her bouncers armed?" Rob asked, knowing that most brothels employed former pugilists to maintain order with fists and truncheons.

"Don't know for sure, but ole Molly, she don't need bully boys. She's the canny one, she is," Dyer said, scratching his head. "She's made lots o' blunt smuggling since the war with Boney started. Ain't stopped since the peace, neither. Every hidey-hole of 'ers has secret rooms and such to stash stolen goods. Last year the Customs raided one o' her sties up in St. Giles Rookery. Found lots o' French brandy and such, but ole Molly had herself an escape tunnel in the basement. Led out to a sewer. The bawd disappeared like fog in sunshine.

"See, Molly don't take no chances," Dyer continued as Rob muttered an oath beneath his breath. "Half the time, she's up in Kentish Town, living like a nob. But with this kind o' auction, she'll be at the Goat for sure. Too much quid selling an honest-to-God little angel. She'll want to handle it 'erself, but if she smells trouble, mark me, she'll get out and take the gel with 'er."

Burleigh slumped into a chair and put his face in his hands while Grace placed her arms around his shoulders and offered silent consolation. "There must be something we can do," she said desperately.

Rob stood, rubbing his chin, his thoughts whirling as

various ideas played out in his mind. He sorted and rejected one after another with growing frustration. "We need a bloody diversion," he said, then flushed. "My apologies, ladies," he quickly added.

All three women shrugged, indicating they did not blame him. They had heard far worse on many occasions during their varied life experiences.

Rob began to pace back and forth, now thinking out loud. "A fire, perhaps? No, in such a crowded area of wooden buildings, we could endanger the child. A brawl outside the place—we could incite a good fight—but then Molly might take Millicent and run, if she's half as wary as Mr. Dyer indicated."

"If I might suggest a better alternative?" Amber said, breaking into his conjectures. Everyone looked at her with interest, most significantly Rob, who nodded.

"What is it you have in mind, Lady Fantasia?" he asked.

"I have heard that the despicable men who take part in purchasing children often do so based on an old superstition." She flushed slightly beneath Rob's stare but continued. "Grace and I have had this particular request made of us and refused any further admittance to the men for even suggesting such a thing. . . ."

Grace could see that Amber was struggling with her embarrassment in front of the earl. She picked up on the cue, saying, "Yes, some aging rakes who have lost their ability to perform," she explained as Sergeant Coulter's mouth dropped in silent amazement, "believe that if they bed a very young virgin their potency will return. If we had an older man feign interest in such a cure . . ." Now she looked over at Burleigh, who was beginning to comprehend.

"I would be that old rake," he exclaimed. "I shall offer a huge amount of money—get the door open so the rest can rush inside when I gain admittance."

"Ye're onta something there, Your Honor, ladies," Dyer

said, clearing his throat nervously before he continued. "But, ya see, an old bloke what's lost his, er, manhood, well, that just ain't our way inside. Molly might figger it'd take too long, er . . ." Now it was Dyer's turn to flush red as a spring beet.

"Please, do continue, man," Burleigh commanded as Grace nodded encouragement.

"She'd never chance 'ow long it might take for 'im to get it up." He stopped and clapped his mouth shut abruptly, then doggedly resumed. "What I means to say is it'd be best to have Your Honor pretend to be wanting a cure for the pox."

"Yes, the only cure for it, according to many leeches, is having a young virgin. Fools believe the pox can be drawn out of the man and transferred into the girl," Grace clarified as neatly as any Sunday school teacher explaining the miracle of turning water into wine at Cana.

Dyer nodded gratefully. "Just so, Mrs. Winston." He turned to Chipperfield. "If Your Honor was to offer, after a bit o' hagglin', say three hunnert pounds for only a few minutes, Molly would think she could clean up the gel and still auction 'er off later that night as a virgin. Old bawds knows 'ow to fake it. Double her profit, it would."

Rob nodded with an expression of extreme disgust. "Filthy business, but it might just work."

"I'll do it!" Burleigh exclaimed. "I could use my old walking stick, pretend to hobble, flash about some money and gain entry. Then—"

"Then we rush in and seize Molly before she can escape," Rob said, seeing how it could play out. "The trick will be convincing her to come to the door and haggle." He looked at the baronet.

Chipperfield's face was set. "I will drive a very hard bargain."

Rob evaluated the older man. He was built like a tree trunk, broad shouldered and rock solid. There was not an ounce of fat on him. And, judging by his expression, he could keep control of his emotions sufficiently to play the part.

Grace held her lover's chin in her hand, saying, "My dear, you look too healthy. We shall apply some of my paints to make you appear ill and older in dim light. Come now, let us prepare." She and Burleigh stood up.

As Dyer furnished Chipperfield with a brief explanation about how to approach a bawd such as Motley Molly Chub, Amber and Jenette exchanged whispered words. "There will be other children in that place, won't there?" Amber asked her friend, knowing the answer.

"A woman as evil as this, *oui*, I imagine she buys many unfortunates, stolen off the streets, even sold by their own starving parents . . ." Jenette gave a helpless shrug indicating that she had seen far too much in her own brief lifetime. "I know what are you thinking, *ma coeur*."

"We cannot just rescue Millicent. We must save them all."

Jenette nodded with a hint of a smile. "I agree. What do you suppose the gentlemen will think when you suggest it?"

"I shall not merely suggest it but demand it. And what is more, you and I shall accompany them—although we will not tell them that . . . just yet!"

Chapter Eighteen

•

"Much as I would wish to save them all, it is too dangerous, Fantasia," Rob said firmly when she demanded they
rescue all the children in the virgin house. "We have no way
to transport them. They could be killed—"

"Do you think life after being raped by poxed old lechers
will be worth living for those children? How long do you
imagine such young ones survive in that kind of place before
they die of disease or abuse?" she asked with rising anger.

Before he could reply, Jenette cut in. "We have two closed
carriages—they are large and will conceal the little ones.
How many do you believe there might be, Monsieur Dyer?"

The runner shrugged, considering. "Maybe few as four or
five, or many as a dozen. No more'n that at the Goat."

"Even twelve children would fit easily in two coaches,"
Amber said stubbornly. "We have two boys who are excellent drivers. Grace and I rescued them from the streets, so
they know how to take care of themselves. You must bring
out all the children as soon as Burleigh has found Millicent
and driven away with her."

Rob looked from her implacable face to Jenette's equally
determined albeit less combative expression. When Grace
moved forward, he threw up his hands in defeat. "All right,
we will round up all the children we find in that den, but my
driver Frog will handle the lead coach. Will that satisfy
you?" he asked Fantasia.

She nodded regally. He did not see the wink she exchanged with Jenette.

* * *

As dusk thickened and a light fog swirled over London, Rob and the two sergeants inspected their men's weapons and horses, making certain everyone understood how they were to be deployed when they left the mews behind the House of Dreams. When the earl was satisfied that all was ready, he returned to the house just as Burleigh stepped outside.

"I can scarcely recognize you, sir," he said in amazement. The baronet looked to be tottering on the verge of death, his gray skin hanging in creases and his eyes sunken back in the sockets.

Theatrically, Burleigh hunched over his walking stick, seeming to use it to support his weight. A larger size of clothes concealed his robust build and made his body appear as wasted as his face. "I think the doorman at that hellish place shall feel safe allowing me inside," he said grimly.

"Just remember, once you've gained entry, wait for us," Rob reminded him, still concerned that the older man's fear for his granddaughter might lead him to act rashly.

"He knows his part, m'lord." A woman spoke behind his back.

Recognizing Fantasia's voice, Rob turned around—and blinked as if trying to clear cobwebs from his mind. "Fantasia?" he said, looking over the dirty stable boy's shoulder for a beautiful woman in a bright yellow gown. Standing before him was a slim lad sporting a cap as grimy as his soot-smeared face. A baggy shirt hung over his ragged, torn breeches. His toes peeped out of holes in the scuffed boots on his feet. Both were liberally caked with manure.

"My stable boy Wally's clothes," she explained, turning around for his inspection. Seeing him and Burleigh wrinkle their noses, she added, "He had just mucked out the stalls when I asked to borrow them."

"Where do you think you are going in that absurd disguise?"

Rob asked, already knowing the answer. She had a percussion-lock pistol shoved in her waistband.

Amber watched him cross his arms over that impossibly broad chest and glare. She glared right back. Burleigh straightened up off his walking stick and made haste toward his coach, saying, "I shall be ready to leave as soon as you, er, settle matters."

"You have no idea what kind of hellish place and dangerous people we are dealing with."

"And you do? Come, m'lord. Before you first came here, had you ever visited any sort of bordello?"

"I've inspected factories and almshouses in the worst slums and gone in disguise into flash houses as well. Why do you think my speeches before Parliament have been so vivid? I'm a veteran of the war on the Peninsula. You—"

"I have seen more cruelty than you might imagine," she snapped. "M'lord, we are wasting time. I am going and so is Jenette," she said as her companion rounded the corner, also disguised as a grubby lad. She, too, carried a pistol tucked in her wide leather belt.

"This is insane. I know you can shoot well, Fantasia, but two women, no matter how skilled they are with firearms, will only be in the way."

"How will those terrified children react to a group of hard-faced soldiers storming in and trying to carry them off during a fight with Molly and her men? Once inside, we can take off our caps and the little ones will see we are women. We can calm them and get them to climb into the carriages waiting by the door. Quickly, safely."

"She is right, *mon seigneur*," Jenette said softly. "You will require our assistance, *oui?*"

"Remember what Mr. Dyer cautioned us," Rob argued. "We dare not fire shots. Bow Street is nearby and the last thing we wish is to have the authorities intervene."

"*Certainement.* I am prepared," Jenette said in a deceptively quiet tone as she slipped a wicked-looking blade from her belt.

Something in her eyes reminded him of the Spanish partisan women he had met during the war. "I believe you, but Fantasia—"

"I am coming, too. I'm strong enough to wield a cudgel. Any of your men might be forced to fire a shot. We will be as careful as they to see that it is not required."

He looked from Fantasia to Jenette. "What would you do if I refused? Shoot me? No, on consideration, please do not answer that." He sighed and muttered an oath, then stared at Fantasia with narrowed green eyes. "When we reach the Goat, you will remain with the carriages until we clear the place. Then I shall signal for you to come in and attend to the children, is that understood?"

"It is understood, *mon seigneur*," Jenette replied, dashing off toward the stable and the carriage.

Amber nodded. "I understand." *But that does not mean I shall obey.* "As you reminded me, you are the one with military experience." *But I know what it is like to be held prisoner.*

Fantasia's two coaches, with Amber and Jenette in the first one, headed down Charing Cross, their plain black exteriors and shabbily dressed young drivers attracting little attention in the twilight. When they neared the virgin house, they pulled up, one at each end of the street. They were far enough away from the Goat as not to cause alarm. If not for Dyer's description, they would never have recognized the virgin house. There was no identifying sign hanging over the door, which was made of stout, well-scarred oak. It would take a battering ram or a cannon shot to break it down.

As Boxer's men trickled in from above South Street and hid themselves, Rob dispatched three of his men to slip around the rear of the big ugly frame building with peeling gray and green paint. They took their places, one in the alley and the other two at the sides, to make certain no one escaped through a window or a back door.

Satisfied that everyone was in position, Rob dismounted, handing his reins to Sergeant Coulter, who already held the reins of the other horses. "As soon as O'Keefe, Cooper, and I lunge out of Chipperfield's coach and breach the door, everyone rushes in on the double," he said. "Watch that no one fires a weapon unless absolutely necessary."

Coulter resisted the urge to salute, but said, "Yes, sir, Captain! Er, m'lord." He watched the earl stroll casually around the next corner to where he knew Burleigh's coach waited at the prearranged rendezvous point.

Frog sat on the driver's perch, appearing unconcerned, as Rob quickly leaped inside. O'Keefe and Cooper were seated across from the baronet. The two burly men had served with Rob and Coulter during the war. They all exchanged nods of grim understanding. Then the earl rapped on the roof and Frog snapped the reins, heading for the Goat.

When Chipperfield's coach stopped at the entry, Rob whispered to him, "Remember, you must get the bawd to come to the door."

"I will do it," Burleigh replied.

It was difficult to credit that the old man climbing down from the coach was the robust baronet. He hobbled to the door and knocked. Rob and his men watched, poised to leap out. "All right, Burleigh, all depends on your being as good as Kean," the earl murmured.

Everyone except for the men behind the Goat observed from their scattered vantage points when Chipperfield struck the door with his walking stick and waited.

A small spy window in the door opened and a hoarse voice challenged, "Wat ye want?"

Burleigh gave a good imitation of a racking cough and spat on the cobblestones at his feet, then said, "I'm of a mind to sample the virgin that's supposed to be auctioned tonight—if the chit really is a virgin." He spat again.

"Sure 'n he could've convinced me," O'Keefe whispered to Cooper.

"Come back at midnight and bid with the rest o' the toffs," the doorkeeper said, starting to slam the little window closed.

Burleigh beat upon the door once more and yelled, "Look at this, you carbuncle-faced cork brain!" As soon as the window reopened, he shoved a fistful of banknotes toward it. "My leech says a real virgin will draw off this damnable pox. The younger the gel, the better. Word is around the gaming hells that you have a real one and I'll pay double for her!"

The pockmarked doorkeeper's eyes widened as he saw how much money the old devil was practically shoving in his face. "Er, I gotta ask the mistress. Just wait."

Burleigh grimaced in satisfaction. Excellent. Motley Molly Chub was coming to the front door herself. She would not escape with his precious Millicent!

He coughed a few more times, loud enough to be heard through the heavy door. After several minutes, the window opened again and a handsome female with eyes as glacial and dead as an arctic winter peered out at him.

"We are holding an auction at midnight," she said with diction so precise that Burleigh was certain she had practiced to erase any trace of her flash house upbringing.

However, she did not close the window when he again raised his fistful of banknotes. "I know about the auction but have no desire to make my plight public. Besides, I only want to use the gel for a few minutes to draw off my pox. I'll pay fifty pounds for the treatment and then you may sell her to the very devil for all I care."

Molly Chub had not come from a St. Giles flash house to become owner of a far-flung smuggling and prostitution empire without recognizing a business opportunity when she saw one. She studied the wasted face and expensive clothing of the man at her doorstep. He looked sick enough to be desperate and rich enough to pay far more than the fifty he clutched in his fist.

In and out. She smirked, knowing that the sick old rake would only use the chit for a few moments. Then she would have time aplenty to treat the little brat with warm alum water to tighten and shrink the torn tissue. When she bled the second time, the drunken auction winner would believe he had been the cause of it. A handsome profit for one night's business. But first, this transaction.

"The chit is only twelve, a golden-haired little angel. I could not sell her virginity for less than a hundred."

Burleigh felt the bile rising in his throat. Just hearing the evil woman describe his Millicent in this manner made him want to tear the heavy iron hinges from the door and smash it down on her. But he controlled his fury and bartered back, "Seventy-five pounds."

Molly's eyes narrowed. "One hundred or you may wait and appear in public at the auction."

Chipperfield coughed again and cursed, giving voice to the rage boiling inside him as he replied, "Very well, a hundred it is, you mercenary bitch!" To spur her to open the door, he reached into his waistcoat and extracted more banknotes.

As the door swung open, Burleigh deliberately stumbled against it as he entered. Motley Molly Chub stood directly in his path, backed by a hulking giant of a man with no front teeth. The woman wore a gown of pale blue satin and as skillfully applied face paints as his own—to the opposite effect. She was stunningly beautiful in an icy way with snow white hair arranged in elaborate curls on top of her head. The diamond necklace at her throat glittered almost as much as the greed in her dead gray eyes.

Shark's eyes. He had read of the great killing beasts. Here was a smaller version, every bit as deadly . . . and far more brutal. To feed her greed, he reached into his pocket and pulled another fistful of banknotes out, shoving them into her bejeweled claws.

"If you will follow me up the stairs," she said, turning her back as she began to count the loot.

The toothless brute guarding the entrance started to reach for the door when Chipperfield dropped his walking stick directly in front of him. The baronet bent to pick it up, blocking his opponent as the door to his coach sprang open and his three companions leaped out. The gatekeeper tried to step around the old man, but Burleigh grabbed him behind his knees and attempted to throw him on his back. It was like trying to lift one of the Elgin Marbles. The huge doorman must have weighted twenty stone. Chipperfield sank to his knees as a ham-sized fist started to crash down toward his face.

Hearing the commotion, Molly dashed for the stairs, money flying as she clutched it to her bosom with one hand while the other raised her skirts so she could run in heeled slippers. She screeched an alarm, dropping banknotes like a maple shedding leaves in a high autumn wind.

To avoid being smashed in the face, Burleigh ducked his head into the giant's crotch and sank his teeth into the bulge of his indecently tight breeches. The gatekeeper let out a squeal of pure agony. The supposedly sickly old man's arm reached between the guard's legs to grab his belt. The brute froze, afraid to punch because of the blindingly painful hold his opponent had, clamped on like a leech.

As Rob and Cooper dashed past him in pursuit of Molly, O'Keefe stopped to intervene. Burleigh opened his mouth just enough to growl, "I bite again and you'll be singing soprano!"

At that instant the big Irishman struck the doorman on the head. As he crumpled unconscious to the floor, Chipperfield shoved himself free and spat in disgust. "I do thank you, Mr. O'Keefe."

"You done as you said, he'd be the one thankin' me!" O'Keefe replied with a broad grin, helping the baronet to his feet. Both of them followed the chase up the stairway.

Coulter and Boxer with the rest of the men came pouring into the Goat just in time to see three street toughs running down the hallway from the back of the building, each one as large and battle scarred as the doorman. Former pugilists employed for their brute strength, they wielded truncheons and knives, but were no match for the sabers of trained cavalrymen.

None of the combatants saw two slight, ragged figures slip into the dimly lit hallway and race up the stairs after Burleigh and O'Keefe. "The children must be up here somewhere," Amber whispered to Jenette, who had drawn her knife.

Amber stopped at the landing where a small table sat with a heavy long-necked vase on top. Grabbing the fresh flowers from it, she threw them on the polished oak floor and picked up the vase. "This ought to serve," she muttered, following her friend to the top of the steps where the clang of steel echoed from down the long hallway.

Rob was at the end of it, engaged with a tall figure improbably dressed in a stylish red jacket and brandishing a sword with considerable skill. The earl's saber was awkward in close quarters but he had the advantage of a heavier blade. With a few well-placed strokes, he broke the slender sword near its hilt, then backed the man against the wall, the business end of his weapon pressing into the man's throat. "Now, where is the young blonde girl you intended to auction tonight?"

Molly's paramour rasped out, "Behind you. That door."

Overhearing, Chipperfield turned the knob and entered, then said in a soft voice, "Millicent, do not be afraid. Grandpa's here to bring you home, dear child." The terrified little girl was bound to the bed with ropes. Hands trembling, he began to unfasten them, silently cursing human depravity and praying in gratitude at the same time.

"Down on your knees," Rob commanded the pretty-faced whoremaster outside the door, forcing him to kneel, then raising his saber. He used the butt of the hilt to smash the fellow on his head.

Cooper backed a huge brute against a wall with his saber while O'Keefe clubbed him unconscious. Neither soldier saw another denizen of the Goat slip from a door behind them, a gun aimed at the Irishman's back. Before he could pull the trigger, Jenette seized hold of his long greasy hair with her left hand and jabbed the tip of her blade into the side of his throat with her right, drawing a trickle of blood. "Lower the pistol, *s'il vous plait*," she whispered in a deadly voice.

His gun clattered across the floor.

Both soldiers looked at the "boy" in surprise. "We owe ye, boyo," O'Keefe said as Cooper dealt with the unconscious pugilist. The Irishman shoved the second attacker down. They rolled both men over and started to bind their hands.

Giving a low grunt, Jenette stooped down to pick up the pistol, not seeing Molly slide open the door to her quarters. The bawd, too, had armed herself. Taking in the situation, she prepared to shoot the youth who blocked her pathway to escape.

Amber sprang forward and swung the vase in a backhanded stroke just as the bawd heard her and whirled around. The pottery caught Molly full in the face. She crumpled to the floor in a puddle of blue satin and red blood. A huge gash opened across her forehead and ran in a jagged line down to her jaw. "A tiny bit of my debt is paid, my friend," Amber said to Jenette.

"Blimey, there be two of 'em," Cooper said, rubbing his eyes.

"Ain't ye the lady from the House of Dreams?" O'Keefe asked Amber.

Before she could reply, Rob answered for her. "Yes, the disobedient chit is." As he spoke, he scanned the hallway doors, expecting more armed men to appear, but none did.

"We have no time to waste. You dispose of these . . . creatures," Amber said. "Jeni and I shall free the children." She opened the first door and slipped inside with the Frenchwoman following close.

"Cooper, O'Keefe, drag these men to the top of the stairs and roll them down," Rob commanded, hearing Boxer's and Coulter's voices from below. They obviously had the situation there well in hand and were binding their captives according to plan. Just then Molly moaned and stirred. "Tie her up, gag her, and while you're at it, find something to cover her face so she doesn't frighten the children." With that, he walked quickly to the door the two women had entered.

Burleigh finished freeing Millicent, then helped her sit up. "Wait here, child, while I see if 'tis safe to come out," he said gently.

Before he could stand up, she threw her arms around his neck, begging, "Please don't leave me, Grandpapa!"

He patted her back and held her, uttering a prayer of thanks as he heard Rob issuing orders down the hallway. At last, the nightmare was over! He lifted his granddaughter into his arms and carried her swiftly down the hall and out the door to his waiting carriage.

In the first room they entered, Amber and Jenette found two little girls tied to beds, one about Millicent's age, the other slightly older. Both recoiled in terror until the women removed their caps and let their hair fall around their shoulders as they approached, speaking soft, soothing words.

Rob watched as Jenette sliced away the cruel ropes binding them and Fantasia comforted them, rubbing their abraded arms gently. *She is as natural at this as my mother would be.* Rather than voice that startling thought aloud, he said, "I'll check the next room."

Amber turned to the elder of the two girls. "Are there more children held here?"

"Yes," she said, gulping in air as if drowning. "Me two twin brothers is next door, I think. Our ma, she couldn't feed us . . ." Her voice faded away in misery.

The younger girl asked, "What 'appened to that mean witch with the white 'air?"

"I broke her broomstick—and her head," Amber replied with a smile.

The child returned it shyly. "Good," she said quietly.

Rob and Jenette made a systematic check of every room on the floor and found six more children including the twin boys. As they guided all of them down the hall, Amber whispered to Rob, "What makes men so utterly evil that they will buy six-year-old boys to abuse?" She shuddered in revulsion as their charges filed down the steps.

"I saw things during the war . . ." His voice faded as he recalled all the senseless bestiality he had witnessed and described to Gaby. Shaking his head, he vowed that he would never speak of that brutal part of his life again.

"That was war. This is . . . London," she replied as they helped the little ones into the coaches. "When first I came here, I hoped for better, but it took a while to find it," she said.

Rob wanted to ask her where she had come from, what she had fled before she ended up at the House of Dreams, but Sergeant Coulter interrupted. "No alarms raised. Got 'em all trussed up tight as Christmas geese, Captain." He waited expectantly.

Rob nodded. "Do it," was all he said.

Amber looked at him, puzzled. "What are they doing?"

she asked as Coulter, Boxer, and four of their men filed resolutely back into the house.

"Meting out justice, eh, *Capitaine?*" Jenette said with a knowing look. "What of the bawd?"

"She will have scars enough from Fantasia's hand, I think, to serve as a reminder," he replied.

Amber realized what they meant. "They're going to flog them," she said, nodding her approval. "I have never enjoyed seeing anyone bleed as much as I did Molly Chub. But will it deter her from selling children?"

"I believe the message might require a bit of reinforcement," Jenette said, exchanging a look with Amber.

"Molly will be scarred for life," Rob said. "Lesson enough."

"And what of the children? What scars has she inflicted on all those we were too late to rescue?"

Jenette slipped his blade from its sheath. "I will deliver a message that she will remember." When he started to refuse, she raised her hand. "A threat, not a killing. I can be . . . most convincing." At his nod she walked quickly inside.

"Miss, where will ye take us?" the girl with the twin brothers asked Amber from the coach door.

"To a very kind woman who will see that you all find good places to stay. Her name is Mrs. Winston," Amber replied.

"Me brothers be fearful hungry. W-will she feed us?" she asked.

Tears gleamed in Amber's eyes. "Not only feed you, but give you warm, clean beds. You shall go to school and learn to read and write."

As she asked the girl's name and those of her brothers and the other children huddled inside the coach, Rob looked on, amazed at her way with them. Within moments, the men and Jenette returned. As she passed Rob to climb into the second coach, the Frenchwoman murmured to him, "Molly will never deal in children again—and, *non*, she has no further marks on her. I only made her a . . . promise."

"I take it she believed you," he said dryly.

Chipperfield and Millicent had already departed in his coach. Now the other two, filled with children, took off, headed for the House of Dreams.

By the time the tall case clock struck ten, all the young ones had been fed and bathed and were sleeping on the spacious third floor of Grace Winston's home. Amber came downstairs, exhausted but jubilant, her eyes gleaming in her still-smudged face. She had taken no time to change from her stable boy's clothes, so eager was she to help care for the little ones. None had been molested yet! Her relief in learning that made her cry with joy.

She found Rob sitting in her office, nursing a cup of coffee and a snifter of brandy. "I have received word from the Elijah Woodbridge School for indigent children," he said. "They've offered to take all of the children."

"Oh, Rob, that means they will receive an education and have a chance in life!" she said, launching herself at him as he stood up. She practically dragged him across the floor and yanked on the bellpull, then wrapped her arms around his neck and began raining light kisses all over his face.

Bonnie peeped her head inside the door, hearing the commotion even before being summoned. "Bring us champagne, Bonnie. We must celebrate!" The little maid grinned and nodded, closing the door to fetch it.

Rob returned Fantasia's embrace and whirled her around in a circle, laughing as he said, "The children are clean but you still smell of manure!"

"I don't care, I don't care," she practically shouted.

Rob had never seen the cool, controlled Lady Fantasia in such girlish high spirits. She was filthy and wearing rags, but she had never seemed more lovely, he thought as he looked down into her smiling face. When they stopped spinning across the room, he let go of her with one arm and reached into his pocket for a handkerchief. "Let me at least clean off the soot before we toast," he murmured, wiping away the smudges marring her perfect features.

His gentle ministrations took away the makeup beneath the stable dirt. That was when he saw the small scar on her cheekbone.

Chapter Nineteen

*H*is hand froze but he kept his other arm around her waist. He pressed her closer. Squeezing his eyes closed, he rested his chin on the top of her head, drawing her to melt against his body. Then he murmured in French, "My little one."

Without being aware of what she did, Amber automatically replied, "My heart, my own," also in French. She felt his whole body shudder and realized what had just happened. He dropped his arms to his sides and stepped back from her. Unconsciously, she raised her fingertips to the scar.

Watching her touch the scar made him blanch. "Perfect . . . Parisian . . . French. You've taken everything I had to give, every secret, every hope, dream." His voice cracked. "What a fool I've been, Fantasia—or should I say Gaby? Amber?"

"Amber Leighigh is my name." Her voice sounded hollow to her own ears. What could she say that would erase the pain and betrayal she read in his eyes? He looked physically ill. She raised her hand beseechingly, not knowing how to begin, what to confess first. "Rob—"

"I've given you no leave to use that name, only Gaby . . . and now I find that she does not even exist. Congratulations on your best fantasy yet. Please cash the banknote. You were a most excellent teacher. You've earned it."

With that he turned and walked silently from the room. As she crumpled to the floor, she heard the rear door close softly and his great black horse's hooves clatter across the cobblestones.

A moment later Jenette pushed open the door and walked in, her face alight as she held up an icy bottle of champagne. The instant she saw her friend, huddled sobbing on the carpet, she set the bottle down and took Amber in her arms. "What has happened, dear one?"

Grace, who had been following directly behind her, said softly, "The inevitable." She looked at Jenette and said, "I believe we shall require something a bit more potent than champagne."

Jenette poured three glasses of Lady Fantasia's excellent cognac.

Rob rode through the night for hours, his mind in turmoil. Gaby, his sweet, gentle confidante, did not exist. He had stripped his soul bare before her, believed her tragic tale about being a victim of Napoleon's tyranny. He had confessed the horrors of Spanish battlefields, described experiences in the war that he had vowed never to speak of. Worse yet, he had babbled about his sexual inadequacy, the intimate details of his first marriage, and the guilt he felt over Credelia's death. How understanding she had been. How wise. How consoling.

How false!

Why had Fan—no, Amber, he corrected himself savagely—gone to such lengths? Why deceive him in such a cruel way? She had even deceived his mother, and Abigail St. John was no one's fool. But he had been.

As dawn began to glimmer over the eastern rooftops of the city, he led his tired and sweating stallion into the mews at the back of his city house. The stableman took one look at the brooding expression on the earl's face and accepted the reins, saying only, "I'll see 'e's rubbed down good and fed, m'lord."

Rob made his way inside, handing his coat and weapons to his butler, Settles, without uttering a word. The discreet elderly servant knew something was badly amiss but accepted the articles, then followed the earl upstairs. Asking no questions, he merely said, "I shall have a bath drawn, and Cook will prepare a light repast since you missed supper last night."

"Please do not bother Cook. All I require is the bath and a bottle of brandy. No, make that two bottles of brandy," he corrected, yanking off his shirt and tossing it on the hall floor. He progressed into his bedroom, shedding his remaining articles of clothing and employing the jack to tug off his boots. As he slipped on a robe and belted it, Settles picked everything up. "Very good, m'lord."

The butler bowed and left to do as he was bidden.

Within a half hour, Rob had sunk into a tub of warm water and sipped his third glass of brandy. He had gulped the first two as he paced back and forth across the large room, alone with his demons. "And they are legion," he said, raising the cut crystal of amber liquid in a mocking toast. Amber. How ironic. Was it truly her name? Why should he care? He would never see her again.

But memories of her filled his mind. As Fantasia with her razor-sharp wit, so cool and elegant by day. He squeezed his eyes shut tightly to blot out the image of golden eyes and cherry-colored hair . . . and remembered Gabrielle, so passionate and sweet in darkness. He could smell her lilac scent. He muttered an oath and took another swallow of brandy.

Rob could not shut out the soft cadence of whispered words of love and passion uttered in that flawless French. He heard the magic of her rich laughter. He fought the desire to clamp his hands over his ears as if he could drown out the sounds. But they were inside his head, trapped there forever. "I will never forget you . . . either one of you . . . whoever the hell you are," he slurred, finishing the brandy.

The bottle on the tub-side table was half-empty. He started to pour a refill, then changed his mind. Setting aside the glass, he drank directly from the bottle. How could he have been so dense? So besotted with newly discovered sexual gratification that he dismissed the idea that they were one woman, especially after he danced with Fantasia at the Chitchester ball? Her English was far too good for her to be a French émigré. Her French was so authentic that she must have lived in Paris for some time. Jenette, he suspected, held the answer to that question. But there were many others.

Who wanted to kidnap her? Why did she hide her face and name? Why would a woman possessing such education and refinement live in a bordello, even the most elite one in London? Somehow he would have to explain to his mother that they had both been deceived. How the devil he would accomplish that without confessing his involvement with a courtesan, he had no idea. His head began to pound.

He let the now empty bottle slip from his fingers. It rolled across the floor while he hung his arms over the sides of the tub and fell into an exhausted sleep.

After Grace explained Amber's masquerade as Gabrielle to Jenette, the Frenchwoman attempted to console her friend, insisting that the earl was in as much pain as she. Far from assuaging her guilt, that only intensified it. She suffered the well-meaning ministrations of her friends, forcing down the cognac, eating a few bites of bread and cheese, then taking a bath to scrub the filth of the stable boy disguise from her body. When she finally shooed everyone from her quarters, she started for her bedroom, only to see the bank draft Rob had written for Gabrielle lying on her desk.

Her eyes were blurry with unshed tears when she reached for it. *"You earned it."* She blinked, letting the tears roll down her cheeks as she tore the draft into tiny pieces. She watched the bits of paper float to the carpet and felt as if her heart had been sundered the same way.

* * *

"Barrington spoke on kidnapping children and forcing them into prostitution in Lords yesterday," Grace said to Amber as she folded that morning's *Chronicle* and lay it aside. A week had passed since their bitter parting, yet Amber remained in her quarters, licking her wounds. "If he can recover himself and go back to his work, you must do likewise, my dear," Grace admonished.

Amber sat in her robe, idly stirring cream into a cup of coffee. She had always drunk it black, but now it seemed more appealing if the color did not so closely resemble her mood. She made no reply.

Sighing, Grace stood up and came around the table to place her arms around Amber's shoulders. "Jenette has visited the children at the Elijah Woodbridge School every day. They all ask after you. I know it would do you a world of good to see how well they're doing." When that elicited nothing more than a nod, Grace paced across the carpet to the window. "I should never have instigated this whole tangle," she said, hugging herself in misery.

Amber looked up at Grace's forlorn figure. Her face appeared haggard in the harsh morning light. A pang of guilt touched Amber. "Please don't feel you are to blame. It was something I wanted, else I would never have come to you when he asked for my help." She walked to Grace and hugged her. "I do not regret loving him, you know. Even if it could not last, he did love Gaby and even Fantasia just a little bit. At least I have learned what love is."

Grace looked into Amber's eyes as her own filled with tears. "Jenette is certain that he will come about. If he loves you half as much as you do him . . ."

Amber shook her head. "You know 'tis impossible. Even if I were not the notorious Lady Fantasia, I am still a married woman."

"That will be remedied shortly," Jenette said from the doorway. She was dressed in a vibrant rose traveling suit

trimmed with snowy white lace. "La Comtesse de St. Emilion is expected in Northumberland Thursday next. The
Marquess of Eastham will be dead within a fortnight."

"No, Jeni, I beg you, do not do this! They will kill you and
you will die horribly—then how could I live knowing I was
the cause of it?" Amber rushed over to her friend and hugged
her. "Please, you—"

"She will do as you would if your positions were reversed,"
Grace said firmly.

"*Ma petite*, have you no faith in me after all I have survived?" Jenette asked in a scolding tone. She took Amber by
the shoulders and held her at arm's length, then cocked her
head and smiled. "I shall eat nothing from his kitchen and
watch Mrs. Greevy as if she were Foche himself. Never fear.
Now, wish me *bonne chance*," she said, bussing Amber lightly
on both cheeks.

"Everything has been arranged," Grace explained to Amber. "A large house rented, servants hired from the village,
and half a dozen French émigré soldiers are accompanying
her, in addition to two of our most loyal veterans. She will be
safe."

"Think of this as ridding the world of a monster and
also keeping his poor son from following his father's evil
ways," Jenette said. "Now, you will see that she does not
languish until I return," she instructed Grace, bussing her
cheeks in farewell. Before she headed for the door, she said
to Amber, "Then we shall discover how to bring your earl
back, *oui?*"

Each day when he entered Lords, Rob could not stop himself
from scanning the gallery seats for a woman in black. He
found it difficult to concentrate during debates, missing op-
portunities to challenge his opponents' inconsistencies in
logic and legal precedent. His colleagues in both houses of

Parliament commented upon it and speculated as to why the earl appeared so preoccupied.

Some laid the fault with Baroness Oberly, whose pursuit of him had tongues wagging across the ton. Too polite to bluntly dismiss the lady, he performed the minimal courtesies at social gatherings where she contrived to accidentally meet him, which was sufficient fuel for many discussions over scandal broth.

Others were certain the problem was political in nature. The Tories insisted that he had grown disenchanted with radical causes and broken with the reformers over increasing Luddite violence in the countryside.

No one had the slightest idea that he was in love with a courtesan. From her daughter's house in the country, Abigail read the London newspapers with increasing dismay and continued writing admonitions to her son regarding Amber. When she received evasive replies, she resolved to give him a serious set-down as soon as the session of Parliament ended and he returned home.

Since Jenette's departure for Northumberland, Grace insisted that Amber keep busy lest she lose her mind worrying about her friend. When her duties running the House of Dreams allowed, she took to visiting the Woodbridge School, something Grace strongly encouraged. Sharing the innocent joy of children was healing, even if no one but Rob St. John could completely mend her broken heart.

Early on a warm, sunny Monday morning, Grace, their cook, two kitchen helpers, and Bonnie set out to do the weekly marketing, intending to have luncheon in a nearby alehouse. Grace tried to cajole Amber into joining the outing, but she declined, saying that she needed to spend the day taking care of bookkeeping. After they departed, she summoned Sergeant Major Boxer and convinced him that she would be perfectly safe at home while he visited his niece who had just given birth to a son named Waldo in his honor. He agreed only upon her pledge to remain indoors until he returned.

An hour later Amber was engrossed in her ledgers when a commotion downstairs interrupted her concentration. Setting aside her pen, she pulled a scarf across her face and walked to the head of the stairs. A gentleman of middle years dressed in a good but dusty suit argued with two of her footmen. The one assigned to guard the front gate had allowed the disheveled gentleman to approach the entry. The door stood ajar with her two employees blocking his entrance.

"I tell you, the older woman in the accident kept repeating this direction! Mrs. Winston was obviously a lady of breeding. No gentleman would refuse to aid her, especially in such dire circumstances. She could barely speak—"

Amber rushed down the stairs and shoved the guards aside. "What happened to Mrs. Winston and the others?" she demanded.

"It was a terrible smash with a dray about a mile down Alpha Road," he said, bowing politely to the lady in the blue morning dress. "My coach and driver were involved also, but we were spared injury. Another older domestic and several young maids were also hurt, one with red hair is most probably dead. I could not be certain . . ." His voice faded as he mopped his forehead, shoving back thinning gray hair that stuck up in unruly tufts. His eyes were wide with horror and he was trembling.

"Has help been summoned?" Amber asked, resisting the urge to shake the panicked man.

"Yes, another gentleman on horseback has gone to fetch a leech and notify the authorities. I thought it best to come here."

"Is your coach undamaged?" she asked. When he nodded,

she said, "Please rest in the sitting room for a few moments while I prepare. Clifton, bring Mr.——" She stopped and looked at the messenger.

"Samuel Abercrombie, at your service, m'lady," he replied with another bow.

"Bring Mr. Abercrombie a glass of cool water while he waits. I shall be back very shortly." Clifton showed the guest into a nearby sitting room. As soon as they were out of ear-shot, she said to Jonathan, "Fetch horses for yourself and Clifton. I'll require your assistance with the injured."

She raced up the stairs and called out to Lorna, "Come with me!" Lorna hurriedly followed her into Grace's quarters. Amber snatched a pen and a sheet of stationery from the escritoire and scrawled a street address. "Send word immediately to Mr. Boxer at this direction. There's been a terrible carriage accident and he's to return at once!" She shoved the paper into Lorna's trembling hands.

As soon as the young woman rushed off to summon a boy to deliver the message, Amber gathered bandages, ointments, and other medical supplies from Grace's cabinet, all the while praying that Mr. Abercrombie had been wrong about Bonnie. Already heartbroken over Rob and frantic with worry over Jeni, she simply could not lose another person she loved. Not her faithful young maid and not Grace. *Please, God, not either of them!*

As an afterthought, she seized her LePage pistol and shoved it in a reticule before heading back downstairs. When she gathered up Mr. Abercrombie and Clifton, the three of them headed out the front door. Jonathan rode up with a second mount for his companion. Under their watchful eyes, Abercrombie's driver assisted her into the open carriage and the five of them rode pell-mell down Alpha Road.

Two hours later Sergeant Major Boxer whipped his horse up Alpha Road. When he saw no signs of a carriage accident, he became alarmed. By the time he reached the house, a frantic Grace was waiting at the front door, chalk-faced, wringing her hands. "Where is Lady Fantasia?" he asked, knowing the news would not be good.

"In the hands of the devil! Jonathan returned with a pistol ball in his shoulder. Clifton is dead. Amber was taken in by a charlatan who convinced her we'd been in a carriage accident. She and the men rushed into a trap. They were met by half a dozen armed ruffians. The charlatan just sat back while his driver disarmed Amber. At the same time, Clifton and Jonathan were shot."

"You know for certain who did it?" Boxer asked grimly.

"Jonathan was left for dead and only regained consciousness as they rode away, but he heard one name—Hull!"

Boxer's ruddy face turned gray. "Have you sent for him?"

Rob stood in his office with the message crumpled in one fist. Stunned, he smoothed out the heavy velum and reread the spidery writing, obviously scrawled in terrified haste:

M'lord,
  Amber has been kidnapped. When her captors deliver her to Wolf's Gate in Northumberland, she will die a slow and horrible death at the hands of the Marquess of Eastham, her husband.
G

Some pieces of the puzzle that was Lady Fantasia now fell into place. She was the wife of that brutal old bastard Wolverton! Small wonder she had run away and now hid her face. Stuffing the missive into his pocket, he yelled for Settles. "Send for Sergeant Coulter and his men at once! Tell them to prepare for a long, hard ride and arm for a fight."

"I shall lay out riding clothes as soon as I have done, m'lord," the butler said, scurrying from the room.

The earl moved quickly to the cabinet where he kept his weapons. They would require all the firepower they could muster to rescue Amber from the legendary lair of a former member of the Hellfire Club!

Within the hour Rob and Coulter, along with six former dragoons from his old command, rode furiously down Alpha Road. He told the men only that one of the ladies who had helped them rescue the children had been kidnapped by the "Mad Marquess," and would die if they did not reach her in time. No one questioned him.

When they reached Grace's place, he had the men follow him upstairs. The moment he strode into the room, he could see from Grace's and Boxer's haggard faces that the situation was dire. She gave them a quick outline of the abduction and the sergeant major explained Hull's destination, speculating that only a driver and possibly one guard might accompany him. Then Grace asked the earl to follow her into her office so they could speak privately for a moment.

As soon as they were alone, she said, "There is one thing you must know. Since Amber fled Wolverton, no man has touched her—until you." Before he could frame a reply to the terse statement, she went on to describe Jenette's mission and where they could find her when they reached their destination.

"I always suspected she was more than a lady's companion," Rob replied, trying to absorb everything.

"She is a lady, the sole survivor of a noble family who died at the hands of Napoleon. She eluded Foche's secret police and worked as a spy for His Majesty's government during the war. Now, let us rejoin the others."

"We will save her," Rob said as he opened the door for her.

Grace placed her hand on his arm and said softly, "Thank you, m'lord."

Rob swallowed hard, trusting himself only to nod as they rejoined the anxious group of veterans.

Boxer, looking grim-faced and armed to the teeth, nodded to the earl, then exchanged a quick glance of understanding with Grace. Both were relieved that the earl had come and brought seasoned campaigners with him. They would require all the help they could muster. "We have to ride fast, m'lord. I've picked the best mounts from our stables, an extra for each man."

"I've done the same with a few more to spare," Rob replied as Boxer nodded his approval. "Have you a map of the countryside between here and Northumberland?"

"Yes," Grace replied, standing over Amber's big desk where she unrolled a large piece of paper. Rob, Boxer, and the rest of the men crowded around to study the map. "Amber marked the route to show Jenette before her first journey. She did not require it for the second trip."

"A good spy always possesses an excellent memory," Rob said as he traced the carriage route. "They will keep her concealed in a carriage until they reach . . ." He looked down at the map, then pointed to a less populated area disturbingly close to Eastham's lair. "Until here, they will travel fastest by remaining on the coaching roads."

"Can you stop them before they reach Wolf's Gate?" Grace asked hoarsely.

Rob studied the location of the small village Amber had circled in Northumberland, only a few miles from Eastham's fortress. "I dislike our chances since they are well over four hours ahead of us at the least. We would be wise to devise a plan to infiltrate his castle."

"Here is Jenette's direction. 'Tis on a hill midway between the village and Wolf's Gate. You cannot miss it," Grace said, offering him a sheet of paper with the rental information on it. "She is familiar with that devil's ghastly den."

Rob accepted the paper and slipped it inside his shirt. "Good. She will be a formidable ally," he said as he handed the map to Coulter.

As he led the men down the stairs and out the door, Grace clasped her hands and did something she had not done since her youth. She prayed.

Amber returned to consciousness slowly, the pounding in her head echoed by the pounding of horses' hooves as they thundered down the road. The conveyance she was in rocked with every bump and turn, tossing her like a rag doll. She blinked and saw that she was in semidarkness. It was only when she tried to reach for the curtain to let in more light that she realized her hands and feet were bound.

"Ah, I see that you are returning to the living. For a bit there I feared the stupid driver had permanently damaged you and deprived me of a hefty reward for the return of Eastham's runaway wife."

Everything began to come back to her as sharp shards of pain lanced through her brain. She recognized the nasal voice and northern accent of Edgar Hull even before she could make out his form seated across from her in the dim light. "You ever were a stupid, greedy little weasel, Edgar. Eastham will not pay you. He will kill you," she said, raising her hands to rub the knot on the side of her head.

"I think not," he purred, "but he *will* kill you . . . after he has a bit of fun. I extracted a promise from him that I be allowed to watch." Edgar Hull slouched in his seat, holding on to a coach strap to keep from being pummeled side to side in the small, lightweight carriage he had secured for a fast trip north. Amber tumbled right, left, forward, and back, bracing her legs so as not to fall into her dissipated captor's arms.

"Mr. Abercrombie was quite convincing," she said, trying

not to dwell on what lay in wait for her when she was delivered into the hands of Wolverton.

Hull gave an ugly laugh. "That 'kindly gentleman' was an actor from Drury Lane, paid enough for a good drunk. Cressy promised to see that he never sobers up to repeat what he witnessed."

"Cressy?" she echoed.

"A runner in my employ," he said smugly.

"You mean Wolverton's employ, do you not? You apparently do not have enough of the ready to pay for a jacket that conceals your increasing girth." She stared at his ill-fitting clothing with disdain.

"I was smart enough to bait the perfect trap for you," he snapped. "Once your female companion disappeared and that interfering earl stopped his visits, that left only the old soldier. All I needed to do was wait until he left you unguarded and make up a tale about the old bawd and her servants being in a carriage wreck. I knew you would come rushing out," he boasted. In fact, it had been Cresswel's plan, but Hull would never admit it.

What a fool she had been! Half a dozen armed ruffians had burst onto the deserted road from a stand of trees only a short distance from the house and shot both of her men. Poor Clifton and Jonathan had died because of her reckless actions! Before she could reach the pistol in her reticule to aid them, the driver had turned around and struck her on the head. After that . . . her reticule! The pistol! Trying not to move suspiciously, Amber rubbed her head again, looking down. Had Hull found it, or was it still at her waist?

"If you're hoping I overlooked that nasty little firearm in here," he said, holding up her reticule with a sneer, "you hope in vain." He had anticipated her carrying a good bit of extra blunt in it but was furious to find nothing more than the weapon.

"At least I shall have the satisfaction of seeing you die before I do," she said to Hull.

He tsked at her. "Such venom. 'Tis I who have every right to wish you dead. I offered to marry you—"

"Even if I had been so foolish as to agree, my father would never have allowed me to wed a drunken sot such as you, turned out by your family for your wastrel ways."

"There would have been no way to prevent his giving me a dowry for you once we'd eloped," he replied angrily. "But no, you had to have your season, to look for some fancy toff in London! Well, I took care of that."

"Yes, but I was sold to a man willing to pay for me, not given to one hip deep in dun territory," she replied, curling her lip in contempt.

He raised his hand preparing to slap her, then lowered it. The marquess had been most explicit about having his "merchandise" delivered undamaged. The blow to her head was necessary, but he dared risk no further marks. Damn, he wanted her to pay for ruining his youthful schemes.

Amber had hoped she could bait him sufficiently so as to be able to wrest the reticule with her pistol from him in the pitching coach, but when he did not strike her, she could see that he had grown cunning over the years. Then he pulled a flask from his jacket pocket and took a swig. He always had been a drunk. Better to wait until his tongue loosened. Perhaps she could learn how many others were with him. With Hull out of the way, they might accept a bribe to release her.

She held fast to that thought. Grace would pay a fortune to have her returned safely. And that would keep Jeni from placing herself in danger if she learned Amber had been taken prisoner. At all costs, she had to keep Jeni from doing something rash!

But first, she must dispose of this evil worm who had plotted her downfall for the past decade. How ironic that he never understood the truth about her relationship with her family. She pushed the ugly memories from her mind.

Unbidden, an image of Rob came to her. Would Grace send word to him? Would he come? A part of her hoped he would, but she quickly squelched the thought. That would mean he, too, would be in terrible danger. She must outwit Hull once more. She had accomplished it as a green girl—how much easier should it be for her now?

But he was the one who led you to ruin and Eastham! No! The only way to remain sane was not to dwell on Lytton Wolverton.

Rob and the men sat around a small fire, resting their horses after the moon set that night. All were exhausted from the hard day's ride. He calculated it would take another even longer one before they reached their destination. That meant they would only stop for an hour at a time, taking turns napping and eating cold biscuits and bacon from their packs.

"Rather like bein' back in Spain, ain't it, sir?" O'Keefe asked his captain between bites from the tough bread.

As he nodded agreement, Rob could see there was no relish in the Irishman's remark. Every man here admired the lady who had been so kind to the children and clubbed Molly Chub over the head. He remembered Grace's piercing eyes when she told him Amber had been with no man but him since fleeing Eastham. Did he believe her? Damned if he knew. Damned if he cared.

He was certain of only one thing. He loved Amber Leighigh.

There was no doubt of it from the moment he read Grace's terrifying message. No matter what her past sins might or might not be, he was in love with Wolverton's wife. But she would truly be a widow once he got his hands on that madman and wrung the life from him. As Boxer kicked out the fire and they prepared to mount up, Rob bowed his head and did something he had not done since leaving England for the Peninsula.

He prayed.

Northumberland

By the time they reached the small village in the bleak, isolated hills, the small troop had ridden for nearly forty hours. They had taken only brief stops to rest and switch out their mounts, eat, and relieve themselves. Rob knew Amber's captors would have been forced to do the same.

But scouting ahead, Boxer had reported back that they had money enough to pay for fresh horses at the public coaching stations along their way. Several of the hostlers remembered a small carriage with the curtains tightly closed in spite of yesterday's inclement heat. The driver had been impatient and rude, cursing the stablemen for not moving fast enough. As nearly as they could tell, there had been no other riders accompanying the carriage. Hull had to be inside with Amber, keeping her quiet. Was he alone? There was no way to know.

If only they had been able to overtake the carriage . . . but it had proven impossible. Rob had driven his men hard, but it had been Sergeant Major Boxer who reminded him that they could do the lady no good if they rode their horses to death and were left stranded in the wilds of the north.

Rob reined in his winded black on the crest of a hill and peered into the darkness below, trying to fix his bearings now that the moon had set. "Lady Jenette's stone manor house should be just over that ridge," he said, pointing to the east.

"She be a game one, even if she is a Frenchie," his sergeant said with admiration.

"We need to reach her before the villagers start to stir."

"No one down there will lift a hand to help Wolverton. They'll dance in the streets when he's dead," Boxer said.

Rob grunted, then gave the signal for the rest to follow him.

Amber shivered in the cold darkness of Wolverton's cellar. She wore only the light cotton day dress she'd had on when she rushed to the supposed carriage wreck. In this dank lower level behind thick stone walls, the temperature better suited storing wines than accommodating people. But she was certain that was why the marquess had her brought here. To tremble in terror while she awaited his appearance.

Well, it was an effective ploy, she admitted. Hull had delivered her in the dark of night. This far belowstairs, she had no idea if the sun had arisen or how long she had waited. One dim torch flickered on the other side of a crack at the bottom of the locked door.

During the journey, the coach had been stifling with the curtains drawn and the sun beating down upon them. Each time they reached a coaching station, Hull had used her own pistol to guarantee her silence, a conceit he found amusing, although she knew he had another gun inside his jacket. To her dismay, he remained sober enough to foil any plan of escape. His hate was palpable in the confines of the coach and only grew with the passing of each hour.

When they finally reached the castle—she had always thought of the huge stone monolith as a medieval castle, never a manor house—Hull and the driver had awakened a terrified servant to summon the marquess. Rather than come to see his prize, he had ordered Hull and the servant to drag her down to this dungeon to await her fate. She could still hear the echo of Edgar Hull's vile laughter as he walked away.

She had searched the dark room, groping blindly, praying to find something she could use as a weapon before Wolverton arrived, but found not so much as a stool to sit upon. She could hear the evil rustling of rats in the distance, but they did not come near.

This is worse than the prison in Paris. The thought brought Jeni to mind. Amber prayed her friend would not attempt another rescue by herself. If Grace sent the sergeant major and the other men, perhaps there was hope. She would do her best to survive in the meanwhile. *Best to conserve my energy for now.*

She sank down against the wall next to the door and laid her head on her bent knees. Sleep claimed her immediately, but she had only drifted off when the clank of keys in the rusty lock awakened her. Amber stood up quickly, smoothing her now damp, filthy clothing. The marquess strode into the cramped room. A servant held a torch behind him to light his way.

Outlined in the flickering light, he looked like Lucifer himself, tall and rawboned with powerful shoulders and a horseman's muscular legs. But his face had aged. Lines made vertical creases above his eyebrows. Always heavy, they had grown together into one thick downturned curve shadowing winter-gray eyes. Those eyes had sunken deeply into their sockets. His mouth was a thin angry slash, now split into a chilling smile.

He still has all his teeth. She forced her chin up and returned his malevolent stare. Without a word he moved forward and gave her a hard backhanded slap.

Amber stumbled against the wall. Quickly righting herself, she wiped the blood trickling from her lip and said as coolly as possible, "So good to see you again, too, Lytton. 'Tis comforting to know the years have not changed you."

The grooves on his high forehead deepened in a furious scowl. "They certainly have changed you, slut. You were my marchioness. Now you're a common bawd."

"A position much to be preferred," she snapped back,

knowing she was goading him. But he fed on fear. She vowed never to give him the satisfaction of showing it.

"In the months you lived here," he went on in a silky voice, ignoring her insult, "you never had occasion to see the only functioning dungeon left in all of England. Now I shall give you an opportunity to observe how well it works . . . firsthand."

Chapter Twenty

$\mathcal{H}$e motioned to the guard, a skinny fellow with greasy yellow hair and eyes the color of mud. The vile-smelling fellow grabbed hold of her arm, bruising the soft flesh as he dragged her behind the marquess. She bit back a cry of pain and struggled to keep her footing. *He will not see me crawl!*

The room was as hellish as any description from Dante's *Inferno,* filled with ancient torture devices of unimaginable horror. Did the iron implements owe their rusty color to the blood of those who suffered in this evil place? Torches hung from the walls, their flickering light dancing on the cobwebbed wooden rafters and straw-strewn floor.

"Inventive people, my ancestors," he growled softly.

"Your ancestors still lived in wattle huts and painted their bodies blue when the Norman invaders built this fortress," she said scornfully, earning another slap.

"We will see how brave you are after you spend a few hours inside this lady." He gestured to an upstanding metal box in the shape of a man. Its front lay open, revealing sharp teeth protruding all around the interior. "Place her in it," he instructed the servant, whose eyes took on an eerie yellow cast as he dragged her to the hideous device.

"You're too small and thin for it to do much damage, but after a few hours holding yourself rigidly erect to keep from falling against the rusty spikes . . ." He let his voice trail away. Amber kicked and pummeled the man holding her until Wolverton seized her other arm and pushed her against the now dull spikes. "Struggle more and you will sustain serious

injury," he cautioned, his voice silky with relish as he closed
the front of the device and locked it.

She heard the echo of footsteps as the marquess and his
toady walked out of the chamber. Thank heaven he was
right in assuming the device was too large to impale her. But
she could feel the icy press of metal spines around her head
and torso, even her legs. She dared not move an inch. *If I fall
asleep . . . No, don't think of that!*

Jenette's face was a hard mask. She paced back and forth in
the manor's kitchen where she had taken Rob and his men
to study the drawing she had made of the marquess's for-
tresslike house and grounds.

"Most useful," Rob said as he tapped the map.

"Do you know why I am here?" she asked. When he nodded, she said, "*Bien.* This will provide the perfect opportunity to finish it."

"First we find Amber," Rob said flatly.

"Amber is the reason that I will not act rashly, *mon capitaine*, no matter how much I long to see that *batard* dead."

He would have to rely on her experience, which according to Grace and Boxer was considerable. "Do you know
where the sentries are?"

"*Certainement.*" She indicated their locations on her drawing. "They are mercenaries, hired killers who are very dangerous. This man is so hated he must pay for loyalty."

"Once that mad marquess is dead, they won't fight," Boxer
said tightly.

"*Oui.* But we must get past them to reach the *batard.* That
means we quietly eliminate them . . ." She paused to see if
the earl would object to the obvious meaning of "quietly
eliminate." When he did not, she continued. "We enter
here. My servants have heard rumors about a torture chamber in the bowels of that hellish place." Her finger trembled
the slightest bit as she pointed to the stairs to the wine cel-

lar. "After that, I do not know what catacombs lie below, but I am certain that is where he would take her."

Rob studied the twists and turns of the back hallways leading to the wine cellar door, then turned to Boxer and Coulter. "After we're inside, Sergeant Major, you and your men secure this area. Coulter, here and here." He pointed to various spots on the map. Both men nodded. "If at all possible, deal silently with anyone you encounter. Lady Jenette and her men will come with me."

"After you have Amber, I deal with Wolverton," Jenette said.

"If he's harmed her, you will not have the opportunity, mademoiselle," Rob replied.

Jenette and her men led the others toward the stone manor that loomed evilly on the horizon. As they dismounted, O'Keefe gave a shiver and whispered to Sergeant Coulter, "Sure 'n it looks like the very entrance to hell itself."

Silently, Rob motioned for the men to move into position, scattering around the barren grounds, using the cover of trees and rocks as they stalked their prey. They had done a good deal of night work behind enemy lines during the war. Slipping up on the guards proved easier than Rob had anticipated. The lethal Frenchwoman, dressed in black shirt and boys' breeches, dispatched one herself. She was a tall woman, but the guard topped her by half a foot.

They slipped in the back of the still-dark manor that had been built centuries ago to replace the original keep. It was like entering the maws of hell, the only light furnished by flickering flames in the kitchen fireplace. The cold gray walls dripped with moisture, and a musty smell of old evil seemed to leach out of every stone in the cavernous room. A twisting labyrinth of hallways filtered out in every direction. Without Jenette's drawing, they would have wasted precious time. They dispersed silently to deal with the guards who would be arising shortly to take their turn at sentry duty.

Jenette led Rob and two of her men to the cellar door. Just as she touched the knob, the sounds of a scuffle came from the servants' quarters. "*Merde*, that will alert the others," she whispered. "*Se presser*—hurry!"

Rob could see the dim flicker of torchlight at the bottom of the steep stone steps. "See if they need help. I'll find Amber."

Elvira Greevy lay in her bed, staring morosely at the ceiling, unable to sleep. She had heard the carriage pull into the courtyard in the dark of night and watched as Hull dragged that harlot into *her* house. But when she had come down, the master had ordered her to return to her quarters. Seething with frustration, she had obeyed.

She bolted upright on the bed when a loud thump and the sounds of scuffling echoed from downstairs. Throwing back the covers, she seized her robe and secured it, then took a small poison-tipped dagger from her armoire and placed it in her pocket. It would kill within seconds after only a good scratch. She picked up the lit candle from her bedside and tiptoed to the door, peering down the darkened hallway. No one was in sight. She crept down the steps to see if the master was in danger.

In the dungeon below, Amber could hear soft footfalls. Wolverton? Hull or the yellow-haired man? No, they had no reason to be quiet. Daring to hope, she cried out, "Here! Please help me!" Her chin scraped one of the spikes when she opened her mouth. Gritting her teeth, she tried again. "I'm in here!"

"Amber! I'm coming, love," Rob replied with his heart leaping in his chest. He ran toward the light at the end of the long passageway.

"Rob!" Her voice shook with emotion. No, she must be dreaming. He had called her his love! In seconds the clasp rattled and she blinked when Rob raised the door. "You are not a dream," she said hoarsely.

He saw the horrible spikes and froze for an instant. "Don't move!" he commanded as he reached inside to lift her out. The moment she was free, she flung her arms around his neck. He held her tightly and pressed her to his heart. "My love, my love, what a fool I've been," he murmured, raining kisses across her face.

"I never dared hope—I thought I would never see you again," she said, kissing him back.

Sounds of gunfire and open fighting echoed down the stairs. "Do you know where Wolverton is?" he asked her, glancing around the huge chamber.

"He locked me in here and left," she replied.

Rob gritted his teeth, nodding. "I'll deal with him after you're safe," he said, taking her hand. "Stay behind me."

She followed as he led the way upstairs. All around them men fought with pistols, knives, fists, and sabers. As soon as Rob saw Jenette dispatch a brute twice her size with a lightning dagger thrust, he yelled to her, "Get Amber out of here!" He turned to his love. "Go with her."

"Rob—"

"For once, Lady Fantasia, follow my orders," he said. Giving her a swift kiss, he shoved her to Jenette.

The Frenchwoman tore an unfired pistol from the fist of a downed guard and handed it to Amber, then practically dragged her to the front entry, away from the fighting. The enormous foyer was encircled by a huge flight of stairs leading to the second floor. Seeing no one above them, she yanked open the massive door. "Come, *ma coeur*! We retrieve the horses for our escape."

Amber looked back at Rob, who had returned to the thick of the melee. Where was Wolverton? Impatiently, Jenette shoved her through the door, then ran toward a grove of trees where one of Jenette's men had been left standing guard. "Francois, untie them quickly and bring them to the back door. Wait there. At the first sign of danger, leave the other horses and take her away from this place as swiftly as you can."

"No, Jeni, I will not leave without you and Rob!"

Jenette took hold of her shoulders and stared levelly into her eyes. "I have sworn to Grace that you will live. So will your earl. Now do as you are told so we may do what we must, *comprenez-vous?*"

"Yes, I understand," Amber replied. "Go, but watch for Hull. As far as I know, he's still inside."

Jenette curled her lip in disgust. "That one is nothing," she said, giving Amber an appraising look. It would be a waste of time to argue further. Best to kill Eastham and be gone. She gave Amber a quick kiss on each cheek, then raced back to the manor.

As Amber and Francois began unfastening reins, a twig snapped behind the Frenchman. She saw a dim figure raise a pistol. "No!" she yelled, lunging forward to shove Francois aside, but was too late. The shot struck him in the back and he pitched forward.

"Well, you are a clever little bitch," Edgar Hull said with a nasty chuckle. He tossed away the spent pistol and pulled a second one from his jacket. "You really should have married me when you had the chance, m'dear." He patted the fat bulge in his coat pocket. "Now I no longer need your dowry since I've taken a fortune from the marquess's library. Pity I shall have to kill you," he said, raising the weapon.

A shot rang out. "No pity at all," she said coldly. Dropping the pistol Jeni had given her, she turned to calm the frightened horses and seize the reins of those loosed already. As soon as she secured them, she knelt to see if Francois was still alive. Feeling no pulse, she took his unfired weapon and mounted one of the calmer horses, leading the others toward the manor.

The fighting must be fierce. *Please let Rob and Jeni and all the others be safe!* She confined the horses in the small paddock at the back of the servants' quarters, then ran inside the kitchen. Old memories clawed at her, filling her with terror, but she forced them aside. Steeling herself, she slipped down the hall.

From the shadows, Elvira Greevy lunged out and knocked the pistol from her hand with one bony fist. "Now I will deal with you," she whispered, holding out a deadly-looking knife. "One tiny prick . . ." Her eyes glowed with insane glee.

Amber was certain the blade was poisoned. She backed into the kitchen. "I never harmed you, Mrs. Greevy," she said soothingly, glancing around for anything to block the knife.

"He married you and you ran away to become a whore, you ungrateful little bitch! He took you to his bed, just as he did that next mewling little breeding sow. At least she gave him a son." She sneered. "The master needed an heir, but I convinced him to send the boy to his milk-and-water brother in Newcastle."

"All the better for the child, to escape this hellish place once his poor mother died bearing him," Amber said, glancing around the room.

Elvira laughed. "She did not die in childbirth. I killed her as soon as she fulfilled her obligation to my master! Just as I'll kill you and that Frenchie whore."

"I do not think we are so easy to kill, *oui?*" Jenette said sharply.

Elvira whirled around, the blade flashing toward her new antagonist.

"It's poisoned, Jeni!" Amber cried, reaching for a heavy wooden bowl on the kitchen table behind her. She raised it, but before she could strike the housekeeper, Jenette seized hold of the older woman's wrist and twisted viciously with one hand while she drew her own blade across Elvira's throat.

For a moment suspended in time, the two women glared at each other. Then the glow of madness in the narrow gray eyes faded as the deadly weapon slipped from her fingers. She dropped to the floor, gurgling her last breath.

"I feared you would not wait outside," Jenette said as Amber stepped into the hallway and retrieved the pistol.

"Hull killed Francois. I killed Hull," she said succinctly. "I'm going to find Rob."

Sighing, Jenette followed, muttering in French about idiots in love.

Furiously, Rob fought his way from room to room, searching for the vicious brute who had placed Amber in an iron maiden! This monster could hold her here, and there was no court in all of England that would stop him. She had spent ten years of her life in hiding, surrounded by guards, and still the bastard managed to have her kidnapped.

Rob entered the massive library. It had been ransacked, books pulled from their cases, desk drawers smashed open. But Eastham did not cower in the last hiding place on this floor. If he had gathered up some hidden cache of money to flee, surely he would have known where it was kept. No, someone else had done this mayhem. The earl ran into the front entry and looked up the wide stone stairway twisting in a semicircle to the second floor.

Taking no time to reload the spent pistols in his sash, he started to climb, clutching his saber in his fist. He reached the top and stared down the cavernous hall, ready to kick in every door until he found the craven animal. Like the main hall below it, this one also looked like a medieval armory, lined with antique suits of chain mail, lances, pikes, and battle-axes.

"Eastham, you cowardly bastard, do you hide under a bed now that you must fight a man instead of torture a woman?" he roared, kicking open the first door to a dark room with gargoyles carved on the huge four-poster bed. Ripping the heavy velvet draperies apart, he stepped back. Light poured in. He tried not to think of Amber as a young bride raped and brutalized on that ugly bed.

A door adjoining the next room stood ajar. After satisfying himself that the marquess was not hiding in the master suite, he entered the large dressing closet. Rob threw open trunks and overturned clotheshorses draped with velvet and ermine robes. Just as he turned to leave, he caught a flicker of movement at the edge of his vision—a large man stood in the doorway, raising a pistol.

"Your men have kept me from reaching your whore, but I have laid a trap for her whoremaster," the madman purred. He squeezed the trigger just as Rob ducked.

The earl felt the burn of the bullet as it cut through his jacket and nicked the top of his shoulder. Wolverton threw the pistol at him but missed, then spun around with startling swiftness and slipped through the door to the hallway. Rob gave chase.

"There's nowhere to run, Wolverton. Stand and fight," he yelled as the marquess made for the stairs. Then he saw what his enemy was after—one of a pair of crossed battle-axes mounted on the wall. Eastham was as tall as Rob but heavier with a massive frame that still held considerable muscle on it. He reached the axe and ripped it from the pegs holding it in place, then turned with a feral grin, eyeing Rob's saber, a flimsy defense against his new weapon.

"You and your whore will die today," he snarled.

"You will die today, like the vicious cur you are," Rob said, raising his blade, bracing for the marquess's swing. The air hissed when the gleaming edge of the axe missed his head by inches as he danced back.

"I keep these weapons in perfect condition," Wolverton said, swinging again, this time forcing Rob to use his blade to parry the blow. The saber snapped in two pieces, but Rob held on to it as the marquess grinned like the madman he was and raised the cumbersome weapon once more. The earl lunged beneath Eastham's upraised arms and rammed his shoulder into the marquess's stomach, knocking him back against the wall.

Jenette crested the stairs with Amber just behind her. Amber started to aim her pistol, but her friend quickly shoved it aside. "*Non*, you might hit the earl."

Amber could see it was true. The two men spun around, each gripping the weapon hand of the other. Wolverton's heavy axe fell from his grasp when Rob slammed his foe's arm against the stone wall, but his own broken blade, still a lethal weapon, remained immobilized. The marquess's huge hand encircled Rob's wrist so tightly that his arm started to go numb. The earl twisted with all of his strength and wrenched free but dropped the saber in the process.

Without hesitation the two men dived at each other with fists. Eastham was heavier but Rob was lean and fast. He delivered several swift punches to his enemy's beefy face and took a vicious blow to his stomach that sent him staggering backward toward the heavy stone railing overlooking the foyer below. Jenette tried for a shot, but the bellowing marquess was immediately upon the earl in a blur. With his hands grasping Rob's throat, they rolled along the railing.

The earl punched the bigger man in the chest, the stomach, the ribs. Coughing, Eastham finally loosened his grip. Rob twisted around and head-butted his foe in the face. The women could hear the satisfying crunch when Wolverton's nose broke, but still neither man released the other. They grabbed for purchase with their hands, ripping apart clothing, striking with fists and elbows.

"Your earl, he fights like *un sauvage*," Jenette said with admiration, watching the contest as the men battered each other. Barrington had speed on his side while Eastham had brute strength. They were evenly matched.

Amber felt her hand tremble and gritted her teeth to steady her grip on the pistol. She might only have one chance before that madman killed Rob! After a hard, fast punch from Rob's fist sent him back near the railing once more, Wolverton aimed a vicious kick at the earl's groin. Twisting away at the last second, Rob grabbed the marquess's raised leg and shoved him backward. Eastham hit the railing hard. The groan of ancient mortar giving way quickly turned to the screech of sliding stones.

Feeling the railing crumple at his back, Wolverton seized hold of Rob's torn jacket, trying to pull his enemy down with him. Amber steadied her arm to fire at the marquess's arm, but his weight did the work without her. Rob's jacket lapel ripped off as the earl stepped backward. Eastham fell in an avalanche of rock and mortar, screaming until he hit the stone floor fifty feet below.

Jenette peered down at the big man's grotesquely twisted body lying half buried under a pile of masonry and murmured, "Hell has waited long enough to claim its own."

Amber dropped her pistol and flew into Rob's arms. He picked her up and swung her around, well back from the ugly scene. From below in typical sergeant-major fashion, Boxer barked orders to his men to stand back after he saw Jenette calmly walking down the stairs with an unfired pistol in her hand. "Tell what is left of this carrion's men that they will not be paid, even if they fight to the death," she said to him.

"Consider it done, m'lady," he said with a satisfied grin.

As their footsteps faded, Rob and Amber stared at each other. "I beg your forgiveness for the way I behaved. I hope you can give it one day," he said, caressing her face with his fingertips.

She took his hand in hers and kissed the bruised and bloodied knuckles. "There is nothing to forgive, m'lord. I deceived you and caused you great anguish. 'Tis I who should apologize."

"You have nothing to apologize for," he said, placing a kiss on her forehead as he cradled her head in his hand. "Now we must go." He led her down the long winding staircase.

As she descended, Amber realized that this was the last time she would ever set foot inside Wolf's Gate. When they reached the body of the marquess, she stopped and stared at the ruin. "I have lived with fear and guilt for so long," she murmured.

"You have nothing to fear any longer and never had any reason for guilt. He was a monster. You were right to flee him."

She looked up at him. "Did Grace tell you about him?"

Rob shook his head. "Only his name and that he was your husband. I once overheard my uncle Reginald and his friends discussing Eastham. He had been banished from polite society for such excesses that even the most hardened of the ton's rakes were appalled. The gossips called him the mad marquess."

She shivered in his arms as the old memories washed over her. "'Tis over at last. You have freed me."

"If not for the kidnapping, Jenette would have done that without my help," he said wryly. "I hope one day you will tell me about how the two of you met, but now we must leave before anyone from the village sees us. I doubt any will mourn Wolverton, but the death of a peer, even a degenerate such as this offal, will mean the local authorities must investigate."

As he led her down the hall and out the back entrance, he murmured low, "When we return to London, we must discuss the future."

She made no reply as they joined Jenette and the others. The group rode away from the hellish manor, taking a circuitous route, stopping to patch up those who had been wounded before rejoining the busy coach road.

* * *

We must discuss the future. Those words hung like a portent over Amber's head as she lay soaking in a tub of warm, oil-scented water in her quarters. Grace fussed over her even more than Bonnie, and all of those who worked for the House of Dreams were overjoyed that she had returned safely. She was grateful to be home. This was her home now, and there was no more need to hide behind stifling black veils. She should be overjoyed to have the shadow of East-ham removed forever.

But Rob's words troubled her. He had acted as if he hoped they could build some kind of future together. She could not allow him to jeopardize his career for her. Grace had agreed to his request for tea this afternoon without consulting her. She could not put off saying good-bye any longer, but this parting would be the most painful of all.

Now he knew who she was and still wanted to keep her in his life.

Amber climbed from the tub as Bonnie came in carrying a pile of bath linens and a robe. "I laid out two afternoon dresses so ye can choose, m'lady," she said with a shy smile as she wrapped a towel around her mistress's body.

Thanking her, Amber dried off and removed another towel from around her head, rubbing her long cherry hair vigorously as she strolled into her bedroom. She eyed the gowns and felt certain Grace and Jenette had made the se-lections, a brilliant peacock-blue silk and a rich golden mull. Both were of sheer fabrics and the necklines were cut low. Matching jewelry had been added as well, aquamarines to contrast with the deep blue and topazes to set off the gold . . . and match her eyes.

"It would serve the conspirators up properly if I were to dress in my widow's weeds," she muttered wryly. At last they were appropriate.

After short deliberation, she sighed and chose the gold.

Bonnie was back in a trice with a heated curling iron and pins for her partially dry hair. She suffered the ministrations, saying, "One would think I was a girl preparing for her first season the way you're fussing, Bonnie."

"Perhaps you are," Grace said from the doorway.

"Don't be absurd. I never had a season and am too long of tooth by far now."

"Barrington does not think you 'long of tooth' at all," Grace replied with a chuckle.

Amber turned and stared at her with narrowed eyes. "What has the earl said to you—and you to him?" she asked suspiciously.

"What was sufficient," the older woman replied serenely. "He awaits you in your office downstairs."

Rob paced back and forth in the room where they had first met on a dark, foggy night. Today brilliant sunlight poured in the bow window facing the elaborate gardens at the back of the rambling house. He had been nervous, indeed frightened, about what he was going to say then. Now he was not nervous. He was terrified. How could he convince her? What could he say? How ironic for the most skilled debater in Lords to be at a loss for words yet again. He tried to gather his wits. When she entered the room silently, he knew even though his back was to her.

Turning, he said, "Attar of rose. It suits you."

"I thought you preferred Gaby's lilac," she said nervously. She had hoped to study him for a moment before those brilliant green eyes swept over her.

He appeared to consider the merits of both perfumes, stroking his chin as he closed the distance between them. Amber remained near the door as if poised to flee. A soft smile curved his mouth. "Lilac is a soft and yielding essence, but the rose is bold and self-assured, the queen of flowers."

"I pretended to be both when I was neither."

He shook his head. "You are both, my love, and so much more to have survived Eastham and built a life here, helping others."

"A life as a courtesan," she said flatly, trying to remind him of who she was.

"Grace told me from the day you fled the marquess you allowed no man to touch you . . . until you came to me."

"Are you gloating, m'lord?" she asked, trying to goad him to anger.

Instead, he reached up and touched her chin, lifting it as he smiled sadly. "I am honored, m'lady," he said simply.

"I was your hired tutor for bed sport."

"Was that why you had a messenger send back the initial money I gave you and destroyed the bank draft I wrote the day we parted? No, Amber, you did not come to me for money. Any more than I continued seeing Gaby for crass physical gratification—although," he confessed wryly, "bed sport does provide unimaginable gratification . . . if two people are in love. I love you, Amber, and I believe you love me."

How could she deny her own heart? This was not working the way it should. She had to make him accept that they could not have a life together. "What either or both of us may feel is not to the point," she equivocated. "You are going to marry a noblewoman—"

"Correct! You are a marchioness, the daughter of a viscount," he countered. "I see no impediment to our marriage."

Amber felt her knees weaken and her heart start to pound. "Marriage! No impediment!" she cried out, shoving the door closed behind her as much to lean upon it as to keep anyone from overhearing. She had thought he wanted her to become his mistress. Never in her wildest imaginings had she thought that he would ask her to marry him!

Understanding softened his face as he took that final step toward her, leaving a scant inch between them. He inhaled her fragrance and felt his body respond as it always did.

"Amber, Amber, how could you believe that I would dishonor you by asking you to be my mistress?" he asked gently, bending to kiss her lips.

She quickly turned her head away, trying desperately to stiffen her resolve. "I could not bear sharing you, no—but that does not mean that I expected marriage," she hastily added.

"We are adults, both with terrible marriages behind us. We love each other. There is no reason we cannot wed. Only your trusted friends and servants know the identity of Fantasia. Eastham, Elvira Greevy, and Hull are dead. Clyde Dyer has even disposed of Alan Cresswel to avenge his cousin Clifton. No one alive will ever accuse you of being Lady Fantasia."

She shook her head, trying to clear it. With him standing so near, towering over her, she could not think. All she wanted to do was lay her head against his chest and wrap her arms around his neck. "B-but I'm dead!" she said. "Eastham buried some poor village girl in the Wolverton family plot with my name on the headstone. If I return as Amber Leighigh Wolverton, that will disinherit his poor son, not to mention creating a perfectly horrid scandal if you had a wife who fled her first husband and vanished mysteriously for over a decade. Your career in Lords—all the good you can do—would end. I cannot allow any of that to happen."

"I will not live without the woman I love as my wife," he persisted, framing her face with his hands. He kissed her, long, slowly, and thoroughly, waiting patiently as she had taught him for her to open her lips and admit his tongue. When she sobbed and did so, he gave a soft growl of triumph.

He deepened the kiss, pressing her against the door. Amber could not help kissing him back with all the pent-up fervor she had so long denied in her disguise as Fantasia. Her body melted against his. Every hard contour of it was so dearly familiar now, but when she felt his erection pressing against her belly, she broke away. "We must stop while we are still able!" she pleaded, pushing against his chest until he released her.

Breathing as if he had run a long race, Rob stepped back. "That is the first sensible thing you've said since you stepped in here. What we must do now is find a way to fashion you yet another identity."

"Impossible," she said, letting the anguish show through on her face, in her voice as she paced across the floor, placing distance between them.

"Perhaps I have the perfect solution," a thick French-accented voice purred. Jenette stepped inside the room with a cat-in-cream smile on her face.

Chapter Twenty-one

"Jeni, no!" Amber said. She disliked the devilish gleam in Jenette's eyes.

"Please come in, m'lady," Rob said, offering her a chair. He took Amber's hand and drew her to sit beside him on the sofa.

"Please forgive my eavesdropping, but for a moment, I did not feel it wise to interrupt," she said with a sly smile.

Amber blushed like a schoolgirl, but Rob asked, "What would you suggest?"

"That Amber assume *my* identity."

"Masquerade as a French émigré? I am English, born and bred," Amber protested incredulously. "My family—"

"Your father is dead, your mother a recluse, and your brother has fled to Scotland to escape his debts." Jenette shook her head and sighed, looking at the earl. "At times she has the wooden head." Ignoring Amber's snorted protest, she continued. "You have the ear—your French is perfect, *ma coeur*. My code name during the war was the Dark Angel, and the Englishman at Whitehall to whom I reported was called Charon."

Rob's eyebrows lifted. "Rather mixed theology, but I believe I understand where you're leading," he said with a grin.

"*Bien.*" Jenette nodded. "You will both go to France. I will accompany Amber, but you shall travel separately, m'lord. There, with my help, you will write to Charon, *ma petite*. Although he does not know mine, I have learned his name— Lord Hillsborough. In this letter you will inform him that you are Lady Collette Solange de Beaurivage, known to him as the Dark Angel."

"Your cousin, b-but she is dead," Amber said, horrified.

"*Oui*, she is," Jenette agreed sadly. "But no one here knows that. You will explain that you were sent to England for an education as a small child and remained until you were old enough to return home. When your family was killed by the Tyrant, you became an agent for the English."

"Surely this Hillsborough will know 'tis a hum."

"He is a man, *oui*? He knows only what I allow him to know."

Rob sat forward. "No one in England has ever seen the Dark Angel, have they?"

"*Non*. You, *ma petite*, with my help, will feed Hillsborough bits of information that only the Dark Angel could know . . . and he will eat it up like the greedy gosling. If ever anyone asks questions, Whitehall must admit that you are French nobility and a heroine of the war."

"I see your plan," Rob said, warming to the clever idea. "We shall marry in Paris and return home. I will call you Amber because of your beautiful golden eyes."

Amber felt those eyes welling up with tears. Could this impossible scheme work? "I want so desperately to agree. . . ."

"Then do! We are getting married," he said, clasping her hands in his.

"What of your mother? We cannot deceive her, Rob."

"I shall send for her to be present at the wedding in France. Of course, once we return, she will insist upon a proper Anglican ceremony," he said chuckling. "We will explain why you were forced to hide from Eastham until his death. As to where you hid . . . in time, we'll tell her that as well. She will accept it."

Amber sighed in relief, realizing that Abigail would indeed understand. "I would never lie to your mother . . . but would it be too awkward to have Grace present, too? She has been like a mother to me."

"We shall include everyone you wish, my love, Sir Burleigh, even the sergeant major," Rob replied.

"Then all is settled," Jenette said, rising. "Now I shall tell Bonnie to begin packing for a trip to Paris."

When she had closed the door, Rob turned to Amber and said, "The gossips will think it terribly romantic that an English earl married a mysterious French noblewoman while visiting Paris."

"We must wait until after this Hillsborough agrees that I am the Dark Angel before we dare marry, Rob. I will not burden you—"

He kissed her gently, shushing her. "Have you always been so dutiful and self-sacrificing, my love?"

"I have never thought of myself that way, merely as . . . a survivor. I must tell you about Amber Leighigh. Perhaps, once you know all my dark secrets, you'll change your mind about making me your countess."

He caressed her cheek with his hand and smiled gently. "I feel some splinters from that wooden head," he teased. "Amber, my love, nothing in your past will deter me from marrying you. But 'tis only fair that you should tell me everything that has made you who you are since I have confessed all of my dark secrets to you."

Amber took a deep, shaky breath. "Very well, let me begin with Edgar Hull."

"You were more than justified in killing the blighter after he took you to Eastham."

"There is more. Hull and I grew up on adjoining estates. The second son of an impoverished baron, he hoped to wed me for my dowry." She gave a mirthless little laugh. "I refused his suit just before my father sent me to London. I was instructed to find a wealthy husband during my come-out.

Hull enlisted a few of his drunken friends to kidnap me from the carriage on the road to the city."

"He intended to rape you and then your father would be forced to allow his suit." Rob wanted to kill Hull himself . . . slowly.

"The taking of my maidenhead was reserved for Wolverton," she said bitterly. "Edgar had a penchant for strong spirits. When we reached the tawdry inn where he intended to do the deed, I encouraged him to drink several bottles of port. He passed out before he could touch me and I climbed out an upper window while his companions celebrated belowstairs."

"Always clever and resourceful, my love," Rob said warmly.

She returned his smile, but then it faded. "When I came home . . ."

"Your father considered you ruined anyway," he supplied. "But what of your mother? Surely—"

"My mother despised me since the day I was born. I ruined her figure when she carried me, and then I had the exceeding bad grace to be born female. She had to have a second child, who to her relief was a boy. My father then returned his attention to mistresses and horse racing. My mother, having done her duty, retreated to her private quarters, where she has drunk herself stuporous ever since."

"If I did not already consider myself blessed with a wonderfully happy childhood, this would convince me of my great good fortune," Rob said, waiting to see if she wanted to continue while he rubbed her back gently.

"The scandal of my abortive 'elopement' with Edgar Hull became the talk of Durham. My father was desperate to rid himself of me but would never consider the wastrel Hull. He cast about for someone who needed to buy a wife—even if she were *ruined*."

"Eastham."

"Just so. I was packed off to Northumberland and the nightmare began." She shivered in revulsion.

"Even if I had not heard of his evil reputation, just seeing you in that torture chamber would be enough to make me want to kill him all over again."

"I have the consolation of knowing that he will answer for his sins in the next life," Amber said fervently. "After months of enduring his brutal rapes, I still did not conceive. He called me barren and worthless. Often he beat me until I could scarcely move. When I overheard him and Mrs. Greevy discussing whether or not to poison me, I knew I must flee. Late that night after he had left my bed, I took the household money Elvira had hidden and a horse from the stable.

"I made it south to Durham before the poor beast gave out, but I knew my family would not help, so I walked the rest of the way to London, stopping at remote inns for bits of food and sleep. Foolishly, I believed once here that I could find decent employment as a governess. I had a good education because of my brother's tutor. Although Chandler was not interested in his lessons, I was eager to learn. Perhaps the old man, Mr. Quinlen, took pity on me. . . ."

"In spite of a formidable education, you found no work in London without references." Rob had seen enough desperate young women on the streets. It explained why Fantasia took in so many unfortunates.

"I had used up all the money from Wolf's Gate by then and lost my lodging. Grace found me walking aimlessly in Eastcheap and had her driver pull over."

"She treated you as her own daughter," he said, remembering how intent Mrs. Winston had been when she told him that Amber had never been a courtesan. He knew she had told the truth.

"She had rescued many young women, but only those who wished to become courtesans did so. The others she found respectable work for, but I was different. None of them were pursued by Eastham. She sent me abroad, hoping that he would give up and assume me dead. I studied in Florence and Bern for a year, then went to Paris for two more. I always had an affinity for languages. I could pass as French during the war—that is, until I ran afoul of Fouche."

"Napoleon's head of secret police?"

"Although I did not suspect, one of the women with whom I roomed was a royalist sympathizer. She was found out and quickly executed, along with two other poor innocent girls who shared our small apartment. I was scheduled to die next, but Jenette and her associates rescued me. She smuggled me out of France at great risk and brought me back to Grace. When the war ended, Jeni returned to London, where Grace offered her employment as my bodyguard.

"Since Wolverton remained a threat, I became Lady Fantasia, never allowing patrons to see my face, hiding behind widow's weeds when I left the safety of this place with Jeni at my side."

"Gaby's childhood—it was Jenette's, wasn't it?" he asked, certain of the answer after she had described her own bitter upbringing.

"Yes, her father was a baron with an estate in the south of France. He was much beloved by his people. Her family remained intact in spite of the violence across the countryside during the revolution. But when Napoleon came to power, that changed. Their land and fortune were confiscated and they all died in prison. Jeni was the only one to escape."

"I can see why she became a spy for our country."

"Without her I would have no new identity. I could not marry you," Amber said.

He lifted her chin and looked into her eyes. "We *are* going to Paris and you *will* become my wife. For that I will be forever in her debt." He lowered his mouth to hers and bestowed a soft kiss on her lips.

Amber returned it and their ardor grew until a quick rap on the door interrupted and Bonnie asked, "Is it all right for me to start packin', m'lady?"

"A capital idea. The sooner we reach Paris, the sooner we can be married," Rob whispered to Amber.

"Yes, Bonnie, please do come in and begin the packing. We shall be gone for a long time," she said, smiling at her earl.

Paris, France

After sending the letter Jenette composed to "Charon" in Whitehall, several anxious weeks passed before Hillsborough replied. His Majesty's grateful government would be honored to welcome Lady Collette Solange de Beaurivage, also known as the Dark Angel. Rob immediately arranged passage for Abigail, and Amber sent for Grace and an entourage of friends.

As the earl had predicted, his mother readily accepted the partial story of Amber's past and the need for her to assume a new identity. Now that she was really a widow, she was free to become Robert's countess. No one was more delighted than Abigail that her son had found such a suitable bride. As Rob had also predicted, she asked that they have a quiet Anglican ceremony with all their family present. Both Rob and Amber readily agreed.

The day Amber and Jenette visited the modiste for a final fitting on her wedding gown, Jenette waited until the seamstress left them alone in the dressing room, then said, "I have something to tell you, *ma petite*. You must promise to be happy for me, *oui*?"

Amber took her friend's hand in hers and tugged her over to a small settee. "What is it, Jeni? You have seemed . . . preoccupied ever since we arrived."

"*Oui*, I have been. You see, I have brought with me a map given to me by *mon pere* before he died." She paused to compose herself as Amber placed a consoling arm around her shoulder. "This map, it will show me where he buried all he could of our family's treasures before those pigs took us. I am going to find my birthright."

Amber realized why Jenette looked so apprehensive. "You will remain here in France then, won't you?"

Jenette shrugged. "For a time. You see, I will have arrangements to make. Buried with the family's heirlooms is a list of banks in England where *Pere* had funds transferred when he saw the upheavals coming. He invested wisely in many things over the years. He promised me that I would be a very rich woman when I laid claim to the money—and I swore to him that I would use it to help any of our faithful tenants and servants who survived."

"Very well. But now you must swear to me that you will come visit us as soon as you are able," Amber said, hugging her friend.

Jenette smiled. "But of course! I must return to England to become 'a very rich woman,' *oui*?"

"You will visit often," Amber insisted.

"You are the sister of my heart, Amber, the only family I have left. Besides," she added with a big smile, "I must come to spoil all of those beautiful *bebes* you and your earl will make!"

"*Oui*, Aunt Jeni," Amber said, hugging her dearest friend.

Rob raised his flute of champagne to his new bride, and the crystal chimed magically when hers touched it. They stood before a large window overlooking the Seine in the lavish suite where they would spend the next week.

All the wedding guests had gone off to celebrate elsewhere, leaving them alone. By mutual agreement, they had not made love before the crossing or after they were reunited in Paris. This would be their first time without secrets, each knowing the other's true identity and accepting it, a joining so special that Rob and Amber agreed it must wait until they were married.

"Ever since the first time I saw your beautiful face unveiled, I have wanted to make love to you in daylight," he said.

"Does this mean no more love lessons at midnight?" she asked, setting aside her half-finished champagne.

He studied the cherry-haired woman swathed in glittering gold silk, devouring her with his eyes. "I am certain we shall continue teaching each other many delights, night and day . . . for the rest of our lives," he murmured, drawing her into his arms. "Gaby was an extraordinary teacher . . . and according to her . . . I have been an apt pupil," he said between nuzzling kisses to her throat.

"Keeping Gabrielle and Fantasia's identities separate was very difficult," she said breathlessly.

He chuckled. "'Tis ironic how often I thought if Gaby's shy sensuality were combined with Fantasia's keen wit, she would make the one perfect wife for me. Now my fantasy has become real," he said, sweeping her up into his arms.

Amber held tightly to him as he carried her through the door leading to a large bed in the center of the room. He walked over to it and stood her on her feet while pressing her close. "Allow me to take Bonnie's place and undress you," he murmured.

"Only if I may perform Settles's work and be your valet," she whispered, holding on to the lapels of his suit.

His fingers were deft and clever. She hummed as he slipped the loops on the back of her gown free from their buttons. Her own hands were busy untying his cravat and tossing it to the floor. When her bridal gown slid from her shoulders, she watched him throw his jacket across a chair, allowing her access to his waistcoat. By the time she had removed it and opened his shirt to bare his chest, he smoothed the whispery silk gown over her hips and let it puddle at her feet. As they undressed each other, they exchanged soft sounds of pleasure and love words.

After he pulled the lacy chemise covering her breasts open, he gasped, reaching up to cup a perfect breast in each hand. "I have waited for so long to see what I have tasted. Such pale pink perfection at the tips."

He brushed his fingers across them and took joy in her gasp of excitement, then bent his head and suckled until both nipples hardened into tight nubs. When she arched and moaned, he let out a growl of satisfaction as his hands slid the chemise down her arms. He quickly unfastened the tapes to her sheer linen petticoat, then stepped back as the last of her clothing dropped to her ankles. Her slender body glowed like ivory in the soft light filtering in from the bedroom window.

"Just allow me to look at you for a moment." His eyes swept from her face to her breasts, then down past the dark reddish curls enticing him at the juncture of her thighs, lower yet to take in her legs, the curves of her calves and the delicate turn of her ankles. He walked around her, studying her body from every angle, savoring what was to come. "You are even more perfect, more beautiful than I ever could have imagined," he said in awe.

Amber basked in the heat of his hungry green gaze, as she reached out one hand and placed it against his bare chest. Her palm felt the rapid pounding of his heart, yet he made no attempt to rush. How well they had learned together! "Now, 'tis I who would see you unclothed," she whispered, shoving his shirt off his muscled shoulders.

He shucked it away, then said, "My shoes must be removed before I can proceed any further." His eyes danced with a dare.

"Sit on the edge of the bed and raise your leg. I said I would be Settles."

"I am ever so grateful you do not resemble him," he said

with a chuckle, doing as she asked. Amber straddled his leg and began to tug off a shiny black shoe while he admired her small derriere from an exceedingly good position. By the time she had removed the second one, his breeches had become unbearably tight. Sitting up, he held her hips and planted a swift nip on each cheek, eliciting a startled laugh from her.

"Not sporting unless I may do the same," she cried, watching as he stood and began to unbuckle his belt. Her mouth watered when he started to peel down his tight pants. "You are like a Greek statue, only with a larger . . ." Placing her fingers over her mouth, she let out a rich chuckle. "Have I shocked you, m'lord?"

"M'lady, how could any man ever be displeased to have his body described thus?" he replied, smiling ruefully. "Once I believed that my naked body was repellant to women."

"Ah, but you were so very mistaken. If you stood thus next to the Elgin marbles, the female audience would be enormous and they would not be there to admire the marbles." She placed her hands on his chest and ran her fingers through the crisp hair. Her mouth followed, tongue flicking one hard male nipple, then the other.

"Darling, I am no marble statue," he said hoarsely.

She pressed her hips to his lower body and felt the hard probe against her belly. "But this part of you is hard as marble, only warm and alive," she murmured, taking his staff in one hand. "No cold lifeless stone but heated, steely velvet. How often I have felt this buried so deeply inside me. Now I may see and stroke its beauty."

"Do not stroke too much, love, lest you suffer the fate of Pliny, inundated by an eruption of Vesuvius." He stilled her busy fingers. "Here, allow me to take down your hair, so I may see it flowing freely as I have felt it in the darkness." He reached up and began to unfasten the pins holding her elaborate coiffure, tossing them carelessly away until he could run his fingers through the thick satiny curls as they tumbled to her waist.

Amber combed her fingers through his inky locks. "From the first time I watched you pacing across my office, I wanted to do this."

He picked her up and knelt on the mattress with one knee, laying her on the soft linen like the most precious treasure on earth. And she was to her earl. She stared up at him. He looked down at her. Both drank their fill.

Her hair spilled like cherry satin over the snowy pillows. "At last, at last," he whispered, lying down beside her. She turned into him and wrapped her arms around his neck. He twined her hair in his fists and drew her mouth to his.

They kissed slowly, languorously, caressing and examining every part of each other's bodies with eyes wide open. How often had they done this in darkness? How familiar was every inch of skin? Yet much greater pleasure came now that they could love without darkness or subterfuge between them. Rob sat up, bracing his hands on each side of her body as he bent his arms, lowering his head to suckle her breasts again, then moving to her belly . . . and the fiery curls below.

When she opened her thighs, he bestowed a soft kiss on the creamy petals, eliciting a moan from her. "You are beautiful here, too," he whispered, returning to the caress. When he saw her body bow up on the mattress and felt the tiny spasms signaling the start of her first culmination, he raised himself up and covered her, plunging deeply inside her welcoming heat. He held his body rigidly still, waiting for the blissful storm to pass.

Amber felt his powerful thrust add to the blinding pleasure surging through her. But he did not move. She watched his face above her, set tightly as he held his own release in abeyance to give her more pleasure. *What woman could ask for a husband to love her more than this?*

In response, she slid her hands up his sleekly muscled

arms and drew him down to her, kissing him fiercely, arching her body hungrily even as the contractions slowly died away. "Now we will continue our lesson, yes?" she whispered once again in French.

"Oh, yes, a thousand times, yes," he murmured, stroking slowly until her fire once again matched his own. She clenched his body between her thighs, gasping and writhing with every slow, delicious stroke he made. He knew the moment she began to ascend the heights again. When she cried out his name, urging him to go faster, he let go of his hard-won control and spilled himself deeply inside her.

Amber felt his whole body shudder in release. And watched him through her own heavy-lidded eyes, even as he watched her. This was the ultimate communion of body and soul, mated together. And they would share this for the rest of their lives.

He collapsed on top of her, being careful to take his weight on his elbows as he rolled to his side. She curled against him and they lay, silently, each listening to the other breathe. When she regained composure sufficient to speak, she placed her hand on his chest and whispered, "I could never imagine our coming together could grow better than what we experienced in London. Now I know I was wrong."

He twined a curl and let it slide between his finger and thumb. "Seeing you this way . . . free in the light . . . I have waited so long. Yes, this is even better than before."

"And will it grow better each time we love?" she asked.

His chuckled. "We have only to keep loving and find out." With that he started kissing his countess once again. . . .

One dim candle burned by the side of the bed and the remains of a cold collation of cheeses, fruits, roast pheasant, and crusty bred lay on a nearby tray. An empty bottle of what had been fine claret sat beside it. They had fed each other between bouts of making love until both were utterly exhausted.

Amber nodded off in a light sleep, her hand placed over his heart. When she felt the rumble of a laugh building up, she opened her eyes. "What is so amusing, m'lord?"

"I was just thinking . . . once I was the most ardent of reformers. Now I am a veritable polygamist, wed to an aristo spy, a penniless French innocent, the notorious Lady Fantasia—and to triumph all, a dead marchioness. I have a luscious harem made up of all these amazing women in you, my Amber love."

"Aren't you the fortunate husband, then, m'lord Pasha? Every member of your harem is madly in love with you!"

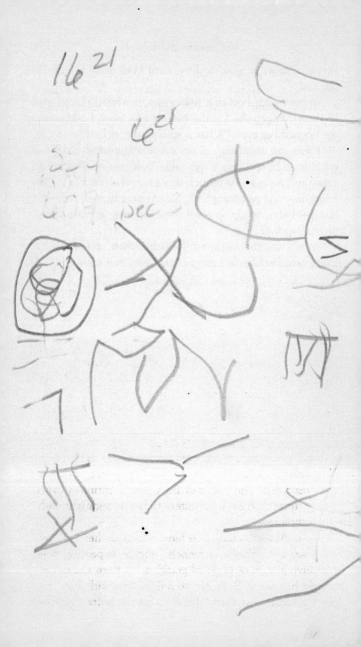

Author's Note

I was delighted but caught by surprise when my editor asked me to return to writing Regencies. What unique idea could I come up with that had not already been done in this, the most popular subgenre of historical romance? Of course, I asked Jim to brainstorm with me. We each retired to our offices and did what any writer does in these circumstances. Wait for a miracle to appear on the blank computer screen.

Was the hero a rake in need of a good woman to tame him? Nah, that's been done a lot. Was the heroine a noblewoman posing as a courtesan or a courtesan posing as a noblewoman? Hmm, what if she was both? But what hero would want such a woman? Then some magical muse must have had a slow day and decided to favor me with an inspiration. What about a "good boy" hero, rather than a rakehell such as Alex Blackthorne from *Wicked Angel* or Jason Beaumont from *Yankee Earl*?

Creating the Earl of Barrington, Rob St. John, was a real challenge, a reformer who wants to stop prostitution. But he needs to learn how to please his potential bride in bed. Where can he find such help but with a courtesan? Because of his concern for a lady's sensibilities, he must have the "lessons" take place in the dark.

Amber Leighigh, a marchioness in hiding from a brutal husband, poses as Lady Fantasia, owner of the most exclusive bordello in London. After her experience with the "mad marquess" she has had no physical intimacy with men . . . until Rob St. John comes to her at midnight with his startling request.

Here is Amber's chance to have a man do her bidding. She poses as Gabrielle, a French émigrée, expecting only to receive a taste of physical gratification from the devastatingly handsome Rob, not to fall in love with him. He feels the same about Gabrielle. But then he is drawn to the brilliant, witty Lady Fantasia. Which woman does he love? When Amber admits to herself that she loves Rob, how can she explain her deception? And what about the mad marquess waiting in the wings?

I pitched the story to my editor and she loved it, so I dug right in. Amber's character worked beautifully. But it took me over a hundred pages to grasp what motivated the reformer Rob. In more than thirty historicals, I have never written a good-boy hero. Why should I? After all, I married my very own bad-boy hero!

In spite of this, Jim really liked my concept. Together we brainstormed plot twists and did research, but when it came time to turn in the finished manuscript, he said he felt his name should not appear as collaborator. "Why?" I asked. "Because you wrote a Regency and a woman's fantasy," he replied. I said that if we could stay married for years there must be a few elements of nobility in his soul, or else I would have killed him by now!

That's when Jim came up with the idea for the authors' photo in the back of this book, taken on our wedding day. He may still be a semidomesticated bad boy, but he does have a good idea now and then . . . in spite of the caption that he wrote!

Shirl

Jim's Note

I suggested that we use a wedding photo for the back cover of this book! I? Me? That's about as likely as a condemned man suggesting that a photo of his execution, swinging by the neck from the gallows while he's dressed in a diaper, be sent to the *New York Times*. Hey, I may have been dumb enough to get myself married to a bossy redhead, but I ain't into public humiliation!

Just look at that coy supercilious smile on Shirl's face as we cut the wedding cake. Sure, why not? She won. Now, look at that frown on my face. Her lawyer was informing me that this would be the last time I was allowed to be near my wife with a sharp knife in my hand. We didn't have a prenuptial agreement. We had a bloody armistice. But then, I guess that is why we've been married for 87 years . . . or maybe it's only 78. A person has a way of losing track of time in purgatory.

But I have to admit that Shirl's idea for this book is a brilliant one, although her note gets some of the details a bit wrong and omits others I found fascinating. The Earl of Barrington wants his "love lessons" conducted in a dark room, not out of consideration for his future wife. That's only an excuse. He wants the darkness because he is unsure and embarrassed by his uncertainty. Amber/Fantasia realizes this immediately and offers him this advice: Ask your lover what pleases her and then do it. Fantasia realizes that such a question is so much easier to ask in the dark. Of course, modesty forbids me suggesting where Amber/Fantasia and Shirl got that idea.

However, Shirl correctly outlines Rob's psychological quandary when he believes he may be falling in love with two women, entirely different in every way. What she glosses over is Amber/Fantasia's growing "schizophrenia" as the "lessons" continue.

Having created the passionate, nurturing Gabrielle—Rob's lover and her own alter ego—Amber/Fantasia begins to think of "Gabrielle" as a separate woman and her rival. She becomes jealous of her Gabrielle persona, the recipient of Rob's passion and the confidant with whom he shares his deepest and most painful secrets. She becomes a victim of the deception that she has created to control the hero. Now that's poetic justice. Once again, modesty prevents me . . . Hey, deceit is how I've survived marriage for 67 years to a willful, obstinate creature . . . or is that 76?

Jim